'A compulsive thriller with sufficient twists and plot turns to keep the most action-avaricious of readers satisfied. Haynes treats the subject matter of domestic violence delicately and with gentle self-assurance. Hers is clearly a name to watch.'
*Bookgroup.info*

'Compelling and disturbing. This book is disquieting, believable and has a realistic twist.'
*Mystery Women*

'This beautifully dark and disturbing novel is, amazingly, the first book by Elizabeth Haynes. It is seamlessly put together and the clever juxtaposition of chapters from the present and the past keeps the reader on the edge of their seat. It's impossible to guess the ending of the book and the storyline digs deep into your psyche, teasing you and tempting you to check that your own doors and windows are locked and secure. I love this book. Elizabeth Haynes is a very talented new face in the murky world of crime fiction and definitely a name to look out for in the future. Very highly recommended.'
*Eurocrime*

'This psychological thriller is fast-paced and chilling, with a realistic twist. The impact of OCD and Post Traumatic Stress Disorder on victims of abuse is sensitively handled and believable. Lock all your doors and settle down for one of the most gripping reads of the year!'
*Pamreader*

'A nervy, heart-racing page-turner. It's a one-sitting, impossible-to-put-down kind of book.'
*Bookrambler*

'Domestic violence, OCD and murder in a book that exerts a nerve-shredding grip on the reader, with a sympathetic heroine and a truly loathsome baddie.'
*Crimetime*

*For an exclusive extract, turn to p.351*

## About the author

Elizabeth Haynes grew up in Sussex. She works as a police intelligence analyst and lives in Kent with her husband and son. Her first novel *Into the Darkest Corner* was Amazon's Best Book of the Year, winner of Rising Stars and featured on the Specsavers TV Book Club. *Revenge of the Tide* is her second novel.

# ELIZABETH HAYNES

# REVENGE OF THE TIDE

**Myriad Editions**

Published in 2012 by
Myriad Editions
59 Lansdowne Place
Brighton BN3 1FL

www.MyriadEditions.com

1 3 5 7 9 10 8 6 4 2

A CIP catalogue record for this book is available from the
British Library.

ISBN: 978-0-9567926-4-8

Printed on FSC-accredited paper by
CPI Group (UK) Ltd, Croydon, CR0 4YY

*For David*

# One

It was there when I opened my eyes, that vague feeling of discomfort, the rocking of the boat signalling the receding tide and the wind from the south, blowing upriver, straight into the side of the *Revenge of the Tide*.

For a long while I lay in bed, the sound of the waves slapping against the hull next to my head, echoing through the steel and dulled by the wooden cladding. The duvet was warm and it was easy to stay there, the rectangle of the skylight directly above showing the blackness turning to dark blue, and grey, and then I could see the clouds scudding overhead, giving the odd impression of moving at speed – the boat moving rather than the clouds. And then, that discomfort again.

It wasn't seasickness, or river-sickness, come to that: I was used to it now, nearly five months after I had left London. Five months living aboard. There was still a momentary shock when my feet hit the solid ground of the path to the car park, a few wobbly steps, but it was never long before I felt steady again.

It was a grey sort of a day – not ideal for the get-together later, but that was my own fault for planning a party in September. 'Back to school' weather, the wind whistling across the deck when I got up and put my head out of the wheelhouse.

No, it wasn't the tide, or the thought of the mismatched group of people who would be descending on my boat later today. There was something else. I felt as though someone had rubbed my fur the wrong way.

The plan for the day: finish the last bit of timber cladding for the second room, the room that was going to be a guest bedroom at some point in the future. Clear away all the carpentry tools and store them in the bow. Sweep out the boat, clean up a bit. Then see if I could cadge a lift to the cash-and-carry for party food and beer.

There was one wall left to do, an odd shape, which was why I had left it till last. The room was full of sawdust and offcuts of wood, bits of edging and sandpaper. I'd done the measurements last night but now, frowning at the bit of paper, I decided to recheck it all just to be on the safe side. When I had clad the galley I'd ended up wasting a load of wood because I misread my own measurements.

I put the radio on, turned up loud even though I still couldn't hear it above the mitre saw, and got to work.

At nine, I stopped and went back through to the galley for a coffee. I filled the kettle and put it on to the gas burner. The boat was a mess. It was only occasionally that I noticed it. Glancing around, I scanned last night's takeaway containers hurriedly shoved into a carrier bag ready to go out to the main bins. Dirty dishes in the sink. Pans and other items in boxes sitting on one of the dinette seats waiting to be put away, now I had finally fitted cupboard doors in the galley. A black plastic sack of fabrics and netting that would one day be curtains and cushion covers. None of it mattered when I was the only one in here, but in a few hours' time this boat would be full of people, and I had promised them that the renovations were almost complete.

Almost complete? That was stretching the truth a little thin. I had finished the bedroom, and the living room wasn't bad. The galley was done too, but needed cleaning and tidying. The bathroom was – well, the kindest thing that could be said about it was that it was functional. As for the rest of it – the vast space in the bow that would one day be a bigger bathroom with a bath instead of a hose for a shower, a wide conservatory area with a sliding glass roof (an ambitious plan, but I'd seen one in a magazine and it looked so brilliant that it was the one project I was determined to complete), and maybe a snug or an office or another unnamed room that would be wonderful and cosy and magical – for the moment, it worked as storage.

The kettle started a low whistle, and I rinsed a mug under the tap and spooned in some instant coffee, two spoons: I needed the caffeine.

A pair of boots crossed my field of vision through the porthole, level with the pontoon outside, shortly followed by a call from the deck. 'Genevieve?'

'Down here. Kettle's just boiled, want a drink?'

Moments later Joanna trotted down the steps and into the main cabin. She was dressed in a miniskirt, with thick socks and heavy boots, with the laces trailing, on the ends of her skinny legs. The top half of her was counterbalanced by one of Liam's jumpers, a navy blue one, flecked with bits of sawdust and twig and cat hair. Her hair was a tangle of curls and waves of various colours.

'No, thanks – we're off out in a minute. I just came to ask what time we should come over later, and do you want us to bring a lasagne as well as the cheesecake? And Liam says he's got some beers left over from the barbecue, he'll be bringing those.'

She had a bruise on her cheek. Joanna didn't wear make-up, wouldn't have known what to do with it, so there it was – livid and purplish, about the size of a fifty pence piece, under her left eye.

'What happened to your face?'

'Oh, don't you start. I had a fight with my sister.'

'Blimey.'

'Come up on deck, I need a smoke.'

The wind was still whipping, so we sat on the bench by the wheelhouse. The sun was trying to make its way through the scudding clouds but failing. Across the other side of the marina I could see Liam loading boxes and carrier bags into the back of their battered Transit van.

Joanna fished around in the pocket of her skirt and brought forth a pouch of tobacco. 'The way I see it,' she said, 'she should keep her fucking nose out of my business.'

'Your sister?'

'She thinks she's all clever because she's got herself a mortgage at the age of twenty-two.'

'Mortgages aren't all they're cracked up to be.'

'Exactly!' Joanna said with emphasis. 'That's what I said to her. I've got everything she's got without the burden of debt. And I don't have to mow any lawn.'

'So that's what you were fighting about?'

Joanna was quiet for a moment, her eyes wandering over to the car park where Liam stood, hands on his hips, before pointedly looking at his wristwatch and climbing into the driver's seat. Above the sounds of the marina – drilling coming from the workshop, the sound of the radio down in the cabin, the distant roar of the traffic from the motorway bridge – the van's diesel rattle started up.

'Fuck it, I'd better go,' she said. She shoved the pouch back into her pocket and lit the skinny cigarette she'd just managed to fill. 'About seven? Eight? What?'

I shrugged. 'I don't know. Sevenish? Lasagne sounds lovely, but don't go to any trouble.'

'It's no trouble. Liam's made it.'

With a backward wave, Joanna took one quick hop-step down the gangplank and on to the pontoon, running despite the boots across the grassy bank and up to the car park. The Transit was taking little jumps forward as though it couldn't wait to be gone.

At four, the cabin was finally finished. A bare shell, but at least now it was a bare wooden shell. The walls were clad, and the berth built along the far wall, under the porthole. Where the mattress would sit, two trapdoors with round finger-holes in the board gave access to the storage compartment underneath. The rest of it was pale wood in neat panelling, carved pine edging covering the joins and corners. It would look less like a sauna once it had had a lick of paint, I thought. By next weekend it would be entirely different.

Clearing away the debris of my most recent foray into carpentry took longer than I thought it would. I had crates for the tools. I hadn't bothered to put them away since I'd started work on the bedroom, months ago.

I lugged them forward into the bow, through a hatch and into the cavernous space below. Three steps down, watching my head on the low ceiling, stowing the crates away at the side.

It was only when I made the last trip, carrying the black plastic sack of fabric from the dinette and throwing it into the front compartment, that I found myself looking into the darkest of the spaces to see if the box was still there. I could just about see it in the gloomy light from the cabin above; on the side of it was written, in thick black marker: KITCHEN STUFF.

I had a sudden urge to look, to check that the box still had its contents. Of course it did, I told myself. Of course it was still there. *Nobody's been down here since you put it there.*

Stooping, I crossed the three wooden pallets that served as a floor, braced myself against the sides of the hull, and crouched next to the box. KITCHEN STUFF. The top two-thirds of the box was full of rubbish I'd brought from the London flat – spatulas, wooden spoons, a Denby teapot with a crack in the lid, a whisk, a blender that didn't work, an ice cream scoop and various cake tins nested inside each other. Below that was a sheet of cardboard that might, to the casual observer, look sufficiently like the bottom of the box to deter further investigation.

I folded the cardboard top of the box back down and tucked the other flap underneath it.

From the back pocket of my jeans, I took out a mobile phone. I found the address book and the only number that was saved there: GARLAND. That was all it said. It wasn't even his name. It would be so easy to press the little green button now and call him. What would I say? Maybe I could just ask him if he wanted to come tonight. *'Come to my party, Dylan. It's just a few close friends. I'd love to see you.'*

What would he say? He'd be angry, shocked that I'd used the phone when he'd expressly told me not to. It was only there for one purpose, he'd told me. It was only for him to ring me, and only when he was ready to make the collection. Not before. If I ever had a call on it from another number, I wasn't to answer.

I closed my eyes for a moment, for a brief second allowing myself the indulgence of remembering him. Then I put the screen lock back on the phone so it didn't accidentally dial any numbers, least of all his, and I shoved it in my pocket and made my way back to the cabin.

# *Two*

Malcolm and Josie were the first to arrive, at six. It was an unofficial arrival: they stopped for a chat and didn't leave again. I was on the deck tipping the ice I'd just got from the cash-and-carry into a big plastic crate, and Malcolm heard the chink of beer bottles from his narrowboat. Seconds later he was chatting amicably from the pontoon about this and that, three bottles of French red wine tucked under one arm.

'We've got loads more if you run out, Genevieve,' Josie said, when they came aboard. 'We went to France last weekend. Stocked up for Christmas, you know.'

'I thought you didn't drink wine,' I said, handing the bottle opener to Malcolm so he could crack open his first beer.

'Don't, really,' Malcolm said. 'Dunno why we bought so much of it, tell the truth.'

I'd cleaned up as much as possible. It could have been better, but the worst of the mess was out of the way, and the galley wasn't looking too bad. Maureen had given me a lift to the cash-and-carry and I'd taken a taxi home, with two crates of beer and several bags of ice, jumbo packets of crisps, and a large block of cheese that had seemed like a good idea at the time. I wasn't very good at party food, to be honest – but at least there was plenty of alcohol.

Josie had brought garlic bread wrapped in tinfoil. 'I thought it could go on your stove,' she said.

'I wasn't going to light it. I think it's going to be roasting with lots of people in here.'

Malcolm, the designated expert in the room who had provided advice on living aboard more times in the last five months than I could remember, snorted. 'You'll freeze in the night if you haven't got your stove on.'

For a moment we all stood contemplating the wood-burning stove that sat on large tiles in the corner of the main cabin. It wasn't cold now, but Malcolm had a point – not good to be lying in bed at four in the morning, freezing cold.

'I'll light it, if you like,' Malcolm said at last. 'You ladies go up on deck and admire the sunset.'

On the way past the galley I took hold of the bottle opener and, as I opened two bottles of beer, not as cold as they should be but cold enough, Josie said something about leaving the man to build his fire. 'He loves it. We were going to have central heating put in at one point but he kept putting it off and putting it off. He even starts piling up logs in the summer, just in case it gets a bit on the chilly side. One of these days he's going to chop down one of the trees on the rec.'

I looked down and along the pontoon to the *Scarisbrick Jean*, the narrowboat Malcolm and Josie shared with their cat, Oswald. Not long after I'd moved in, I had heard them talking about 'Aunty Jean' and for a while I'd thought they had a third person living on the boat with them, until I realised that *Aunty Jean* was their affectionate name for the boat itself. A friendly name. Maybe I should think of a pet name for mine.

The first time I saw the boat, I knew it was the one. It was above my price range, but my finances had seen a recent improvement and as a result I was looking at boats I'd previously discounted. It needed work, but the hull was sound and the cabin was bearable. I could just about afford to buy it and do the renovations for a year or so, provided I budgeted carefully and did the work myself.

'*Revenge of the Tide*. Odd sort of a name for a boat,' I'd said, the day I decided to spend the bulk of my savings on it.

Cameron, the boatyard owner and the broker for boat sales, was standing beside me on the pontoon. He wasn't a fabulous salesman; he was in a hurry to get on with the countless other tasks he had waiting. He was fidgeting from one foot to the other and was clearly only just managing to hold back from saying, *'Do you want her or not?'* It was a good job for him that I'd already fallen in love.

The *Revenge of the Tide* was a seventy-five-foot-long barge of a type known as a Hagenaar, named for the canals of Den Haag, under whose bridges the boat was low enough to pass. It had been built in 1903 in the Netherlands, a great beast of a boat, a workhorse. The masts had been removed and a diesel engine added after the Second World War, and it had been used for transporting goods around the Port of Rotterdam until it was sold in the 1970s and moved across the English Channel. Ever since then, a steady stream of owners had been using it either for moving cargo, for pleasure trips or as living accommodation, with varying degrees of commitment and success.

'The owner bought her just before his second divorce,' said Cam. 'He managed to con his missus because he bought the boat with all the savings he had stashed away. He wanted to call her just *Revenge*, I think, but it was a bit too obvious so he called her *Revenge of the Tide* instead.'

'I might have to change the name,' I said, as Cam took me into the office to sign the paperwork.

'You can't do that. Bad luck to change a boat's name.'

'Bad luck? What, worse than having a boat named after a failed marriage?'

Cam grimaced.

'Anyway, the last owner changed the name, didn't he?'

'Yeah. And he's just getting divorced for the third time, and having to sell his boat to pay for it. What does that tell you?'

So I left the name as it was, because I didn't need any more bad luck in my life. Besides, the *Revenge* had character, had a soul; living aboard such a majestic, beautiful boat made me feel a bit safer, a bit less lonely. And it looked after me and hid me away from view. Boats were supposed to be female, but I always thought of the *Revenge* as male: a big, quiet gentleman, someone who would keep me safe.

'So what time are your London mates turning up?' Josie asked.

'Oh, lord knows. Late, probably.'

Josie was like a warm cushion, fleecy and brightly coloured. There was barely room for the two of us on the narrow bench. Her greying hair was fighting the breeze to escape from the loosely tied ponytail on the back of her head. At least the sun had come out, and the early evening sky overhead was blue, dotted with white clouds.

'What are they going to make of us lot, do you reckon?'

'I'm more worried about what you'll make of them.'

A few days after I'd moved in, I had poked my head out of the wheelhouse to be greeted by the sight of Malcolm sitting on the roof of the *Scarisbrick Jean* smoking a roll-up and wearing nothing but a pair of boxer shorts. It was early, barely light, and the spring air was so cold that Malcolm's breath came in clouds. His hair stood up on one side of his head as if it had been ironed.

'Alright?' he'd called across to me.

'Morning,' I'd said, and had almost gone back down below when curiosity got the better of me. 'You okay over there?'

'Yeah,' he'd said, taking a long, slow drag. 'You?' As though it were entirely normal to be sitting on the roof of a narrowboat at five in the morning wearing nothing but your underwear. I hadn't known his name then. I'd seen him coming and going, of course, and we'd exchanged nods and greetings, but it still felt a bit peculiar to be sharing the dawn with a man who was just a scrap of grey flannel away from naked.

'Aren't you cold?'

'Oh,' he'd said, with dawning comprehension. 'Yeah. Fucking freezing. But I can't go inside: Josie's just had a shit and stunk the whole boat out.'

In the first few days and weeks of boat ownership, living in the marina had felt like being in a foreign country. The pace of life was slower. If someone was going to the shop they would shout at you and ask if you wanted anything bringing back. Some of them turned up unexpectedly and sat on your boat and talked about nothing for three hours and then went away again, sometimes abruptly, as though the flow of conversation had dried up or some other, more pressing engagement had surfaced. Sometimes they brought food or drink with them. They helped you fix things, even if it wasn't immediately apparent that the thing in question needed fixing. They gave you advice about which chemicals you should use to keep the toilet working. They laughed a lot.

Some of the boats were owned by people who only turned up at the marina at the weekends, or less often if it was rainy. One of them, a narrowboat in a state of considerable disrepair, was owned by a man with wilder hair than Malcolm's. I'd only seen him twice. The first time, I'd called a cheery hello on my way past his boat, and got a vacant stare in response. The second time, he'd been walking across the car park with a carrier bag that looked heavy and chinked as though it was full of glass bottles.

Then there was Carol-Anne. She lived in a cabin cruiser that should by rights not have been moored in the residential marina, but she got away with it because she did actually live there. She was divorced, with three children who lived with their father in Chatham. She would say hello and then try and talk to you for hours about how grim things were and how difficult it was to manage. All the other liveaboards tried to avoid her and, after a couple of weeks, I did too.

The rest of them were wonderful.

Joanna had turned up with a plateful of dinner once. 'You eaten? Good, we made too much.'

We'd sat together at the dinette, Joanna drinking from a can of lager which she'd found in my fridge, while I tucked into shepherd's pie and peas.

'I'm not used to people bringing me dinner,' I'd said when I'd finished.

Joanna had shrugged. 'It's no bother. Glad not to throw it away.'

'People here are very friendly,' I'd said, aware at the same time of what an understatement this was. It was like suddenly finding yourself part of a big family.

'Yes. It's the whole boat thing. You get used to it, after a while. Not like living in London, huh?'

*Not like living in London*, I'd thought, *not at all*.

Mixing London friends with marina friends had the potential to be a recipe for pure disaster: they'd have nothing in common, other than perhaps that Simone occasionally read the *Guardian* on a Saturday. Lucy would turn up in her vast, tank-like all-terrain luxury vehicle that did about twelve miles to the gallon and had never been outside the M25; Gavin would be wearing incredibly expensive designer shoes that would be ruined in the muddy puddles around the dock that never seemed to dry up.

And then there was Caddy. Would she even come?

At some point in the future, the *Revenge of the Tide* would be a fantastic party boat, big enough for lots of people to socialise in and crash out on – but not yet. If they all turned up, some of them would have to sit on the deck, and some of them would probably never even set foot below deck – there simply wouldn't be room. They would all have a laugh about it and then they would walk back up to the main road and go to the pub. The other liveaboards would make some remarks about city dwellers, laugh a lot, drink more beer and end up going back to their own boats in the early hours.

They would be here soon. Josie closed her eyes against the low sun and breathed in, a smile of contentment on her face as though she were sunbathing on a yacht in the Mediterranean instead of an old Dutch barge on the Medway.

'We'll love them,' she said at last. 'We love everyone. Unless they're real snobs.'

It had got to the point where I didn't actually care what my city friends thought. At the start of this year I had cared very much. It had mattered what I thought, what I wore, what I said, what music I listened to, what pubs I drank in after work, and what I did at the weekends. London was a vast social network where you met people in bars and clubs, at the gym, at work and at events, in parks and at the theatre, at salsa dance nights in the local pub. You spent enough time with them to establish whether they were on your wavelength, and eventually decided whether they could be classed as friends. People came and went in and out of your life in a transitory fashion, and it never really seemed to matter. There was always someone else to go out with, always an invitation to some party or gathering. So I had plenty of people I knew, and in London they would generally be called friends, or mates. But were they? Were they people you could call on in a crisis? Would they stay with you if you were ill, or in danger? Would they protect you, if you needed protecting?

Dylan would. Dylan had, in fact.

'They're not snobs, not really. But to be honest I think it's going to be a bit of a shock for them. I think they're expecting some kind of gorgeous loft apartment squeezed into a boat.'

'Rubbish, you've done a fabulous job.'

'I've still got a long way to go. And there isn't a single thing on my boat that I've bought new. Unfortunately that lot don't really get the recycling ethos.'

'Seriously? But your boat's looking fabulous. And you've done it all yourself. Not many of us have done the fitting out on our own.'

'At least the tide's coming in.'

The hull was presently sitting comfortably on a cushion of mud, the boat steady. When the tide came in, it would rise on the water and, depending on the weather, rock gently for six hours or so, until the tide ebbed again. The boat looked much better when it was floating, and of course the mud didn't always smell particularly nice.

Josie looked across the pontoon. 'Who's this?'

The sight of the shiny 4x4 pulling into the marina car park meant that some of the London lot had arrived, and in fact it turned out to be most of them. Lucy was first to jump down. She'd made an effort to dress down in jeans and boots, but the boots still had heels on them. Almost immediately she sank down into the earth and from our position on deck we heard her shout, 'Fuck!'

From the back came Gavin and Chrissie, and someone else, from the passenger side – at first I couldn't see who it was, and then he came round the front of the big bonnet and I could see him, in all his glory.

'I don't believe it,' I murmured.

'Ooh, he looks nice,' said Josie.

'It's Ben.'

'What, the gorgeous one?'

'Yes. The one in the jacket is Gavin. I used to work with him. The blonde girl is Lucy, and the other one is Chrissie, she's a model.'

I stood up on the deck and waved. It was Ben who saw me and returned the wave, and then they all started picking their way across the car park towards the marina, carrying various things between them. Gavin was almost hidden behind a huge bunch of flowers. 'You'll need a great big vase for that lot,' Josie said under her breath.

'Mm. I think I've got a milk bottle somewhere.'

We laughed conspiratorially and for a moment I wondered why I'd decided to hold this party in the first place. It was like a crashing together of two worlds, two different planets that I'd inhabited – one of them had been home before, and the other one was home now. I had a foot in both worlds, and to be honest I wasn't completely comfortable in either.

'Hello!' Lucy had reached the end of the pontoon and was looking at it uncertainly. 'Can I walk on this?'

'Of course you can,' said Ben, marching past her. 'Can we come aboard?'

He was at the bottom of the narrow gangplank. Even from here I could see how blue his eyes were.

'Sure,' I said. 'Come up.'

He made it on to the deck, taking my hand for balance although he didn't need it. It was enough reason to pull me into a hug. He smelled delicious.

'I didn't know you were coming,' I said.

'I didn't know either. I was round at Lucy's and she said I could tag along. You don't mind?'

'Of course not.'

'Er, hello? Someone give me a hand?'

Ben held out his hand for Lucy and she wobbled up the gangplank, followed by Chrissie and Gavin at the end.

'Guys, this is Josie.'

Josie stood up, a little awkwardly. 'Hi. I live on that boat down there.' She pointed down at the *Scarisbrick Jean*, sitting forlorn and slightly at an angle on the mud. Oswald was lazing on the roof enjoying the sunshine, one leg elevated elegantly in the air while he cleaned his bottom.

'Oh, cool,' said Lucy. 'It's – oh. A lovely boat.'

There was a pause, and then, just when it was about to get awkward, Malcolm appeared through the door to the wheelhouse, wiping the back of his sooty hand over his sweaty forehead, and said, 'I've put the garlic bread on the stove. Alright?'

# *Three*

It got better as the evening wore on, which was a relief. By the time I had done the first tour, Carla and Simone had arrived by train and taxi, and after the second tour the boat and the deck and the pontoon were full of people, most of them from the marina, outnumbering the townies and making the party come alive.

Joanna and Liam came with the lasagne and two whole cheesecakes, Maureen and Pat brought more beer, Roger and Sally brought a keg of their homebrew and a bag full of homemade bread. Diane and Steve came without their children but with a two-way baby monitor, which worked just fine given that their boat was only about ten feet away. Joanna had also brought a present of a couple of strings of fairy lights, which were duly strung up around the deck and made the boat look pretty and festive as the sun set at last and darkness fell.

There was no sign of Caddy. I wondered if I'd been enthusiastic enough with my invitation. For a long time she had been the closest thing I had to a best friend in London, and I missed her, I wanted to see her again. If I couldn't invite Dylan, there was nothing stopping me asking Caddy. But she hadn't made it.

I'd only spoken to her a few times since I'd left. She still hadn't forgiven me properly for leaving in such a hurry. When I called her, it seemed to take her several minutes to thaw out before we could relax enough to have a laugh.

'What sort of a party?' she'd asked.

'Oh, you know. Just a party. Maybe to show off the boat.'

'Will there be any nice blokes there?'

A mental image of Malcolm had flashed through my mind. 'Well...'

'Oh, alright, then. I guess so. You'll have to text me the address.'

'How's the club?' I'd asked, the way I always did.

'It's alright. Quiet at the moment. New girls started last week, crap most of them. No real competition any more.'

There was a pause. She knew what I was really asking and she always left me hanging. Sometimes she made me ask it; sometimes she took pity on me.

'Dylan's not been in the club much. Fitz has got him doing something, I think.'

'How is he?'

'Grumpy, same as always.'

And she'd laughed.

Where *was* she?

I found myself penned into the corner of the dinette by Malcolm and Joanna, somehow involved in a protracted discussion with Lucy about the toilet system and how it worked.

'But what about the shower?' Lucy shouted above the chatter in the cabin. Joanna was heating up bread in the galley, banging cupboard doors open and shut in the vain hope of finding a baking tray.

'What about it?' Malcolm said, his voice challenging. He had a thing about his hair – he never used shampoo to wash it, which wasn't a problem as far as he was concerned, but he got defensive if he thought someone was suggesting he was in some way grubby or unkempt.

'Well,' said Lucy, 'not putting too fine a point on it, it's a hose.'

'I know it's a hose,' I said. 'It won't always be a hose.'

*Oh, God, I'm drunk*, I thought. *I'm drunk already.*

I looked at my watch. Caddy should be here by now. Why wasn't she?

Malcolm said, 'Most people have bathrooms on board but, just in case, there's showers near the office. They're kept really clean and nice.'

'Oh, you mean like on a campsite?' Lucy said, although the closest she had come to camping was two half-day visits to Glastonbury, and even then she had stayed in a hotel.

'Yeah, kind of. But cleaner,' Malcolm said.

'Look, I'm building a bathroom at the end. A proper one with a bath,' I said, anxious that she wouldn't think I was intending to spend the rest of my life roughing it.

Malcolm coughed.

'I'll have it ready by Christmas, honest. It's going to have a proper bath, and after that I'm going to install an outdoor shower in my conservatory.'

'Your what?'

'I'm going to put a sliding roof on, beyond the bedroom. There's going to be about ten feet or so of deck that I can open up to the elements, with a shower. Then right at the bow I'll put another room – maybe an office or a snug or something.'

'It sounds like a lot of hard work,' said Joanna with a sympathetic smile.

'It's alright,' I said. 'I can work at my own pace.'

'How's the money side of it? Five months without an income would kill me,' said Lucy.

*That's because you spend all your money on clothes*, I found myself thinking. 'It's not going too badly. I've still got savings.'

'I thought you spent it all on the boat?'

'Not quite all of it.'

There was a pause. I was waiting for her to say something else – daring her. Malcolm was looking from me to Lucy and back again.

'So what job was it you did in London?' he asked.

18

'Sales,' I said, before Lucy could answer. 'You heard of ERP software? It stands for Enterprise Resource Planning. It's a big software package: you sell the core system to multinational organisations and then after that you keep trying to sell them bolt-on modules. You know, accounting modules, human resources, that kind of thing.'

Malcolm's eyes had glazed over.

'It's sales, basically,' I went on. 'Doesn't matter what you sell, the same principles apply. Except in our case it was high-pressure because we were accessing buyers at boardroom level, and trying to persuade them to spend hundreds of thousands of pounds.'

'And ninety per cent of the time,' Lucy chipped in, 'we were selling to blokes. And the rest of the sales team were all blokes. They try and say that sexual inequality is a thing of the past, but let me tell you it's alive and well in the world of corporate ERP sales.'

Malcolm had stopped listening, but Joanna was still with us. 'You were the only two women on the sales team? Out of how many?'

'Twenty in total,' Lucy said. 'And we were the first two they'd ever had. It was like being the first girls allowed to play in the treehouse.'

'I bet that was tough,' Joanna said.

'Still is,' Lucy said. 'Except I'm now the only girl in the treehouse, since Genevieve walked out.'

Joanna and Malcolm both looked at me in surprise.

'I'd had enough,' I said. 'All I wanted was to save up the money for the boat. After that I didn't want to hang around.'

'Must have been a good job, though, to earn you enough to buy a boat.'

Lucy dived in before I could stop her. 'Ah, well, Genevieve had two jobs, didn't you, Gen?'

'Most of the money was from sales,' I fibbed.

'Genevieve worked in a club,' Lucy said. She was looking directly at me, her expression unreadable.

My face felt hot. Across the other side of the cabin I could see Ben talking to Diane; both of them were laughing. He was so tall that he was almost stooping slightly, even though the ceiling was above six feet. He looked beautiful, and unreachable.

Liam appeared at the top of the steps. 'Joanna? Where's that scoopy thing for this cheesecake?'

'What "scoopy thing"? You mean a spoon?'

'Yeah, spoon, whatever. You got one?'

She got up from the dinette and rifled through the drawer in the galley, banging things about.

'There's a big spoon on that hook there, look,' I said.

Joanna unhooked the slotted spoon and, wielding it like a weapon, went up the steps to assist with the cheesecake.

'You worked in a club? What, like bar work?' Malcolm asked, animated.

I glared at Lucy, but either she didn't notice or she chose not to.

'Genevieve used to be a dancer,' Lucy said, a note of triumph in her voice. 'Didn't she tell you? She was really rather good. That's what I heard, though of course I never went in the club where she worked – more of a men-only place, if you get my meaning.'

Malcolm's eyes were like saucers. *Bitch*, I thought. I wished I hadn't invited her. And Caddy wasn't coming, clearly, otherwise she'd be here by now. I hadn't realised until that moment that I'd been looking forward to seeing her more than anyone else. And she would have been a useful ally against Lucy in any discussion about the moral or feminist aspects of dancing – nobody would have argued with Caddy.

'Do you ever get that feeling,' I said, more to myself than either of them, 'I don't know, sort of like impending doom? Like something bad is about to happen? I've had that all day.'

'I get that sometimes,' Lucy said. 'Usually when it gets to after two in the morning and I'm still drinking and I've got to get to work by seven the next day.'

It lightened the mood a little, but even so I had no desire to sit here and make small talk with Lucy any more. If she wanted to share any more details about my past, she could get on with it without me. I excused myself and Malcolm moved to let me out of the dinette. Squeezing past all the bodies in the galley, I climbed up to the deck.

I looked across to the car park, half-hoping to see Caddy being dropped off by a taxi. But everything was quiet. Josie sat with her back to the wheelhouse with Roger and Sally and, of all people, Gavin, who had taken off his jacket and his handmade Italian shoes and was sitting barefoot and cross-legged, telling them the story of when he went travelling and accidentally sold his passport in Thailand. They had the keg of homebrew balanced on a bucket in the middle of their circle and were helping themselves to it.

'Here,' said Ben, at my shoulder. He handed me another bottle of beer.

'Oh – thanks.'

The evening was starting to feel a bit surreal. We walked to the other side of the wheelhouse and looked to where the lights from the motorway bridge reflected in the water. The wind had dropped. From the opposite bank, the distant bass beat from the nightclub throbbed.

'I've not been drunk for months,' I said.

'I've not been drunk for – oh, I don't know. Days. Hours, more probably,' said Ben.

We sat on the roof of the cabin.

'I missed you,' he said.

I laughed at that. 'You big fibber,' I said. 'You never miss anyone, or anything.'

He looked a little bit hurt, but I knew it was an act. Despite all these people, despite everything that had happened between us in the past, he was just angling to stay the night.

'You've done a great job with the boat,' he said.

'Thank you.'

'I like the bedroom.'

*Here we go*, I thought.

'I like the skylight. It must be wonderful to lie there at night and look up at the stars.'

I smiled. 'Actually, it's more of an orange glow. Light pollution isn't just confined to London, you know.'

'I was trying to be romantic.'

'I know you were, Ben. But you forget I know you too well. It doesn't work on me any more.'

'Genevieve! What happened?'

'You have to ask? I saw you with that girl when you were supposed to be going out with me. Did you forget that?'

The words were easy to say now. At the time it had broken my heart.

Ben shook his head. 'Christ, you've got a long memory. I didn't mean that. I meant, what happened to you in London? You left so suddenly. Nobody knew where you'd gone. Lucy thought you'd been kidnapped.'

'Nothing happened. Don't be so dramatic.'

'Genny, you quit your job and walked out. You literally walked out.'

'Who told you that?'

'Who do you think? Lucy, of course. She said it was the most exciting thing that had ever happened in your office. She said you marched in to the CEO's office while he was having a meeting and threw your letter of resignation on the table. Then you just grabbed your coat and left. She said she had to empty your desk for you, and when she took the box round to your flat you were all ready to move out.'

I didn't speak for a moment. That feeling was back: the sense of disquiet. The tide had started to rise and in another few hours it would be at its highest point. Already the boat was moving, just slightly, the comforting feeling of the *Revenge* holding me up and cradling me. And yet, with the boat full of people, it didn't feel quite right.

From the skylight next to us on the roof, I could hear genial conversation coming up from the galley below changing subtly into more heated tones. Joanna and Malcolm, by the sounds of it – and, on the other side of the exchange, Lucy and Simone.

'All I said was – '

'I know what you said, and I know what you meant.' That sounded like Joanna.

'You lot are all the same, you haven't got a clue – ' and that sounded like Malcolm, the edges of his words blurred and slurred by cheap beer ' – you think just 'cause we live on a boat we're somehow inferior, just 'cause you choose to live in a house…'

'I didn't say anything of the kind!'

'Well, why was you going on about the bathroom, then? I tell you, when this boat's finished it'll be palatial, and you lot will all be blinded by jealousy.'

Lucy laughed. 'I don't think so somehow.'

On the deck above, I put my head in my hands. 'Oh, God. I knew this was a mistake.'

Ben took the opportunity and put his arm around my shoulders. 'They're just drunk, Genny. It'll all be forgotten in the morning.'

'Ben! Where the fuck are you?' Lucy was coming up the steps into the wheelhouse, stomping with her high-heeled boots on the varnished pine. 'Gavin? Let's go to the pub.'

'Want me to stay here?' Ben asked me quietly. He still hadn't been spotted.

'No,' I said. 'You go with them, it's fine.'

'I could always come back later.'

His voice sounded so hopeful that for a moment I looked up. *It would be so easy to say yes*, I thought. *It would be easy to have him here, to share my bed with him tonight and put him on the train to London in the morning*. Would it hurt, one night with Ben? Five months since Dylan, five long months waiting for him to make contact with me again. He obviously wasn't missing me as much as I missed him.

'Where the fuck's Ben?' Lucy said.

'What's up, princess?' Gavin asked, getting to his feet.

'I want to go somewhere else!'

'Have some of this,' Roger said soothingly, 'it'll make you feel better, I promise.'

'What is it?' Lucy sounded suspicious.

'It's magic potion,' said Gavin, giggling.

'What?'

'No, seriously, Luce. Give it a try. I've never had anything like it, honestly: it's like drinking the earth and the moon and the stars…'

'Gavin, you're so crap, you've been smoking skunk again, haven't you? I thought you said you hadn't got any left?'

'Rog here gave me a puff. But I tell you what, lovely Princess Lucy Loo, it's not nearly as good as this stuff. Here.'

'Eww! It tastes like shit!'

Laughter from the wheelhouse and the deck.

Ben was kissing me. He'd taken my face in his hands and kissed me, before I had a chance to protest, before I could say no, before I could move away. He was good at it. I could feel my barriers, my resolve and my resistance disappearing. It would be so easy to tell him to come back later on. Nobody would even notice. There was a good chance that the other liveaboards would all just disappear back to their own boats in the next hour or so. Once Lucy and the other London lot had gone to the pub, then on to Rochester or Maidstone or even, if they were desperate enough, back to London, the boatyard would be empty and quiet and nobody would even see him come back; nobody would ever need to know…

'Ben! There you are!'

The kiss ended abruptly. Lucy fixed me with a hard stare, as though it was all my fault that she had been irreparably insulted by these river people, the man with the mad hair and the girl with the black eye; clearly now to find Ben down here in the semi-darkness, with his mouth on mine and his hand inside my top, was pretty much the final straw.

'Are you staying here or are you coming with us?' Lucy asked, her voice chilly.

24

Before he had a chance to answer, I stood up. 'You should go,' I said softly.

'Why?'

Lucy had gone to herd up the rest of them, including Simone and Carla. Presumably they were expected to fit in the boot of the car.

I gave a little shrug.

'You've got someone else?'

'I've got a different life.'

He tried again, with his best cheeky smile to go with it. 'I'm not talking about any sort of commitment, Genny. Just one more night. Go on. You want me really, don't you?'

Despite myself, I laughed too.

'Amazing as the offer sounds, Ben, I would rather be on my own than have you here, even for one night. But thank you.'

He gave up, at last. 'Suit yourself,' he said, and turned his back on me to find Lucy.

They left, with promises to text or phone, hugs, professions of what a fabulous night it was and such a shame it had to come to an end, while I hugged them all in turn, and all the liveaboards carried on with the beer and the lively conversation and the last few bits of Liam's lasagne.

As I waved them off and the motion sensors triggered the lights in the car park, Lucy tripped over something and fell on her face – fortunately on the grass. Malcolm let out a hooting laugh.

Diane and Steve went soon after that. The baby monitor gave every indication that the children had got out of bed and were playing some kind of console game on board their boat – either that, or the boat had been stormed by terrorists who were shooting everything in sight.

Downstairs in the main cabin the conversation had turned to milder topics.

Joanna handed me a beer.

'Sit down and join us,' she said.

'I'm sorry they were such louts,' I said.

'They weren't louts.'

'I thought they were alright, on the whole,' piped up Malcolm, who seemed to have forgiven Lucy already.

'Thanks,' I said. 'You lot are lovely.'

'I think you should have shagged that Ben, though,' said Josie with a chuckle.

'What?'

'You think we couldn't hear you? He was begging for it. Absolutely begging.'

'Yes, he was a bit, wasn't he?'

She gave me a hefty nudge. 'I wouldn't have turned him down, if it were me,' she said.

'Oi,' said Malcolm, 'you old hussy. You'll end up kipping on the roof if you keep that up.'

I laughed. 'He's not all he's cracked up to be. Ben, I mean.'

'Ooh,' said Josie, 'you've been there before, then?'

'Been there, done that.'

'And he's no good at it? Blimey. Who'd have thought? He looks like a right one to me.'

I considered this for a moment. This wasn't a conversation I'd particularly planned to have.

'It's not that he's no good,' I said. 'It's just that he's not the sort of person I want any more.'

'You got your eye on someone else?' said Joanna.

'Not really. I just think I'm better off on my own for a bit, you know? Busy with the boat, and all that.'

'Ah, the boat,' said Roger. 'She's married to the boat already. Happens to us all. You still haven't shown me the new room.'

'Help yourself,' I said. 'Go and have a look.'

Malcolm took it upon himself to act as a tour guide, taking Roger to see the newly clad room, while I stayed in the saloon and finished off another bottle of beer. Too many, I thought. The woodstove was burning low and the saloon was warm

26

now that the door to the wheelhouse was closed. We all sat with our feet up, feeling the gentle rock of the boat on the water, lulling us to a doze.

I realised that I hadn't thought about Caddy since Ben had started flirting with me. Where was she? Maybe she'd had to work after all.

'We should do this more often,' Josie said drowsily.

'We always say that,' said Sally. She was curled like a child into the big, soft sofa, a patchwork blanket I'd bought from a charity shop over her feet.

'I like your boat,' said Joanna. 'Did you know that? You have one of the best boats out of all of us.'

This was a conversation we had regularly – who had the best boat and why. We never seemed to reach a conclusion.

'The *Souvenir* is my favourite,' I said.

Sally laughed. 'You're just saying that because you're sweet and lovely.'

'I like the *Souvenir* too,' said Joanna. 'I think the *Souvenir* is the best boat at the moment, but if Genevieve manages to pull off the conservatory with the sliding glass roof then the *Revenge* will be the best one.'

'You're right,' said Sally. 'We can't top a conservatory. All we've got is three pots and an allotment in Rochester.'

'What are you going to grow on your deck, Gen? Have you thought?'

I was wondering whether this was Josie's roundabout way of asking me to grow some cannabis for her and Malcolm, but before I had a chance to answer Malcolm and Roger came back.

'You do realise Liam's asleep on your bed, Genevieve?'

'Shit,' said Joanna. 'I wondered where he'd gone. I thought he'd fucked off back to the boat.'

She got up and went to try and rouse her partner from his beer-induced slumber.

'We should go,' said Malcolm. 'Busy day tomorrow.'

'Oh?' I said. 'What's happening?'

'We're going to look at dresses,' said Josie. 'My niece is getting married soon, and Malcolm's promised to take me shopping.'

'And before you ask,' said Malcolm, although none of us had said anything, 'I'm having me hair cut before the wedding, alright?'

# *Four*

Not long after that they all went, off my boat and back on to the pontoon, swaying back to their boats and the warmth of their respective woodburners.

I stayed in the saloon once I'd shut and locked the wheelhouse, gazing unfocused at the glow of the fire and finishing off my last bottle of beer. I was trying not to think about Ben. I wondered where they were staying. I didn't have his number, which was a good thing. I probably would have given in and texted him, and how desperate would that have looked?

The galley was a state – bottles and glasses and dirty plates everywhere. The floor was scattered with crumbs, from the garlic bread. Joanna and Liam's empty lasagne dish filled the sink, burnt-on bits glued to the edge. I wondered how much soaking it would take before I could present it back to them, clean.

Something was digging in...

I reached into the back pocket of my jeans, and there it was. Dylan's phone. I went through the menus again to the address book. GARLAND. Why that word, of all words? It was just a word, he'd said. It was supposed to be random. It was supposed to be something that nobody would suspect, if the phone got into the wrong hands.

'What if I want to contact you?' I'd said.

'Why would you want to contact me?'

He had no idea, none at all, about how I felt. I wasn't even sure of it myself, right then. I just knew that the concept of not seeing him was a difficult one to grasp.

'What if something goes wrong?' I said.

'Nothing's going to go wrong.' He was getting impatient. 'It will be fine, I promise you. Nothing will go wrong. When I'm ready, when I've got everything sorted out here, I'll ring you and we can meet up somewhere. Alright?'

That had been more than five months ago. All that time, I'd kept the phone on me, kept it charged up, and I'd never used it. Not once.

I tossed the phone clumsily on to the wooden shelf behind the sofa. There was no point sitting here thinking about Dylan. Wherever he was, he certainly wasn't thinking about me.

The toilet, which I'd emptied only this morning, was full and backed up. None of the liveaboards would have left it like that. I felt desolate, and alone. I should have said yes to Ben. It would have been nice to have just been here with him. He wasn't Dylan, but he was someone.

I turned the lights off, and climbed into bed.

I dreamed about the phone, Dylan's phone. It was ringing, the name GARLAND coming up on the display as if to emphasise further that this was it, this was the call; but every time I pressed the green button to answer, nothing happened.

I was half-awake and half-asleep for most of the night, opening my eyes to see the square of inky blackness above my head. Then Ben was in my dream, too. He was lying here with me.

'You lied about the stars,' he said.

I looked up to the skylight and it was full of stars, so bright that they blended together, just one dazzling light shining down on us.

Then I opened my eyes for real, and it was still just dark. There were stars – I could see them – but they were faint.

*Alcohol always does this to me*, I thought crossly.

I was properly awake, because I needed the toilet. I remembered mine was backed up and I wasn't about to go across to the shower block in the middle of the night, so I crawled into the storage space at the front of the boat and found the bucket I used to mix adhesive in. It was clean, which was a bonus. I left the bucket in the bathroom after I'd used it and went back to bed.

For a while I lay there listening to the lapping of the water against the hull. The tide must be going out by now. Before too long the boat would settle back into the mud and lie still, and then it would start to get light.

As well as the water, there was another sound. It started out as a gentle bump, distant, as though the bow had nudged the pontoon or one of the fenders had lifted in a sudden swell and fallen back against the hull. It was easy to ignore at first. But then it came again, and again, rhythmic now – part of the song of the boat, the percussion of the river.

The gentle bumping became a knocking, more insistent. A soft thud, a scrape of something along the hull. I was awake again, listening to the sound and trying to work out what it was. It sounded as though something was trapped between the boat and the pontoon, just outside my bedroom. And the tide was receding, which meant it was unlikely to be washed clear again. It would stay there, knocking, until the hull of the boat came to rest on the mud. Which was still hours away.

With a sigh, I sat up in bed, listening. It was coming with the rise and the fall of the water, a rhythmic bump. It was nestling against my boat, big enough to make a sound. What could it be? A plastic container, something like that?

Shivering, I pulled my jeans on in the dark, a sweater from the pile of washing. The boat was cold now; the stove had long since gone out. Just inside the hatch to the storage area was my torch, big and powerful and cased in rubber. I'd had a Maglite but I'd dropped it in the water during my first week on the boat and never got it back again. One of the first pearls of wisdom Malcolm had dispensed was: 'Put a float on anything important.'

I opened the door to the wheelhouse, my teeth chattering. It was bitter up here, freezing, the sky above barely grey. I slipped on the trainers that were by the wheel; they were cold and damp, but better than bare feet on the wet boards outside.

No sign of anyone. The boats in the marina were all silent and dark, the ones on this pontoon still rising and falling gently on the outgoing tide, the ones nearer to the shore already sitting on their bank of river mud.

To my surprise, I heard a noise from the direction of the car park – a door shutting? Then the noise of an engine starting up, and tyres on gravel. A dark shape of a vehicle driving out of the car park. No rear lights, no headlights. Why didn't they put their lights on? And why hadn't the lights come on in the car park? They were motion-sensitive. I remembered someone complaining to Cam that the lights shone into their cabin when the foxes were out by the bins. Solution – the bins were moved. But surely the lights should come on if someone was in the car park?

Silence, apart from the lapping of the water against the bow. Even the motorway bridge was silent. Then it came again. A soft bumping, accompanied now by a gentle splashing as a little wave drifted over whatever it was. It must be something big.

I crept along the port side of the gunwale, holding on to the side of the cabin for support. I was still a little bit drunk, the gentle rocking of the boat making me nauseous.

For some reason I felt afraid. Out here, away from London, it felt wrong to be awake at this time of the night.

When I got roughly alongside the bedroom, I turned on the torch, surprisingly and suddenly bright, a powerful beam shining out from it and hitting the vast conifers that rose behind the marina office. Then I directed the beam down into the space between the *Revenge of the Tide* and the pontoon.

I couldn't tell what it was, at first.

A bundle. Something covered in fabric.

My first thought, my first crazy, misplaced thought, was of the black plastic sack full of random fabrics that I'd thrown carelessly into the storage space in the bow. But it couldn't be that. This was clearly something heavy, judging by its sluggishness, its reluctance to be moved by the water. It was floating, knocking into the side of the hull – right where my bed was.

I went back to the wheelhouse and found my boat-hook, a long pole which had come with the boat and to my knowledge never been used, not by me at any rate – the *Revenge* hadn't left this mooring since I'd moved in. The hook was heavy and unwieldy, and for a moment I contemplated leaving everything where it was and going to sleep on the sofa with my duvet, but it was no good. The knocking was regular but not regular enough – just random enough to slowly but surely drive me crazy.

I tucked the boat-hook under my right arm and clutched the torch in my left, but the hook was too heavy – it needed both hands. I put the torch down on the roof of the cabin, its beam shining across the tops of all the narrowboats and all the way over to the office.

I fished around with the boat-hook until it made contact with the object. I jabbed at it. It was solid, and heavy. I tried a couple of times to grab at it with the hook but, when it finally connected, the bundle was too heavy for me to lift. I felt it roll, turn, pulling the pole almost out of my grasp, so I wriggled it until it was free and peered over the edge of the gunwale into the darkness below.

Something pale, something shapeless, part of the object but somehow different from it. I got the torch, shone it down into the space – and Caddy's face looked back up at me. One eye closed, one eye half-open, gazing up at me in a bizarre, twisted sort of a wink. Her hair, a dark tangle, swirling and washing over her face in the muddy water.

I dropped the boat-hook. It clattered at an angle on the gunwale and tipped over on to the pontoon, rolling to a stop. I was breathing fast and hard and then I found my voice and screamed, screamed louder and harder than I ever had in my life.

# Five

By the time it was daylight, the shock started to kick in. Josie, who had been a paramedic in a former life, sat with me in the saloon of the *Souvenir* and was keeping a close eye on me.

The police were on my boat.

Malcolm had called them. He and Josie had been the first ones to get to me, although not long after that the whole marina was awake and milling around in various states of undress, waiting for the police to arrive. They all took turns to look down the side of the boat with the torch, at the body. Eventually Malcolm had shouted at everyone to go to one place and wait for the police – they were contaminating the scene – and most of them went back to their boats.

One police car had arrived, and two patrol officers. We'd met them in the car park of the marina. The automatic lights still didn't appear to be working, so it was dark and by that time I was shaking, shaking from head to foot. One of them asked me questions about what I'd seen and heard while the other one went to look.

I hadn't cried. Instead I'd found myself making a sound that started out like a wail of panic, something I couldn't control, a noise from somewhere inside which came from fear and horror at finding her like that; finding Caddy of all people, my beautiful Caddy. The noise went on and on, rising and fading again as I ran out of breath, while Josie held me against her bosom and shushed me and rocked me, and I held on to her.

When I'd calmed down again, they made me go with Sally and Josie to the *Souvenir*. More police cars came, and a motor boat came up the river with other police on it. They put some kind of net over the end of my boat and tied the other side of it to the pontoon, presumably so the body didn't float off on the outgoing tide, although it didn't seem to want to go anywhere. Now it was daylight, low tide, and I was sitting in the saloon with two blankets around me, one around my shoulders and the other across my knees, but even so I was shaking. I couldn't stop thinking about how filthy my trainers were, and whether anyone would notice if I took them off.

People kept asking me questions, and to each of them I gave the answer, 'I don't know, I don't know.' I was only half-aware of all the people in the cabin, and people were talking about me as though I wasn't there at all. In truth, my presence was mostly physical.

Caddy was dead. An accident? Had she tripped, somehow, in the darkness? Had she come to the party earlier, and I'd not realised? Had she fallen over, stumbled against something and hit her head on one of the posts? Why hadn't I heard anything? Why hadn't I noticed?

'What's happened?' It was Roger. He'd managed to sleep through it all.

'It's a body in the water. Against the *Revenge of the Tide*.'

'Is she alright?' Malcolm's voice.

'She'll be fine, I'm keeping my eye on her. She just needs a bit of peace and quiet for a while, that's all.'

'Genevieve?'

'I said leave her alone, Malcolm, alright? Honestly, you should know better.'

'I just wanted to ask her if she wants me to talk to the police for her, you know, kind of like a liaison…'

'What's she want a liaison for, you big twat? Honestly, she's perfectly capable of speaking to the police when they need her to. Anyway, she didn't see anything, she just found the body. Could have happened to any of us.'

'Her boat's nearest the river. It must have come down the river from Cuxton. Her boat's the one that would catch it first if it came downstream.'

'Who says it went in at Cuxton?'

'I never said that. I said it must've come from the Cuxton side, that's all. That's where the last one came from, remember? That bloke that got stuck in the mud. Last Christmas.'

'You're wrong. The last one was that stupid fool who jumped off Aylesford bridge in the summer.'

'That one ended up in Gillingham, not here.'

'I *know* that, I was just saying, that was the last body.'

'Why are you all arguing about it?'

This last voice was Sally's. She'd been crying, off and on, not noisily but dabbing her eyes with a tissue, mourning someone she didn't know.

They were all silent for a while.

I said, in a voice that sounded somehow different from my own, 'Aren't you going shopping?'

It felt as if they were all staring at me and my face grew hot.

'Oh, don't you worry yourself about that,' Josie said. 'We can go later.'

'Shall I get you a drink, Genny? A cup of tea?' Sally said.

She'd made one for me an hour ago. It was still there on the table, cold.

'I don't know,' I said again. 'No. I don't think so.'

'Wonder who she was,' said Malcolm.

'Let's not talk about it any more,' said Josie, patting me on the knee. 'Plenty of other things to talk about, after all.'

But that didn't work either. A man came down the stairs from the deck, a man in a suit. He had thinning grey hair cut short, dark eyes, a lined face.

'Morning,' he said. 'Detective Sergeant Andy Basten. I'm looking for Genevieve Shipley?'

They all looked at him and then at me, despite themselves, and almost imperceptibly they all seemed to move a fraction closer to me as if to afford me some sort of protection.

He showed me his warrant card and his badge. The badge had rubbed against the card in the tatty leather wallet and you could hardly see his picture, let alone his name. He looked as though he liked a beer or two.

The *Souvenir* was a big boat, but not as big as the *Revenge of the Tide*, and it felt crowded in the saloon with all these people.

'We'll – er – leave you to it, shall we?' said Malcolm.

'I'm staying here,' Josie said, 'unless she wants me to leave.'

I wanted her to stay. I wanted her to tell him to go away, the policeman; tell them all to go and leave us alone. I wanted to rewind to last night and that terrible, insistent noise and, instead of going to look, turn over and put my hands over my ears and go back to sleep.

'I'm alright, Josie. Honest,' I said at last.

They all went up on deck, leaving me there with the policeman.

'This won't take too long,' he said. 'Must have been a terrible shock for you.'

I nodded, rapidly. My head felt wobbly, as though it wasn't connected to my body properly. 'I was half-asleep. It woke me up very quickly when I realised what it was.'

He sat down on the armchair opposite me and took out a notebook. 'I know you've been through all this with the officer earlier. I just want to check we've got things straight. You said you heard a noise?'

'I heard a knocking on the side of the boat. It woke me up. I went to find out what it was.'

I was repeating myself already, babbling. My mind wasn't functioning properly; it was working at least three beats behind my mouth. *Think. Concentrate. Don't say anything. Don't tell him anything.*

'That sort of thing happen often?'

'No. Sometimes rubbish gets caught against the boat when the tide goes out. That's what I thought it was.'

He nodded. 'It's a nice boat,' he said. 'Live there alone, do you?'

'Yes. I'm renovating it. I had savings from my job in London. I'm taking a year out to do the boat up. I've been here five months already, I've done most of it by myself. All the cladding. The plumbing.'

I was rambling now, but he didn't stop me. Just watched me with tired-looking eyes.

'I'm sorry it was such a mess in there. We had a party last night. Why did you need to go in my boat, anyway?'

'We're finished with it now,' he said. 'Just needed to check it wasn't part of the crime scene, that's all. Birthday party, was it?'

'Kind of a boat-warming, I guess. Some of my friends from London. Lots of people who live here.' I indicated the marina with a vague sweep of my hand.

'I'll need to get you to write me a list. Everyone who was here last night. That okay?'

'Of course.'

'And you all had a good time? At the party?'

I nodded.

'The woman you found,' he said, 'she wasn't one of your party guests?'

I stared at him. 'They all left. All the London lot. They all went early. I saw them leave the car park.'

His question had reminded me of something and, before he had a chance to ask me anything else, I said, 'There was a car, last night. I've just remembered. In the car park. When I went outside to see what the knocking noise was, I heard a car driving off. I thought it was odd because it didn't have its lights on and it was still dark. And the light's supposed to come on in the car park, it's on a motion sensor, and it didn't work. The light didn't come on.'

The sergeant was noting all this down and when I ran out of words he was still writing. 'You didn't see what sort of car it was? Registration number? Colour?'

'It was dark. I mean the colour. That was all I could see.'

He nodded slowly, made another note.

'Do you know who it is?' I asked, trying to keep the trembling out of my voice.

'You mean the body? Did you recognise her, Genevieve?'

'No,' I said, quickly. 'I couldn't really see the face, anyway. I just saw that it was a body and I started screaming.'

He didn't say anything. He was looking at me curiously, as though he knew something I didn't. As though I'd said something particularly interesting.

He'd written everything down, laboriously, on three sheets of lined A4 paper headed with various official titles, and he handed them to me. I looked at them blankly, at the rounded letters on the page, thinking how his handwriting was girlish, not what I'd expected at all.

'I need you to sign it,' he said.

'What is it?'

'Your statement. You need to read it through carefully and check that you agree with everything I've written. Then you need to sign the bottom of each page. There – see? And there.'

I read through it. He'd written it on my behalf, as though I'd done it myself. It was odd seeing my words summarised in that curiously rounded script. I kept thinking how I would have phrased it differently – 'it was dark and I didn't see the face of the person clearly' – but I couldn't bring myself to question it. I signed each page with a rough approximation of my signature and handed it back to him.

'Can I go back to my boat now?'

'Not just yet. We'll come and find you when we're ready, okay? Are you feeling alright?'

'I think so.' I unwrapped myself from the blankets slowly, as though I was peeling off bandages. My body ached as though I'd fallen over. I felt a wave of relief: maybe I'd got away with it.

'We'll come and talk to you again, maybe tomorrow,' he said. 'Can I take your phone number?'

I recited it to him. 'I don't think I can tell you any more,' I said. 'It woke me up, I went to look, and I found it. That's it.'

'Yes,' he said, giving me his card. *Detective Sergeant Andrew Basten, Major Crime.* 'But you never know. You might remember something else. Like the car in the car park. Your brain does funny things when you've had a shock; it's like it only lets you remember one thing at a time.'

He led the way up the steps on to the deck of the *Souvenir.* Sally and Josie were sitting on the wooden bench, with Sally's petunias and pelargoniums, just starting to look autumn-bedraggled, in pots around them.

'Alright?' said Josie when she saw me coming up the steps.

'I'm fine. Thank you.'

'You look terribly pale,' said Sally.

Basten cleared his throat. 'I'll leave you to it,' he said. 'Let me know if you think of anything else in the meantime.'

He didn't head for the car park; instead he climbed off the *Souvenir* and headed towards the pontoon where the *Revenge of the Tide* was moored. There were still lots of people around; crime scene tape fluttered across the start of the pontoon and he lifted it and ducked beneath it. At the end of the pontoon, two figures dressed in white boiler suits were on their hands and knees doing something. The whole area was illuminated by lights on metal rigging, as though they were preparing to make a movie. It was daylight, and yet still cloudy enough to make the lights necessary. I thought about what they were illuminating, down there, and shivered. The space between the end of the pontoon and the side of the hull was draped in a huge blue tarpaulin.

The tide was out now.

'They've not taken anything away,' said Sally. 'I think the body must still be down there.'

Along with all the other cars in the car park, a black Transit van with 'Private Ambulance' in grey letters on the side had arrived. At the main gate, two police officers were standing guard to prevent vehicles entering or leaving.

'I heard one of them say they were going to move it soon. Before the tide turns.'

We watched the activity as people came and went. The road filled up with spectators and a constable was stationed there to move people on. Then the press arrived, and spent the rest of the morning hanging around trying to take pictures of anything interesting. Sally made sandwiches. Josie ate two. I stared at them because I didn't want to look at anything else. In the end I lay on the sofa in the saloon of the *Souvenir* and tried to sleep. I could hear them talking, on the deck, commenting on the action in the marina. I tried to block out the sounds, but they still came through.

What seemed like hours later, I heard Basten on the deck of the *Souvenir*, telling Sally that I could go, if I wanted to.

I went up to the deck but he'd already left.

'He said you can go back,' Sally said. 'They're still working down there but you can go back if you want to.'

I looked doubtfully down to the pontoon, where the *Revenge* was still surrounded by people in white boilersuits. Josie pulled me into a hug. She was big and warm and soft. 'You poor girlie,' she said into my hair. 'Do you want me to come with you?'

'No, thanks,' I said. 'I think I'll just go back to bed and try and get some sleep. I'm so tired.'

I was tired, it was true, but there was no way I was going to be able to sleep. I just needed to be alone. I needed them all to leave me on my own, so I could think. So I could work out what to do, without having to worry about accidentally giving something away.

'Alright, then. I'll come and look in on you later.'

I stepped off the *Souvenir* gingerly, my legs shaking. I felt as if I'd been ill, or asleep for a long time. The bright lights lit up the scene dramatically; I couldn't think of a time when I'd seen so many people in the marina.

A young policewoman tried to stop me when I got close to my boat.

'He said it would be okay for me to go home,' I said, pointing at Basten.

'Oh, it's your boat? Let me just check.'

The sergeant was at the end of the pontoon, talking on his mobile phone. The police officer got his attention and pointed back to where I stood behind the flapping strands of blue and white plastic tape.

I heard him say, 'Yeah, let her through.'

She gave me a smile and beckoned me forward. 'Must have been a shock for you,' she said, before I had time to reach the gangplank.

'Yes, it was,' I agreed. I had no desire whatever to go through all this again.

'Take it easy,' was all she said. Her smile was warm.

I stumbled down the steps to the cabin, my legs like jelly.

I picked up Dylan's phone from where I'd thrown it the night before. My hands were shaking as I scrolled through the menus to the address book, selected the only name in there: GARLAND. I pressed 'call'.

It was ringing. My heart was pounding at the thought of talking to him.

'Yeah?'

Oh, the voice. It had been so long and yet I remembered it instantly, it came flooding back – everything.

'It's me.' My voice was low, urgent. I didn't want to risk anyone overhearing.

'Yeah. What do you want?'

I hadn't been expecting an especially enthusiastic response, given his unequivocal instructions never to call him, but I hadn't been prepared for quite such a hostile tone.

'It's about Caddy.'

'Caddy?'

'She's dead, Dylan. I found her last night. She was in the water, next to the boat. I heard this noise, and I went to look, and then I found her in the water.'

An indrawn breath, a pause. 'What a fucking mess. What the hell was she doing there?'

'She was supposed to be coming to my party, and she didn't turn up, and – '

'Why the fuck did you invite her to your party?'

It registered somewhere in my foggy brain that he didn't seem that shocked that someone we both knew well had met such a horrible death. And was this somehow my fault – was he blaming me? Because I'd invited her to come to the party?

'What should I do?' I asked miserably.

'Did you tell them anything?'

'No. Nothing. I didn't say I knew her. What should I do, Dylan? I'm so afraid.'

There was a pause. I couldn't hear any noise in the background, no traffic, no voices. I wondered if he was at home, or in the car. I longed to be there, wherever it was. If I could see him, if I could see his face, this nightmare wouldn't be quite so awful. I felt another lurch of misery, like a jolt.

'Just keep your head down, right? I'll be in touch.'

I went to say something else to him, something – what? That I missed him? That I wanted to see him? – but I didn't get the chance. He'd disconnected the call.

I'd waited so long to talk to him again. And of all the conversations I'd imagined, none of them bore any resemblance to that one. Despite the exhaustion, the panic, one thing registered above anything else: he already knew. He knew Caddy was dead.

# *Six*

The cabin was still a mess. I'd been staring at it for half an hour and not seeing it, my brain trying to process the image of Caddy in the water through a fog of tiredness and alcohol.

I set to work clearing up, sweeping up the breadcrumbs, soaking the dishes in the sink and then working my way through them methodically, my back to the scene of chaos behind me. The clouds had cleared, and through the porthole above the sink I could see the river, peaceful and sparkling in the bright sunshine. It looked like it did on every other sunny day, and for a moment I could focus on the task in hand and forget about last night.

When everything was washed and dried I was almost tempted to wash it all again, just so I could stay in the warmth and safety of that moment. I put it all away, leaving the lasagne dish on the table in the dinette. I would take it back to Joanna later on. The bathroom smelled very bad, but I had no intention of emptying the toilet cassette while the pontoon outside was swarming with police officers. I used the bucket again, and closed the door behind me.

The new room was just as I had left it, the woodwork soft with the last of the sanding, a shaft of sunlight dancing with specks of sawdust. It smelled of fresh timber. It would almost be a shame to paint over it all.

The smell of the wood reminded me of my dad, as it always did. Certain smells took me back to his workshop, a large shed behind our house built of corrugated asbestos and breeze blocks: linseed oil, turps, pickled onions, barley sugars, and engine oil. My dad was a practical man. He could fix anything, build anything and repair anything. He scoured car boot sales for lonely and discarded items that could be recycled, reworked or otherwise brought back to life with a bit of care and attention. His workshop had rows of old pickle jars half-full of screws, nuts, bolts, nails, capacitors, resistors and fuses, nailed by their lids to the cobwebby beams overhead. As well as random bits of machinery, he collected cars that now would be called classic: a Ford Escort Mark II, a Citroën 2CV, and a Lotus which, even with his best effort and constant tinkering, never travelled another mile under its own power. My mother tolerated it all, since it kept him out of the house and out of her way.

I was never excited by the cars. I watched him as he tinkered and fixed, but I never felt that same drive to see those old things working again. But when he got out his workbench and the woodworking tools I was always there, ready to help. I built a chair when I was nine years old. There was something about the transformation from the rough wood to the beautiful, practical lines and curves of the finished article that I found inspiring.

He died the day I sat my final exam at university. I'd rung home when I'd finished, but there'd been nobody there. He had suffered a massive heart attack in the shopping centre at lunchtime. My mother had told me she knew he was dead the moment he fell.

I went back into my bedroom, looking for something to do. This was turning into the longest day of my life, and it felt as though I'd been awake for a week. It was too early to go to bed, but it looked so tempting, the duvet thrown back. Just as I had left it last night when I went to investigate that noise.

I took off my jeans and lay down on the bed, pulling the duvet over myself. I was shattered, my head aching with the remains of what was probably a hangover from all that beer I'd drunk last night.

I lay there for a while, dry-eyed, wondering why I wasn't crying. Caddy's body was outside, probably less than two metres away from where I was lying, in the mud of the river Medway. Dylan had answered me as though I was the last person on earth he wanted to speak to. There were so many things wrong with this that I couldn't begin to understand what could have happened.

Thinking about it made my head hurt. And my heart.

It was impossible to sleep, to rest, even to think. I could hear them talking out on the pontoon – just the impression of voices at first, but when I sat up in the bed I could make out phrases.

'...could be worse, at least it's not been raining...'

'...get out of here before it starts...'

I wanted to know how she'd died. I wondered if they would tell me, if I asked.

She couldn't have been there when the party started. It must have been afterwards, after everyone had gone. I'd sat in the saloon, looking at the mess, and Caddy was – where? Outside, on the pontoon? In the car park?

Had she come for the party after all, slipped and fallen into the river? No, she hadn't. I remembered that first glance, what I'd seen in the beam of the torch, the shock that it was Caddy – and her face had been misshapen, her head – some kind of wound, too deep for an accidental blow – she'd been hit.

Why hadn't I heard anything? Why hadn't she made a sound, screamed?

She hadn't just fallen in the water. She hadn't floated downriver from Cuxton or anywhere else upstream. Someone had killed her, and dumped her body in the water, next to my boat.

Outside, on the pontoon, a mobile phone rang.

It was no use. There was no way I was going to sleep. I got out of bed and went back to the saloon, got a clean glass out of the cupboard and ran the tap. The water still didn't take the taste away. Last night's beer, last night's panic.

I heard the sounds of footfalls on the deck above and then a sharp knock on the door to the wheelhouse.

'Yes?'

The door opened and a man in a suit appeared at the top of the steps. But it wasn't Basten: this one was younger, with dark hair and dark eyes and – unexpectedly – a nice smile.

Just as I was thinking how easy it was to spot police officers, I realised he was looking me up and down. Knickers. Cropped T-shirt, displaying an expanse of midriff.

'Sorry. Didn't realise you were – er…'

'I was just trying to get some sleep,' I said, even though I was patently standing in my saloon and not in the bedroom.

'Miss Shipley?'

'Yes.'

'I'm DC Jim Carling.' He showed me his badge. Like Basten's, it was scuffed and worn so badly that the image was unrecognisable.

'I already spoke to somebody.'

'I know. I just wanted to let you know that they're bringing the body up now. Didn't want you to get another nasty shock.'

'Oh,' I said, my voice rising. I looked across to the porthole without thinking, at the several pairs of legs that had now gathered on the pontoon.

He came down the steps into the cabin, so he was on my level. 'I'll stay with you for a bit, if you like,' he said gently. 'Here.'

He'd taken the crocheted blanket from the sofa and put it around me, guiding me to the sofa to sit down so my back was to the porthole. For the first time I felt tears starting.

'It's alright, Genevieve,' Carling said. 'It'll be fine.'

He was nice, really, I thought. He had a kind face.

Like Dylan. Dylan had a kind face. He had a face that only a mother could love, he'd said once. He did look like a right bruiser, broken nose from boxing when he was a kid, misshapen ears, shaved head – but then, an unusually sensual mouth, and beautiful eyes, kind eyes. He wasn't what any girl would describe as handsome. Maybe that had been a blessing, otherwise I would have fallen for him sooner than I did, and then everything would have been different.

As it was, I only really realised how special he was once I'd left London and it was too late to go back. And now, five months later, he didn't sound as if he wanted to know me any more.

Carling was in the armchair, looking around the saloon. I wondered if he'd ever been on board a houseboat before today.

'Do you want to have a look round?' I asked.

'Hm? Oh.' He looked curiously embarrassed, as though I'd caught him out, looking at something he shouldn't. 'That's okay. I just – I think it's nice in here. You've done a good job.'

'Thank you.'

'What made you want to live on a boat, then?'

I smiled at him. 'I don't know. Just something I always wanted to do: buy a boat, spend a year doing it up.'

'Cost lots of money?'

'I had a good job in London for a few years, saved up.'

'What are you going to do when the year's up?'

'I don't know. I might stay on the boat, try and get a job around here. Or go back to London.'

From the pontoon came noises, shouts. They were hauling up the body. Josie told me afterwards that there were four of them were in the mud, wearing waders. Another four on the pontoon. She watched the whole thing from the safety of *Aunty Jean*. They'd put a tent up, perched on the end of the pontoon and rocking in the wind because they had nothing to anchor it to, because the car park was starting to fill up with press. Cameron was talking to the journalists, while next to my boat they lifted her out of the mud and on to the pontoon. She was tiny, Caddy, probably weighed no more than seven stone, but it took eight of them to lift her up.

'It'll be strange, going back to a nine-to-five after this, won't it?' he asked. His voice was jovial, a little forced. I think he was trying to distract me.

'It will. I don't know if I'll be able to do it. But the money will run out soon enough.'

'Does this thing work? I mean – does it go anywhere?'

'It could do, I guess. I've never tried the engine but it does have one. That part of it is beyond my technical capability at the moment.'

'You should take it on a journey, before the money runs out.'

'Maybe I should.'

There was an awkward pause. I wanted to ask about him about his job, what it was like. I wanted to ask if he was married, what he did when he wasn't working. But none of it would come out. It sounded wrong, to be asking such things, given what was happening outside.

'Would you like a drink, Mr Carling?' I asked at last. 'Coffee?'

He smiled, a warm smile. 'That would be great. Thank you. And call me Jim.'

'Jim. Alright, then.' I pushed the blanket to one side and went to the galley, filling the kettle from the sink and putting it on the gas burner. At least I'd managed to clean the kitchen this morning. If he was going to spend time on my boat, he might as well see it at its best.

'It's an odd name for a boat,' he said. 'In the circumstances.'

'I guess so. It was already called that when I bought it. Apparently it's bad luck to change the name.'

I turned from the galley and caught him looking at my legs. He blushed, just a little. Poor man. I should really put some jeans on.

'I couldn't be having much worse luck, really, could I?' I said.

'I guess it's not really luck. Your boat is the closest to the river; if it was going to wash up anywhere it would be here.'

I wondered at what point Caddy had changed from a 'she' into an 'it'. The thought of it made me want to cry.

Carling stood.

'I think,' he said, 'I would really like to look at the rest of the boat. You don't mind?'

'Go ahead,' I said.

From here I could see down the corridor to the end, to the hatch leading to the storage area at the bow. He wouldn't go in there. If he did, I told myself, he would just see boxes, carpentry tools, tubs of emulsion and paintbrushes. But he wouldn't go in there. Not with his suit on, at any rate.

He stopped at my bedroom and looked inside. 'I like the skylight,' he called.

'Yes,' I said. 'It's nice to wake up to. I like it when it's raining.'

He said something else, but the kettle was starting to whistle on the stove and I missed it. I poured water in the coffee mugs and left them, and went to find him.

He was in my bedroom, looking up at the skylight.

'I didn't hear what you said, I'm sorry.'

He started a little and turned. 'Oh, I just said… it's cosy.'

We stood for a minute facing each other. My jeans were on the floor by his feet, the duvet a tangle on the bed.

'I should… um… put my clothes on.'

'Oh, yes. Sure. Sorry.'

'You could finish off making the coffee, if you like.'

His cheeks were pink. He squeezed past me and went back to the galley, while I pulled my jeans back on and found a thin jumper, one that didn't make me look like an ancient mariner.

'I wouldn't go in the bathroom,' I said as I went back to the galley. 'Toilet needs emptying.'

'You have to empty the toilet?' he said, handing me a mug.

'Yes. You get used to it. When I do the bathroom up I'm going to put one in with a bigger cassette, then I won't need to empty it so often. Or maybe a composter.'

'It's starting to sound a bit less idyllic,' he said.

'I'm not looking forward to the winter, to be honest. It gets really windy here.'

A mobile phone rang and it made me jump out of my skin. Carling fished in his pocket for his phone while my heart raced.

'DC Carling. Okay… thanks. No worries. Bye.' He drank his coffee. 'They're all done out there now,' he said. 'Will you be alright?'

I nodded. 'Yes. Thank you. It was kind of you to stay with me.'

'Thank you for the coffee. I'll have to see the rest of your boat another time, maybe.' He scribbled his mobile number on a scrap of paper. 'Call me if you remember anything else.'

I wondered if policemen always said that.

When he'd gone, and I'd shut the door of the wheelhouse and locked it behind him, the boat felt very empty, and very big. I stared at the closed door, thinking about what circumstances could bring him back here again, and whether giving him a tour of the rest of the boat would be an option.

I stood for a moment in the silence. I should eat something, I thought, but I had no appetite. My coffee was going cold and I didn't even have the stomach for that. I should try to sleep, but I knew I would just lie there thinking about it all.

In the end I started by wiping down the woodwork in the new room, getting the dust off everything so that I could paint it. Autopilot kicked in, which was a blessed relief. I put the radio on, which meant I could block out the sound of feet tramping up and down on the pontoon outside – what were they doing out there? Surely they'd looked at everything, sampled everything, photographed everything?

The boat had been my dad's idea. It was one of our main topics of discussion, in his workshop. There was some unspoken understanding that it was only to be mentioned in that sacred space, between us: that if my mother knew of this, she would flip. He shared his dream with me. One day, he said, he would buy a boat and do it up, then he would take it around the canals and rivers of Britain. We spent hours discussing the merits of the narrowboat over the barge, whether to do just the fitting out ourselves or whether to buy a rusting shell and tackle the welding too. He sneaked in boat magazines which he secreted in a box under the workbench and we pored over the classified ads, choosing our dream boat and then changing our minds, over and over again. We set ourselves imaginary budgets and planned interiors. I had different names for my boat every week, but Dad's was always the same. He was always going to call his boat *Livin the Dream*. I tried to tell him how naff this was, but he didn't care. It was his dream, his decision.

My mother found his magazines when she ventured into the workshop for the first time, two months after the funeral. She'd burned them in the back garden, along with a whole pile of wood that he'd been planning to make into a chest of drawers.

When the woodwork was clean and everything in the room smelled of damp pine, the floor swept and washed too, I realised it had gone quiet outside. I stuck my head out of the wheelhouse. There were police cars in the car park, and the gates were shut – all the other cars and people outside the gate. Cameron must have evicted the press. The pontoon was as it always had been – empty, and starting to move on the rising tide. If there was anything left to find down in the mud, their chance had gone.

I seized the opportunity to head for the disposal tank, and emptied the toilet cassette and the bucket I'd used in the night, cleaned them both and scrubbed the bathroom from top to bottom. Then I took a bagful of washing up to the laundry and stuck it in the washing machine, leaving it to its own devices while I took a hot shower in the shower block. The hose was alright. It had been fine in the summer. But now the weather was turning chilly I should think about sorting the bathroom out next; I couldn't keep coming out here when it was getting darker in the evenings.

I felt better once I'd showered, and back at the boat I made myself a fresh cup of coffee. After that I went back to the laundry and transferred the washing into the drier. Cameron was in the car park, up a ladder.

'How's it going?' he called.

'Okay, I guess,' I said. 'Are you fixing the lights?'

'Yeah. Something's snagged the cable.'

'Really?'

He climbed down the ladder and showed me the section of cable he'd just replaced. It looked as if it had been caught around something, twisted.

'I guess that means there wasn't any CCTV either,' I said.

Cam shook his head. 'The camera one was alright; that feeds directly into the office. It's only the lights that have gone. Of course, without the lights the camera's not going to have picked up much, but they might be able to see something. I dunno.'

The police cars were still in the car park, two of them, but there was no sign of their occupants. The lights were on in the *Souvenir*, and in a couple of the other boats. The sun had gone in and the wind had picked up a little, and the clouds were making the afternoon feel darker and later than it was.

Back on the boat, the woodwork in the new room had dried off and I decided that now would be as good a time as any to paint it. I went to the end of the corridor and opened the hatch into the storage area. It was dark in there, and cold. The torch I usually kept just inside the doorway was missing. For a moment I hunted around for it, and then I realised it was probably still on the roof of the cabin where I'd left it last night.

I turned on the light in the hallway, one I rarely used, and it shone brightly enough into the cavernous space to show me where the tub of undercoat was, and the brushes in a carrier bag.

The light shone directly into the bow and illuminated the box at the end. KITCHEN STUFF. I tried not to look at it.

If I ignored it long enough, I would forget it was even there. But, once I'd got the paint loaded into the tray and started work on the plain pine cladding, the thought would not leave me alone.

I had to get rid of it. I had to get rid of the parcel.

Dylan should have come to collect it. A few weeks, he'd said, maybe a couple of months. Five months was really pushing his luck. And it couldn't stay where it was. If the police took it upon themselves to search the boat properly, they would find it and then I would be in big trouble.

I worked fast, splashing paint on to the wood. Missing bits. Going over other bits twice.

On my first night on the boat, I'd lain awake on the sofa in the saloon – the only really habitable space on the boat back then – and thought about all the hiding places, all the options. It had to be somewhere safe. It had to be close by, where I could be certain that it was still there, that it hadn't been tampered with. It had to be dry, and well-hidden enough that someone wouldn't accidentally come across it.

The very front of the bow was the place I chose. If I'd realised I was going to have to hide it for all this time, I would have incorporated a better hiding place into one of my build projects – a false wall maybe, a hidden compartment behind the cladding. Too late for that now.

The porthole was a dark circle, nothing beyond it but black. The boat rocked gently, almost imperceptibly, beneath my feet on the river. The wind was blowing waves up from the estuary, and after a while I heard rain on the skylight in the hallway outside.

I finished painting. It wasn't a very good job. I would put another coat on in the morning, and try harder to concentrate.

I turned the radio off and the quiet was like a blanket that descended on the boat. Just the tickling of the rain on the roof of the cabin, on the skylights. It was a lonely night to be on board a boat this big. I washed the brush out in the sink and thought about making something to eat, a proper meal. I still had no appetite.

I couldn't bring myself to think of it, and yet it was there, all the time. Waking up, still half-drunk. The sound. Caddy's body, against the side of my boat. The cable to the automatic light in the car park, mangled and snapped. The car, driving away with its lights off.

# Seven

I hadn't expected to be able to sleep, but somehow I did. I kept both phones by the bed, mine and Dylan's, and neither of them rang. Apart from the rain, which grew heavy, and the gentle rise and fall of the river, nothing stirred all night.

When I looked out of the wheelhouse the next morning, one of the two police cars was still parked in the car park. No sign of anyone in it.

It was still raining, so I pulled on my thick waterproof jacket and took a plastic bag over to the laundry room with me. My clothes were in a laundry basket by the side of the drier, neatly folded. The washing machine and the drier were both whirring. The room was warm and humid and smelled of fabric conditioner. As I was transferring my clothes to the plastic bag, Josie came in to check on her clothes.

'Did you fold these?' I said. 'That was kind. I'm sorry I didn't take them out of the drier last night.'

'It's no bother. How did you sleep?' She was eyeing me, concerned.

'Not bad, considering. You?'

She laughed. 'Oh, I always sleep like a log. Nothing ever wakes me. Good job too, with Malcolm's snoring.'

'Josie,' I began, talking quickly so I didn't have a chance to change my mind, 'I was wondering if Malcolm would help me with something on the boat.'

'Oh, love, you don't have to ask. You know he'd love to. What is it?'

I hesitated, the momentum gone. 'I think – um… I think I'd like to see if I can get the engine started.'

She stared at me. 'What's brought this on?'

I shrugged. 'Nothing really. I just thought – you know. It might be nice to take the *Revenge* on a trip one day.'

'There's a lot more to it than just getting the engine started – you know that, don't you?'

'Mm. I just thought, shame to have a boat that never goes anywhere. I need to have a new project, that's all.'

'Well,' she said uncertainly, 'I'll ask him. Maybe if you wanted to go on a trip he could go with you. Where did you want to go?'

This was all starting to get a bit too detailed. I should have asked Malcolm, rather than Josie – he wouldn't have batted an eyelid at the idea.

'Nowhere special. Look – just forget I asked. It's not a problem.'

'Genevieve,' she said sternly, 'are you worried about what happened yesterday? Because I'm sure it was just a one-off. We don't often get bodies washed up here, you know. I know your boat is the one nearest to the river but you don't need to worry about it happening again, really you don't.'

I picked up my bag full of washing. 'It's fine, Josie, honest. It was just a thought.'

I was putting the washing away when I heard a knock at the door to the wheelhouse. It was Malcolm.

'Morning,' he said cheerily.

'How did the clothes shopping go yesterday? I forgot to ask Josie.'

'Ah,' he said. 'Didn't happen, in the end. Far too much going on here.'

He filled the kettle and put it on the stove, as if this were his boat and not mine. I didn't mind, although I probably wasn't at the stage yet where I could stroll on to *Aunty Jean* and help myself to whatever I wanted.

'The police, you mean?'

'Yeah. The gavvers.'

'Did they talk to you?'

'Oh, yes. They wanted to come aboard the *Jean*, but I told them it was too cramped and we sat in the office instead. Good job too.' He gave me a lopsided smile. 'I'm not too keen on the gavvers. Although this lot weren't too bad, to tell the truth.'

'I thought they were alright.'

'Yeah, but see, there's all sorts of things wrong with that body being there. I don't think it was washed downriver, for one thing.'

'I've been trying not to think about it, to be honest with you.'

'And it didn't just fall in.'

'No, I guess not,' I said with a sigh.

He helped himself to two mugs from the cupboard, spooned coffee into each. 'The police are starting a murder enquiry.'

'Really? Are you sure?'

'You don't get that number of cops for a suicide, or even an accidental death. And they don't know who it is. Generally by the time they find a body in the river they know exactly who it is that's missing. That means, either they've not been reported missing, or they're not from round here. Maybe from London or somewhere, I dunno.'

'Why London?'

He pulled a face. 'It's handy here, innit? Straight down the A2. First river you come to. First bit that feels like countryside.'

'I guess so.'

'What gets me,' he said, pointing a teaspoon at me, 'is why your boat? Now that's intriguing me.'

I stared at him. 'Maybe they just thought it would get washed out to the river if they put it at the end of the pontoon.'

'Maybe,' he said. The kettle was starting a low whistle. 'Feels to me like it was put there deliberate.'

'What?' My voice sounded dull, a long way off.

'You come here from London, yeah?'

'So?' I felt sick all of a sudden. How could I get out of this? How could I wind the clock back, to before the laundry, before I asked Josie for Malcolm's help? I felt as if I'd managed to give myself away.

'You never mentioned moving the boat before,' he said.

'It was just something that policeman said,' I replied lamely. 'He asked if I'd taken the boat out on any trips. It hadn't really crossed my mind before that. That's all. It's got nothing to do with the body, not really.'

He smiled, as though he didn't believe me. Nor should he.

'You shouldn't be scared, Gen.'

'I'm not.'

'You shouldn't lie to me, either.' The kettle screamed its final, loudest note and he turned off the gas.

Malcolm handed me a mug of coffee and we went to sit in the saloon. I felt as if I was at a job interview that was going badly wrong.

'Well, of course I'm bloody scared,' I said lightly. 'I came face to face with a corpse last night. That sort of thing doesn't happen in Clapham. Not often, anyway.'

'When I was in the army I saw all sorts. I saw a lot of bodies, in Bosnia, and other places. It fucks with your head. You think you've dealt with it, but you haven't. It takes years.'

'I didn't know you were in the army,' I said.

He sniffed. 'Don't like to talk about it really.'

I sipped my coffee. It was chilly in the saloon. I wondered whether to ask Malcolm to light the woodburner again, to give him something to take his mind off the topic of starting the engine.

'I never felt scared here before, never worried about being here alone. This place always felt so safe.'

'You're not alone. You've got all of us now.'

'Yes, I guess so. I'd still like to try and start the boat, though. Just to see if it works. Will you help?'

Malcolm's whole face brightened. 'Of course I'm going to help, you big jessie.'

An hour later, Malcolm was up to his armpits in the engine.

I'd looked at the engine when I bought the boat; Cameron had pointed out all the various parts and I'd nodded and smiled as though I knew what he was talking about. As though I was listening. Thanks to my years of training with my dad in his workshop, I was fully prepared to do all that needed doing on the boat in terms of renovation, and I'd done a lot already: I'd learned as I'd gone along and I'd made the *Revenge* into a habitable, comfortable boat. But the engine was just a step too far.

Of course, Malcolm scarcely stopped talking. It started with a low whistle when we lifted the hatch down to the engine space.

'Nice.'

'Is it?'

'Looks good from here,' he said. 'Maybe it just wants a good clean. Have you tried starting her up?'

My blank expression told him everything. He went up into the wheelhouse and fiddled with various controls. Nothing happened. 'Charged the battery?'

Of course I hadn't.

'You've got a decent generator, you know.'

'Have I?'

'Bloody good job too. A new one would cost you a small fortune, and you need a decent generator, if you want to take her upriver. What you going to plug her into, otherwise?' He indicated the pontoon and the electricity and water hook-up.

'I hadn't thought.'

'Lots of things you probably haven't thought. Got a cloth?'

I found him some old rags from the storage and crouched on the deck next to him, watching as he cleaned black gunk away from joints, dials and levers.

'So,' he said cheerfully, leaning back on his heels, 'while I'm doing this, you can tell me all about what happened in London.'

I hesitated. 'There's nothing to tell.'

He stopped what he was doing and gave me a pointed look.

'You don't have to tell me,' he said. 'Just trying to make conversation, that's all.'

And he went back to tinkering with the engine.

It wasn't that I didn't want to tell him. Lord knew, it would be good to tell someone – it was just where to start.

And then I had a picture of myself, dancing. How it felt to dance. How free.

'Well, you know I used to be a dancer,' I said, quietly.

He carried on tinkering.

'I started with ballet, when I was very small. I carried on with it until I was twelve. I was good at it, but not quite good enough for ballet school. When I got turned down for that I concentrated on gymnastics instead. I was alright at that, too.'

'What happened?' he asked, without turning.

'Well, for a start, my body changed and suddenly I was the wrong shape for it. Then I got too busy with A-levels, then university. That was it, basically. Then, when I was working in London, I started looking for dance classes – something to do to keep fit. I thought, I'd enjoyed it before; it might be a good way to tone up. And – well – what happened was, I found a pole fitness class.'

'What's that?'

'Pole dancing.'

'Ah!'

'Yes. You can laugh.'

'I'm not laughing. Sounds like a good idea to me. Pass me that spanner? No, the other one.'

I watched him for a moment, wondering whether I should carry on with this.

'So – you went along? To the class?'

'Yes. It was good fun. Not as easy as it looks, you know. You have to be fit, and physically strong – it's not like other dancing classes where you can get away with it if you have a good sense of rhythm. And it was a fitness class really, but I loved it straight away.'

'I bet you were good at it. What with all that dancing you'd done. And gym, and that.'

'Yes, I was. Have you been to a club where they've done it?'

He coughed a little. 'Well, yes. Not very good though. I bet you were better.'

I found myself laughing. 'Probably, yes, I was.'

Malcolm said, 'Right, that's all I can do until you get the battery charged up. We'll have another try tomorrow.'

I felt a bit bereft all of a sudden, until I realised that he had no intention of ending our conversation there. He wiped his hands on the dirty rag, and handed me his coffee mug. 'I think I'd like a cuppa tea this time, if it's all the same to you. I'll just go back to *Aunty Jean* and get some Swarfega. Back in a minute.'

Ten minutes later we were sitting back in the saloon, steaming mugs in front of us. I was glad of the warmth of the mug. I'd started the fire in the woodburner but it would be a while before it started throwing out any real heat.

'I was good,' I said. 'The instructor was a girl called Karina. She'd worked in some of the big clubs, earned loads of money doing it. She said I was better than she'd been. She said I should try it. Dancing in a club, I mean.'

'And you did.'

'I needed the money,' I said. 'I'd got this plan that I wanted to buy a boat. You know there were times I loved the sales job, times when I hated it too, but I knew I couldn't do it forever. It's bloody hard work, very pressured. When everything's going well, it's great, but if things start to slip then it's just hideous, just like fighting uphill, all the time. And I had a sort of relationship with Ben – that one from the party – that had gone all wrong. So I wanted out. I wanted something to look forward to – an end to it all. And I decided I was going to take a year out and do up a boat.'

'Bit of a difference from working in London,' he said.

'Exactly. I'd got money saved up, from bonuses and stuff. But nowhere near enough to buy a boat, and I was getting so sick of it, so sick of the stupid job and the crazy fucked-up people I worked with.'

'So you were dancing in a club? Like, a strip club?'

This was where it started getting difficult. 'It was a private members' club called the Barclay, near London Bridge. Karina introduced me to the owner. Fitz, his name was. I had no idea what those places were like; I'd never been in one. But it seemed alright. The membership for it was hundreds of pounds. The drinks in the bar were – shit, I don't know – stupid money. The whole place reeked of cash. They had separate rooms, bars. VIP area. It was good money, easy money in a lot of ways.'

I was waiting for his reaction. I'd had lots of different ones, from the few people I'd told, or the people who'd found out for themselves. Shock was a common one. Hostility, sometimes. Occasionally I was lucky enough to get a 'Good on you, girl' and a pat on the back.

'Well, it's like an art form, innit,' Malcolm said. 'That's what I've always thought, anyway. You have my complete admiration.'

'Thank you.'

He raised his mug of tea in salute.

'So. That was London.' I said it with finality, thinking that might satisfy him. 'It's not the sort of thing you can just tell people, after all.'

'That's it?'

'I was good at it. I earned a packet, more than I was earning in the sales job, just for a few hours at the weekends. I saved it up until I had enough to leave my job and buy this boat.'

He nodded, slowly. 'Makes sense.'

'Yes.'

'I bet some dodgy stuff went on, though.'

'What do you mean?'

'Them places, full of drugs and shit like that.'

'I guess so. Some of the girls used to take stuff to keep themselves awake. I kept away from all of that side of it, really. I had better things to do with the money I was making.'

He sniffed and finished his tea. 'You don't want to be messing with all that stuff, you know. There are some nasty people run them sorts of clubs.'

'Yes,' I said.

He looked at his watch. 'I better shoot off. I told Josie I'd only be ten minutes.'

I felt a huge weight of relief. 'Oh, okay. Thanks, for, you know – the engine.'

'No worries. I'll have another look tomorrow when you've got the battery charged. She still wants me to take her shopping for this bloody wedding outfit, I dunno why we can't just go as we are; got enough bloody clothes stuffed into that boat as it is.'

'Right you are.'

At the steps he paused and looked back at me, his lined face serious. 'You're not on your own, Gen. You know that, right? We all stick together here. You don't need to worry.'

I smiled at him. 'Thanks.'

I watched from the door of the wheelhouse until he went below decks on the *Scarisbrick Jean*. The boat was silent; even the rain had eased off.

# *Eight*

If it hadn't been for Karina, I would never have met Dylan, or Caddy – for it was Karina who arranged the appointment at the Barclay. An audition, I suppose it was – with Fitz, the owner of the club.

'He's alright,' she'd said. 'You'll get on with him. And he's gonna love *you*.'

He didn't show up very often; he didn't need to. In fact I found out later that he didn't audition all the girls; he mainly left that up to the club manager, David Norland. For some reason, Fitz had wanted to see me personally.

Karina and I had worked out a rough routine between us. It had been good fun dancing around one of five poles in an upstairs studio in Clapham, me, Karina and several other girls of varying sizes and abilities. It had been a laugh, even with bruised legs and friction burns on the palms of my hands and the insides of my thighs until I got used to it. Like everything, the more you did it, the easier it got. I'd worked my way through all the basic moves, the intermediate and the advanced, and now I was developing new moves and combinations myself or trying ones I'd seen on the internet. It wasn't just fitness, by that stage. It was like a challenge. And then I'd had that conversation with Karina.

'You should train to be an instructor,' she'd suggested. 'You could help me out with classes.'

'Nah,' I said, pulling my jeans back on after class one evening. The other girls had gone; I'd stayed behind to help her dismantle the poles and put them away in the storage room.

'You're good enough,' she said. 'You could earn some extra money.'

'Thanks for the offer, but I need lots of money. Lots and lots. More than this would give me.'

'How come?'

So I told her about my plan. We ended up walking out of the studio together and, without even really discussing it, into the pub next door. It was full of blokes, post-work, ties loosened. Sport on the huge flat-screen TVs.

'You should think about dancing properly, then.'

'What?'

'In a club. You'd earn an absolute packet.'

'You mean, like in a strip club?'

'A gentlemen's club, they're called.'

'Really? You think I could do that?'

'Of course you could.' She was looking at me, her big blue eyes wide.

'How come you don't do it any more?'

She laughed. 'Past my sell-by date,' she said. 'No – I guess I could still do it. But it's the late nights, you know? Difficult, with the kids.'

At the time I laughed it off a bit, finishing my drink and listening to Karina telling me about the clubs, how much fun it was at times, how hard it was at other times, but above all how much money you could get if you were any good at it.

The week after that, I asked her about it again after class. She offered to introduce me to a guy she used to work for, the owner of a club on the South Bank. She made the call on her mobile phone and before I could change my mind she'd made me an appointment to go and see him. Fitz.

To be honest, I hadn't really taken the idea seriously when Karina had first suggested it. It would have been great to have had another source of income, in addition to the day job. I'd thought it might be fun to spend the night in a posh nightclub and earn money at the same time. But if he'd said no, I would have turned my back on the place and never looked back. That was why I turned up at the club with plain black underwear underneath the skirt and blouse I'd worn to work – nothing special. I can't even remember if I was wearing make-up.

The club wasn't open; it was seven o'clock on a Friday evening. I rang the bell of the main front door of an imposing Georgian terrace near the river. A man in a suit opened it.

'What?'

'I'm here to see Mr Fitz,' I said, using the same voice I used when I was trying to access a senior buyer. I wondered what he thought of me. He was tall and almost as wide, a tattoo on his neck, unreadable gothic lettering tangled in a swirl of lines. A chunk of his ear was missing.

'You mean Fitz,' he said, leading the way up a flight of stairs into a plush, quiet corridor. Artwork on the walls. Chandeliers. 'Nobody calls him mister.'

Fitz was in one of the club offices, talking on a mobile phone, his backside perched on the edge of a desk that was bare except for a telephone and a new-looking monitor, wireless keyboard and mouse.

He waved me in and pointed to a chair in the corner. While he talked in south London gibberish to whoever was on the other end of the call, I took in the expensive suit, the hand-made shoes. He had dark hair neatly cut, eyes hidden behind sunglasses. Indoors. I thought he looked like a twat.

'...yeah, mate. Nah. No, not seen it.... Yeah, if you like. Whatever. Right. See ya later, then, fella.' And he hung up.

I gave him my best smile.

'You must be the divine Genevieve,' he said. His accent lost the Peckham twang with barely a hesitation.

'It's nice to meet you,' I said, offering my hand.

'Karina tells me you're something special.'

'You should really decide that for yourself.'

He nodded, appraisingly. 'You've not done this before?'

'No, I haven't.'

'Have you been in a club like this one before?'

I shook my head.

'Very well,' he said, offering his hand to help me to my feet. 'Let's see what you can do, Genevieve. Afterwards I'll ask David to give you the tour. Got any preference for music, or shall we just see what's playing?'

We went back downstairs and through a door at the end of the corridor, which opened up into the main nightclub. There were private booths, tables and chairs around the edge of the dance floor, heavy drapes, cushions, discreet lighting. In this bar were three stages, each with a pole. I wondered if he expected me to strip all the way. I hoped not.

He pointed me to the largest of the three. 'Off you go.'

From an unseen DJ booth, the opening beats to Elbow's 'Grounds for Divorce' came through at deafening level. I stepped out of my shoes and started by circling the pole with bare feet, my hand on it, before lifting myself up into a curl and swinging round... and I was away. I wriggled out of the skirt quickly and did the rest of the routine in my underwear, unbuttoning my shirt and letting it swing around me as I moved. I worked my way through the routine I'd worked on with Karina, adjusting it as the music slowed, and after the first half-minute I got into my stride and actually started to enjoy myself. I even added in a few extra cartwheel kicks. The song was over sooner than I expected it to be, and, other than a slight flush to my cheeks, I hadn't really exerted myself.

From the seating area below the stage came a slow handclap. 'Very good, my dear. Very good. Different, but not in a bad way. What do you think, David?'

A second man was with him. I'd not noticed him arrive, but he was seated with Fitz. A sharp grey suit, a thin face, blond hair cut short. 'Yeah. She'll do.'

'Come and sit with me, lovely Genevieve.'

I slipped back into my skirt and stepped down from the stage. I crossed the carpeted floor, buttoning up my work blouse again, and went to sit at the table with the two men. My demeanour, as I sat down, was back to businesslike.

Norland told me the rules.

'Okay, here's how it goes. You can start tonight on a trial basis. If the customers like you, we'll call you back for a full night. That's a minimum of five dances on the stage, more if you get requests. You can do private dances on the pole; that will be in the Blue Room. In between your stage dances you sit with the clients and drink with them – you get commission on that and you get thirty for a lap dance. You don't do extras. You don't take phone numbers, you don't piss about outside the club with customers. If you take guests to the VIP area you get paid for your time, two hundred per hour, plus tips. The house fee is fifty a night. Sound fair?'

'And if I don't like it?'

The men both laughed.

'You're not keen on earning upwards of a grand a night?' said Norland.

'I can earn that in my day job easily enough,' I said. It wasn't entirely true, but they weren't to know. 'I'm doing this because I enjoy dancing.'

Fitz smiled, a smile that was surprisingly warm. 'You'll like it, I promise you. If you don't, then you don't have to come back. Alright?'

I nodded. 'Thank you.'

'Stage name,' said Fitz. 'What do you reckon, David?'

'I think Genevieve is pretty cool anyway,' he answered.

'Don't be a fuckwit,' Fitz replied, looking at me steadily. 'She can't use her real name. How about Viva?'

'Viva,' I repeated.

Norland nodded. 'I'll add her to the list for tonight.'

When he took me on the tour of the place I was struck by two things: firstly, the place was full of money, real money; and secondly Norland was a complete cock. He was patronising and sly and sure of himself. He wore his aftershave like a weapon.

'These are the dressing rooms,' he said, leading me through a discreet 'Staff Only' door behind the stage. 'You can fight with the other girls for a dressing table when you're on.'

'Don't we get a dressing table each?' I asked. I should have kept my mouth shut.

'There's a lot of girls working here at the weekend,' he said. 'We don't have room for egos.'

We went back out to the club and down a corridor to the side. Away from the dance floor, the carpets were thick and our footfalls were silent. The doors along the right wall of the corridor were named: Harem, Justice, Boudoir. Norland stopped outside the last door. On it, a brass plaque: 'The Blue Room'. It was called that because of the décor, I supposed: rich blue wallpaper and gold fittings, heavy velvet curtains held back with thick gold braided rope. In the centre of the room was a round parquet floor and a gold pole rising from it. The ceiling in this room was higher and the pole went all the way up to the ornate plasterwork cornicing.

'Wow,' I said, running my hand up the pole.

Norland smirked.

'Size is everything, huh?'

I didn't respond.

'Can you get up there?' he asked, nodding upwards.

'Of course I can,' I said coldly.

'Not many of the girls can. In fact, the last one to do it was Karina, and that was five years ago.'

I liked the idea of the height in this room. I never felt the poles were enough of a challenge. I liked the idea of working my way to the top of the room and spinning back down. I would have to work out some new move combinations to make use of the whole length of the pole.

He showed me round the rest of the Barclay Gentlemen's Club. The two main bars, one of which was downstairs with a separate entrance on to the side street; the reception area, the cloakroom; the various private booths and VIP rooms around the main dance floor.

'Find something nice to wear later,' he said, when we found ourselves back in the foyer. The place looked more like a hotel than a club. 'You'll need an evening dress before twelve. Then you can change into something that shows more flesh for your dances. Get yourself some decent underwear.'

'Alright,' I said. The man was a slug.

'Come back any time after half-ten. When you come tonight, ask for Helena. We'll put you on probably around two, three o'clock. As long as you're here for your dance, you'll be alright. If you're ever late you'll get a fine and you might not get to go on. Sorted – yeah?'

'Fine,' I said, and I was back out on the London pavement.

# Nine

I ate toast for dinner. It was the first solid food I'd had for more than twenty-four hours, and even so it was a struggle. It felt dry and rough and tasted of nothing.

I was sitting at the dinette, looking at the bit of paper that Carling had given me, with his phone number on it. Next to it on the table was Andy Basten's business card.

### Detective Sergeant Andrew Basten
### MAJOR CRIME

Why didn't Carling have a card like the other one? And which one should I ring, if I was worried? Basten's neat, official card, with the crest of Kent Police? Or Carling's number handwritten on a bit of paper, scrawled but legible? Just a mobile. I wondered what he did when he was off-duty. Did he go home to his wife? Wife… and kids, maybe? And a dog. There would have to be a dog. And a wife with a noble profession, maybe a teacher. Or a nurse. Or maybe she was a police officer too. And two children at the dining table busy doing their homework when he got in from his hard day chasing criminals. He would kiss the tops of their heads – a boy and a girl – and he would ask his wife what was for dinner, while the dog chased around his feet wagging its tail with delight. He would open a bottle of wine and they would finish it – Jim Carling and his wife – when the kids were in bed.

Or he was divorced. He had that pissed-off look about him, I decided. Maybe his wife had run off with someone else – another police officer; they all did it – and left him behind to try and look after a great big house all on his own.

Or he was married, and yet he had affairs with people, people like me, vulnerable women he'd come across in his day job. Victims. He picked ones he fancied and got them to sleep with him.

I wasn't a victim, though, was I? Not yet, anyway.

For some reason, my next thought was of Ben. He could have phoned me, at least to say thanks for the party. None of them had. None of them had any idea about the nightmare that had followed their departure. They'd all fucked off to the pub and thence God knows where, back to London in the end, without so much as a thank-you-goodbye. Shits, they were, all of them. Especially Lucy. I remembered what she'd said to Malcolm, the tone of her voice when Malcolm told her she'd be jealous of my boat one day.

'I don't think so somehow.'

I didn't care what she thought about it, anyway. Her opinion had ceased to be valid for me a long time ago.

Lucy was one of the people who'd had a real problem with me dancing.

It had been Ben who'd told her, of course; she would never have known about it otherwise. I think it was his revenge for my ending our stupid pointless disaster of a relationship. Lucy and I were in the pub one Friday after work, drinking big glasses of chilled white wine and unpicking the nightmare of selling high-end software solutions to boardrooms full of men. We took a lot of shit for it. The blokes on our team were highly competitive, driven, occasionally downright nasty. Lucy got by because she was the daughter of the managing director, but she was bitter about all the testosterone she had to deal with. I wasn't as bothered as her about the gender thing because I got by through working hard, which usually meant I hit my bonus targets. We had an alliance, of sorts, because Lucy needed someone to moan at. But beyond that we had little in common.

'Ben told me where you were last night.'

I drank my wine and looked at her. We'd been out with clients last night, and I'd disappeared early instead of staying on as we usually did and getting pathetically drunk. I'd told her I had a headache, but instead I'd gone to the Barclay.

'You're a stripper,' she said.

'I'm a dancer.'

'You take your clothes off for money.'

'Good money.'

There was a flicker, I saw it – a moment where I'd almost justified it to her. She knew about money and the pursuit of it. She was about to ask the question: *How much money?* But then the moment passed.

'It's exploitation,' she said. 'You know how hard we bloody work, twice as hard as some of them, and we still don't get the same recognition.'

'That's got nothing to do with working in the club. I'm there because I want to be there,' I said. 'And if anyone's being exploited, it certainly isn't me. Men come in and spend all their money watching me do something I enjoy. It feels great, to be honest.'

Just at that moment three of the guys on the sales team had come over and joined us and the conversation turned to the normal topic of who had the biggest car, the biggest sales deal, the biggest set of balls. Lucy had never mentioned it again, not until last night at the party. Despite her supposedly feminist convictions, I couldn't shake the notion that, actually, she was a little bit jealous.

Apart from Lucy and Ben, most of my friends hadn't known what I did every Friday and Saturday night and sometimes Thursdays and Sundays too. I didn't need to be at the club until eleven, so I carried on with my normal social activity and when they went off to clubs, or back home to bed, I went to the Barclay and earned myself a fortune.

It had crossed my mind to tell them, more than once. If any of them had asked me a direct question, I wouldn't have lied. But none of them seemed bothered; when I said I was going somewhere else, they just said things like, 'Okay, cool,' and waved me goodbye as they disappeared off to some club or other, or back to someone's house, or off to another party.

I was lying awake, in bed. The skylight was a square of black that was somehow lighter than the black in the rest of the room. When I closed my eyes, I could still see it. It was like the opening, the entrance to a tomb.

I was physically tired, but my mind was spinning. Malcolm was right: I was scared. During the day it was easy to pretend this wasn't really happening, easy to believe that maybe the body hadn't been Caddy after all. I'd only caught a glimpse of her face, the dirty water of the Medway washing over it, a flash of white in the beam of my torch. It could so easily have been someone else: a body from upstream after all, a suicide, a missing person.

At night, things were very different.

From the first day in the marina, I'd never really felt alone. Even after dark you heard noises from the other boats, the faint voices from someone's television, shouts from Diane and Steve's two children, traffic on the motorway, the rattle of the Eurostar or the Javelin rocketing along the high-speed rail link a mile or so away. The other liveaboards were never more than a shout away; I'd proved that last night, I tried to reassure myself. I'd screamed, and in under a minute at least five people had come out of their boats to see what was going on. And yet I couldn't relax.

A mobile phone was ringing.

I sat up in bed, my whole body tensed and alert. It sounded a long way off, as though it was coming from one of the other boats.

I pushed back the duvet and opened the bedroom door. The noise of the ringing grew louder.

In the saloon, it was louder still. It wasn't my phone, which was charging on the dinette table – it was Dylan's.

Finally I found it, buried down the back of the sofa, where I'd thrown it when Carling came down into the cabin. It was still ringing. The name on the display: GARLAND.

I had a surge of joy, overwhelming relief.

'Hello?'

There was silence on the other end of the phone.

'Is that you?' I said, my voice trembling.

Still nothing. Someone breathing? I was certain someone was there. 'Talk to me,' I said, 'please, say something. Please.'

Nothing.

I disconnected the call and threw the phone back on to the sofa, and cried. I waited a second to see if it would ring again, but it didn't. There was nothing, just the silence of the boat and the sound of my own sobs.

Even though he'd not said a single word, it felt like a goodbye. He knew about Caddy; he must have some idea of the spinning chaos of my life... why wasn't he here? Why hadn't he called to tell me what to do, to arrange to meet, even? He didn't care about me at all, not really. Whatever it was we'd had, that one single night together that I had interpreted as magical, had been nothing to him, nothing.

I went back to bed and buried my face in the pillow until the tears were gone.


Hours later, still lying awake staring at the skylight, dry-eyed and too tired to move, I had worked my way all around the theory that he didn't care about what happened to me and found myself in a different place entirely.

He had called, after all. And he hadn't, despite my miserable self-doubt, said goodbye. He'd said nothing at all. Why would he do that? With a rush of fear I wondered if he was in trouble. Had he tried to call, but been prevented somehow? Did he need help? And what could I do about it if he did?

# *Ten*

I'd always prided myself on my ability to adapt to any changes to my working environment, but dancing at the Barclay was a steep learning curve.

After my audition, I hunted through my wardrobe for something that I thought might be appropriately dramatic and sexy. Eventually I settled on the dark blue velvet dress I'd worn at the last conference dinner. A few tops and skirts that I wore out clubbing with my friends. And lingerie. Black lace with a pink ribbon trim.

I had no idea if that was okay.

I wasn't even nervous when I went back. The club was already filling with people, the music at a level loud enough so the girls had to lean forward to chat to the guys in the bar but not so loud that they couldn't hear someone calling them over.

I found Helena behind the bar. She was a small woman in her forties, with an expression which said 'don't give me any shit'. She never looked happy in the time I worked there; even when she laughed she looked pissed off. She had dark hair piled on her head, which gave her an extra few inches, and sharp heels.

'You worked before?' she said, writing my name on a list behind the bar.

'No,' I said. I didn't think she was referring to work in general.

'Did they tell you the rules?'

'I guess so. No fraternising, that sort of thing?'

She smiled at me, or maybe it was a grimace. '"No fraternising." I like that. If you're any good and they want you back, you have to be here ready and out in the club by eleven. If you're late you get fined.'

The dressing room was still crowded even though a lot of the girls were already out in the club. I found a tatty bar stool and dumped my shoulder bag next to it, changing out of my jeans and into my dress while the girls around me ignored me completely. They were all talking at once, laughing, shouting, and the room was a confusing mess of fabrics and make-up and clouds of competing perfume.

'Mind if I sit here?' I asked, pulling my bar stool up to the edge of a mirror. A blonde girl was finishing off her look with lip-gloss.

'Whatever,' she said, 'I'm done.'

I had the mirror to myself. Within a few minutes the room had emptied of everyone except me and another girl. She was shorter than me, even wearing improbably stacked heels; she had long brown hair, big baby blue eyes.

'You new?' she said.

I nodded. 'Is it obvious?'

'Only that you're not out there yet. You're wasting money.'

'I'm not on until later.'

She laughed. 'Christ, you are new, aren't you? Just 'cause you're not on stage doesn't mean you're not working. You should be out there hustling.'

I looked at her blankly.

'You go out and chat to people, get them to buy you drinks, do a few dances, try and get them in the VIP area.' She took pity on me. I must have looked scared, or lost, or maybe just dumb. 'Want me to show you?'

'Yes, please.'

'Okay,' she said, 'but if any of my regulars come in you're on your own, right?'

'Thanks. What's your name?'

'My club name is Kitten,' she said, 'But back here you can call me Caddy.'

'Caddy? Like in *The Sound and the Fury*?'

She looked at me, glossed lips in a perfect O. I thought she was going to ask me what the fuck I was talking about, but it turned out we'd underestimated each other. 'You read it?'

'Yeah.'

'I've never met anyone else who's ever read that book. What's your name?'

'Genevieve. I think they're calling me Viva.'

'Viva. Isn't that a type of old car? My dad had one.'

We both laughed, and it was the birth of a friendship – Viva and Kitten. The other girls in the club came and went; the Russians and the Polish girls stuck together, hustled in and out of the club, bent the rules in every way they could. Other girls formed cliques and went out with each other on their nights off; but I never got close to them, not the way I did with Caddy.

On that first night she took me out into the club and we strolled around saying hello to people, stopping for brief chats. I watched and learned, feeling a bit like the new girl at school.

'Mind if we sit with you for a bit? ... Special occasion, is it, lads? ... Ah! Congratulations! Are you going to come and have a dance with me? ... Yes – this is Viva – she's new. I know! ... Don't worry, I know you'll look after us, won't you? ... Ah, I'll have to leave you to it, then – I'll get told off if I sit here too long... well, let's go to the VIP area, then you can have my undivided attention for as long as you like... You guys need to be doing shots, especially if it's his birthday...'

I felt a bit nauseous, thinking that within the next couple of hours I was going to be taking all my clothes off in front of a room full of complete strangers. It felt surreal, and watching the other girls take their turns on the pole made it somehow worse. I kept one eye on the stage as Caddy and I sat and chatted with the various groups, trying to get some idea of how it all worked. Someone announced the girl on to the stage in a barely intelligible voice that reminded me of fairgrounds. There would be a ripple of applause, maybe, just audible above the music. She would dance for two tracks, the first with clothes on, then stripping off in the second. The first girl was good, plenty of turns and spins, inverting in her second dance. She got a good cheer when she came off the stage, a little crowd forming around the pole. The second one, by contrast, was rubbish – just a lot of walking around the pole, a few dips and turns, a half-hearted spin and then she was done.

That was something of a comfort. Even I could do better than that.

As it turned out, I had to do my first lap dance before I even went on the pole. Thankfully I had the chance to watch Caddy doing one first, and, although mine was a clumsy effort, the young lad I was entertaining was already so drunk he was barely conscious.

'It'll get easier,' Caddy said to me as we walked back to the club to look for our next targets. 'The trick is going for the ones who are pissed but not so pissed they've forgotten what they're doing here. It's a fine line.'

After that, it was my turn for the pole. My heart was pounding as I stood off the stage waiting for my name to be called. *It's just a job,* I thought. *You can do this. You can nail it.*

'Give her a big cheer, it's her first night – it's Viva!'

For the first minute or so, nobody was particularly paying attention. I started off with some easy climbs and spins, but that wasn't much fun. Carousel spin into back hook – that got some attention. And then a quick invert, splits at the top. Stripping off my clothes while dancing around the pole wasn't as easy as I'd thought it was going to be – but it didn't seem to matter. By this time the gathering around the stage had grown and I was getting some half-hearted applause. This made me braver. Spin to the floor, little peek-a-boo, knees together, bum out. End of song. I grabbed my clothes and my shoes and skittered off the stage.

Caddy met me as I was coming out of the dressing room a few moments later. 'Come and meet Nigel and Tom,' she said. 'They loved your dance, they've been asking after you.'

I was breathless and perspiring a little, full of adrenaline. I couldn't keep the smile off my face. I'd done it, and it hadn't been so bad really – actually, it had been fun. I'd caught glimpses of faces in the crowd, watching me – they liked me, and I'd only just started.

Hours later, so tired I could barely think straight, I was next to Caddy in the dressing room as she peeled the fake lashes off her eyelids. 'You did really well,' she said, 'for a first night.'

'Thanks. I wouldn't have had a clue if it hadn't been for you, though.'

'No biggie. Want some more advice?'

'Sure.'

'Get yourself a decent tan,' she said, waving a make-up-caked wipe in my direction. 'You're bloody dazzling them under the lights.'

I had a lot to thank Caddy for. Not all the girls were quite as helpful – since we were all, in effect, competing for the same limited pot of money in the wallets of the men in the club on any given night, it was horribly similar to the day job. Dancing on the stage was the pitch. You started off showing your skills as a dancer, before moving on to add value to your pitch by showing them that you had a good body to back it up. At the same time, you were scanning the room for potential customers to target later. Once you came off the stage it was all about establishing a proper rapport with your customer by chatting them up, before closing the deal by getting them into the VIP area, which was the most financially rewarding part of the job, or, failing that, by going for an interim close by getting them to pay you for a private dance.

At least I understood how the sales environment worked. Once I applied that to the Barclay, I could start to earn some serious money. As for taking my clothes off, after the first couple of times it didn't bother me. It was acting, just as selling was. You spotted the guys who were paying particular attention to you, the ones that made eye contact, prioritising the ones who were already drinking champagne and shots, and therefore had plenty of money and were already half-drunk. The rest was easy.

'Half the blokes in here are expecting you to make them come,' Caddy said, 'and the other half are expecting you to fall off the pole. That's what we're here for. Entertainment, whichever way you look at it.'

Every so often she would come out with corkers like that: classic Caddy quotes that summed up the experience of working in the club in a way I would never have been able to do.

The first night in the Barclay I made two hundred quid, after taking off the house fee. I'd had fun, got a fairly decent workout and enjoyed chatting to the customers. And I'd made a new friend. This would be easy, I remember thinking. This was going to be a complete piece of piss.

I had absolutely no idea.

When I woke up, it was raining. I'd slept through the dawn, the hours where the lightening of the skylight above my head usually woke me. It was nearly ten.

I got dressed, waterproof jacket on, and took my bag with me down to the office. My bike was in the storage room behind the main building. I unlocked it and set off for the city centre, the rain falling more heavily and stinging my eyes.

The city of Rochester was beautiful, even in the rain. I left the bike chained to a bike stand and walked past the pubs and the Indian restaurants. Today there was a food festival, and an Italian market was lining the cobbled high street. Some of the stalls had given up, drawing tarpaulins over bowls of olives and baskets of fresh bread. I looked at cheeses and jars of relish and chutneys. At the corner, a stall with a huge pan was selling hot farmhouse sausages in a baguette. The smell was enticing and I bought one, but a few bites in I realised I still had no appetite.

I browsed through charity shops and second-hand bookshops, looking for things for the boat. I was very careful about what I bought. I didn't have room for piles of crap.

The rain fell steadily and I walked up the hill to the castle, through the castle grounds and back down to the cathedral. I wanted to walk until I was tired... until I was beyond tired.

I felt lonely today. I didn't want Malcolm, or Josie, lovely as they were. I wanted someone who knew who I was, knew what had happened in London. I needed Dylan. Part of me wanted to phone him again and demand to know exactly what had been going on in the club, how Caddy had looked, what she'd said – everything I'd missed from that last day right up until the moment she'd appeared in the water.

But I couldn't get the sound of his voice out of my head, that tone when I'd called him. I'd disobeyed his instructions. I'd pissed him off. Where was he? If something had happened to him, would I ever find out?

When I got back to the boat I made a hot drink and sat at the dinette looking at Dylan's phone, and at the scrap of paper with Carling's number on it.

Fuck it, I thought, and reached for the phone.

And, this time, it didn't even ring. There wasn't even an option to leave a message.

*The number you have dialled is currently unavailable. Please try later.*

# *Eleven*

The first time I met Dylan I was afraid of him, although I was careful not to show it.

I'd been dancing at the Barclay for two weekends already, and I had arranged to meet Caddy for a drink on a Saturday evening. I woke up zinging with such energy that I decided to go to the Barclay first, to practise. It didn't cross my mind that this was something out of the ordinary – it just seemed like the perfect way to spend a few hours, even though I'd only got to sleep at four that morning.

The door to the Barclay was locked. I rang the bell and waited. Then I rang again, and knocked, and sat down on the top step and debated what to do with myself. I had my earphones in and was listening to a playlist of potential dance music and so I didn't actually hear the door open behind me, wasn't aware of his presence until I got a little kick on the bum.

I jumped and looked up, and there he was. A mountain of a man. I pulled the earphones out.

'What do you want?' he said.

I got to my feet and got on to the top step so at least I was on his level before answering. In fact, he was still at least a foot taller than me but I didn't let that stop me. 'Thanks for the welcome. I'm here to practise.'

'Practise?' he repeated, and laughed as though I'd said something hilarious.

I ignored him and walked in through the open door, into the main club. The place was empty, though the lights were on. No point bothering with the changing rooms if there was nobody here. I kicked off my boots and wriggled out of my jeans. Pole lessons with Karina had always been barefoot, and the one thing I found difficult was dancing in heels. The first few evenings in the Barclay I'd started off in heels and then kicked them off as soon as I started to do climbs and spins, but nobody else danced without their shoes. So in my bag were a pair of platforms I could just about manage to walk in, with ankle straps, and impressive spike heels that were sturdier than they looked.

The air-conditioning was on and it was chilly, so I stretched and jumped up and down on the spot a few times to warm up.

Heels on, then. I walked around the room in them to start off with, trying not to look at my feet, trying to be purposeful, trying to 'own the room'. I felt silly, but better to be doing this here on my own rather than stumbling in front of a club full of potential paying customers.

'You look like you're walking into a boardroom,' someone said.

He was sitting in one of the booths near the door, almost in darkness. I was getting used to blokes watching me, but having him there without my realising it was just plain creepy.

'Like I said, I need to practise,' I replied. 'I could do without you watching, thanks all the same.'

'Only trying to help.'

He didn't move.

Creepy as it was, he had a valid point. I tried to put a bit of a swing into my hips, one foot in front of the other, head up, back straight…

'Better, but now you look like you're going to pounce on someone. Try smiling.'

I ignored him this time. I was warm enough now anyway, and I was feeling more confident in the shoes. I climbed up the steps on to the stage into the glow of the lights. That was better. I couldn't see him.

I walked around the pole a few times to get used to the additional height the heels gave me, both ways so I didn't get dizzy. The floor seemed a long way down, my heels clomping inelegantly on the laminate stage.

Without warning, a heavy beat started up. He was in the DJ's booth. He turned the volume down to a reasonable thud.

He wanted a show, I thought. Whoever he was. And I realised that actually I was better off with an audience. What was the point of practising on my own? And the music helped.

I started off with some easy climbs and spins, mixing it with some filler moves and kicks, then I gripped the pole and inverted, my head back against the pole, my ankles crossed and my legs providing the friction to hold me steady. Normally doing this I had enough grip in my legs that I could let go with my hands, but I didn't know if I could trust my grip with the shoes on, and my legs felt so much heavier with them. It felt very strange. I transferred the grip back to my hands and opened my legs into the splits, spinning slowly to the floor and standing up, snaking my body against the pole. A hook and spin around the pole to get my breath back, then back to an invert, splits, back down into an attitude spin. The trick was allowing those few extra inches to land both feet back on the floor despite the heels. If I spun too far down, it would be harder to stand up, and not very elegant.

I was so engrossed in the shoes and how different it felt moving around the pole with them on, I almost forgot he was there.

'You're a good dancer,' he said.

He was near the stage now, sitting to the side at the bar.

'Who *are* you?' I asked, back to the pole, sliding to sit back on my heels before kicking my leg up in front of me. Then a pivot on my hand, holding the pole above my head, bum out, straighten, toss head back.

The song ended and before the next one started I stepped down from the stage and went to stand next to him. Seated precariously on a bar stool, he didn't seem quite as intimidating as he had out on the front doorstep.

'Dylan,' he said, holding out a hand like a shovel.

I shook it. 'You work here?'

'Sort of.'

'Haven't seen you before.'

'That's because you're new,' he said.

I got a water bottle out of my bag and drank from it, watching him. 'You don't have to hang around, you know,' I said.

He stayed where he was. It dawned on me that he didn't trust me, that he thought I might be here to nick money from the tills, or something. His presence was intimidating and I was here on my own with him.

His mobile phone rang then and he answered it, heading for the door of the club. I stood watching him until the door shut behind him.

I went back to the pole and tried some more spins. The track was much slower. I concentrated on getting on and off the pole with these stupid shoes on, trying to make it look effortless when it wasn't. Despite the door between us I could hear Dylan's half of the phone conversation and that was also putting me off.

'…I don't see it like that, mate. He said he'd have it for us tonight… It's not good enough, is it…? Tell him if he doesn't pull his fucking finger out, he's going to get a kicking…'

Inverted, looking up at my feet in those ridiculous shoes, I thought, *I should get a pedicure, some nice neon pink, something classy like that*. The pole was thicker than the poles I'd learned to dance on. It made it easier for the climb and sit, harder for the hand grip.

'…he doesn't get it, though, does he? You tell him one thing and it's like he's not fucking listening…'

There was no point having routines here. You didn't get to select the music you were dancing to unless you were doing a private dance in the Blue Room. It was better to just get used to going with the flow, building the momentum of your spins if the music was faster, concentrating on snakes and hip circles when it was slower.

'...no, you tell him. Seriously, mate, this is a warning, yeah? My contact is going to be fucking unimpressed. We need it tonight or else he's going to have some big regrets, you getting me?'

I was back on my feet, looking towards the door. Being here on my own, half-dressed, with this huge lump of a man didn't seem like such a bright idea right at that moment. The call was over. I saw him through the glass in the door, shaking his head. He still had his back to me.

I kicked off the high heels and put them back in my backpack. Jeans on, socks, boots. I was lacing my boots when the door crashed open with a bang, as though he'd kicked it.

When he appeared next to me he was breathing hard, as if he'd been running.

I gave him a hesitant smile. 'I'm off now,' I said cheerily. 'I'm going to meet Caddy for a drink.'

'Are you, now?' he said, raising an eyebrow. 'Hope you behave yourselves. Come on, I'll show you out.'

The sunshine was bright after the darkness of the club. I turned to say, 'See you later,' but the door had already been shut firmly behind me. Above the noise of the traffic I heard the sound of the locks turning.

I left both phones on the table and pulled my boots on. I had had enough of being alone.

Joanna was on board the *Painted Lady*. She was watching telly while cleaning out her gerbils and seemed pleased to see me.

'Liam's gone into town about a job,' she said. 'Hope he gets it.'

As far as I knew, Liam worked sporadically and seasonally, building and sometimes painting and decorating, taking cash-in-hand jobs where he could. The *Painted Lady* was a narrowboat like the *Scarisbrick Jean*, clean and tidy but cluttered. As well as the gerbils, two cats lived aboard. I sat at their dinette and folded the pile of washing on the seat next to me, while Joanna emptied damp sawdust on to sheets of newspaper next to me. Behind her the portable TV mounted at head-height was showing the news.

'Has it been on the news?' I asked.

She shook her head. 'Nah. How are you feeling today?'

'Alright,' I said. 'The boat just seems very quiet. Can't be arsed to do anything.'

'It was a good party,' she said. 'Your mates are interesting.'

I laughed and then she did too.

'They're not really my mates,' I said. 'Not any more. I think I've moved on.'

'Good job too. You're better off with us.'

The gerbils were scratching around in the bottom of a big plastic tub, the same tub that Joanna used for transporting her washing up to the laundry. I could hear rain on the roof of the cabin, a rapid pattering.

'Haven't seen any police for a while,' she said. 'Do you think they've done everything?'

'I guess. Did they interview you?'

Joanna nodded. 'They interviewed all of us. I had a call from Rowena; she's not been near her boat for at least a month and they still went round to her house and talked to her.'

Rowena was one of the people with a boat at the marina that was just used sporadically, at weekends. With the cooler weather, she visited it less and less frequently.

'What did they ask you?'

'Oh, you know – what happened at the party, what time we went back to the boat, what we saw, heard. Didn't have much to tell them, to be honest. First we knew about it was when we woke up and heard you yelling.'

'Sorry about that,' I said.

'Are you kidding? Most exciting thing that's happened here in ages.'

One of the cats was peering into the plastic tub. 'Jasper, no,' said Joanna, picking him up under his belly and throwing him up the steps on to the deck, shutting the door. 'He's always trying to get at them, poor little things.'

'I wonder why they wanted to know about the party,' I said.

'Maybe they think it's linked. Can't see how, though.'

'When you went back to your boat,' I said, 'did you notice if there were any strange cars in the car park?'

She stopped scooping clean sawdust into the gerbil cage and stared at me. 'The police asked us that too. No, can't say I remember. In fact if I'm honest I don't remember much at all. Too much of that homebrew. It's a wonder I even heard you yelling.'

The cage was ready. She crouched over the plastic tub and crooned encouragingly at the gerbils that squeaked and scrabbled in frantic circles until she managed to grab first one, and then the other.


I was twenty minutes late meeting Caddy in the bar, but she hadn't even noticed. The place was busy already, even though it was early evening, and she was sitting in a booth with a long drink in front of her, playing with her mobile phone.

'You missed the excitement,' she said, leaning towards me as I slipped into the seat next to her.

'Why? What happened?'

'Chanelle was in here with one of her regulars. She didn't see me, though. They just left a few minutes ago. Probably gone to the hotel round the corner.'

I must have looked blank.

'Chanelle. You know – Summer? The one with the tattoo going up the back of her leg? Christ, you're hard work.'

'I know the one you mean. What's exciting about seeing her in here, then?'

'Ah,' Caddy said, sipping her cocktail through a little straw, 'it's not that she was in here. It's who she was with. We're not allowed to meet up with customers. House rules.'

'Maybe she's seeing him, or something.'

'She's got a boyfriend. He's a primary school teacher, poor sod.'

'They're tough with the rules, then?'

'Pretty tough. It's for our benefit, though. Means we don't get blokes trying to take advantage the whole time.'

At that moment two guys came and sat down next to us. Casually dressed, already quite drunk by the look of them. 'Ladies,' the taller one said, 'you need to let us buy you a drink. What are you having?'

The shorter of the two, his blond hair spiked with gel at the front, rested his arm on the back of the seat behind me.

'Do you mind?' I said, my voice frosty. 'We're having a private conversation.'

'Ah, don't be like that,' he said, breathing beery fumes over me. 'We were just thinking, you two look like two girls in need of a drink and some sensible conversation...'

Caddy laughed at this.

'We can buy our own drinks, thanks all the same,' I said.

'And we can manage a sensible conversation on our own, too,' Caddy added.

'Seriously, girls,' said the one leering all over Caddy, 'you could be missing out on the chance of a lifetime.'

'I'll risk it,' Caddy said, to my relief. 'Can you please piss off?'

They gave up, and without a further word of protest headed to the bar to look for other prey. We looked at each other and giggled.

'I went to the club to practise this afternoon,' I said. 'I met this hulking great bloke called Dylan. Wouldn't like to get on the wrong side of him.'

'Oh, Dylan's alright,' she said. 'He's pretty decent once you get to know him.'

'Really?' I was remembering the one-sided telephone conversation – something about someone getting a kicking.

'Yeah. At least he sticks to the rules. The others, and most of the doormen – they take back-handers from the foreign girls. They turn a blind eye to things in the VIP suite – and they keep an eye out for the regulars, give the girls a nod so they don't miss out.'

'Don't they do that anyway?'

'Not unless you give them twenty quid every night.'

'Is it worth it? Surely we can keep an eye out for our own regulars?'

'It can give you a boost if you need more cash one month,' she said. 'And it's not just your regulars. They know who the big spenders are. When the club's busy, if you get stuck talking to someone and you don't notice who's come in... or they come over and let you know who's just arrived, who's in the cloakroom before any of the other girls see. Gives you a bit of an advantage.'

It was looking more and more like sales and less like a girls' night out.

'But Dylan doesn't do that?'

'Not that I've ever seen. That's why the foreign girls all steer clear of him. Plus he doesn't serve up drugs to them; they have to go to Gray for that.'

'Gray's a drug dealer?'

She laughed at me. 'You're so funny! No, he's not really a dealer. He just gets stuff for you if you need it. They don't take on girls who've got a serious habit, but if you need a bit of a hit to put the sparkle back in your eyes Gray is the man to ask.'

'I like Dylan a bit more now,' I said.

Caddy went to the bar and got us some more drinks, although it didn't look as though she'd had to pay for them, judging by the sweet little flirtatious chat with the barman and the wiggle as she walked back to our table.

'He's a cutie, that guy behind the bar,' she said to me.

'I guess he's fair game,' I said, 'since he's not a customer.'

'You think I should give him my number?' she asked, sipping her drink.

'Why not?'

She didn't answer, just glanced back across the room to where the barman was still watching. She looked sad for a moment, thoughtful.

'You've got someone,' I said.

'No,' she said, quickly. 'But it's not easy to keep a relationship going with our line of work. Ask Chanelle.'

'How did you get into dancing?' I asked then, curious.

'I started doing it to earn some extra cash,' she said. 'I was waitressing at the weekend; one of the girls there started and after a couple of weeks she left the restaurant. I bumped into her in a bar a few weeks later; she was raving about it and going on about how much money she was making. She made it sound so easy.'

'So you started at the Barclay?'

'No,' she said. 'I started working in a strip pub. Very different sort of place from the Barclay. Still good fun, just not quite so – refined. And you can earn good money because there isn't a house fee. You only pay commission to the bar.'

The barman was still looking. Caddy was ignoring him now.

'Anyway, did you seriously turn up at the Barclay to practise? What did Dylan say?'

'He was kind of giving me tips,' I said.

Caddy laughed, pushing her hair out of her eyes. 'I bet he thought all his Christmases had come at once. Did you strip for him?'

'No!' I said, shocked. 'I just did a bit on the pole. I wanted to try keeping my shoes on.'

'And?'

'I'll get there. Feels weird, especially inverting. The shoes make my legs feel heavy.'

I thought back a few hours: Dylan sitting by the side of the stage, watching me. His face expressionless, waiting for me to hurry up and finish so he could get back to whatever business he'd been dealing with before I'd rung the doorbell. 'What does he actually do?'

'Who?'

'Dylan. Is he a doorman?'

'No. He helps them out sometimes when the club's busy – they all do, if they have to. Dylan works for Fitz, not for the club. He's been with Fitz for years.'

'Doing what, exactly?'

Caddy shrugged, smiling at the barman again in preparation for getting us another round. 'I guess he's like Fitz's enforcer.'

# *Twelve*

After I left Joanna, I went up to the office to check my mailbox. The rain had passed over and the sun was shining. It was almost warm.

Cam was in his office, feet up on the desk, talking to Maureen. She was standing in the doorway with her arms folded. They had conversations like this on a regular basis: Maureen would be complaining about something, Cameron would placate her and do nothing, and so things went on as normal.

'...all I'm saying is, you should be doing something about it, not just sitting there.'

'And, as I said, I'll get some quotes. I can't do it overnight.'

I turned the key in the lock of the mailbox and Maureen noticed me for the first time.

'Ah, Genevieve! You think we need locking gates, don't you?'

'Um – well, I...'

'After what happened. We could all end up murdered in our beds, like that poor girl.'

'She wasn't murdered in a bed,' Cameron said helpfully.

My mailbox was full of junk as usual – free newspapers and pizza adverts – even though I had a sign on my box which expressly requested post only. I sifted through them in case something important had slipped in.

'I don't see what the problem is,' Maureen said, her voice rising. 'Surely it's a straightforward thing to do. Lord knows we pay enough to live here; the least you can do is make sure we have some degree of security. And that man, last night! Honestly, it's the final straw…'

'What man?' I asked.

Maureen turned to me again. 'Pat saw a man hanging around in the car park yesterday evening. She called the police, but by the time they got here it was pitch black; there was no sign of him.'

'What did he look like?'

'She didn't get a good look. He was standing by the side of the office, just out there, skulking around. Obviously up to no good.'

'Probably one of those journalists,' Cameron offered.

'It doesn't matter who he was!' Maureen said. 'It's that he was there at all, and he had no business to be. If we had proper gates, it wouldn't have happened!'

'What did the police say?' I asked. 'Did they have a look around?'

'Well, no, I don't think they did. They were here for about twenty minutes. Then they said they would keep an eye on the place overnight. Not good enough, really, but of course what can they do?'

'I've fixed the lights again,' Cameron said, 'and I'll ask for some quotes for the gates. These things aren't cheap, you know.'

'You can't put a price on safety,' Maureen said.

Cameron's mobile phone rang then and I thought that would be the end of the discussion, but Maureen showed no signs of moving. While he spoke to someone on the other end of the line about booking the crane for a hull inspection, Maureen turned her attention to me.

'We should put some sort of petition together,' she said.

'A petition? To Cameron?'

'To make him get some proper gates!'

I left them to it then, despite Cameron flashing me a pleading look. As I locked my mailbox again he swivelled in his chair to face the wall.

On the pontoon Oswald the cat was enjoying the sunshine, stretched out with the end of his tail flicking. His eyes were half-closed but I could tell he was watching the young gull sitting on the roof of the *Scarisbrick Jean*. When I approached, the gull flew off and Oswald jumped up and wound himself around my legs, the way he always did whenever anyone came near. I scratched the top of his head.

'Hello, old mate,' I said. 'Is it nearly dinnertime?'

He followed me to the *Revenge* and sat at the bottom of the gangplank, twisting to lick his shoulderblade.

The cabin was chilly, despite the sun. I put the kettle on the burner and turned on the radio for some company.

Pat had seen a man outside yesterday evening, near the office. Could it have been Dylan? Maybe that was why he hadn't been able to speak when he called me last night. Maybe he had been outside, waiting for the right moment to come to the boat, and instead Pat had called the police and he'd had to go away.

I didn't go back to the Barclay to practise again. I got used to working there, just as I got used to walking and dancing in the heels. I learned the best and quickest ways to make money, too. And I learned that being a good pole dancer opened up opportunities to maximise my income.

For a start, I realised pretty quickly that I was one of the best dancers on the pole. Caddy was good, too, but she was better at the lap dances. A lot of the girls had never bothered to learn to pole dance properly, and mostly what they did was walk around the pole, snake against it and do an occasional easy spin.

The real money was to be made on lap dances and in the VIP area, so for most of the girls dancing around the pole was a waste of time, tolerated only because they could spot their regulars from the stage and head straight for them as soon as they finished.

But the pole was the best part of it for me, and, although some of the girls thought I was mad, I got more adventurous as my confidence grew. My pole routines attracted more attention and as a result I found it easier to approach people afterwards. I was getting better at the lap dances, but I was still no better than average. So I increased my chances of getting private dances by impressing them on the pole.

Two weeks after my afternoon practice session, I saw Dylan again in the club. I was doing my first pole dance of the evening, warming up with some swings and wriggles, waiting for the beat to kick in so I could climb and spin, all the while looking out for the potentially lucrative customers. And there he was – sitting at the back in one of the VIP booths. I saw him first because he was watching me, and then I realised he was sitting with Fitz, who was busy talking to another guy to his right – the bloke with the tattoo on his neck who had let me in when I'd come for the audition. With them were several other men, on the table a bottle of vodka and several ice buckets holding half empty bottles of champagne.

I hadn't seen Fitz since my first visit to the club.

I got a ripple of applause and a few cheers when I climbed the pole and inverted – I think they all expected me to fall off, to be honest – and then did an inverted splits. They loved that one. I was keeping my eye out for one man in particular, someone I'd met here last Friday. Karim had ended up spending the rest of the evening with me in the VIP area, telling me about his business and buying me bottles of champagne and not noticing that he was drinking most of it. At the end of the evening he'd promised to come back.

By the time the music slowed and I went into my second dance, the one where the clothes came off, Fitz and the other guys were paying attention too. I saw Dylan say something to Fitz, who was nodding.

At one of the other VIP booths, a group of guys in suits were applauding me enthusiastically, much to the disgust of two of the girls who were sitting with them. I blew them a kiss, and when the song finished I grabbed my clothes and scooted off to get dressed again.

When I came out a few moments later one of the girls had given up and moved on to try her luck at the bar. I sauntered past Fitz and Dylan, feeling their eyes on me, and put a hand on the shoulder of the nearest, drunkest of the group. 'Hi, guys,' I said, 'are you having fun?'

'You're good at dancing,' one of them said. He was wearing a decent suit. I was getting better at spotting them.

'Thank you,' I said. 'May I join you?'

I sat down in between two of them. Across the table, another girl, Crystal, was busy chatting up two of the younger guys, laughing at them and swigging down the champagne.

One of them poured me the last of their bottle of champagne, and another bottle was ordered – and I sipped mine while topping up their glasses, pretending to drink more than I was. Crystal wasn't so cautious. Some of the girls knocked it back then did a couple of lines of coke to sober themselves up every now and again. I aimed not to get drunk in the first place.

'Come and have a dance,' I heard her saying to one of the guys.

'I've got no money left,' he protested.

'You're a fibber, Jason, I just saw your wallet! You've got cards.'

He made a noise of weak protest, but she was winning him over.

'You can get tokens at the bar. Come on – you know I'm the best,' she said, with the good grace to give me a wink.

'We should have a competition,' I said to the table in general. 'Crystal and Viva, you decide the winner!'

We took them off to the private area one after the other and Crystal and I danced side by side for each of them in turn. A nice little earner, and an hour or so later we'd depleted their credit cards and the score – thankfully – was determined to be a dead heat.

I got a glass of iced water from the bar and drank it quickly, scanning the room for my next target. Still no sign of Karim.

Dylan appeared beside me, his bulk putting me in shadow. 'Fitz wants a word.'

I followed him over to the booth. Two other men had joined the group, and Caddy was there too, sitting on Fitz's right side and sipping champagne. She gave me a smile and a wink.

'Viva! Come and join us,' Fitz called when he saw me, patting the seat next to him. 'Guys, this is the lovely Viva. She's just been here a couple of weeks.'

Fitz poured me a glass of champagne while I said hello to them all. I wondered if any of them were Caddy's regulars. I didn't want to tread on her toes.

'So, are you enjoying yourself, Viva?' Fitz asked.

'Oh, definitely,' I said. 'It's like having a brilliant night out with your mates every week.'

I wasn't exaggerating. I'd had a laugh every night I'd worked so far, particularly when I was working with Caddy. The downside was that it was a bugger to get up for work on a Monday morning, but other than that I was having the time of my life. And earning money doing it.

'That's good,' Fitz said. 'I like to know my girls are happy.'

'Viva,' Caddy said, 'your mate's just turned up.'

I followed her gaze and saw Karim at the bar. He was watching me and I felt a fizz of excitement. I gave him a little wave. 'Would you excuse me?'

'Of course,' Fitz said. 'We mustn't keep you.'

I stood and went over to the bar, smiling my best Viva smile.

Karim was my first 'regular'. Over the following weeks, I collected quite a few more, but he was the one who earned me the most. Some of them, Karim included, became good friends: people I liked and trusted and respected. And, as Caddy had said, the more regulars I had, the easier it was to make big money.

# *Thirteen*

In the middle of January, the club was quiet and I found myself bored for the first time.

There were so few customers that the girls almost outnumbered them. I was sitting at the bar talking to one of Caddy's regulars, trying to persuade him to come for a lap dance with me. He was so drunk he could barely stand, and making conversation with him was hard work.

'So where's Kitten tonight?' he asked for the third time, breathing over me.

'She's on holiday,' I explained again. 'She'll be back next week, though, Pete. And in the meantime I promised her I would take good care of you if you came in…'

I saw Dylan out of the corner of my eye, crossing the floor of the club directly towards me. He stood the other side of Pete at the bar and Tracey put a drink in front of him.

A few moments later, Pete stumbled off in the direction of the gents' and I turned back to my glass of water.

'It's so quiet in here tonight,' I said to Dylan.

'It's always like this in January,' he said in reply. 'Won't get any stags in till they get paid. Anyway, I came to find you. Fitz wants a word.'

I wondered if I was in trouble. I followed Dylan up the stairs, struggling to keep up in my heels. I heard voices and laughter from up the corridor, faint, deadened by the heavy fabric and thick carpets.

'...like he said, he needs to learn who's in charge...'

'...not this time, not after what happened...'

'...look, boss, we can fucking do it in an hour. Just give us the nod, alright?'

'...lads, lads. All I'm saying is, he owes me, right? It's not about the money. It's about the respect.'

Dylan was at the door. 'Fitz.'

'Genevieve! Come in, come in.'

I gave him a wide, innocent smile that should have fooled no one, least of all him. He put an arm around my bare shoulder, and drew me into the office. It smelled of whisky and testosterone.

They were all in there, comfortably lolling in armchairs and sofas. The desk held a bottle of aged malt, three-quarters gone, and piles of cash in bundles.

'Nicks, Gray, this is our new star, Genevieve. You know Dylan already, of course.'

Gray was the man with the tattoo on his neck, the one who'd let me in on the first day. The guy next to him must have been Nicks – smart suit, leaner than Dylan and Gray, but his eyes said he wasn't someone you should consider messing with.

Fitz had been drinking; I could tell how by unsteady he was on his feet.

'Did you want me to wait outside for a minute?' I said to him.

'Not at all, my dear, we were just finishing anyway. Have a seat. Drink?'

'I'd like a glass of water, please.'

It was Dylan who was sent up to the bar to get me water. I watched him retreat from the room, pulling a face as he did so. He was built like a tank.

'I wanted to put a proposition to you, Genevieve,' said Fitz. He was behind the desk now, fingers steepled. The other men were talking among themselves.

'Oh?'

'I wondered if you'd be interested in earning some extra money.'

'I'm always interested in that, Fitz. What did you have in mind?'

He regarded me steadily, as though still uncertain whether I could be trusted. Dylan came back with a tray, a glass bottle of mineral water, frosty, an iced glass with a slice of lemon on a small silver dish, a matching silver bowl of ice. He placed it on the table next to my seat. I looked at him but he didn't meet my gaze, a face carved out of solid stone.

'I'm entertaining some clients at home next weekend, a private evening – just a few select guests. I wondered if you'd dance for us.'

'What's the room like?' I asked. I didn't much care about the room, to be fair; I was stalling for time, to think about whether this was a good idea. Decide how badly I needed the money. I poured some water into the glass, squeezed the lemon, licked my fingers delicately.

He nodded as though this was a legitimate question: I was showing my professionalism and he appreciated it.

'It's good,' he said. 'You could come and check it out first, if you like. The guys would be close by, the lighting brighter than it is in the club, but the normal club rules apply: no touching, nothing lairy. My guests are all wealthy individuals. I can guarantee you would get good tips if you agreed to do it.'

'How much?'

'Two grand, for the night. As many dances as they want, although we're talking business too so I don't reckon there would be time for more than four or five. Tips on top of that – you might be looking at doubling the pay.'

I looked into his eyes, saying nothing. One of my favourite sales techniques. He met my gaze resolutely for a few moments, and then laughed. 'You're good,' he said. 'Very cute. And cheeky.'

I smiled my best cheeky smile.

'Alright,' he said, 'I give up. Two and a half, plus tips. Final offer.'

I'd reached his best price. 'What about Caddy?'

'What about her?'

'Isn't Caddy doing it too?'

Fitz looked at me for a moment, considering. 'Nah.'

'Why not?'

'Caddy probably won't want to do it,' he said. 'Think she thinks it's beneath her these days. You can ask her if you want; I don't mind paying for two as long as she's prepared to work for it.'

I thought about it, sipping from my glass of water. Something about it made me uneasy. As I'd found this week, as much as I was getting used to working and dancing at the Barclay, it wasn't nearly so much fun without my mate. But then, the money…

'I'd love to,' I said at last. 'What would you like me to wear?'

When I went to go back downstairs to see if Pete was still around, Dylan walked with me, in silence. I hadn't asked for him to accompany me, and to my knowledge nor had Fitz; maybe there had been a private nod from him behind my back, some signal. He walked a pace behind me, like my shadow. I wondered if there was something going on in the office, some extra part of the meeting that I wasn't allowed to hear.

'Thanks,' I said to him, when I was back outside the dressing room.

He smiled at me, looked me in the eyes for the first time. 'You're welcome,' he said.

When he smiled, he was a different person. I decided finally he was alright, in the same way that I'd decided Norland was a piece of shit.

He hesitated at the doorway.

'What?'

'Just wanted to say,' he said, 'I'll be there. Next weekend. I'll make sure there's no trouble.'

'Thank you,' I said.

He walked off down the corridor and I found myself wondering whether I should have been expecting trouble. I hadn't factored that into the calculations, but, to be fair, I couldn't really expect two and a half grand for an evening's work without there being some additional drama to deal with.

When Caddy got back from St Lucia a week later I told her about my meeting with Fitz. We were in the dressing room, and I was waiting for her to finish getting ready so we could go out into the club.

'He wants us to dance at a party at his house,' I said. 'He wants both of us – you and me.'

She stared at me for a moment, then let out a short laugh. 'Really? Why didn't he ask me himself?'

'You were away,' I said, hoping that this would sound plausible. 'What do you think? Go on, it'll be a laugh if you're there.'

She set her mouth in a firm line. 'I don't know, Gen. Too much hassle,' she said. 'I've done them in the past. Don't really want to do them any more.'

'Hassle? How come?'

She didn't answer, pulling on a pair of sandals and tugging at the strap.

'I thought it would be good for the money,' I said.

'Yeah. It's just what you have to do for it.'

'Fitz said...'

'I know, I know – same rules. All of that shit. Just be prepared, is what I'm saying. Think about what you're willing to do for it. If you don't want to do anything, he'll be okay with it, but you won't be the top dog after that.'

'What? You mean he's going to ask me to fuck his friends?'

She laughed. 'No, not you. He'll just bend the rules a bit, that's all.'

We were both ready to go but neither of us moved. It felt as if there was something she wasn't telling me.

'He doesn't seem to be here that often,' I said, changing the subject. 'What's he like?'

'He's alright, as long as you don't piss him off.'

'What happens if you piss him off?'

Caddy stood up abruptly. Nicks was at the door. I wondered how long he'd been there, listening.

# *Fourteen*

I couldn't get the thought of the man Pat had seen by the office out of my head. The more I considered it, the more convinced I became that it had been Dylan. Who else could it have been? I tried to call him for the third time in as many minutes, but still the same result:

*The number you have dialled is currently unavailable. Please try later.*

In the end I put a second coat of paint on the spare room. With another coat, the paintwork on the cladding was looking less patchy and more like a reasonable coverage. I would make curtains next, put in a chrome bar at the bottom to tuck the curtain into so that it didn't swing when the tide came in and the boat rocked. I would build a shelf unit for the walls, use it for books. I might even build a cabinet for bed linen and towels.

I turned the radio up loud and thought again about the process of building the conservatory, wondered how much it would cost to get a bespoke glass roof made and whether it was something I could actually make myself, or if it was beyond my level of expertise. I needed something waterproof for the bad weather, with a reasonable degree of insulation, so that even in the dead of winter my plants would survive. I thought about how feasible it would be to have an outside shower, draining via a duct straight into the river – no detergents out there – and whether I could put in a coil radiator so I could even use my shower in the winter when it was cold outside. Showering in the snow – imagine that! But how cool would that be?

As hard as I tried to distract myself, the thought of Dylan kept coming back to me. Where the hell was he? Why wasn't he answering the phone?

By the time I was at the sink cleaning the brushes again, it was dark outside and the marina was quiet. Tomorrow I would start planning the bathroom. I'd put it off long enough, finishing off the easy jobs first. It would be a new project, something to get my teeth into; something that would take all of my time and tire me out every day.

The radio was still blaring in the spare room. I should turn it off; it was getting late to be playing music so loud. The instant the radio went off, the silence descended again.

Something was wrong.

A sound, from overhead – on the deck? No – on the roof of the cabin, directly above my head.

I froze, listening with my whole body. No sound, nothing – just the waves lapping against the side of the hull.

A scrabbling, a scattering sound. It was probably a bird, I thought, exhaling. A gull... sometimes they landed on the pontoons and on the boats, especially when it was windy.

I went back to the sink and rinsed it with bleach, trying to cover up the smell of the paint. After that I decided to have a beer, maybe two. My nerves were jangling as it was; alcohol might numb them a little. Was every night going to be like this from now on? Waiting to get tired enough to go to bed and sleep?

I heard another noise from outside when I'd just opened my third beer. It wasn't on the deck, and it wasn't a bird, I was sure of it. It was an animal noise, a yowl, a yelp. Maybe Oswald was having an argument with the foxes.

Alcohol made me brave.

I unlocked the door to the wheelhouse, which made a noise, and took enough time to scare whoever was out there away.

I stepped outside.

'Hello?' There was no figure on the pontoon. The marina was in darkness all the way up to the car park, a brisk wind blowing from the water, bringing with it the smell of rain.

I took a step forward on to the deck and stood for a moment, looking across the water to the lights on the opposite bank. I looked down on to the pontoon and I could see a dark shape lying on the wood at the end of it. Whatever it was hadn't been there this afternoon. I went down the gangplank, trying to get a closer look, my arms folded across my chest against the chill of the wind.

The pontoon was completely dark; even right next to the object, staring down, I couldn't see what it was. I nudged it with my foot and it moved – something soft. I crouched low, feeling with my hand.

Fur, soft fur. Cold. Wet. I stood and lifted my hand to the little light that came from the motorway bridge. I could see dark on my fingers.

'Oh my God, oh my God,' I found myself muttering under my breath. Again, looking out across the pontoon, over to the office, the car park. There was no sign of anyone.

I went back up the gangplank and turned on the light in the wheelhouse, the one I never bothered using because it attracted moths in the summer – and when I went back to the pontoon I saw what it was. A bundle of fur, black. Blood on my hand.

It was Oswald. Malcolm and Josie's cat. Someone had killed him and thrown him on to the pontoon.

I bit back a scream, my breathing shallow and fast. I had a sudden notion that whoever had thrown the cat on to the pontoon had had no time to leave the marina and was probably hiding somewhere in the darkness, just out of sight.

I ran back up the gangplank, turned off the light in the wheelhouse and jumped down the steps into the cabin, slamming the door and locking it as fast as I could.

From outside came the sound of footsteps, someone walking away quickly, fading and then louder again on the gravel in the car park. Whoever it was had been just the other side of the *Scarisbrick Jean*.

I stood in the galley in a panic. Everywhere I turned were the black circles of the portholes. Anyone outside on the pontoon would have been able to see in, to see me. I washed my hands in the sink, rinsing the blood away and scrubbing with soap, tears pouring down my cheeks.

Who could I call? Who could I talk to? I tried Dylan's number again. The same message.

I kept coming back to the same, reluctant thought. He was probably at the club.

I didn't even stop to think about what I was going to say to him. I put Dylan's phone back down and picked up mine. I rang the office number for the Barclay and waited an age for it to be answered.

'Hello?'

I could hear the music, a low, thumping bass in the background. It sounded like Helena's voice, but I couldn't be sure.

'Can I talk to Dylan, please?'

'He's not here.'

'Do you know where he is?'

'Who is this?'

'Genevieve.'

'Who?'

'Genevieve. Viva. I used to work there?'

'Hold on.'

The music cut out and was replaced by an 'on hold' bleep. I waited. *This is ridiculous*, I thought: *what am I even going to say to him if he's there?* What could I say about Caddy? Was he grieving for her, or had he not given her death a second thought?

'Genevieve.' Fitz's voice was loud and took me by surprise.

I swallowed. I should have disconnected the call the moment the woman had told me Dylan wasn't there. I just hadn't quite believed her.

112

'Hi,' I said, as cheerfully as I could manage. 'How are you?'

'Well, this is an unexpected treat. What can I do for you?'

'I just – just wanted to see how you all are. And I wanted to say I'm sorry – about what happened to Caddy.'

There was an awkward silence, a long one. I could hear him breathing and, muffled this time, the low percussion of the music.

'You don't really want to know about everyone, do you? You were asking for Dylan. He's not here, though. You want me to pass on a message?'

'No, no,' I said, too quickly. 'Is he in tomorrow? I could try then. It's not urgent.'

'Yeah, alright. I'll tell him you rang, shall I?'

'Whatever,' I said, hoping that I didn't sound as panicky as I felt. 'If you like.'

'So what are you up to, these days?' he asked then.

'Oh – nothing much. I moved out of the city,' I said.

'How'd you hear about Caddy?' he asked, his tone casual.

I had no idea what to say. My hands were shaking and then I felt the tears starting at the horror of it, the shock at finding the cat, covered in blood, and the madness of ringing the Barclay and ending up with Fitz, of all people – and that Dylan was obviously fine, still happily working there and deliberately not answering my calls.

I couldn't think of anything to say and the prolonged silence had become too much to deal with. I disconnected the call. Cut him off. *Well*, I thought. *That was an unbelievably stupid thing to do.*

There was only one place left to turn. I took the bit of paper with Carling's number on it from the table and turned all the lights off in the galley and the saloon. I went through to my bedroom and scrambled on to the bed, the far corner, tucked into the side of the hull. Above me, the skylight – anyone looking in would not be able to see me, here, in the shadows – but I would see them, outlined against the dark sky.

I crouched into the corner and dialled the number.

It rang for ages and I thought he wasn't going to answer.

And then: 'Hello.'

It took a long moment for me to find my voice, so long in fact that he said, 'Hello?' a second time.

'Is that Jim Carling?'

'Yes. Who's this?'

'It's Genevieve.'

There was a pause. I wondered if he was trying to remember who I was.

'Hi. How are you?'

'I'm sorry to call you so late,' I said. My voice was hoarse. 'I'm… I'm afraid. Something's happened.'

'What is it?'

'I was here on my own and I heard noises outside. I heard a bump on the deck. I went up to look, and… and…'

'It's okay,' he said gently. 'Take your time.'

'Someone's killed Oswald. I found him outside. I don't know what to do.'

'Oswald?'

'The cat. Malcolm and Josie's cat. He's lying outside and I'm afraid, I'm so scared. Please help me.'

There was a pause. I realised that maybe I should have just dialled the number for the police, whatever it was. Called the main switchboard.

'I'm sorry. I didn't even ask if you were on duty. You said I could ring you.'

'To be fair,' he said, wearily, 'I did say to call me if you remembered anything else, not if you found a dead cat.'

I felt very small and suitably chastised.

'I'm coming over,' he said.

'Really?'

'Yes. Don't go anywhere, okay? I'll give you a ring on your mobile when I get to the marina, so you won't get a fright when I knock on your door. Alright?'

'Thank you,' I said. 'Thank you so much.'

I shrank back into the corner in the darkness and waited. On the deck above my head I could hear more noises. Bumps, scrapes. As though someone was crawling over the roof of the cabin. I stared and stared at the skylight, but all I saw was the dark, stormy sky.

# Fifteen

I didn't even have to get myself to the venue for Fitz's private party: he arranged for Dylan to pick me up in the BMW X5. It meant I had to be ready early, of course, but on the other hand getting a lift to wherever it was was certainly preferable to public transport.

Dylan rang the bell for the flat, and when I went downstairs he was holding the rear door of the car open for me.

I laughed. 'Are you my chauffeur, Dylan?'

'Something like that,' he growled, and climbed in the driving seat.

'Does Fitz not trust me to get there on time, do you think?' I asked, as we headed towards the main road.

'Don't ask me. I think he thinks this is a perk.'

'A perk for you, or for me?' I asked cheekily, then instantly regretted it. He gave me a look through the rear view mirror, a look that said, *Don't take the piss.*

The busy streets of London gave way to the leafy, dark suburbs. I had no idea where we were; I hadn't been paying attention. And that, I thought with a sudden understanding, was probably the real reason I was being driven – so I didn't know where I was going.

'So how long have you worked for Fitz?' I asked.

'Years.'

'You like working for him?'

A brief shrug of the shoulders. A few moments later he turned up the music, loud enough to prevent further conversation. I looked out of the window and watched the world gliding past.

About half an hour later we pulled into a driveway and tall wooden gates swung open automatically. The driveway continued ahead of them, and we drove for several more moments before the car stopped in front of a large house, mock Tudor. *If I didn't know we'd headed west*, I thought, *I'd have been certain we were in Essex.*

Fitz was home. His guests hadn't arrived yet, he told me. He showed me the downstairs, the wide living room with the huge leather sofas and abstract artwork on the walls, the white carpet, glass everywhere, crystal. Through a heavy door to the left was the room I'd be dancing in. There were several comfortable chairs and sofas grouped around the centre, and the pole. I went across to test it, trying a few gentle swings to see if it felt solid. It did. I kicked off my shoes and climbed it, one hand over the other, and flipped over at the top, spinning back down to the bottom. Not easy, wearing jeans. It would be a piece of cake with bare legs.

Fitz watched all this with an expression that was hard to read. He shook his head gently. 'Does me in,' he said, 'when you do that.'

Dylan was standing in the doorway, arms folded across his immense chest.

'Have you eaten?' Fitz asked. 'Want something to drink?'

I didn't want to eat or drink – neither was particularly good just before cavorting around a pole – so I sat on a stool at a marble-topped breakfast bar talking to Dylan until the guests started arriving.

'So am I the only one here?' I said in hushed tones.

'You're the only one dancing, put it that way,' he said.

'What does that mean?'

'There's other girls here. You're the only one dancing.' Dylan was tucking into a bowl of olives, removing them delicately between finger and thumb and placing the stones into a little dish on the marble surface.

'Why don't the girls in the club like him?'

'No idea.'

'Do you like him?'

He stopped chewing and looked at me. 'You're full of questions today,' he said. 'What am I supposed to say to that?'

'The truth?' I suggested.

At least that made him laugh. 'He's alright,' he said. 'Don't fuck with him, and he's fine.'

Almost the same thing Caddy had said to me. I wondered what happened to people who didn't follow that advice.

I watched Dylan eating for a moment. He had a glass in front of him, like mine, except mine contained water, his vodka.

'So,' I said, trying to lighten the mood a little, 'who's coming to this party? Anyone I know?'

I'd been at the club long enough by this time to recognise some of the regulars, many of them friends of Fitz's.

'Doubt it.'

'Who are they?'

'Seriously, Genevieve, you ask too many questions.'

I laughed. His tone wasn't as hostile as the words implied. 'Well, you're not exactly a natural conversationalist, Dylan. I'd rather not sit here waiting in silence.'

'Me too.'

'So, you ask me some questions. Balance it out a bit.'

He gave me a smile and again I was struck by how much less threatening he looked when he smiled.

'Alright. I've got a question for you. What are you doing with all this money?'

'What?' He'd taken me completely by surprise.

'You're earning an absolute packet,' he said. 'You take twice as much in tips as Lara, and she's always been the best dancer we've had. She's got a whole fan club of blokes who've come to see her every weekend for the last four years, and since you started at the Barclay you've made her income look like a pittance. So what are you doing with it?'

I flushed. I didn't really have an answer for him. Telling him about my dream, to renovate a boat, sounded ridiculous in this context.

'You're not a druggie,' he said.

'How do you know?'

'Oh, give over. I know everything there is to know about drug addicts, believe me.'

'Well, you're right. I don't do drugs.'

'So what are you spending it on?'

'I'm not spending it. I'm saving.'

'You're *saving*?' As though he'd never even heard the word before.

From the hallway came the sounds of guests arriving. The caterers started moving platters of food into the dining room and all of a sudden the kitchen was a hive of activity.

I nodded. 'I can't stand my job much longer. I hate it, in fact. I'm just waiting until I've got enough, then I'm going to hand in my resignation and take a year off.'

His face lit up. 'Travelling?'

I stood up. 'Maybe. I'm not sure. Just as long as I don't have to do that job forever, that's all. I need something to look forward to.'

Afterwards, of course, I had a different perspective on that cosy little chat with Dylan in the kitchen of Fitz's vast house. He'd stuck with me because he'd been told to keep an eye on me. He wasn't eating olives with me at the breakfast bar out of choice. He was my minder, just in case I decided to go snooping into other rooms.

And he'd asked the question he needed to ask. Not for Fitz, but for himself. I didn't know it then, but Dylan had an agenda of his own.

# *Sixteen*

When the mobile rang, I jumped out of my skin. I didn't recognise the number and for a moment I hesitated before answering.

'Hello?'

'Genevieve? It's Jim Carling. I'm in the car park, I'll be two minutes. Okay?'

I went to unlock the door to the wheelhouse. It was still pitch black out there so I turned on the light. I could just make out the tangled pile of black fur lying on the pontoon. I would have to do something with the body: wrap it up in a cloth or a towel, or put it in a bag.

I saw a figure making its way down the pontoon towards the boat. I couldn't see it was definitely him until he was right at the gangplank.

'Evening,' he said with a smile.

'It's there,' I said, 'look.'

He turned back to where I was pointing. 'Alright. Go inside, I'll be in in a minute. Put the kettle on, eh?'

I did as I was told. I presumed he was having a look at the body, trying to determine how Oswald had met his end, or doing whatever it was that detectives did. He was such a lovely cat, so friendly, I couldn't see why anyone would want to hurt him. But they had. I thought of the man Pat had seen last night, the man I'd stupidly been convinced was Dylan. It couldn't have been him, after all.

The kettle was boiling when the wheelhouse door finally opened and Carling came in. He was dressed in jeans and trainers, with a dark waterproof jacket over the top. He looked very different out of the suit, younger. He went to the sink and washed his hands.

'I'm sorry to ring you. I didn't know what else to do,' I said, putting two mugs of coffee down on the table in the dinette.

'That's alright. I wasn't doing anything particularly exciting.'

'It must be hard on the home life, this job,' I said. Unsubtle. I felt my cheeks colouring.

'It can be,' was all he said in reply.

We drank our coffee.

'What do you think happened? To Oswald, I mean?'

'Difficult to say,' he said. 'Not easy to see any injuries in the dark. Have you told the owners?'

I shook my head. 'I had a feeling that someone was on the pontoon. I didn't want to go out, in case they were still there.'

'Who's "they"?'

I stared at him. 'Whoever it was that killed Oswald.'

He sighed, and ran a hand through his hair. 'See, I get the distinct impression that there's stuff going on that you're not telling me about, Genevieve. And it's very difficult for me to help you when I don't know the full story. Do you understand?'

I nodded. 'Really,' I said. 'There's nothing going on. I'm just scared. I've just been shaken up since I found – you know – the body.'

'Candace Smith,' he said.

'What?'

'That's her name, Candace Smith. We've identified the body.'

'Was she – local?'

Carling shook his head. 'From London. We still don't know what she was doing down here.'

'So she drowned?'

'The cause of death was drowning, but the post mortem showed a head wound. If she'd been outside the water she would have died of the fractured skull soon enough.'

I turned away, thinking about Caddy and her face, her lovely face, shattered and swollen, the muddy water washing over it. I felt sick at the thought of what had happened to her, and my eyes filled with tears. I wiped them away with the back of my hand, took a deep breath in.

'You think she hit her head on the pontoon? Like, she fell over, or something?'

His look said it all.

There was a silence. I fought back the tears. She had been so lovely – so kind to me. And I was never going to see her again.

'I'm scared. I'm afraid to be on my own.'

'You know I can't stay,' he said.

'Oh, of course. I hope you didn't think…'

'Didn't think what?'

'That it was some sort of… I don't know… come-on.'

He smiled, warmly. 'That's a shame. I was rather hoping it was. Never mind – in either case, I can't stay. It just wouldn't be right.'

'Are you seeing someone?' I asked, his flirting making me bold.

'No. Are you?'

'No. It's just me and the boat.'

'Right.' He finished his coffee. 'I've wrapped up the cat in an old towel I had in the back of the car,' he said. 'Have you thought about what you're going to do?'

'I'll have to go and see Malcolm and Josie in the morning. They'll be beside themselves.'

'I'm not sure if it might not be kinder to tell them the cat was run over, to be honest.'

'Would I get away with that? I mean, does it look like he's been run over?'

'Maybe they won't look too closely.'

122

I felt sick. 'Who would do something like this? Seriously, what sort of sick fucker?'

'The same sort of sick fucker who fractured Candace Smith's skull, I expect.'

I flushed, and looked at my hands. They were trembling.

'Look,' he said, 'I can't force you to tell me. But whoever killed that girl seemed to deliberately put her next to your boat. And now it looks as if someone's left a very unpleasant message for you to find. And you seriously have no idea who's behind it?'

He was looking at me, studying my face. I wondered how it was that I was giving away secrets without telling him anything. My cheeks flushed and I stood up, uncomfortable, took my mug to the sink and poured the last of my coffee away. Behind me he made a sound, like a sigh that turned into a low growl of frustration.

Carling stood up and brought his mug over to me. Without saying anything, I took it and washed it up in the sink.

'Candace Smith was a stripper. She worked in a nightclub in London, a place called the Barclay. Have you ever heard of it?'

I tried to stay as relaxed as I could. This was not something I wanted to talk about, not with Carling.

'I'm scared, Jim,' I said.

'I know you are.' He put a hand on my shoulder.

I turned away from the sink to face him. He'd been about to say something else and he stopped himself. He was very close. I could have moved away but there was something about him, something about his nearness. I could feel warmth from him.

'You don't have to be scared,' he said, so quietly I barely heard him.

He took a step towards me and kissed me. Despite his nearness, it took me by surprise. For a second it was gentle, and then he pushed me back against the sink and the kiss was forceful, demanding. I should have resisted, I thought vaguely, at the same time realising that it felt good and there was no way on earth I was going to do anything other than kiss him back, just as hard and maybe even a bit harder.

When we parted, breathless, I whispered, 'I'm sorry,' as though I'd assaulted him. As though it had been my idea.

'I can't help you,' he said softly, 'unless you tell me.'

'I can't,' I said. 'I just can't.'

'Right.' He took a step back from me. 'It's late,' he said.

'I know, I'm sorry.'

And then, as though there was some kind of magnetic field pulling him back, he kissed me again, his arm around me, his hand in my hair. I could feel how hard he was. For a moment I thought, *Is he going to want to stay? Are we going to have sex? Is that what I'm hoping for?* And then he pulled away from me again, right away this time. He backed off and leaned against the dinette.

'Shit,' he said. 'Sorry about that.'

'Don't apologise, Jim,' I said. The expression on his face made me laugh. How the hell had we ended up snogging like a couple of teenagers?

'I should go,' he said.

'Sure,' I said.

'Do you want me to stay?'

I thought about this. I thought about Dylan and my heart gave a lurch: the last man I'd kissed. The last man I'd slept with. I'd waited five months, and now it was clear he wasn't interested. He wasn't bothered about me any more; maybe he'd never really liked me at all.

'Look,' he said, 'I don't want to make things worse for you. Do you want me to stay until you fall asleep?'

That did sound like a very good compromise to me – and while he was here, at least, I was safe.

'Yes,' I said. 'That would be very kind.'

He took me into my bedroom. I took my jeans off and got into bed. He pulled the duvet up around me and sat on the edge of the bed. After a moment I said to him, 'You can lie down if you like.'

124

'I don't want to fall asleep,' he said, but he lay down anyway. We lay together on the bed, side by side, looking up at the skylight. He was holding my hand. I could feel the tension in him through his skin.

'When you're asleep, I'll go. You'll be alright. I'll call you tomorrow, is that okay?'

'Yes,' I whispered.

The clouds had cleared and above us was the night sky, black like a blanket, a few tiny stars like pinpricks of light. I closed my eyes, afraid that I'd see a face or a shape in the dark rectangle. Despite myself I felt sleepy. I felt his bulk beside me, his warmth. I wanted to snuggle up to him, to throw my arm over his middle so that he would not be able to slip away without me noticing.

'I'm glad you called me,' he said.

'I thought you'd be angry. Or, actually, no – I didn't think. I just knew I wanted to see you. I knew you'd make me feel better.'

'I can't believe I kissed you.'

'I can't believe it either.'

'I've been thinking about kissing you for days.'

'Really?'

'You know...'

'What?'

'You know this can't happen, don't you? Not now. Not with the investigation and everything.'

'Do police officers never find themselves being tempted into immoral situations by witnesses, then? Does this never happen?'

He laughed. 'Not to me, no,' he said. His fingers were stroking the skin on the back of my hand. It was soothing, so gentle.

'I like you,' I murmured.

'I like you too.'

We were silent for a bit and I wondered if I kept quiet long enough maybe he would fall asleep too; maybe I'd wake up and he would be still here and daylight would be showing through the skylight instead of darkness.

But what happened was quite the opposite: I fell asleep, and, when I woke up, he was gone.

# Seventeen

In total, I estimated that there were no more than five guests at Fitz's party. They were vastly outnumbered by caterers, a waitress, heavies they'd brought with them that weren't officially participating, and by Fitz's entourage, including various other men, Gray, Nicks, Dylan, and me.

I got changed in a downstairs bathroom before my first dance. Dylan had taken a CD with all my favourite music, plus some extras for spares, and uploaded it on to Fitz's sound system.

I'd gone to town on the outfit, although it never consisted of much more than underwear with something stretchy over the top that I could remove over the course of the dance.

In fact, I'd spent most on the shoes – two hundred pounds on a pair of sandals that buckled with thin straps all the way up to just below the knee. The heel on them was five inches. I'd had to practise dancing with them on, as much of my grip came from the skin on my calves down to the ankles, but when I tested them out it was fine. The only danger would be if one of the buckles snagged on another when my legs were crossed at the ankle.

Dylan came to fetch me. Despite my attire he didn't so much as look at me twice. 'You're on,' he said.

The first dance went well. I opened to my favourite dancing track, the one I'd had at my audition with Fitz – Elbow's 'Grounds for Divorce'.

I swung around the pole at full force to start off with, and it was my first chance to have a look at the men grouped on the chairs and sofas. They were all smartly dressed, and they'd all had a drink or two – including Fitz – but they weren't drunk yet and I needed a spectacular start to get their attention. They were still talking and laughing amongst themselves when I started, but they stopped within the first ten seconds of my routine and then I had their undivided attention – vertical, upside-down splits with a spin, my hair flying around in an arc so fast that they should have been able to feel a breeze from it.

Fitz watched me, and looked at his guests, glancing from them back to me with an expression that was hard to read. Approval, definitely. Arousal? I could never tell, not with him.

The next morning I went to the *Aunty Jean* to see Malcolm and Josie, but the boat was empty and the hatch shut and locked. Liam was on the deck of the *Painted Lady*, tinkering with something. He waved at me, and I went across the pontoon to where he was.

'Morning,' he said.

'How are you doing?'

He pointed with the screwdriver he was holding, towards the office. The ladder was resting against the wall. 'That light's gone again. Maureen's just been out there having a go at Cam.'

'Gone again? What do you mean?'

'Someone's cut the cable. Maureen said Cam should put electronic gates on the car park and keep them locked at night. She's trying to get a residents' meeting together for tonight. Hasn't she been round to see you yet?'

I shook my head. 'I saw her yesterday; she was going on about it then, too. Liam, have you seen Malcolm and Josie?'

'They went to the supermarket, 'bout half an hour ago.'

'Oh. Thanks.'

I still had no idea what to say to them about Oswald. I'd tucked him inside a cotton shopping bag, still wrapped in

Carling's towel, and put him in the wheelhouse so he wouldn't get wet if it rained. He would need burying – maybe on the recreation ground? Roger and Sally's allotment? It all seemed so bloody horrible.

I couldn't get Carling out of my head. He'd asked me about the Barclay and I'd stalled him. He knew where Caddy worked. Which meant it was only a matter of time before he found out that I'd been a dancer there too, that we were friends. I needed Dylan, needed him so badly. Why wasn't he answering his phone? And then Carling – lying on my bed next to me. This morning that just felt awkward. If I ever saw him again I would be embarrassed by it.

'What did Cam say about the gates?' I asked.

Liam laughed. 'You know Maureen. Maybe she just asked in the wrong way.'

I went back to the boat and spread my plans and notes out on the dinette table. If I was going to do the bathroom, I would need to lose the storage space at the bow. I would need to start with the conservatory and the sliding roof – in theory a straightforward project, in practice quite difficult.

I rang up a local glazing company and tried to describe what I wanted. I'd done this before, with other companies, and had received a mixed response, including one telling me to my face that I didn't know what I was doing and I would be better off leaving the boat alone and getting myself a nice house.

The local independent glazing company was much better. I spoke to a guy called Kev who promised to come round and have a look.

At some point I was going to need to get the MIG welder and the saws out again and cut a hole in the cabin roof. I'd done it before with the skylights and each time it had made me nervous. But when Kev turned up an hour later, he was more helpful than I'd expected and he offered to help fit the sliding roof as well as supply it. His father owned a boat and he'd often helped out on it. Nothing this dramatic, mind you, but he looked at my plans and at the article I'd clipped out of *Waterways World* magazine that had a boat with a similar sliding roof, and he agreed that it could be done. He even had tracks in stock that we could use to make the mechanism for the slide.

I started to get excited about it again. 'How long would it be before we can do it, if I order everything now?'

'Six weeks, maybe less,' Kev said. 'When they're ready we could pick some good weather days and I'll help you out with the roof.'

I felt much better with a plan. I wrote a cheque for the deposit, and, when I waved Kev off in his van, the sun came out.

Malcolm and Josie were back.

I went to board the *Scarisbrick Jean*, knocking on the hatch. A shout came from below; it might have been 'come aboard' or might just have been 'piss off'. Either way, I opened the door and climbed down the three steps into the cabin.

Josie was packing shopping away in the galley.

'I've got some bad news,' I said.

Her face fell and she stared at me. 'Is it Oswald?'

I nodded, and went forward to hug her as she started to sob.

'I knew it, I knew something had happened to him. I told Malcolm, I said…'

At that moment Malcolm came in from the bedroom. 'What's going on?'

I looked at him over Josie's shoulder. 'I found Oswald.'

'Aw, shit. He's dead? I knew it; he always comes home. Run over was he? Bastards on that road, they speed up and down.'

I didn't say anything else. I should have told them what had happened, but I was afraid they would blame me. I'd done this: I'd brought this to the marina, this nightmare.

'Where is he?' Josie whispered. Malcolm was hugging her now, stroking her back with his huge, bony hands.

'I've got him in my wheelhouse,' I said. 'I've wrapped him up a bit.'

Malcolm nodded. 'I'll come and get him.'

I said to Josie, 'Do you want me to stay with you?'

She shook her head. 'I just need a minute,' she said, her shoulders shaking. 'I just need to be on my own for a minute. You – you go with Malc.'

We got to the wheelhouse and I showed him the cotton bag, neatly wrapped. Malcolm said to me, 'Is there anything you want to tell me?'

The sun shone fiercely on the back of my neck. Just for a moment, it was warm. 'He wasn't run over,' I said. 'I'm so sorry.'

'Right,' he said. 'We won't say anything to Josie.'

'No.'

'What happened?'

'Last night,' I said, 'I heard a noise. Like a thump. When I went outside to have a look, Oswald was lying on the pontoon.'

'You didn't see anyone?'

I shook my head. 'Did you know someone's cut the cable to the light again? Liam told me that Cam was up there trying to fix it again this morning.'

'Yeah. Maureen was bending my ear about electronic gates when I went to the shops earlier. Like that's going to solve anything.'

He picked up the bundle, cradling it gently as though Oswald was still alive. 'I'd better take him back,' he said.

'Can I help? With – you know. Digging a hole.'

He smiled. 'No. I'll do it later. Be fine.'

He left me alone on the deck, taking Oswald with him. I felt so bad for them both, and Malcolm was so kind. Even though it was all my fault.

In total I earned nearly five thousand pounds for one night's effort at Fitz's party. I did work for it, in truth – I lost count of the songs I danced to on the pole, and then lap dances for each of them. Worth it for the tips.

By three, most of Fitz's guests had gone. One guy was left – a hand-stitched suit, silk shirt, open at the neck. Bling on his wrist. Serious money. I'd been talking to him for a while, pouring him drinks and laughing at his crap sense of humour. His name was Kenny. I had an appalling memory, but I'd trained myself at the day job by repeating people's names back to them constantly until they stuck. It felt clumsy to me, but I'd never met a man who'd commented on it. They all seemed to love the sound of their own names.

The flirting ramped up a notch. The same lines, variations of which I heard most weekends in the club.

'Seriously, you're the best dancer I've ever seen. And I've seen a few. What's your name?'

'You know – it's Viva.'

'No, your real name. What is it?'

'Ah, if I told you that it would spoil the magic, Kenny. You'll just have to trust me.'

'You have an incredible body, Viva.'

'Thank you, Kenny.'

'No, seriously. You deserve better than this. Why don't you come out with me? Go on, say yes. I can give you the best time ever.'

'I'm sure you could,' I said, smiling.

'Will you? Let me take you away somewhere. I've got a place in Spain – come with me for a weekend...' He was slurring his words. He wouldn't have been able to stand up without assistance. I topped up his glass.

Behind him, in the darkened room, Dylan looked at me and then at his watch.

'Ah, I can't. I'd love to, but I've got to work...'

'I can pay you,' he said. 'You just tell me how much it is you need and I'll sort it.'

'It's not the money,' I fibbed. 'I love my job. I get to meet gorgeous guys like you, Kenny.'

He sighed heavily, as though admitting defeat. Dylan took a step forward. He was ready to kick him out.

'What about one last dance?' Kenny said, leaning forward unsteadily. 'One last dance, just you and me. You know.'

Dylan appeared at his side. 'It's getting late,' was all he said.

The man said, 'Where's Fitz?'

I took advantage of the distraction and excused myself, and went to the bathroom to get changed. A few moments later Fitz opened the door, without knocking. I was folding up clothes and packing them away into my bag.

'Viva,' he said. 'I need to ask you a favour.'

I stopped what I was doing and gave him a look. It had been a long night.

He came over to me and stroked the back of his hand over my bare arm. 'See?' he said. 'Not so bad, is it?'

'That's not the bit he wants to touch, is it?'

'Viva. This guy – he's going to be very helpful to me. I need to keep him sweet. He really likes you; he's never been bothered with any of the girls before...'

'I'll dance as many times as you want, Fitz. That was what we agreed. You promised me that there would be nothing like this. You want to change the deal, you have to pay for it.'

'How much?'

I told him I would do it for a grand, I would choose my own music, and there was an extra condition: that Dylan was waiting at the door. Fitz was torn, as though I was screwing him over, and at the same time as though he'd just been given the keys to the sweetie shop.

'Seriously, a grand? Who do you think you are?'

He was quite drunk, unsteady. I waited patiently.

He looked at me for several moments, then said, 'Alright. A grand. You're pushing your luck, you know that, don't you?'

A thousand pounds. I'd better make it worth his money.

The music had already started when I went into the room. Donna Summer's 'Love to Love You Baby' – the extended version, sixteen minutes long, complete with Summer's orgasmic moans and cries. Not the three-minute track I'd chosen. Should I make a fuss? I wondered. But it seemed quicker to just get it over with.

He was waiting in the chair, reclining. He looked half-conscious; he would wake up pretty damn soon. I came up behind him, stroked my hand across his shoulders, down his arms. One last look behind me. Dylan was standing at the open door, his face in shadow.

I didn't make him wait too long for the dress to come off. The song made me hot anyway. He'd paid, or rather Fitz probably had, for just about everything he wanted. Even though I knew he wanted me to be close, I was going to start on the pole, since it was what made my dances special. So I spun and swirled and kicked, vaguely aware of Dylan at the back of the room. If he'd been watching Spurs play he would probably have shown more emotion.

As I had more skin to play with, I was adventurous with my dance and experimented with some new moves. I tried some back flips and twists that I'd not done since my gymnastic days, although doing it in heels was a different story, and thankfully I didn't fall or pull a muscle. When the music slowed and pulsed, I came off the pole and went over to Kenny, and I danced for him. I let him have my best moves, up close. At first he didn't touch, then a hand on my backside. I pushed backwards encouragingly. After that, there was no stopping him. When his fingers got too insistent I backed off, smiling as though I was enjoying it, as though he was turning me on. And when I was astride his lap, rubbing the side of my knee against the bulge in his expensive handmade trousers, I glanced up to the shadows. Dylan was still there. Unmoving.

There was a lot of touching. Some of it clumsy, uncomfortable. I had a moment where I thought, *Why am I doing this? This can't be right. I don't give a fuck about this bloke, I don't even like him, and he's got two fingers inside me and the other hand in his open fly and I'm pretending I'm enjoying it. Is it worth the money? Is it really worth a grand?*

The song came to an end, like all things, both good and bad.

Dylan came forward with a large, soft towel and held it out for me as though I'd just swum the channel.

'Goodnight,' I said to Kenny. 'Thank you, that was fun.'

He tipped me an extra two hundred quid, and asked again for my number. I smiled at him and said he should come and see me next weekend in the club. It was a compromise, potentially lucrative – although if I never saw him again I would be secretly relieved. I kissed his cheek and he made a clumsy grab at my breast. I took his hand off me and kissed it. I wondered where his money came from.

Dylan waited for me to get dressed, then he drove me home in silence. I had the feeling he was somehow pissed off with me. He kept his eyes on the road ahead.

'You must be tired,' I said at last, fed up with looking out of the window into bleak greyness of the early morning.

'Not really,' he said.

'Got far to go home?'

He just shrugged.

'Have I done something to upset you, Dylan?'

Even then, he didn't look in the rear view mirror. He was made of stone. 'No.'

'Thanks for getting me that towel, it was kind of you.'

Silence.

When we got back to my flat I half-expected him to come out and open the door for me, but instead he stayed where he was, the engine running, staring straight ahead.

'Thank you,' I said.

He waited for me to get to the door of the flat, and then the X5 sped off into the dawn.

# *Eighteen*

I'd almost forgotten that Carling said he was going to call me until the phone rang on the table in the cabin.

I'd been trying to ring Dylan again, but his phone had been switched off once more. There was no option to leave a message. It was easy to become obsessive about it, to ring every few minutes in the hope that he would have turned the phone on by pure chance since I'd last called.

My phone rang at just gone nine. I was washing up at the sink in the galley, wondering if it was too early to go to bed and whether I would be able to sleep if I did.

'Hello?'

'Genevieve? It's Jim Carling.'

I should really programme his number into the phone so I would know it was him, instead of answering it with such trepidation.

'Hi, Jim,' I said, my face colouring even though nobody was here to see it. Last night he'd kissed me and pushed his body against mine. He'd lain next to me on my bed and held my hand until I slept, and yet this morning once again the only person I could think about was Dylan.

'I'm sorry it's so late,' he said. 'I meant to ring you earlier but it got busy. This is the first chance I've had.'

'That's okay,' I said. 'Thanks again for coming over last night,' as though he'd come over to fix a leaking tap or put up a picture, 'it was really kind of you.'

'How did you get on with Malcolm and Josie?' he asked.

'They were very upset,' I said. 'I think Malcolm's buried the cat somewhere.'

'Did you tell them what had happened?'

'I didn't say much to Josie, she was devastated. Malcolm's no fool.'

'No,' he said. 'I got that impression when I spoke to him the other day.'

There was a little pause.

'Are you still at work?' I asked.

'Yes. Going to be late finishing tonight.'

'You poor thing, you must be shattered.'

He laughed. 'I am a bit. Funny, that. Anyway, I was just calling to check you're okay. You know where I am if you need me, right? Or you can always ring the main number. They'll send someone out quickly.'

'Thanks,' I said. Was that it?

'I'll see you soon,' he said. 'Sleep well.'

I put the phone back on the table, feeling put out. He might at least have offered to check up on me on his way home.

I finished the pots and got ready for bed, cleaning my teeth in the bathroom. I left all the lights on in the cabin and I'd left the radio on since the afternoon, too, the noise from it blocking out the silence. It was the quiet moments that were worst, I'd decided, once the marina had gone to sleep, darkness had fallen over the Medway and the only sounds were the wind and the water lapping at the sides of the hull as the tide rose and floated the *Revenge of the Tide* away from the muddy riverbed. I never wanted to hear that bumping noise again. If I had to leave the radio on every night, I would do it.

I turned off all the lights and crawled into bed. I left the radio on the timer socket, with it set to turn off at one in the morning. There was no way I would still be awake by then, I thought. I would drift off to sleep to the peaceful sounds of Classic FM and I would wake up to bright daylight. Nothing to worry about. No stupid gulls marching up and down the roof of the cabin above my head. No footsteps outside on the pontoon. Nothing bumping against the side of the hull.

I slept, and I think I was dreaming about Dylan. He was there, in any case, on my boat the way he'd never been in real life. He was saying, 'You did a good job with all that money, Genevieve.' I thought then that maybe he wasn't paid as much as me by Fitz. It was a sudden realisation that the time he'd driven me home from Fitz's private party he was probably pissed off because of all the money I'd earned for not doing very much at all. Whereas he'd done so much that evening, minding me and ferrying me around, and stopping me from going upstairs and seeing all the other things that were going on at the party without me having a clue – and he'd likely earned less than a tenth of what I'd taken home in cash.

It was dirty money, I realised that now. But it was all just cash, to me. It was beautiful cash that I could put towards my boat. And I'd been wrong about Dylan, of course. I'd been wrong about just about everything, back then.

The Sunday morning after my appearance at Fitz's private party, I slept late.

When I woke up, it was to a banging on the door. Half-asleep, I answered it – a delivery of a hand-tied bouquet of roses and lilies, so big that I could hardly see the delivery person behind them.

I managed to get them through the door and into the kitchen, and read the card. It said, simply:

*Thanks*
*You were great*

I smiled as I found enough vases to accommodate all the blooms and set about arranging them. I'd enjoyed myself, money or no money, even the last dance for Kenny. Nakedness was just a state of mind, after all. And the clumsy fingers, the grabbing hands? Nothing that a nice hot shower wouldn't put right. He wasn't that bad; in fact if he hadn't been quite so drunk I might even have found him attractive.

I wondered if Fitz liked me. Was that why he'd asked me to do the party? No, of course not – he was entertaining his guests, and I was the best dancer he had – he'd told me that often enough, and Dylan had said something similar earlier on in the evening, hadn't he?

One thing was for certain: Dylan definitely didn't like me. In fact, he'd barely been able to look at me on the drive home this morning. The thought of the tension in his shoulders, the way he'd looked steadily ahead as though I weren't even there, made me feel sad. I wanted him to look. I wanted him to smile when he saw me dance, and I had no idea why. It wasn't even as if he was my type. He was taciturn, monosyllabic... a moody shit, in other words.

Fitz was much more like it. Maybe if I played my cards right, I thought, I could get my escape money together sooner than expected.

When I got up it was a beautiful day. It reminded me of the summer, a huge blue sky overhead, so bright that it hurt my eyes to look at it, scored with vapour trails and the occasional wisp of cloud. It was still, the river sparkling. The cabin was warm even though the woodburner had gone out, the ashes cold.

The door to the wheelhouse was sticking. The damp weather was warping the wood. That would be my job for today, something to take my mind off it all. It was cold outside, but the air so fresh and clear I took deep breaths of it for several moments.

The marina was at peace, all the boats quiet. The car park was still; Joanna and Liam's Transit was there, and Maureen and Pat's Fiesta. Another I didn't recognise. The door to the office was open. Everything looked as it should. I'd been half-expecting something else to happen in the night, some new horror to deal with, but this morning was so normal and right that I almost felt silly for my apprehension.

I went back into the cabin to get a jumper, and while I was there I put the kettle on the stove to make coffee. The cool air flooded the saloon from the open door and the steam from the kettle rose in clouds.

I sanded the edge of the wheelhouse door, watching the dust dancing and whirling in the sunshine, as the marina came to life around me. Maureen emerged first, shopping bags in hand. She called to me across the decks of the boats.

'Need anything?'

'Where are you going?'

'Market!'

'No, thanks! Have fun.'

She waved at me and headed off to the car park.

The door was better, but still sticking. I debated getting my workbench out and planing the surface. It wasn't that bad, not yet. I went back to sanding and lost track of time. My shoulder was starting to ache.

The door to Joanna's cabin opened with a bang. Music drifted out. I recognised it straight away, faint as it was – the Velvet Underground, 'Venus in Furs'. I used to dance to this, a lifetime ago.

I could smell bacon cooking, too. I wondered if it was Joanna's. I stopped sanding for a moment to stretch my arms over my head, then I drank my coffee. It was cold, flecks of sawdust floating on the surface.

I'd finished working on the wheelhouse, and the cabin was full of dust. I couldn't be bothered with that now. I left things as they were, went over to the *Painted Lady* just as Joanna came up on deck with a steaming mug and a plate.

She saw me and waved.

'You want some? Liam's making.'

I shook my head. 'No, thanks.'

'Help yourself to a coffee, then.'

I went down the steps into their cabin. Liam was standing in the galley, dressed in a pair of jeans. He was shaking a frying pan that was sizzling furiously, filmy smoke in the air. I was pleased to see that their cabin was in a state of even more riotous abandon than mine.

'Morning,' he said cheerfully. He looked as though he'd not slept.

'Hi,' I said. 'How are you?'

'Not bad. Bit of a night on the sauce. It was Manda's birthday.'

'Oh, okay.' I helped myself to the last remaining clean mug and poured myself a coffee from the pot. I left it black and took it upstairs on to the deck. Joanna was sitting with her face to the sun, hamster cheeks full of bacon sandwich.

'I hear you had a good night. Who's Manda?'

'Sister,' she mumbled, through a mouthful.

'Oh. You made it up, then?'

'Different sister.'

Her bruise was fading to yellow already, a smear under her eye that might have been mistaken for tiredness. The sound of an engine out on the river trundled and rattled closer and then faded again as it passed. The sun was warm on our faces.

'That policeman seems very nice,' she said eventually.

I looked at her. She had a mischievous smile on her face.

'You mean Jim Carling? He is nice. I like him. So where did you go last night?'

'Oh, just in town. George Vaults, a few other places.'

'What time did you get back?'

'Not sure. Late. Why?'

'I just wondered if you saw anything last night. Anyone. In the car park, I mean.'

She looked blank.

When I went back to the *Revenge*, Malcolm was sitting on the pontoon at the stern of the *Scarisbrick Jean*, doing something to the water pipe that connected the boat to the mains. He was bashing at the connection with a spanner, making a loud clanking noise that sounded dramatic, echoing off the walls of the office. His face was pink and beads of sweat stood out on his forehead.

When he saw me, he stopped.

'That looks serious,' I said.

'I think there's a blockage,' he said. 'Water pressure's rubbish.'

I felt like saying that whacking the connection probably wasn't going to improve things much, but he looked so depressed I held it back. 'Fancy a cuppa?' I asked instead.

His face lit up. 'Got any beer left?'

'Sure. Might be a bit warm.'

We were on the sunny side of the deck where I'd sat with Ben nearly a week ago, drinking our beers.

'How's Josie?'

'Alright, considering,' he said. 'She didn't sleep much, so she's having a lie-down.'

'I'm really sorry,' I said.

'What I don't get,' he said, 'is why Oswald? And what were they doing in the middle of the night, killing cats? Don't make sense.'

'I know.'

'Bastards.'

'I heard someone running away.'

'You didn't see them?'

'No.'

He shook his head, took a big gulp of beer and let out a long, soundless belch.

'Why was he left next to your boat, though?'

I shrugged. If I could have thought of a different topic of conversation to turn to, I would have.

'I reckon you must have pissed someone off back in London.'

'Not me,' I said, attempting a laugh.

'You didn't make off with the takings, or anything like that?'

'Nah.'

'Ah,' he said, 'I reckon there's a lot more to it. These London gangsters, they don't mess about, you know. You've obviously done something to piss them off. Or you've got something they want.'

His voice trailed off and I looked out across the river, taking big gulps of beer and trying to swallow it without choking. I hadn't even thought about it – Dylan's stupid parcel. Of course that was it. Of course that was what all this was about.

'You alright?' He was looking at me with concern.

I didn't answer for a moment. Malcolm was eyeing the beer bottle I was holding against my knee. I looked at it, wondering why it was dancing up and down, and then I realised it was my hand shaking.

I put the bottle down by my feet and spread my palms on my knees, rubbing them on the denim to try and keep them steady.

'I've got something,' I said, my voice unsteady.

'What?'

I stood up and took a deep breath in, trying to stop the panic which was rising inside my throat. I put a hand over my mouth.

'Gen? What is it?'

'It's – it's just a parcel. Someone gave it to me to look after, when I left London.'

'What's in it? Drugs? A gun?'

Fuck – a gun? I hadn't even thought about it being a gun. Surely it wasn't that? It was drugs, surely, even though I'd done my best not to think about it, even though I'd just hidden it away and put it to the back of my mind, even though I'd pretended it didn't even exist, not really. It wasn't what was inside it that was important – it was just his parcel. It could have been anything.

'I don't know; I didn't like to ask too many questions. I just promised I'd look after it, that's all.'

'Jesus. Well, that explains a lot, don't it?'

'It might not be that,' I said, at the same time knowing for a fact that it was.

'You need to get rid of it,' he said.

143

'Yeah, thanks for that! I've been trying to get hold of the person that gave it to me. No luck so far.'

'You want me to – take care of it?'

'What?'

'Well, we could find somewhere else to hide it. We could bury it on the rec.'

'No. It's alright where it is. Thanks, though.' It was still Dylan's parcel, and I was supposed to be looking after it. What if he turned up to collect it, despite everything, and I'd got rid of it? He'd be furious.

We sat in silence for a few moments, watching as a small motorboat chugged upstream. The woman sitting in the back of it was wearing a bikini top. Surely it wasn't warm enough for that? I was starting to calm down a bit now. The breeze was fresh, blowing in gusts under the Medway bridge. The woman on the boat waved at us. Malcolm raised his bottle of beer in salute.

'You worked at that club a long time?' he asked then.

'Six or seven months, altogether.'

'You miss it?'

'Sometimes. It was good fun.'

'Why did you leave?'

'I got enough money for the boat.'

He looked at me and laughed. 'That can't be the only reason. Why not work there and do up a boat at the same time?'

He was right, of course. There was a moment when it had all started to go horribly wrong, when things began to unravel. They'd unravelled at the Barclay at just about the same time that my night job collided with the day job, and it had all started the night I recognised my boss in the crowd of customers at the Barclay.

# *Nineteen*

My boss was called Ian Dunkerley, a well-built man with small man syndrome. His way of working was to make you look like an idiot in front of your colleagues, so that you were left not trusting your friends, and despising him.

He'd only taken over the line management for the sales team a few months before. At the time I was one of the top performers, but not *the* top, and that made me a target. Everyone who wasn't actually top of the performance tables was a target. The idea, I suppose, was to encourage us all to be hungry for profit, or at least to make us want to be the favoured one who didn't get picked on or abused, but in practice it pissed everyone off.

Of all the people to see at the Barclay.

I didn't notice Dunkerley at first as I was concentrating on the moves, but during my usual moments when I was pausing in a particularly provocative pose, getting my breath back ready for the next gymnastic flip, I scanned the room as I always did looking for my regulars, new customers, people who looked reasonably well-oiled.

And there he was.

I was so shocked I nearly fell off the pole. I had to put in an extra spin which put me one beat off.

He was sitting in one of the VIP booths with a number of other men – quite casually dressed, I noticed; I was surprised they'd been let in – laughing and joking with a couple of the girls and fortunately paying no attention whatsoever to what was going on on stage.

When I'd finished the routine and run back to the dressing room, flushed, breathless, I contemplated crying off sick for the rest of the night. I'd not missed a single dance since Fitz took me on, but the thought of going out there and dancing in front of that odious man made me feel physically ill.

'Are you alright?' Kay asked me.

Kay was new to the Barclay, a pole dance specialist like me. She had been sent over from one of Fitz's other clubs because she put on a 'challenging' show, mainly due to her outfits, which had more than a hint of S&M about them. Her dance name was Mistress Bliss, but since that was a bit of a mouthful we were allowed to call her Kay, as long as it wasn't in earshot of any of the customers.

'Yes. Thanks – I just... I thought I saw someone I know.'

'What? A punter?'

'Yes.'

She laughed. 'I get that all the time. I saw my old maths teacher when I was working at the Diamond.'

'Really?'

'Yeah. There he was, Mr O'Brien, in the front row, drooling. It was hilarious. Who've you seen out there, then?'

I grimaced. 'My boss.'

'From the day job?'

Not all of us had day jobs. We never mentioned them here, in any case. I had no idea what the other girls I worked with did. 'Yes.'

'Ooh, shit. He doesn't know about this, then?'

'You must be kidding. What makes it worse is that he's not even nice. He's a complete, total arsewipe. What am I going to do, Kay?'

She patted me on the upper arm. 'Do you dress like this at work? What's the chances he's going to recognise you? Lord knows Mr O'Brien didn't recognise me. Hope not, anyway.'

'I feel sick.'

'Go home, then. Don't ask Norland – go and see Helena. You'll be alright.'

'I'm not a quitter.'

'Then you're going to have to go out there and face him.'

It crossed my mind to ask one of the other girls for help, to distract Dunkerley for me. But, other than Kay, none of the girls on tonight were particularly friendly. Caddy wasn't here to ask. There were a bunch of Eastern European girls who stuck together; they worked the room hard and concentrated on the lap dances, putting in a half-hearted show on the pole and then doing their best to hustle in the club. If I asked them for help, they'd be less likely to oblige by providing a distraction and more likely to use it as an opportunity to get one over me by deliberately pointing me out to him.

I sat miserably putting make-up on in the hope that it would work as a disguise, borrowing someone's tongs to put a few loose curls into my normally straight hair. Kay was probably right. The chances of him recognising me, with my hair down, wearing these clothes, in the dark, in that context in fact... it was all a bit unlikely.

And yet, he was a sharp little fucker. I wouldn't put anything past him.

My next dance was slower – Portishead's 'All Mine'. The lights in the club were low and I could almost hear the conversations going on around me as I danced. I loved this song, it was easy to block him out, to take myself off to a private space where I was alone and dancing for myself.

When I looked over to the table where he'd been sitting, near the end of the track, he was gone.

Malcolm went back to the *Scarisbrick Jean* after two beers. Josie had popped her head up and seen us sitting together, feet up on the gunwale, laughing about something. I waved at her but she'd already gone in.

'Better go,' he said, downing the last of his beer. He slid the empty bottle into the crate outside the wheelhouse and hopped down the gangplank. When he got to the deck of the *Jean* he waved. 'Cheers, Gen,' he said.

When I stood up, a little unsteadily, thinking that it was probably a bad idea to be drinking beer in the middle of the day, I caught sight of something down in the mud. I put both my hands on the gunwale and peered over the edge.

The mud was disturbed, churned up, around the boat. When I looked properly I realised there were footprints, deep holes with trails between them as though someone had pulled their feet from one step to another, stumbling, leaving a muddy wake with each step. To my left the trail ended in a mess of mud, debris and river weed.

The footprints led away from the boat to the grassy wasteland between the marina and the great concrete legs of the Medway bridge. I followed them with my eyes all the way to an old pontoon, half-submerged in the mud, that was made out of old pallets lashed together with bits of rope. There, more churned mud, and footprints on the wooden pallets leading up to the tussocky grass, the marshy land under the bridge.

Someone had walked from there, down to my boat. They must have struggled in the deep mud, and, judging by the mess, they had probably lost their balance once or twice and fallen over. There was no sign of anyone – nothing moved in the marina, no cars in the car park. In the bushes under the bridge, the only movement was the leaves and branches stirring in the breeze.

This morning I'd felt relief that the night had passed without incident. I'd chastised myself for being foolish, for expecting more horrors when I had no reason to expect any. But as it turned out, I'd been right – someone had been here. Someone who hadn't wanted to be seen by anyone at the marina and so had approached my boat from the river, across the mud.

I leaned over a bit further, dizzy with the beer and with a sudden waft of stinking silt, until I could see that the footprints were right underneath the porthole. The porthole that looked in on my saloon.

# Twenty

I didn't see Dunkerley on Monday morning. He was out at meetings, and as usual it was a hectic day. By home time, I was starting to feel relief where previously I'd been feeling dread, panic. Lord knew he made my life hellish enough as it was. He didn't need any additional weapon to fire at me.

Tuesday was our regular team meeting. Usually this was the time he picked on one of us, the one he perceived to be performing badly and needing a boost. We all dreaded it, every week.

But this Tuesday was different. He scanned the room to see if anyone was missing. I felt his eyes brush over me like an unwelcome grope on a crowded Underground train.

But there was no public humiliation, not for me or for anyone else. He was quiet, writing notes, his skin and bald head pink and shiny with perspiration. He asked for updates on workload, on profits. As soon as that was over he called the meeting to a close and scuttled off.

'What the fuck? What's happened to him?' asked Alan.

We all celebrated our first gentle meeting since Dunkerley had arrived with a coffee and a prolonged discussion about what could possibly have come over him. I had a horrible feeling it might have been related to our encounter in the club, but I kept quiet.

Dunkerley avoided me at work after that, and I started to relax. Maybe he'd been embarrassed by it; maybe he was worried that I would tell everyone he'd been seen in a lap dancing club. I was almost able to enjoy work again, for the first time in ages, without that constant pressure.

Of course, it all changed the following weekend at the Barclay.

He was there early, not with his mates this time. He managed to bag himself a table right at the front of the main stage, and he was sitting there looking up with a kind of joyous anticipation, like a kid at his first pantomime.

I stared at his ugly mug, the door to the dressing rooms open just a crack.

Well, there was no doubt in my mind what he'd come to see, and I had no way of getting out of it.

He was there for all my dances. He only ever moved when I came off the stage. I did my best as I always did, but the force of his stare was off-putting. In my second dance I slipped and only just recovered in time. Even so, he laughed. The bastard laughed.

After that I got fire in me and the rest of my routine was powerful, and faultless. I would show him.

I was half-expecting him to ask for a dance with me, and it was no surprise when Helena came to see me in the dressing room when I still had at least two dances left.

'There's a customer for you,' she said.

'I thought there might be.'

'Thing is, he said he wants a private pole dance with you for free. I told him that wasn't an option. He said I should ask you. Someone you know, is it?'

'Yes. The man's a complete idiot.'

'I take it you don't want to dance for him, then?'

I gave her a look which said it all.

'Is he giving you any shit?'

'Yeah, he is a bit. He's sitting at the front and he's putting me off, to be honest with you.'

'Right,' she said, and marched out again.

When I went back out into the club, he had gone.

I asked Helena when I got a chance to talk to her. They'd taken him out. He wasn't welcome, she said.

I could have kissed her.

I spent the afternoon keeping busy, anything to take my mind away from the churned-up mud under the porthole, but even so the thought of it kept returning. Whoever it was had been there at low tide, which meant first thing this morning. I'd been asleep in bed.

The cabin was still full of dust from the sanding I'd done earlier, so I spent a long time wiping everything down with a damp cloth. I kept glancing across to the porthole as I did it, as though I was expecting to see a face appearing there. In the end it got dark and then all I could see when I looked up was a blank, black circle.

When I'd finished wiping down the cabin, I rinsed out the cloth and left it out to dry. It was early, but I was exhausted. I got ready for bed and, as I drifted off into an uneasy sleep, the tide ebbed away once more and left behind it a clean, smooth surface to the mud outside the porthole, as if the footprints had never been there at all.

The week after he'd been chucked out of the Barclay, Ian Dunkerley avoided me. I thought that I'd escaped somehow, that maybe the heavies at the club ejecting him had put an end to it.

Of course, I was wrong.

It was one of the regular Friday night after-work drinking sessions that I'd participated in with rather less frequency since I'd been dancing; most of my team went, got smashed every Friday on expenses and then either staggered home to nurse their heads, or went off into town and got drunker and drunker at their own expense.

Dunkerley didn't come along often; he'd told one of the supervisors that he felt it was important to allow the team to relax without him, it helped foster an atmosphere of independence. Bollocks to that. It was because he knew we all hated him and if any of us saw him away from company property there was a strong chance one of us would punch him, especially when lubricated by several bottles of wine.

This time, he was in the Highwayman with a large glass of red wine when I made it in there at nearly eight. I'd been working hard to set up appointments for the following week, something I liked to do on a Friday because then I could draw a line under the day job and concentrate on getting ready for the Barclay.

He was already a bit pissed, I noticed, his bald fat head shiny in the lights from the bar. Of course, what I should have done was to turn on my heels and leave again immediately, but I was tired and I'd been looking forward to my two glasses of wine for most of the afternoon.

'Genevieve,' he said, holding out his arm in an arc as though he expected me to snuggle into his sweaty armpit and embrace him.

'Ian,' I said in reply. 'Special occasion?'

He tried to laugh but snorted instead, which made him look like a drunken idiot.

'I was just thinking I'd have a few drinks with my team,' he said in general, and then, in a hushed comedy whisper which was directed at me, 'I might go on somewhere else, later. Anywhere you recommend?'

'I recommend you go home,' I said.

Dunkerley gave me a foul look; clearly, I'd made a mistake.

'Sorry,' I said, with a tight smile. 'It's been a hectic day.'

I got myself a glass of burgundy and took a big sip. One glass, I thought. One glass and I'd be on my way. I tried talking to some of the other guys on the team, but they kept looking over my shoulder at Dunkerley as though he might erupt at any moment.

'He's been acting really weird,' Gavin said. 'It's like he's disturbed, or something.'

I laughed at that, recognising that that was probably exactly what had happened to him. I still hadn't told anyone about the Barclay. I wasn't sure any of them would believe me if I did.

A few minutes later I finished my glass of wine. 'I'm off,' I said to Gavin.

'What? You can't go yet!'

I winked at him. 'I'm afraid I've got a hot date,' I said. Only something of that magnitude would satisfy him.

'Really? Who is it?'

'I'll tell you all about it on Monday,' I said, recognising that by the time Monday rolled around Gavin was likely to have consumed enough alcohol to have killed off all the brain cells that were currently engaged in our conversation.

I kissed him on the cheek and made for the door.

Dunkerley followed. I didn't realise until I'd reached the Underground, and there he was, pressed against me from behind in the crush to get on the District Line. It was still the tail end of rush hour, I'd left the bar so early.

'Where are you off to?' he asked into my ear, breathing wine fumes and cheese-flavoured corn-based snack all over me.

'Home,' I said. 'Why don't you go back to the bar, Ian? They'll be wondering where you've gone.'

I recognised that this was a dangerous situation, despite the crowds of people. I had to be pleasant to him, when all I wanted to do was throw him on the tracks.

'Are you dancing tonight?' he asked, as though to put to bed any lingering doubts I might have had over his recognising me.

'Not tonight,' I lied.

'Shame,' he said. 'I was going to try again for another private dance.'

The woman standing next to us on the platform looked at me, and him, and then focused on the advertisement for coffee on the far wall.

'I don't think they'll let you in, Ian.'

His voice rose, just slightly. 'And who do I have to thank for that, eh? You sarcastic bitch.'

That did it. 'I beg your pardon?'

'I said you're a sarcastic bitch!' His voice got louder and louder and by the last two words they were a full-on shout.

The other platform occupants were torn between staring or looking pointedly in the opposite direction. Of course, no one intervened. He could have put his hand up my skirt and not a single person would have said or done anything.

I felt a gust of wind heading towards us through the tunnel. I turned and started to walk away. As I thought he would, he followed. I had to push my way through the crowds who were surging forward to try and get on the train.

'Where the fuck are you going?' he shouted, over people's heads.

I didn't answer. I was going to get a cab home. He couldn't follow me there, after all. I had a sudden vision of being crammed against him in the train, feeling his skinny little erection pressing into my backside. *I'd rather die,* I thought, *I really would.*

Outside the station, though, there were no cabs anywhere. It had started raining, and everywhere I looked were people patently ignoring this wanker who was standing within my personal space, bleating something about my being a stuck-up bitch who needed to get a grip.

'Leave me alone,' I said. 'Seriously, Ian, fuck off back to the pub. This is getting embarrassing.'

That didn't work either; in fact it seemed to make him even more mad. 'Look,' he said, 'you're moonlighting. You could lose your job. I could sack you.'

'Yeah, course you could. And how would you explain how you found out what I do in my spare time, huh?'

It threw him for a second, but he rallied. 'I don't need to explain myself. If anyone asks, I'll say I got a tip-off.'

'You can't sack someone on hearsay. And in any case, you know what – I don't give a fuck. You tell anyone about my job, and I'll make your life hell, do you understand? Does your wife know where you were? Do you think she'd like to hear about it?' I was getting angry and raising my voice, and of course now people were starting to take an interest. Fortunately for me, at that moment a cab came into view with its light still on, and I waved at it and stepped into the road to force it to stop. I got in and told the driver to go, fast, please just go... just as Dunkerley reached for the door handle and had it snatched away from him as we sped off.

I cried in the cab. I had been afraid of him, the wanker; if I'd been in a different place, with fewer people around, what would he have done? Would he have tried to be more physical with me? Would he have hurt me?

Would I have been able to fight him off, even if I was angry?

'You alright, love?' the cab driver asked me.

'I'm okay,' I sniffed. 'Thanks.'

He drove me home and the cost of it, thirty quid, came out of my savings. Even though I had plenty of money by this stage, it was the principle of it, that that man had taken money out of my boat fund, that made me mad.

I sensed that wasn't the final confrontation between us. Things would not get better, they would get worse from now on. He'd make every day at work a misery for me, until I left. I needed more money. I needed enough money to get out, and soon.

I woke up, with a start – my heart pounding – without really knowing why.

I sat up in bed and shrank back into the corner, away from the skylight, even though it was still dark overhead – grey clouds. Too early to be awake.

Something must have woken me up – what? I strained to listen, but there was nothing, except the gentle rise and fall of the boat, the noise of the water. I could distantly hear something else – a car maybe?

And then, a sound, directly overhead. On the roof of the cabin. I froze, listening hard, my heart thumping with panic. I thought of my mobile phone – both of them, mine and Dylan's – on the table of the dinette. Fat lot of good they were there – what if I needed them? I would bring them both to bed with me tomorrow…

In the perfect rectangle of the skylight, framed against the grey sky, I saw the figure of a man.

I took in a sudden gasp of breath and pushed myself back even further into the corner. From here I could just see the dark shape outlined against the sky. I could see him moving as he tried to peer in. And then I heard something else, a voice – but not clear enough to make it out, and a footstep on the deck.

Seconds later and there was a figure in the doorway to the bedroom.

I tried to scream but it was too late. He saw me in the corner and lunged for me, grabbing my pillow and ramming it against my face. My head hit the wall behind the bed and for a second I saw stars. Then I started struggling and kicking, fighting as hard as I could.

'Stop it,' he hissed, 'stop it, you stupid bitch.'

I kicked harder, and he put one hand across my throat until I couldn't get any air. I really panicked then.

'You going to stop struggling?'

I tried to speak but couldn't get a word out with his hand over my throat, so I nodded, hoping he could see me in the darkness. Someone else came into the room.

'What the fuck are you doing?'

'She was fucking right kicking off,' said the first man in a low whisper. He took his hand away from my throat and I gasped and choked, pulling air into my lungs.

He pushed me over on to my front and between them they grabbed my wrists and fastened them with something, pulled it tight, the plastic biting into my skin.

'Genevieve,' said a voice – the second man. 'You want to tell us what the fuck's going on?'

'What? What do you mean?' I wailed. They were whispering but I had no intention of doing that on my own boat.

He lifted my head by my hair and flung it back on the pillow so my teeth knocked against my lip. I felt blood in my mouth and spat it away.

'Don't make it worse. Tell us what you're up to, and get it over with, or we'll just fucking shut you up and have plenty of time to look round the boat. What's it going to be?'

'Fuck off,' I said. 'My boyfriend's coming over when he's finished work. He'll be here in a minute.'

He laughed. 'Like fuck he is. You mean your boyfriend Mr Carling? He's tucked up at home with Mrs Carling. He's certainly not on his way round here. Oh, Genevieve, you're hilarious.'

There was a breeze a fraction of a second before his fist connected with the side of my head, just behind my ear, once, twice – hard; I felt dizzy and sick.

'Don't be stupid. Right?'

I could hear buzzing, a ringing, and for a second I wondered what it was, until I realised it was coming from inside my own head.

'I don't know,' I said, my voice muffled by sobs, by the bedclothes and the pillow, 'what you're talking about.'

Someone else was on the boat. They were throwing things around in the galley.

I recognised the voice of the second man, the one who had stopped the first from strangling me. It was Nicks, Robbie Nicks, one of Fitz's men.

'Nicks?' I said.

There was silence in the room, broken only by the noises from the saloon and the galley.

'Will you shut up, you stupid fucking bitch,' he hissed.

There was a bang like a firework going off in my head, and the room disappeared and everything in it.

# Twenty-one

After the episode with Dunkerley, I spent some time counting up the money I'd saved. Realistically, I needed eighty to a hundred grand for a barge in a reasonable condition. I could have got a narrowboat for much less, but I found them restrictive. I wanted the same space I could get in a house, on a boat. After all, I was going to live on it, not spend summer weekends there. After that, I would need cash to do it up – say another twenty or thirty grand assuming a worst case scenario, a boat with some sort of structural problems or one that needed taking out of the water and welding. On top of that, I'd need enough to live on for at least twelve months, although it was in the back of my mind that I could get a part-time job if I had to, once the process had started.

I had about two-thirds of the amount I needed, and most of that had come from equity from my flat, which I'd sold a year ago. Nowhere near enough to be able to leave the job now. Part of the trouble was that, as much as I earned from dancing, there were expenses too: clothes, shoes, cosmetics – even being frugal I was spending a small fortune on make-up every month. So: another six months at work, assuming I didn't get the opportunity to do any more of Fitz's private parties, and I should have enough money to be able to resign.

I didn't know if I could stand it that long.

Dunkerley went back to keeping out of my way, but he had also returned to his usual dreadful self. Performance targets had been published – an increase for all of us. We were already working as hard as we could. Where the extra was supposed to come from, none of us had any idea. The only reason I stayed was because of the money. Other organisations in our sector were actively making people redundant. I didn't hold out much hope of getting another job if I chose to leave, especially since Dunkerley would be the one writing my reference.

No, I decided: I would have to stay, and just try and manage Dunkerley the best way I could.

It was a week after the incident on the Underground, Friday again, that I first had an indication that Dunkerley was not prepared to let things lie. I opened my desk drawer, and inside on top of the papers was a flyer for a lap dancing club.

I took hold of it and marched into Dunkerley's office. He was in there on his own, pretending to be busy. I slammed the leaflet on his desk.

'What is this all about?' I said, furious.

He grinned. 'I have no idea what you're talking about,' he said. 'What's that – applying for another job, are we?'

'Why are you doing this?' I asked, quieter.

His face changed.

'You know why. You had me chucked out of that club. It was humiliating.'

'I didn't do anything of the kind,' I said, embellishing the truth a little. 'The manager told me you'd asked for a private dance for free. They don't like that kind of thing, as I'm sure you realise. You don't get anything for free in that place and, if you ask, they take it as an insult. So that's why you got chucked out.'

'So if you weren't in the club, would you have given me a private dance for free?'

'No, of course not,' I said.

'Why not?'

'Because you're an odious little shit. Quite apart from the fact that you're my manager and it's inappropriate on just about every level.'

'You complete bitch,' he said. 'Get the fuck out of my office!'

I went to see the Human Resources officer. If he was going to get nasty on me, then I could play the same game. I sat in her office, breathless and flustered and teary, and told her his behaviour towards me amounted to sexual harassment and I was sick of it. She listened sympathetically while I explained that I'd seen him in a nightclub and he'd tried it on, and ever since then he had been making inappropriate suggestions. I showed her the leaflet.

'He put this in my drawer,' I said.

'How do you know it was him?' she asked.

'I went to ask him. He denied it at first and then he – he said something about how I should dance for him.'

'I see.'

She asked me to write her a report detailing all the incidents I could remember, all the times when he had said things to me or done things that I considered inappropriate. I was still anxious, stressed by the whole thing, and she said I should take the rest of the day off and she would sort it out.

I had work to do, and realistically I should have gone back to my desk and carried on with it, especially considering the new targets we were working towards. But the thought of having to face Dunkerley again was making me feel sick, so I did as I was told and went home.

I was looking forward to tonight, and the weekend. Assuming they wouldn't let my cock of a boss in through the door at the Barclay I was going to have a great weekend dancing, seeing my regulars, getting some good exercise and earning money into the bargain.

I opened my eyes and almost immediately closed them again, because the light was too bright and everything hurt, everything, from my head to my feet.

It took me a second to realise where I was, then I saw I was on the floor and someone was talking to me, only I couldn't

160

hear them properly. It was like being underwater – I could hear my own breathing, my heart, the blood rushing through my veins.

'Gen? Oh, thank God...'

'Malc?'

He went off somewhere, saying something – 'Where's the fucking scissors...?'

*In the drawer in the galley*, I wanted to say. Why couldn't I move my hands? Then it started coming back to me – there were men in here, in my bedroom, on my boat...

I started to panic, and struggle, and then Malcolm was back. 'Hold on, hold on. You've got a cable tie on your hands. I can't find any effing scissors, it's a bit of a mess back there...'

'There's a pair of pliers in the hatch... in the box of tools...'

The hatch was a mess, too, apparently. That told me everything. They must have found the parcel. It was a miracle they'd left me alive.

He found the pliers under one of the pallets in the storage room. It hurt like hell, levering the jaw of the tool under the cable tie, digging into my swollen flesh, and then one snip and the plastic tie came free and I let out a scream of pain as my arms were released and the blood started rushing back through my hands and fingers.

For a moment I couldn't move, I just lay on my bedroom floor sobbing, crying my heart out. How did I get into this stupid, crazy mess? What had I done to deserve all this shit?

Malcolm was sitting on the floor, resting with his back against my bed, watching me steadily. 'Take your time,' he said. 'When you want to sit up I'll give you a hand.'

I gasped and sobbed into the carpet. My hands were in agony. 'Oh, God, Malc... I was so scared...'

'Did you see who it was?' he asked.

I shook my head and tried to push myself up from the floor. He stood, and hooked his hands under my armpits, pulling me upright and then helping me to sit on the bed.

'It was dark… oh, God. Have they trashed it, Malcolm? Have they damaged the boat?'

'It's not so bad,' he said. 'I think they've just thrown stuff around. If it was my boat you'd not even notice they'd been in. Perhaps I should ask them to come round *Aunty Jean* next time; they might make it look better.'

I smiled despite myself.

'Do you want me to call the gavvers?' he asked, in a tone that suggested complete unwillingness to do anything of the kind.

I shook my head again. 'I can't.'

'This is shit, Gen, you know,' he said.

'What – not calling the police?'

'No. What they're doing. It must be that fucking parcel you told me about.' He was shaking his head, running a hand through his hair. 'They could come back any time, couldn't they? They could start on us too; they could be threatening us next if they can't get what they want from you, and Josie…'

'Calm down, Malcolm. I'm not even sure that's what they were after.'

'Of course it fucking is! Why else would a load of heavies suddenly start searching your boat and beating you up?'

I wished I'd not told him about the stupid parcel. He was raising his voice now, pacing up and down.

'Look,' I said, 'they've gone, right?'

'How do you know they haven't taken your parcel?'

'I don't know. They might've. But I somehow think they didn't find it.'

'You want me to check for you?'

'No, I don't!' I was losing patience with him now – always this bloody need to help, to interfere. 'Thanks. Honestly, I'll be fine. I'll have a look in a minute, okay? I need to – sort myself out first. I need to tidy up a bit. Will you come round later?'

'Yeah, if you want,' he said.

He looked a bit peeved. He shuffled on his feet, clearly not ready to go just yet.

'I wanted to tell you we buried Oswald,' he said gruffly. 'We found a nice quiet corner of the rec. He used to bring us back presents from there – you know, even a baby rabbit once. He'd like it, where we put him.'

'Is Josie alright?'

'She'll be okay in a week or so. Right as rain. She's already talking about going to the RSPCA at the weekend, look for another rescue cat.'

'That's a good sign.'

He nodded, and then stood. 'Are you sure you don't want me to help you tidy up?'

'I'll be fine, honest,' I said.

'I'll see you later, then,' he said.

'Malcolm – thank you.'

He shrugged. 'Would have come over sooner if I'd known you were lying here bloody well tied up and unconscious,' he said with a smile.

What did he mean? I looked at the clock as he left. I'd been out of it for hours. No wonder I ached all over.

I got up slowly, finding my feet, feeling the room wobble even though the tide was out and the boat was back to resting on the soft mud below.

The cabin was such a mess that I cried out. Paperwork everywhere, my drawings and measurements for the conservatory roof, scattered all over the floor. The drawers in the galley had been pulled out and emptied. The cupboard doors had been ripped off. The dinette seats had been dragged off and the storage space beneath, which was full of odds and ends, bedding, ropes, rigging, spare parts for the engine, had been emptied.

I looked back at the hatch. Malcolm had left the door open and I could see a black space. Was it even worth checking? I knew it had been turned over.

They'd even opened a tin of paint, but thoughtfully emptied it down one side of the hull, presumably so they didn't get any on their clothes and shoes. All the boxes had been tipped up.

And the one at the end, the one helpfully marked KITCHEN STUFF.

I crawled painfully over the pallets to the corner, over tools and bits of hardware and the cordless drill and spare lengths of wood I'd been keeping just in case. Some of them had been broken.

The box was upside down, but as soon as I lifted it I realised that it hadn't been fully emptied. The false bottom hadn't been touched. They had just kicked the box over, seen the kitchen things spilling out of it, and moved on.

They hadn't found it. And at least now I knew who it was, targeting my boat: Fitz. And Caddy must have been coming to warn me. She must have known Fitz had found out about Dylan's parcel, and they'd stopped her before she could get to me. She'd died because of me.

# Twenty-two

That night at the Barclay, Fitz turned up in time for my last dance. The club had been quieter than usual, and although the other girls were all busy I'd just been doing my turn on the stage, interspersed with the occasional lap dance. None of my regulars had shown up. It was cold outside, a chilly February night, but inside the club the atmosphere was sensual despite the cool of the air-conditioning.

I was happy with my dances, enjoying the workout, getting a thrill out of watching the guys at the front of the stage watching me. Sometimes we had stag nights come in, but given the prices in this club they weren't common. There was a group in tonight, however. The giveaway was the age range, considerably younger than the Barclay's usual clientele. The young man who was about to plight his troth was probably the son of one of our club members. He and his friends were all suitably attired in suits and dinner jackets, grouped around the stages and enjoying the show. One or two of them had had dances with some of the other pole dancers, but I suspected they were starting to run out of money.

I put on my best effort for them, even blew the groom a kiss at the end. His mates liked that.

As I was leaving the stage, I saw Fitz in one of the VIP booths, surrounded by his usual mix of steroid-filled associates: Nicks, Gray and the others. Dylan wasn't with them. Not then.

In the dressing room, I wiped the perspiration off and fixed my make-up, and then I went back into the club to look for customers to entice. And maybe I was looking for Fitz too.

He was still in the VIP booth, and to my delight when he saw me he smiled and waved me over. 'Viva! Come over here, gorgeous.'

He waved away the two girls who had positioned themselves either side of him and patted the seat encouragingly. The girls went off in search of other game, leaving me with Fitz. They hadn't been talking business just now, judging by how relaxed they all appeared to be.

I sat neatly on the red velvet cushions next to Fitz. I'd half expected him to touch me, maybe just a hand on my thigh, an arm around my shoulders, but he didn't.

'I wanted to say thank you for the flowers,' I said, when the next dance started and the attention of the men was drawn to the stage. 'I haven't seen you since then or I'd have thanked you sooner.'

'Ah,' he said. 'You liked them?'

'They were beautiful. I appreciated them.'

'Well, you know,' he said with a smile. 'You did a good job. Especially that last dance.'

I'd got him. I could sense it. 'Do you think he got his money's worth?'

'You know he did.'

'I wouldn't have done it for anyone else, Fitz. Only you.'

He laughed, 'And a grand.'

I paused, to hold his eye contact and make my meaning clear. 'I would have done it for nothing, if it had just been for you.'

That was enough. I smiled at him and stood, and went across the floor of the club. At the door which led to the dressing rooms, I glanced back over my shoulder. He was still looking.

Dylan was waiting for me in the dressing room.

'Are you allowed in here?' I said, looking around at the other girls, who were busy either disrobing or getting dressed again, depending where they'd been.

'Aw, leave him alone!' shouted Kay from the table next to mine. 'He's alright, aren't you, Dyl?'

'I'm allowed anywhere,' he said to me.

He was sitting in the seat by my bags. I waited for him to move, but he didn't. I wondered if he was still pissed off with me for some reason. I'd not seen him since the night he'd driven me home from the party.

'Come for a drink,' he said.

'What?' I replied. I didn't know if he meant now, in the club, or… on a date. That would have been just bizarre.

He stood, and offered me his arm.

'I've – er – got to be back on stage in twenty minutes,' I said.

'Liar. You've done your share, right? And the club's nearly closing. So come on.'

Blushing, I took his arm and let myself be steered out of the room, with wolf whistles and cat calls following me out. He took me downstairs to the public bar, of all places. Dances didn't happen in here, but sometimes the girls came down if it was quiet, to try and tempt the regular members of the public into the more exclusive, and more expensive, areas inside the club. They didn't let just anyone in here, but there was always a queue outside, and the bar was usually full of people.

'You're costing me money, you know,' I said. I was only half-joking.

'Get over yourself. You can afford five minutes off.'

There were no free tables or seats anywhere from what I could tell, but Dylan gave a nod to one of the door staff and a few moments later a few lairy-looking lads in suits were being hoofed out of the door and Dylan guided me into their warm seats.

'What would you like?' he asked me.

'Just water, please,' I said.

'I'll have a vodka,' he said to the waitress who had appeared the moment we'd come in. Dylan wasn't Fitz, but even so his presence held a lot of weight in this place. I wondered what it would be like to spend the whole evening on Fitz's arm.

I'd been half-expecting him to squeeze into the booth next to me but instead he sat on the stool opposite. I was used to being stared at here. I had no illusions about it, since I never got this kind of attention in the day job apart from that infernal idiot Dunkerley, and, after all, that was only because he'd seen me here. He'd seen Viva. But Dylan was immune to Viva's charms.

'This is a nice surprise,' I said cheerfully. It was noisy, and I had to speak up so he could hear me.

Our drinks arrived. I squeezed the slice of lemon into my water and licked my fingers, watching his face.

He was completely unimpressed. In fact, he laughed. 'It doesn't work with me,' he said.

'What?' I asked, my face a picture of innocence.

Dylan was serious again, quickly. 'You need to be careful, you know.'

'What do you mean?'

He leaned across the table so he could speak normally. 'Fitz.'

'What about him?'

'You know exactly what I'm talking about. Don't get involved.'

'He likes me. You know he does.'

'Yes, I know he likes you. I'm not blind, or stupid. Just be careful.'

'Why are you telling me this?'

He sighed, took a long swig of vodka, neat, with a grimace to follow it. 'Because you're smarter than the rest of them. You've got a future, and I don't mean in here. Don't get too close to Fitz. Don't piss him off.'

I sat back. He was warning me off. Whatever his motives, he wasn't doing it out of jealousy – all the more reason why I should listen to what he was saying.

'I don't get you, Dylan,' I said.

'You don't have to get me. Just have a word with yourself. It's not a good idea.'

I sipped my water. It was icy cold and if I drank it too fast it would make my teeth hurt.

'Dylan – remember you asked me what the money was for?'

He nodded.

'You still want to know?'

'If you want to tell me,' he said.

'Just between us, right? Nobody else would… understand.'

He shrugged, as though it made no difference to him either way, but I knew I could trust him. I didn't know how, but I knew. After all, nobody else had warned me off Fitz. And he had no clear motive for doing so.

'I'm going to buy a boat,' I said.

To his credit, he didn't laugh or make some joke about a ship called *Dignity*, or any of that shit. 'A boat? What sort of a boat?'

'A barge, preferably – you know, like a houseboat. I want to buy a boat and spend a year doing it up.'

'Why?'

'It's just something I've always wanted. And now every-thing's starting to go wrong here, so I want to get the money together as quickly as I can.'

His expression changed then. 'Hold on. What's going wrong here? You're the top earner in this place, you know that. I thought you liked it.'

I shook my head. 'It's not here, Dylan. It's my day job. Three or four weeks ago my stupid boss showed up in the club and recognised me. He's been giving me shit ever since.'

'Really?'

'Yes. He followed me out of a pub the other weekend; he was making a scene down on the Tube platform. I had to go and get a cab in the end. Now he's started being all suggestive at work. I have to make sure there's always someone there when I see him, that I'm never on my own with him.'

'What's he want?'

'What do you think he wants, Dylan? He wants the same thing they all want. Apart from you.'

'You want me to sort him out?' he said. He was smiling but that didn't mean he was joking.

'No, of course not.'

He finished off his vodka, throwing it down the back of his throat as if it were water and he was dying of thirst. 'Well, just say the word. I've dealt with pricks like that before. Thinking they own you just because you flashed your knickers at them. Piece of shit.'

Dylan waved at the waitress who came straight over, despite the crush of people waiting to be served. 'Another vodka. Viva?'

'I'm fine with this one, thank you,' I said.

'So,' he said, when the waitress had gone. 'A boat, eh? And how much are you short?'

'Quite a lot,' I said, thinking it was none of his goddamn business.

'And this is why you're dancing? To get the money together?'

I sighed and drank some water. This was getting torturous, and I almost wished I'd never told him. 'I have a good job – during the day, I mean. It pays well. I thought I would be able to save up enough to buy the boat at some point, take a year's sabbatical maybe. But it's hard work, high-pressure, so I started doing this – dancing – for a laugh, for some exercise… and what do you know? I'm good at it. I can earn money doing something that to me is little more than a workout. So now I've got two jobs, the money's coming in faster and faster, and the more money I make, the closer I get to my dream. Now, instead of two years away, I could be on my boat by Christmas. And it's making me hungry for it, especially now I've got all the shit with my boss hanging over my head. So yes, I'm earning money, and I want to make more money. And Fitz has got lots of it. Hasn't he?'

'Fitz could buy Parliament,' he said slowly.

'Exactly. And he likes me. What's fifty grand to him? Nothing. He could give me that and he almost wouldn't even notice.'

The waitress appeared with Dylan's second vodka, a large one by the look of it. When she had gone, he drank half of it in one gulp, breathed in through his nose and looked me straight in the eye. 'Have you ever thought where he gets his money from?'

'Of course I have; I wasn't born yesterday.'

'And?'

'I know it's dodgy, if that's what you're asking. And I don't care, personally.'

He smiled, a slow smile, one of those that made him look beautiful. I felt as if I'd crossed some kind of line – as though I'd given the right answer, somehow.

'And,' I added, 'if he asks me to do another private party, I will. I know you think I'm a slut for what I did the other weekend; I don't really care about that. I want my boat. I want to be away from London. I've had enough of it.'

'I don't think you're a slut at all.'

'Why were you so pissed off with me in the car on the way home, then?'

He didn't answer at first; when he did, he looked away. 'I have my reasons.'

'Anyway, why do you care what I spend my money on?' I asked.

He shrugged. 'I think of you and me as mates,' he said.

'What?'

'I don't have many friends, to be honest with you. I like you. I think you're clever, and witty, and you don't sell yourself like some of them do here. When you dance, you do it as a job, and yet you look as though you do it because it's all you want to do in the world. What I'm saying to you is, I respect you as a person who does a good job no matter what the circumstances. You're committed. And you don't interfere.'

'Interfere?'

'That party,' he said, leaning over the table again, 'was a test. Did you know that?'

'I thought I was just there to dance for his private guests,' I said.

'It was a test to see if you could be trusted.'

'With what?'

'With Fitz's business.'

I was confused. 'I wasn't there when they were discussing business. What do you mean?'

'Exactly. You did your job, you did it well, you put your heart and soul into it, and you didn't piss about being nosy about what was going on upstairs, or what Fitz was talking about with his "private guests", as you call them.'

Light was starting to dawn in my head, as well as through the windows to the street outside. 'I don't give a stuff what he does,' I said.

'Good,' Dylan said quietly. The bar was beginning to empty. We were getting near closing time. 'Because the minute you do is the minute you start to become a risk. And that's why I want you to be careful around Fitz.'

'Right,' I said.

'He's going to ask you to do another private party,' he said.

I felt a sudden rush of elation. I wasn't sure if it was the money, or the thought of dancing in front of Fitz and watching his face as I danced, that was making me feel so pleased with myself.

'You'll say yes?'

'Of course. What do you think?'

'If you do,' he said, 'ask for more cash. And now you've set a precedent you'll probably have to do more intimate stuff. You know that, though, don't you?'

'Oh,' I said.

'So, if you do it, he'll make it worth your while. But remember what I said about being careful.'

'Will you be there?'

He smiled at me again. I wished he smiled like that all the time. 'If I have to.'

The waitress had appeared again. 'Can I get you anything else, Dylan? We're just starting to close...'

'It's alright, Tina. We're going back upstairs.'

I followed him up the carpeted stairs to the club, and when we got to the top he left me to go to the dressing room by myself. We'd spent long enough in each other's company. There was no doubt it would have been noted, and it would get back to Fitz. My head was swimming with it all. How could Dylan be loyal to Fitz and just have told me so much about him?

And yet, his smile.

I made a start on tidying, beginning at the front of the boat and working my way back. I put all the spatulas, spoons and various gadgets back in the box marked KITCHEN STUFF and set it back in its position at the very point of the bow.

Some of the other boxes of tools I refilled and placed surrounding the box, a rather half-hearted attempt to disguise its significance. Where was the best place to hide a box but in amongst other boxes, after all?

This wasn't the ideal place for it, I knew that. In a few weeks' time it would have to be moved in any case, as Kev and I would be taking the roof off this section of the boat and my vast storage compartment would become a conservatory, plus another room at the end, which I could use as a junk room until I'd moved on to the final part of the project. Even so, it would be more exposed.

What I should do, of course, was get the thing off my boat.

What I didn't understand in all of this was why the hell Fitz wanted Dylan's parcel – unless Dylan had stolen it from Fitz in the first place. It seemed so unlikely. Dylan wasn't a thief. He was a bruiser, an enforcer, but not a thief.

So if Dylan had decided to branch out in business for himself, how had Fitz found out? And why would he believe he was entitled to come here and take something Dylan had left in my care?

Unless it wasn't about the parcel after all.

What if they thought Dylan and I had some other scheme going? What if someone else had stolen something from Fitz, and they'd assumed, because we were friends at the end, because he'd protected me, that I was in on it?

All that time, five months, that I had no contact from Dylan at all and I'd so desperately wanted to talk to him, to see him again… he should have sorted things out with Fitz – that was the plan, after all.

Maybe Fitz assumed we were together. If it wasn't the parcel, what on earth were they looking for?

My brain wasn't functioning properly – all I had was a lump on the side of my head and a headache the like of which I'd never experienced. I left the bow storage area behind. The paint that had been thrown over the wall could stay there. I was going to clad over it anyway, one of these days.

The state of the kitchen and the saloon made tears start again. That, and my aching head. I picked up all the papers, rearranged them into some sort of order. I replaced everything in the storage area under the dinette, then put the cushions back. Already it looked a lot better, more like my usual mess than an actual burglary.

The only things that were broken in the kitchen were a mug from Dover Castle and the cupboard doors. I didn't tend to buy many fragile things, since it would only have taken a rough spell at high tide for things to get knocked about in the cabin. Everything breakable was either behind a rail or, in the case of the television and music system, fixed to the wall. Most of my plates were melamine. It didn't look as nice, but I was generally the only one using them.

In a pile on the floor I found a pack of painkillers that had been in one of the galley drawers. I took three and swilled them down with a handful of water from the sink.

When Jim Carling rang me at eight-thirty, I was already drunk.

I'd finished the beer and most of a bottle of wine, sitting by myself in the saloon waiting for night to fall. I thought it would be easier to deal with if I was pissed.

I answered the phone the third time it rang, having ignored the first two. I couldn't think of anyone I really wanted to talk to, except for Dylan, and yet again his phone was switched off. 'Hello,' I said at last.

'Genevieve. Why didn't you answer the phone?'

He didn't say 'It's Carling', I noticed. He sounded pissed off.

'I was out on the deck,' I lied.

'Are you okay?' he asked.

'I've had a few drinks,' I said, by way of explanation.

'Ah. Sounds like a good state to be in. I need to catch up,' he said.

I didn't answer, my thoughts drifting away from the phone conversation.

'So,' he went on, 'I was wondering if I could come and see you.'

'Yes,' I said.

'Have you eaten?'

I was going to say that I couldn't remember, which would have been the truth. But that would sound as if I wasn't taking care of myself, and I couldn't face a telling-off. 'Um… not yet. Why?'

'I could bring a takeaway. What do you fancy – Chinese, Indian or fish and chips?'

'Oh, chips. Just chips. That would be great. Thank you.'

'I'll be over in half an hour or so, then,' he said. 'Don't go anywhere, will you?'

As soon as he'd rung off, I tried Dylan's number again.

*The number you have dialled is currently unavailable.
Please try later.*

I tried to tidy up again, half-heartedly, my senses dulled
by the alcohol and by the tiredness. My body still ached;
everything hurt. If I had a bathroom, I told myself crossly, I
could be soaking in a nice hot bath right now. Instead it was a
choice between a shower in the shower block, or the hose.

I took clean clothes over to the shower room with me. The
sky was darkening, the lights across the river reflecting patterns
on the water.

The car park had filled up since I'd last looked this
afternoon. Joanna and Liam's Transit was there, and Maureen
and Pat's Fiesta. I didn't see any cars I didn't recognise.

I had a hot shower and it made me feel better, more awake,
although I kept dropping things. There were marks around
my wrists where I'd spent most of the night tied up, and
when I washed my hair I felt the big lump on the side of my
head, above my ear. I tried pressing it experimentally, but only
the once because the pain was sudden and sharp and brutal.
Fortunately no blood, no broken bones. With a bit of luck
Carling might not notice.

I had no idea how long I'd been in the shower, but when I
came out it was properly dark. I waited for the light to come
on in the car park, but it stayed resolutely off. *Surely it should
trigger?* I thought, standing under the sensor in my trackie
bottoms and trainers. Maybe they'd cut it again last night.
Maybe they cut it every night, and Cam repaired it every
morning. Maybe he wasn't bothering to repair it any more.

I started walking back to the boat, my feet unsteady on the
moving pontoon.

The lights were on in my boat. I tried to remember whether
I'd left the lights on or not, and couldn't decide. My brain felt
as though it were full of cotton wool.

I went down the steps into the cabin and nearly jumped out
of my skin – Carling was standing at the kitchen sink, about
to fill the kettle.

'Fuck,' I said. 'You just gave me a heart attack.'

'You should lock your door when you leave the boat.'

'I only went for a shower.'

He came up to me and took me in his arms. It hurt, and felt good at the same time. He kissed me after that. It felt a bit awkward, not like the kiss we'd shared before.

For a moment, I thought about Dylan.

'Are you okay?' he asked, his expression concerned.

'I'm still a bit drunk,' I said, as if this explained it all. 'I'm sorry. I was miserable and I felt like getting so pissed, the world would go away.'

On the table in the dinette was a big paper bag with two wrapped packets of chips. I fetched sauce, salt and vinegar from the kitchen cupboards.

'I brought more alcohol,' he said. 'I thought you might be running low.'

Two bottles of wine, one white, one red. They looked very tempting. I smiled at him, my best drunken smile.

'You open it,' I said, handing him the corkscrew. 'I've completely forgotten how.'

We ate our chips sitting at the dinette. It was only when I started eating that I realised how hungry I was. I ate all the chips, every one, scraping the last bits of sauce from the paper. He ate his at a more sedate pace, sipping wine elegantly as though he was at a restaurant instead of sitting on a worn velvet cushion in a half-finished Dutch barge on the Medway.

'So,' he said at last, 'why were you miserable?'

I shrugged. I felt a bit less drunk but still vulnerable, as though tears were only a matter of time away. 'I guess I felt alone, that's all. I don't want you to feel sorry for me. I don't get lonely very often, but I did today.'

'Well, not any more. We can be alone together.'

'Sounds good.'

'Why are you looking so sad?' I said.

He laughed, but without mirth, and topped up my wine glass. 'I'm not sad. Just getting old.'

'You're not old.'

'I'm older than you.'

'So what?'

'Alright, then, I feel old today. Which is also a good excuse for getting drunk.'

I smiled at him, starting to really enjoy his company for the first time. 'We need shots,' I said.

'Funny you should say that,' he said. From a holdall which had appeared just beside the steps up to the wheelhouse he brought out a bottle of vodka. 'I hope you like this stuff.'

'Shit,' I said, 'it's better than meths.'

After that, everything seemed funny, to him and to me, and we drank shots while listening to jazz on the radio, which neither of us really liked. Every time one of us grimaced at a discordant note we had to drink. And so we both got drunker and drunker.

The bag and the bottle of vodka told me he was planning to stay the night. He was going to stay the whole night, and judging by how much of the vodka he was downing he didn't need to get up early tomorrow to go to work either. And, once that had filtered through my poor, drunken, battered brain, I realised that tonight, at least, I could relax.

They wouldn't be invading my boat again, not tonight. Dylan's parcel was safe.

# Twenty-three

It was a Friday, again, the next time Dunkerley stepped over the line.

I was looking forward to dancing, and, although it had been an incredibly busy week at work, it was nearly over and I couldn't wait to get to the Barclay later and loosen up.

There was an afternoon meeting, one of the things Dunkerley had initiated that was universally unpopular with my team. On this Friday, to my great misfortune, nobody turned up except me. We'd been so busy during the day that I'd hardly noticed that most of the team were off work. Two of them were off sick. Gavin was in Tenerife. Lucy had taken a half-day to get her nails done. So that left me, and Dunkerley.

I think he'd been told to stay out of my way by Human Resources, while they investigated my allegations. Either way, I'd hardly seen him since that argument we'd had in his office. But now, here he was, sitting across the boardroom table from me, staring at me blatantly in a way that was making me feel increasingly uncomfortable.

We waited in silence, until ten minutes after the meeting was supposed to start, Dunkerley cleared his throat and said, 'Well, Genevieve. Looks as if it's just you and me today.'

'Looks like it,' I said.

'So, what have you got to report?'

I looked down at the performance report I'd printed off in preparation and passed it across the table towards him. I was top this month. It had nearly killed me, but the need to get away from all this had spurred me on.

He read over it quickly and nodded. 'See,' he said, 'what you can do if you try?'

I didn't say anything. I couldn't trust myself to speak.

'Look,' he said, 'I think you may have misunderstood my intentions towards you.'

I raised an eyebrow at him. 'Really? And what were your intentions, exactly?'

'My intentions were to get you to sleep with me.'

Whatever I'd expected him to say, it wasn't that. I must have looked shocked, my cheeks flushing.

He laughed at my discomfort. 'You can't have been surprised. Not in the line of work you do. I mean, your other work, of course.'

'If that's the end of the meeting,' I said, 'I'd really like to go and finish off what I was working on.'

'You're a very hard worker, Genevieve.'

'You know you shouldn't be saying this. How do you know I'm not taping this conversation?'

'Because you're not as clever as you think you are.'

I was getting angry now. I wondered if he realised that he had found the right button to push to get a reaction. 'You're a shit, you know that?'

'Yes, probably. So, are you going to do it?'

'Do what? Fuck you? In your dreams.'

'Not that. Are you going to drop your complaint against me?'

'No,' I said. 'Why should I? If anything you're just giving me more to report.'

'I think you should drop your complaint before everyone else finds out what you do on the side.'

'You know what? Tell them. I really don't give a stuff. In fact, I might well tell them myself. I might just invite them all to the club as my guests and see what they think. Shall I do that? I could invite everybody – except you.'

I stood up abruptly, the chair rocking behind me, and left the room, slamming the door behind me.

We'd finished the first bottle of wine and were a quarter of the way through the vodka before he kissed me again. We were on the sofa together, laughing about something that wasn't even funny, and somehow I collapsed against him and mumbled, 'Sorry,' as he took my face in both his hands, as though he might miss otherwise, and that made me laugh too, and then I couldn't say anything because his mouth was on mine.

While he was kissing me I climbed on to his lap and sat astride him so I could control this, even though I was so drunk I was having trouble balancing. He held me steady, his hands on my waist.

At last I stopped to give him a chance to breathe.

'I seem to remember saying this couldn't happen,' he said.

'Well, I'm not very good at following instructions.'

'Even more so because we're both drunk.'

'You've never had drunken sex before?'

'Of course I have. Is that what's happening, then?'

'What?'

'Drunken sex.'

'Well, maybe we'll sober up eventually. Then we can have sober sex too.'

It was dark in my bedroom, and chilly: the heat from the woodburner had warmed the saloon and the alcohol had warmed us from the inside, but going into the cold room I found myself shivering. I undressed as quickly as I could and got under the clean duvet. Carling took longer to get undressed, folding his clothes and leaving them in a neat pile on the chair on to which I'd already thrown my clothes with far less care. He was thinking about it too much, and maybe I wasn't thinking about it enough.

He had a good body. Even in my drunken state I could tell: he was warm and solid and had kept himself fit, athletic rather than muscular, long-limbed, taut. He climbed in bed with me and immediately pulled me against him. The skylight over our heads bugged me. I still remembered the shock of seeing that face, framed against the dark sky. Was that only last night? It felt like a long, long time ago.

It was drunken sex, but it was still good. Tangled in the darkness, unfamiliar bodies reacting in unfamiliar ways; breathing hard, and sweaty limbs against each other in a sort of desperate dance to which neither of us were certain of the correct steps. The conclusion of it was something of a relief for both of us. He fell asleep straight away, not snoring but breathing heavily, his body firmly between me and the door of the bedroom. If they came for me tonight, they would have to get past him first. Even if it took a lot to wake him from his drunken sleep.

I liked him, that was true. Was it enough? Was it wrong of me to have fucked him when my feelings for him amounted to less than for most of the people who lived on the marina? God, I was even fonder of Malcolm than I was of Carling – but I wouldn't have fucked Malcolm if he was the last man alive.

I thought about Dylan, wherever he was. What he would say if he knew what I'd just done. I could almost picture myself saying it. Him standing there in front of me with his arms folded across his massive chest.

*I fucked that policeman.*

He would raise one eyebrow at me as if to say, *So?* And he would pull that face that implied he had somehow expected better.

I was still angry hours later, when I finally got to the Barclay.

The club was busy, packed out: more than one stag group by the look of it as I wove my way through the throng of people towards the dressing rooms. I saw no sign of Fitz but that meant nothing; it was early. Maybe he'd show up later.

Dylan was talking to Nicks, by the largest stage. They seemed to be deep in conversation, but Dylan looked up as I passed, gave me a nod.

I got changed for my first dance and did some stretches to warm up. Not for the first time, I wished I could choose my own music. I needed something fast, brutal. Something to work off the aggression a little bit, so that I could calm down for my routines later in the evening. When I got on to the stage for my first dance, fortunately it was 'Sexy Bitch' by David Guetta and Akon. That would do the trick. Not exactly girl power, but I would embed my stilettos into the crotch of any man who felt like challenging me about my attitude tonight.

Fifteen minutes later, and my first routine was over. I'd put effort into it, done some high twirls and spins and an upside-down split against the pole that I'd only tried a couple of times before. It looked inelegant if it wasn't done properly. The last time I'd tried it had been at Fitz's party.

I watched the faces of the men gathered around the stage when I finished and I knew I'd done a good job.

In the dressing room I drank water and dabbed the sweat off my skin with a towel. A proper workout to start off with. I scarcely noticed Dylan until I'd finished, and only then because Chanelle called out, 'Dylan! You're perving over Viva – stop it.'

He wasn't perving, of course; he was standing in the doorway like a brick wall, his face impassive. When he'd finally got my attention, he said, 'Fitz wants to see you.'

I checked the clock over the dressing table. I didn't want to waste time; I could be out there in the club, earning money.

Dylan walked up the stairs to the offices and I hurried after him, tottering on ridiculous heels. 'What's it about, do you know?'

'Don't ask me,' he said.

I was half-expecting to see several blokes gathered in the office as usual, but today Fitz was alone. Despite the warmth I'd generated by dancing, I felt a shiver. I wondered what it meant, that he was on his own, and if I had any cause to be afraid.

'Viva. Can I get you anything?'

I wasn't really thirsty but I needed a reason for Dylan to come back. 'Water, please.'

Dylan was dismissed from the room with a nod from Fitz. He crossed the room and shut the door.

I smiled at him.

'Have a seat, my dear,' he said, indicating the sofa.

I did as I was told. No wonder I was shivering. The window was open behind me, the heavy curtain moving gently as the breeze stirred it. I could hear the noise of the traffic in the street below.

'So,' he said at last, 'you enjoyed the party the other week?'

'Yes,' I said. 'It was a good night.'

'Fancy doing it again?'

'Sure.'

'Next weekend?'

Was that it? He could have asked at closing time, or sent a message through Dylan.

He was standing in front of me, his legs slightly apart, hands thrust into the pockets of his expensive silk suit. There was a knock at the door and a few seconds later Dylan opened it. He brought a tray with water on it, exactly as he had done last time. Ice and a slice of lemon on a silver dish. He set it down on the table next to the sofa and left the room again without a word, or a look at Fitz, or at me. He shut the door behind him.

Fitz cast a glance behind him at the door and turned back to me, head cocked to one side as though he were considering something. 'He likes you,' he remarked.

'Could have fooled me,' I said. 'He never so much as gives me a second glance.'

'You had a nice long chat with him last weekend,' he said. 'What was that all about?'

'He was asking me for advice on some girl he fancies,' I said, without missing a beat. Whatever I'd said would have been a lie and I was sure he would have seen straight through it, but I wasn't about to drop Dylan in the shit.

184

To my profound relief, Fitz laughed. 'Sly old dog,' he said. 'I still think it's you he likes. Maybe it was some kind of double-bluff.'

I laughed too, and Fitz went to his drinks tray. He poured himself something that could have been whisky, a tumblerful.

He came and sat next to me on the sofa. Next to me, but a respectful distance between us. 'See,' he said, 'I have a problem with that.'

'With what?' I said, feeling uncomfortable again.

'With him liking you.'

'Why's that?'

Fitz drank from his glass, downed the whole tumblerful as I watched, one gulp after another. Then he sighed heavily and put the glass down on the table, reaching across me as he did so. 'Because, my dear Viva, I like you too. And that big bastard is better-looking than me.'

I smiled at him. 'You like me, Fitz?'

He was watching me coyly from his end of the sofa. 'Come on. You know I do.'

I drank my water to give myself a few seconds to consider how to play this. 'I didn't think you had any free time for girls,' I said at last. 'You're a very busy man.'

He looked at me steadily, as though he was evaluating my response. 'You're different from the others,' he said. 'That's why I like you. You're not going to piss me about, are you, Genevieve?'

'Depends what you mean by that,' I said. 'I work for you and I'm very proud of what I do. If you want to fit me in around my dancing, then that's fine. But I don't want to stop dancing, Fitz. And if anything happens between us, then I don't want that to interfere with work. Do you understand what I mean?'

'You mean you wouldn't mind a fuck every now and then, but you don't want a relationship?'

'To put it crudely, I guess that's probably about right.'

He nodded slowly, as though I'd given the right answer.

'Well,' he said at last. 'You are different from the others. You really are.'

'I need to go,' I said. 'They're busy downstairs.'

'Yes,' he said, 'I wouldn't want to come between you and your dancing.'

He stood and held out a hand to help me to my feet.

At the door he kissed my hand gently. 'I don't do casual fucks, Genevieve,' he said. 'If I can't have your heart I'll have to make do with having you as a valued employee.'

'Thank you,' I said.

I half-walked, half-ran back down to the dressing room, feeling a little as though I'd been in the lion's den and come out again without so much as a scratch. Could that have gone any better? Only if I'd managed to renegotiate my payment for the next private function – the question of my remuneration had somehow failed to come up in the light of the other revelations.

Dylan was waiting for me outside the dressing room and he walked back with me to the door to the club. 'Well?' he said.

I smiled at him. 'He thinks you fancy me,' I said.

Dylan laughed, and I went off to find some nice gentlemen to chat to.

I woke up and my head was splitting with pain even before I opened my eyes.

I was alone – Carling was gone. My head fell back on to the pillow and that hurt, too, the bump on the side of my head jarring with the impact.

I needed water.

I dragged myself upright and found a T-shirt on the floor, pulling it over my head as I went next door to the bathroom. I drank from the tap, ran my hand under it and over my hair, holding a cupped hand of cold water against the bump on the side of my head.

I washed my face and finally looked in the mirror. I'd looked worse, I thought. It would have to do.

It was cold, so I went back into the bedroom and pulled on some jeans and socks. Then I went through to the kitchen.

He hadn't left, after all. He was at the table in the dinette flicking through a copy of *Waterways World* that he must have found on the bookshelf, a steaming cup of coffee in front of him. He was sitting in a shaft of sunlight from the skylight overhead, almost as though he was about to be transfigured. He looked a hell of a lot better than I did.

'Morning,' he said cheerfully.

I cleared my throat. 'Hello,' I said.

He put the kettle back on the stove while I sat down on the other side of the dinette. I thought about the painkillers in the drawer, and wondered if I could be bothered to stand up again to get them.

'You look as if you need to go back to bed,' he said with a laugh.

'Thanks,' I said. 'I'll be alright in a minute.'

'Oh,' he said, pouring the water into the mug, 'I just met your neighbour. Again. I think he was quite surprised to see me.'

'Which one?'

'I remember seeing him last weekend. Fiftyish. Mad grey hair.'

'Malcolm? What did he say?'

'He just said, "Oh," and I said you'd be around later if he wanted you. And he said, "Thanks," and then he went away again.'

We sat sipping our coffee for a few minutes. I wondered why he was still here, torn between liking the feeling of not getting up to a lonely, empty boat and not enjoying the thought of having to make conversation. Although I liked that he stopped reading now that I was here.

'I'm glad you stayed,' I said.

He looked surprised, and pleased. 'Oh, good. I was hoping I hadn't outstayed my welcome.'

'Don't you have to work today?'

'I've got a rest day today, and tomorrow. I was going to head off and do all the stuff I don't get a chance to do during the week, you know, shopping, laundry, all kinds of exciting stuff. How about you? What do you have planned?'

'I was going to go and look at baths,' I said.

'You mean like in a DIY shop?'

'Not unless I have to. Reclamation yards, that sort of place. If I can't find an old bath I like I'll have to go for a new one. Most of them aren't really designed for boats, though.'

A pause. I wondered if he was hungry, and if I actually had any food in the house that hadn't gone off.

'I wanted to ask you something,' he said.

'That sounds ominous.'

'I'm going to ask once, and if you don't want to give me an answer you don't have to. Alright?'

'Sure.'

'What happened to your wrists?'

I looked down at my hands on the table of the dinette. I hadn't even thought about it, stupid cow. I hadn't even thought to put a jumper on, to cover up the marks. Thin scabs had formed in arcs around both wrists, not all the way round but in those sections where the skin had been broken by the cable tie. It looked almost as though I was wearing bracelets, threads of pink.

'If I told you, you wouldn't believe me.'

'Try me.'

I shrugged, still a bit drunk, and too tired to argue or fight it. 'Some men broke into the boat when I was asleep. They tied me up. That's about it.'

'When was this?'

'Night before last.'

'Didn't you ring the police?'

I shook my head. 'Malcolm found me in the morning and cut the ties. By that time there didn't seem to be any point calling anyone.'

He was staring at me.

'What?'

'I can't believe you're so casual about being attacked.'

'What am I supposed to do – lie down and cry? I've got to get on with it.'

'Aren't you afraid they'll come back?'

'Of course I am,' I said. 'But what can I do about it?'

'Genevieve. You can't not report things like this. If anything happens again, you've got to promise me you'll dial 999.'

'Sure,' I said, feeling a bit chilled that he'd suddenly come over all official.

He rubbed a hand through his hair. 'I shouldn't be here,' he said. 'I shouldn't be doing this.'

'I'm not keeping you prisoner,' I said, turning my back on him and heading for the bedroom. 'Shut the door on your way out.'

I stretched out on my bed again, listening for the sound of his feet on the steps up to the wheelhouse, waiting for the sound of the door slamming behind him, and hearing only silence. At least the room wasn't spinning any more. There was just a hint of nausea, and the headache grinding behind my eyes. If I could catch up on some sleep, everything would be fine. An hour or so of sleep, and then I would go out in the fresh air, get on my bike and go and look at baths.

He appeared in the doorway a few moments later. I turned my head to look at him, thinking that I should apologise, maybe; thinking that I should get up, or at least say something. Instead I watched as he came back into the room, pulling his shirt over his head as he approached the bed. This time he didn't bother folding up his clothes, putting them in a neat pile. He got them off as quickly as he possibly could and left them where they fell.

I bumped into Caddy on the way back down the stairs. 'What did he want?' she asked, an urgent whisper above the thumping bass from the main room.

'Another party,' I said.

189

She looked miserable.

'I thought you didn't want to do them?' I said.

'It's not that. It's just…'

'What?'

Dylan passed us, heading back up towards the offices. He gave me a pointed stare, and a quick glance up at the CCTV cameras.

'Look,' I said, 'let's talk later.'

Caddy looked at me as though she was about to refuse, then at the last minute, 'Whatever.'

I had three private dances booked in the Blue Room before the end of the Friday evening. The final booking, when I was already tired, came as a surprise to say the least. I went into the room and found that the only person sitting in there was Dunkerley.

He looked pleased with himself, lounging on one of the sofas looking as if he owned the place.

I wanted to turn around and leave again, but if he was in here he must have paid. If he'd paid, then I was going to make myself very unpopular by asking to have him thrown out.

'Good evening,' I said. 'What brings you here?'

'I wanted to see you,' he said, a smug smile on his face. I had to fight the urge to smack it away.

'That's nice,' I said. 'Would you like a fast dance, or a slow dance?'

'Mm,' he said. 'Surprise me.'

I went through my list of music quickly, trying to find something that was even vaguely appropriate to dance to for the benefit of a man I couldn't stand. All the music was in this list because I liked it and I had routines worked out for all of them. Whichever one I picked I probably wouldn't use again because it would always remind me of dancing for this horrible man.

I found one. Pussycat Dolls' 'Don't Cha'. It wasn't one they appreciated in the club as a rule – it was a little over-used.

I did the dance; I even did some of my best moves, before winding down by gyrating in front of him, spinning and twisting. I watched his self-satisfied smug-ugly face change. At the end, he applauded.

I went straight from the Blue Room upstairs to the offices. Nicks was standing guard at the top of the stairs. Dancers didn't usually come up here unless they'd received a specific invitation, and then only with a chaperone.

'I'd like to see Fitz,' I said to him.

'I'll ask him,' he said. 'You wait here.'

I did as I was told. I felt hot and uncomfortable, not even sure what the fuck I thought I was doing. But knowing I had to do it anyway.

A few moments later Fitz emerged from the main office, at the end of the corridor on the right. He shut the door behind him and came over to me.

'I'm sorry,' I said, giving him my best Viva smile. 'I wanted to ask you something.'

'Come with me,' he said. He led me to the far end of the carpeted corridor. I'd never been down here before. It was a smaller sitting room, almost like a waiting room – chairs and sofas around the edges of the room, a potted plant in the corner. A desk near the door. Fitz sat on one of the chairs and I sank gratefully down into the chair next to his.

'I've been having some problems with a guy at work,' I began. 'He recognised me here a few weeks ago, and he's been making it really difficult for me there.'

Fitz's face was impassive. He was waiting for me to get to the part where it became his problem.

'He wanted me to do a private dance for him but he wasn't prepared to pay for it, so Helena got him to leave. I didn't think he'd come back, but he's here, now.'

Still no response. I was starting to feel like I was making a huge mistake.

'He just booked me for a dance and I did it, so he's changed his mind about paying. But he's staying in the club, he's hanging around, and I don't like it. I think he's going to try and follow me home.'

I had nothing to support this theory but nevertheless I'd finally got to the part that concerned Fitz. While I was working for him, I was almost his property, and anyone seeking to disrupt that easy relationship was not going to be allowed to carry on.

'What's he look like?' he asked.

'Tall, bald head, quite fat, light grey suit, glasses.'

'Sounds a charmer.'

I smiled and looked down at my bare knees. 'I'm not easily scared, Fitz. I can take care of myself normally. I don't like asking for help.'

'I know that,' he said softly. 'But this is bad for business, whether he's paid up or not. I can't have him distracting you while you're at work here. I'll make sure he doesn't follow you home. Alright?'

I nodded gratefully and stood. 'Thank you,' I said. 'I'm sorry to interrupt your meeting.'

'No worries.'

I went back to the end of the corridor and turned at the top of the stairs. He was watching me go. Checking me out, or making sure I wasn't going to try and nose around some of the other rooms? I still wasn't sure he trusted me.

I was just in time for my last dance. I was tired so I made it a slow one, erotic, taking it about as far as it was possible to go without another person. At the front of the audience, looking pink and sweaty, was Dunkerley. At the back, in one of the VIP booths, Fitz, Nicks and Dylan. They were talking, helping themselves from a half-full bottle of Russian import vodka and watching me.

When it was over I blew a kiss to the few men who were still sitting at the front despite the fact that it was nearly dawn and they should have been at home tucked up in their beds next to their wives long ago. I went back into the dressing room and got changed into my jeans and trainers and fleece, wiped off the make-up and tied my hair up in a ponytail behind my head. I said goodnight to the other girls who were still there, and let myself out the back way.

The back street was quiet and grey with the approaching dawn. There was no sign of Dunkerley, or anyone else for that matter. I'd been kind of hoping for an escort to take me safely home, maybe Dylan, or even Fitz – maybe I'd even have been alright with Nicks, at a push – but there was nobody.

I walked round the front to find a cab.

At work on Monday, they told us Dunkerley was off sick, that he was going to be off work for a while. There was a lot of gossip about it, of course. I heard a suggestion that Human Resources had put him on garden leave for some sort of harassment, and that he'd been asked to resign. There was even a rumour going round that he was genuinely ill, seriously ill, and that he might not be able to come back.

All I knew was that I didn't have to see his smug fat head again, and for that I was profoundly grateful.

# Twenty-four

Jim Carling came with me to look for baths. I was grateful for this; despite the cross words first thing in the morning, I was starting to really like Jim. Aside from ferrying me cheerfully everywhere I wanted to go, he kept up the conversation about boat ownership and whether or not it would be possible to make your way around the world in a boat of this size, and, if so, where would you go? We had fun with that one. Jim wanted to go to the Far East. I said I wasn't going to go anywhere in the Indian Ocean because of the threat of Somali pirates. All of this was arbitrary anyway because I had never driven a boat before, much less negotiated the open sea.

We didn't come back with a bath, although there were some reasonable ones in a reclamation yard in Sittingbourne. I was on the lookout for a hip bath, maybe even a genuine Victorian one, something I could manage to connect to the boat's plumbing without too much hassle.

We stopped and had lunch in a café at a garden centre – jacket potato for me, ploughman's for him – with pots of tea. It felt very domestic, this – shopping for home improvements at the weekend.

'Is there anywhere else you need to go?' he asked.

I laughed. 'You don't have to be my taxi,' I said. 'It's very kind of you but I wouldn't want to take advantage.'

We drove home to the marina, and, because it seemed like the most appropriate thing to do with the fading afternoon, we went back to bed. The boat was chilly. I took him by the hand and into the bedroom. He was skilful and patient, his big hands decisive and firm.

By the time we'd tired ourselves out, it was dark. I went to the galley and lit the woodburner to warm the boat up, and then came back to bed. I thought for a moment he was asleep but he moved to let me under the covers, and pulled me against him.

'It should start to warm up soon,' I said. 'The stove's really efficient when it gets going.'

'Mm,' he said. 'I should think about going home.'

'Really?'

'I don't have any clean clothes. And I need to do stuff at home – laundry, you know.'

'Oh.'

He was kissing my arm, making the hairs on it rise in anticipation. 'You could come home and stay with me.'

'No,' I said.

'Why?'

I laughed. 'I don't sleep well on dry land.'

'You don't have to actually sleep.'

It was at that moment that I realised. I wanted to share it with him. Maybe not all of it, but enough to make him understand.

'I have to stay on the boat.'

'Why?'

'The men who came on the boat and tied me up – I think they were looking for something. If I leave the boat, they'll come back.'

'What were they looking for?'

'I'm not sure. I just know that they turned the boat upside down and I assume that means they were looking for something.'

He sat up in bed, bunching the pillows behind him, and turned on the light overhead. 'If you don't know what they were looking for,' he said with impeccable logic, 'how do you know they didn't find it?'

I blinked at him.

'You have to tell me, Genevieve.'

'No, I don't.'

He shook his head slowly. 'God,' he said, more to himself than to me, 'why am I even here? This is fucking crazy.'

'Look,' I said, trying to comfort him, 'I'm not scared of them, not really. They are bad people but I've dealt with them before. I just need to figure out a way to get whatever it is off my boat so that I'm not a target for them any more.'

'Caddy Smith,' he said, 'you knew her, didn't you?'

I nodded my head.

'Why didn't you tell me before?'

'You said her name was Candace.'

'Don't play dumb, Genevieve. You knew it was her when you saw her in the water. You lied on your statement.'

'No, I didn't. It was dark. I saw a body. It looked like her, but I wasn't sure.'

'You've got to tell me, Genevieve. What do you mean, you've dealt with them before? Who are they? What do they want from you?'

I didn't answer.

He got out of bed and started to dress in his clothes which, once again, were scattered all over my bedroom floor. I watched him silently, wondering which bit of the whole bloody mess had sparked off this sudden change in the mood. Just because I didn't want to make everything worse? Just because I didn't want to tell him about all the crap at the Barclay? What was he planning to do, anyway – go and ask Fitz nicely to leave me alone?

He was nearly fully dressed now, pulling his jumper over his head.

'What are you going to do?' I asked.

'I'm going home,' he said. 'Crazy as it is, the offer's still there if you want to come with me. But I'm guessing you won't.' He was so angry. I could tell, it was more than anger, it was fury, and, worse still, disappointment. When he'd finished dressing he came over to the bed and kissed me hard, fiercely, as if it might be the last time. I put my arms around his neck and tried to pull him back to bed but he wasn't having any of that.

It was a kiss goodbye.

It was on my second visit to Fitz's house that everything began to change for all of us: for Fitz, for Dylan, for Caddy, and for me.

I'd been looking forward to it all week, not just because these weekends were going to be giving such an impressive boost to my savings, even if I hadn't managed to negotiate a better pay deal for it; this time, Caddy had agreed to do the party with me.

Added to which, not having to deal with Dunkerley at work was a bonus. Gavin had been promoted to being our temporary manager, and it was pretty much like working for your best mate: we got on with things as we always had, but it felt more as though we were having a laugh about it instead of stepping over each other's twitching bodies in the desperate fight to close deals.

It wasn't Dylan who collected me that evening, but Nicks. He sat in the car outside until I was ready and stayed there; I let myself in to the back seat and then we drove off into the traffic.

'Where's Caddy?' I asked.

He moved his shoulders in some kind of lazy shrug and then barely said a word to me the whole journey. I plugged into my music and listened to it, going over my moves in my head, planning where I could make tweaks, considering what I would do if the option arose for Fitz to bend the rules again. I'd kind of set the precedent now by doing it once; it was more or less accepted that I would be asked to do it again. No matter. The money was the important thing. If it got me closer to the boat, I was prepared to do it. And if he wanted me to go further still? No point worrying about it now. I would decide when the time came.

We pulled up to the rear of the house this time, and I went straight in through the back door to the kitchen. As before, the caterers were busy preparing food, a sit-down meal by the look of it.

I found a comfy chair in the corner and kept myself busy with a notebook I'd brought with me, full of plans and ideas and clippings from various boat magazines. I was so engrossed in it that I didn't even notice Dylan until he was standing right beside me, eclipsing the light from the kitchen.

'Hi!' I said, pulling one headphone from my ear. 'I didn't know you were here.'

He looked at me without expression. 'You're not on till later. They're having dinner in the dining room in half an hour. Fitz wants to know if you'd like to join them.'

'You're kidding?'

'Nope.'

'Just me?'

'You and a few others. There's a seating plan.'

'Oh. Dylan, do you know where Caddy is? She's supposed to be here too.'

'She's upstairs, I think.'

I accepted this without comment, pissed off that my evening of entertainment with my best buddy was not turning out quite the way I'd hoped. What the hell was she doing upstairs? Had she found some nicer room to use as a changing room?

'Am I sitting next to someone I should know about?' I said.

'You're between Fitz and Leon Arnold.'

I dropped my voice to a whisper. 'Who's Leon Arnold?'

He looked at me as though I'd asked the wrong question. 'Owns a yacht. You'll get on well with him. And, if you don't, you should pretend to.'

It was another test, I realised. Good job I'd brought enough outfits with me so that I could select something suitable for an evening meal. I went to the downstairs bathroom and got changed, put make-up on and twisted my hair up into a French pleat that I hoped looked classically elegant.

The dining room was empty but the table was laid for ten; through open doors the other side I heard sounds of polite conversation, a woman's laugh, so I went to the door cautiously and looked through.

They were all in there – Fitz and some other men, one of whom I recognised from the last party. There were women in there too; I recognised a girl from the Barclay – Stella? She'd danced there a few times, but usually she worked at one of Fitz's other clubs. And standing next to Fitz, resplendent in a jewelled black cocktail dress and a pair of killer heels, was Caddy. She gave me a little wave.

Three of the girls were on their own in a corner, giggling over some private joke. I saw Fitz cast a displeased glance over to them before carrying on a conversation with the man to his right. I went over to the girls with a glass of champagne I'd lifted from the tray of a passing waitress and said to them quietly, 'Ladies, aren't you supposed to be mingling?'

Two of them looked worried, but one of them – an acid blonde with pale blue eyes, said, 'Fuck's it got to do with you?'

I treated her to a warm smile. 'Doesn't pay to piss Fitz off,' I said sweetly, 'and he's already looking daggers at you. Just a bit of friendly advice.'

As I left them and headed for Fitz, the girls seemed to come to their senses and they split from their cosy huddle, making their way towards the remaining guests.

'Viva,' Fitz said to me as I approached. 'Come and meet Leon.'

Fitz slipped an arm around my waist and kissed my cheek as I shook Leon Arnold's hand. He was maybe fifty, the same height as me, with a shaved head and capped teeth. A good suit, a diamond stud in one earlobe.

'I'm pleased to meet you,' I said. 'I understand I'm the lucky girl who gets to sit next to you at dinner.'

He looked as though he might take a bit of warming up, but what the hell? I was already thinking of my potential bonus for sorting out Fitz's girls and for softening up Mr Arnold for whatever scheme Fitz had planned for him. What I hadn't reckoned on, though, was the look Caddy was giving me. She wasn't smiling. She was looking at me as though I were something she'd found on the sole of her shoe.

'Hey,' I said to her, as we filed in to dinner, 'I was wondering where you were.'

She didn't seem to hear me. Whatever. This wasn't the time or the place.

Over dinner, the topic of business seemed to be strictly off-limits. Stella told everybody about an audition she'd had, to dance in a music video; one of the other men, a younger version of Fitz, told her he was looking for girls to appear as extras in a film he was producing. After that they were all over him.

I chatted to Leon Arnold over dinner, asked him about his yacht, about cruising around the islands in the Mediterranean. More than once I cast a glance in Fitz's direction to check I was doing the right thing. He gave me a smile which reassured me. The rest of the time he was busy talking to the man who was sitting on the other side of him, an older man with a neatly trimmed grey beard. Caddy seemed to have been tasked with entertaining him – she kept her focus on him and away from me.

I managed to eat most of the soup, and then picked at my dinner, pushing it around the plate even though it looked delicious and in any other circumstances I would have wolfed it and asked for seconds. Not eating allowed me to devote all my attention to Leon, who, despite his yacht and his Rolex Oyster and his unconscionable amount of money, was decidedly dull.

Stella was sitting the other side of Leon, and when her attempts at enlivening the conversation with the dark-haired man on her right failed, she turned her attention to Leon and left me momentarily free to check out the men I'd be dancing for later.

'How's your food?' Fitz asked me.

I felt my face flush a little. 'It's delicious,' I said. 'I'm hoping there might be some leftovers for when I've finished dancing.'

He smiled and under the table his hand made contact with my thigh.

'What time do you want us to start?' I asked.

He shrugged. 'We've got business to discuss, so after that. I'll send one of the lads for you when we're ready.'

'Anything in particular you'd like?' I asked, in a low voice.

He laughed. 'Just your usual Viva magic. Then we'll see if there's anything the gentlemen fancy. Kitten's going to do some private dances, if they want them.'

'Caddy's not pole dancing?'

He gave me an amused smile. 'No, Viva. You're here for that.'

I tried a different route. 'Thank you for inviting me for dinner,' I said.

'You're good at this,' he said.

'At what?'

'At knowing what they like. And you sorted the girls out, earlier. I appreciated it.'

I glanced down the table at the three blondes, who were animatedly discussing their potential careers in the music industry with the three young men.

The girls were all there for sex, I realised. It came to me in a moment even though I'd probably known it all along. When Dylan had said to me last time, 'You're the only one dancing,' I'd thought that meant there would be girls from the club serving drinks, maybe doing lap dances, but when I hadn't seen any other girls I had accepted this without concern or comment. Now, I realised, they'd all been upstairs; and the last time, while I was being touched up by Kenny and dancing for the other clients of Fitz's who'd gathered here, the remaining men had probably been upstairs being entertained by the other girls.

'You know,' I said to Fitz, 'you should think about diversifying the club a bit.'

Another amused smile. 'Diversifying?'

'You could do a couple of ladies' nights – get some men in to dance as well as girls. And maybe a burlesque night, something with a bit more...' I searched for the most appropriate word '...widespread appeal.'

'Ah, but widespread appeal means the profits reduce.'

'But you must admit you're working from a very limited pool of customers at the moment,' I said. 'Think about all the people who wouldn't dream of setting foot in the club as it is now. Couples. Girls' nights out. Hen parties, if you like.'

Leon Arnold leaned over me, one arm heavy across my shoulders. He smelled of whisky and aftershave. 'You want to watch yourself with this one, Fitz, old boy,' he said. 'She's gonna take over your empire.'

My reply was swift. 'Nah, I want to stick to what I'm good at – dancing for gorgeous guys like you, Leon.'

Fitz laughed then, and Caddy scowled at me from the other side of the table.

As soon as dinner was over and I could excuse myself, I went back to the kitchen, found a bottle of water to try and dilute the half-glass of champagne and the half-glass of red wine I'd drunk, and took it with me to the downstairs bathroom. Dylan was waiting at the breakfast bar, munching on a dish of nachos.

'Don't they feed you properly?' I asked cheekily.

He looked up. 'I thought they were going to take you upstairs, with the rest of the slappers,' he cheeked back.

'I'd better get changed,' I said. 'Come in and talk to me if you like.'

Dylan shook his head, 'Fitz wouldn't like that,' he said.

'What?'

'Us having a private chat.'

I thought back to what Fitz had said about having a problem with Dylan liking me. And I remembered the bit about someone having noticed us having a chat in the club.

'Fitz is busy,' I said.

There was nobody else around; the caterers had packed up their kit and gone already. He followed me into the bathroom and sat on the easy chair while I stripped off the evening gown and replaced it with a sparkly cutaway dress in electric blue.

'Do you know what's up with Caddy?' I asked. She'd gone straight into the lounge with Fitz and Arnold, arm in arm with both of them, leaving me no chance to take her to one side.

'What do you mean?' he said.

'She's giving me filthy looks. I don't know what I've done to upset her.'

He stared at me and then a slow smile crossed his face.

'What?' I asked. 'What the fuck's going on, Dylan?'

'You were getting cosy with Fitz,' he said.

'So what? And anyway, I wasn't "getting cosy", I was socialising, which is what I think I'm being paid for.'

'Calm down,' he said. 'I just meant that she wouldn't like you being cosy with Fitz because she's got a thing about him.'

'Caddy and Fitz? They're a couple?'

He smiled again. 'In her dreams maybe.'

Lots of things were starting to make sense. 'But he's not so keen on her?'

'He fucked her once or twice. He used to fuck all the girls, the ones that would let him, that is. Then he had a couple of them go a bit mental on him and he realised it was a bad idea. One of them got pregnant. Trouble is, he didn't quite finish with Caddy, not in any official sort of way, so she still thinks she's in with a chance.'

'Why doesn't he just tell her he's not interested?'

'I don't think he has the faintest clue how she feels. And if she told him straight, he'd get rid of her like a shot. He doesn't like his girls clingy, not any more.'

'No wonder she was giving me daggers,' I said, remembering Fitz's arm around my waist, his wet whisky-kiss on my cheek.

'What do you make of Leon Arnold?' he asked me then.

'Seems alright,' I said. 'Why?'

Dylan scratched his jaw line thoughtfully. 'He's a big player, that's all. Last time you were here, the guys Fitz was talking to, that was all about setting up this meeting with Arnold.'

'Really?' I said, 'I'm glad I didn't know that earlier. I'd have been nervous.'

'I never met him before. Heard of him, of course.'

'You think this deal is a bad idea?'

'Fitz knows what he's doing.'

'What's he want?'

'With Arnold? Same as always – earn his fortune. Like you.' His tone suggested that this would be the last response to any further questions on the topic of Mr Leon Arnold. 'Just better do a good job dancing, is all.'

I pulled my hair out of the pleat, shaking it free, and took off the low-heeled sandals that were useful for socialising with men that were shorter than me. In my bag I had a pair of high-heeled patent shoes with a velvet ribbon which criss-crossed around my ankle and reminded me of the ballet lessons I'd had when I was nine years old.

'I'm glad you're here,' I said.

He shrugged.

'Nothing gets to you, does it, Dylan?'

'What's that mean?'

'I don't know. You must care about something. There must be someone who really means something to you. You married?'

He didn't answer, which I took to mean that he was.

'Come on,' I said. 'I thought we were mates. I thought you said you trusted me.'

'I was with someone,' he said. 'Not any more.'

'Any kids?'

There was a long pause. This was like pulling teeth.

'I've got a daughter. Lauren. She's fourteen.'

'You see her often?'

'Not often enough. She lives in Spain, with her mother.'

'Oh. Spain – that must be hard on you.'

'Yeah, anyway, are you ready?' The conversation was clearly at an end.

'Will you be watching?' I asked him.

'Don't have much choice,' he said.

I went to wait in the kitchen like a good girl, while Dylan headed upstairs to the sitting room to check that the other girls weren't getting too drunk.

When Carling had gone, I got dressed in my jeans and fleece and went to the *Scarisbrick Jean*. Malcolm and Josie were just finishing their dinner: pasta with some kind of sauce that smelled of garlic.

'You hungry?' Josie asked me cheerfully. She looked pale despite her colourful jumper. She'd had her hair done in preparation for the wedding – was it her niece? – and in place of the usual dark threaded with silver it was a warm chocolate colour. It made her look years younger.

'No, no,' I lied, 'I've just eaten.'

'Rubbish,' she said, 'we've got leftovers.'

She spooned some tagliatelle and sauce on to a plate and I sat down at their dinette. 'Your hair looks gorgeous,' I said.

I saw a pointed look pass between Malcolm and Josie. Malcolm's hair, I noticed, had remained resolutely wild.

'Thank you,' she said firmly, as if making a point. I wondered if Malcolm had failed to notice and was somehow living in purgatory as a result. He wasn't looking particularly cheerful.

'How have you been?' I asked Josie quietly.

'Oh, you know. Up and down.' Tears were in her eyes but she blinked them away with a deep breath. She took her plate and Malcolm's to the sink in the galley and started the washing-up, banging and crashing cupboard doors with enough gusto to drown out the rest of the conversation.

'My battery's charged up,' I said to Malcolm between mouthfuls.

He looked up then. 'Yeah. Probably is.'

'And they didn't take it. You know.'

'Right.'

'What's up?' I asked, realising the distinct displeasure in his tone was directed at me.

'You,' he said. 'Fraternising with the gavvers.'

'You mean Carling? He's alright. He helped me look for a bath.'

He looked at me for a moment as though he didn't know quite what to make of me, and then he laughed out loud, his head back.

'Look,' I said, when he'd finished sniggering at the thought of me and a police officer looking at bathroom furniture, 'I needed protection last night, alright? He was happy to stay. So this morning I'm still alive.'

'Whatever,' he said cheerfully, wiping a tear from his eye.

'I need to move the boat, Malcolm. Those people will probably come back for another go.'

'Tomorrow, we'll do it tomorrow. Alright? Too dark now to do anything. You can kip here tonight, if you don't want to be in that boat on your tod.'

I looked up and down the length of the boat. 'Kip where?'

He tapped a bony finger against the side of his nose. 'Aha,' he said. 'You'll need a duvet or summat; we don't have anywhere to keep spares.'

'I can't leave the boat, Malcolm. What if they come back tonight?'

'You could bring it with you. This parcel of yours.'

'Don't be silly. Then I'd be putting you and Josie in danger too. Besides, it's obviously well hidden where it is, right?'

He stared at me for a moment, deep in thought. Then he said, 'I've got an idea.'

I went back to the *Revenge of the Tide* and collected the duvet, pillow and my toothbrush, as well as my mobile phones. When I came back to the *Aunty Jean*, Malcolm was out on the pontoon with some fine-grade steel wire and a pair of pliers.

'What's he doing out there?' Josie asked as I climbed down into the cabin with armfuls of duvet.

'Oh, I don't know – fixing something, I guess,' I said.

'It's going to be lovely having you here. Like a proper sleepover.'

I had no idea what she thought I was doing, sleeping on their boat when mine was just ten feet or so further up the pontoon. Malcolm had told her something about the woodburner needing looking at and that had seemed to satisfy any curiosity.

When all the washing-up had been cleared away, Josie showed me the hidden single bed that slid out from under the dinette like a giant drawer. Of course, while it was out they would need to step over me if they wanted to get from the dinette to the galley or back again, but the likelihood of that in the middle of the night was fortunately quite slim.

Outside, Malcolm was putting the finishing touches to the elaborate set of trip wires he had fixed at ankle-height across our pontoon. If Nicksy or any of Fitz's men came to have another go at the boat tonight they would make enough noise to wake up the whole marina.

Once I got started on the dances, things progressed pretty much as they had for my first visit to Fitz's house.

For the first dance, all the men were present except for Fitz and Arnold. I got the distinct impression that I was there to babysit the other men while they got on with whatever business they had to discuss, in private.

True to his word, Dylan stood in the doorway watching as I worked out, monitoring me and keeping an eye on the guests, as he had been told to do. He blended into the background beautifully, motionless and silent.

I'd just finished when the door opened and Fitz and Arnold came in, bringing Caddy with them. She was a little bit unsteady on her feet. I gave her a warm smile, which she did not return.

'Aw, look, Leon – we've just missed the first dance,' Fitz said, pouring two large glasses of whisky from the drinks cabinet.

I blew a kiss to Leon. 'I'll be back soon,' I said to him. 'Don't miss the next one.'

I skipped out of the room and Dylan shut the door behind me. Just time for a very quick change in the bathroom, repairing make-up, generally making myself presentable again.

The bathroom wasn't empty; two of the blonde girls from dinner were in there doing lines of coke on the polished marble surface of the vanity unit. They shut up as I opened the door and almost immediately started arguing again when they saw it was only me.

'Well, you can fuck right off,' the taller one said. She was wearing a towelling robe and acrylic-heeled stilettos, and most likely not very much else.

'Don't give me that,' came the reply, high-pitched, close to tears, 'it was your fucking idea. Don't back out now, come on!'

'What's up?' I asked casually.

They both stared at me as though suddenly united in their concern that I was going to get involved and therefore somehow want to share the last two lines of powder that were still on the vanity unit.

'She,' said the younger one, pointing with a shaking, manicured finger at the blonde in the robe, 'said we should try and get Leon in for a threesome and we could split the tip, and I said yes, and now she's changed her mind!'

There was a sigh and a hand on the hip in a gesture of defiance. 'It wasn't like that, Bella, you know it wasn't, I was fucking joking, wasn't I, honestly.'

'Could be passing up a very lucrative opportunity,' I said, reapplying lip-gloss.

'That's exactly what I said!' exclaimed Bella.

'But seriously, it would take a lot of fucking money for me to do him on me own, never mind with someone else to fucking worry about.'

'It's called taking one for the team. Don't expect you've ever heard of that, before, have you, Diane?'

'I've had enough of this shit. We ain't got long. Are we doing this line or what?'

Differences set aside for the purposes of ingesting drugs, the two girls bent for their second lines in turn and paused for a moment, before continuing the argument.

'Would you do it?' Diane asked. It took me a second to realise that she was talking to me.

'Why are you two down here, anyway?' I said. 'Shouldn't you both be entertaining the guests?'

'Oh, don't you start. You're worse than fucking Dylan.'

'He's always bloody nagging us. We came down here to get a moment's peace – you know,' said Bella, nodding towards the smear of white residue before picking it up with a moistened finger and applying it to her gums.

'Come on, Bel,' said Diane, 'let's go and find somewhere warmer. Bit frosty in here.'

They left the bathroom to me, and I had a quick check through my bag to make sure my purse and phone were still in there. I wouldn't have trusted them with any of my belongings and I wasn't surprised to find my bag unzipped. They'd probably gone in there to see if I had a stash of coke myself.

When the door opened again I was about to tell them to fuck off and leave me alone, but this time it was Dylan.

'Hello,' I said, turning back to the mirror. 'Don't bother to knock or anything civilised like that, will you?'

'Seen it all before,' he said in reply. He sat himself down on the chair and regarded me thoughtfully.

'What?' I said at last, to his reflection in the mirror.

'Fitz is pissed off,' he said.

'Oh,' I said. 'That's not good.'

'The deal's not going down.'

'Why not?'

'Some of Arnold's lads have been sharing the samples with the girls upstairs.'

'That'll explain why two of them were in here a minute ago powdering their noses.'

Dylan ran a weary hand over his forehead. 'Fuck's sake. They're a fucking liability.' He stood up and made for the door with a sigh.

'Dylan?'

'What?'

'Anything I can do to help?'

He laughed. 'You can cheer Fitz up, for starters. If anyone can put a smile back on his face, it's you.'

'What about Caddy?'

'She's upstairs. In a strop.'

I woke up before it was fully light.

For a second I had no idea where I was, only that I wasn't in my bed; the boat was rocking alarmingly from side to side and, moments later, footsteps near my head. I sat up with alarm.

'Go back to sleep,' came an urgent whisper. 'It's only me.'

'Malcolm? What's going on?'

'Heard a noise outside,' he whispered, crouching down next to the pull-out mattress. 'Think it's just a fox or something, round the bins. Nobody out there.'

'Oh.'

I lay back down on the bed and pulled the duvet up around my ears.

It was chilly now, the grey light enough to see the outline of the cabin and the shapes of the galley cupboards, the woodburner, burned out and cold. I guessed it was about four or five, the same time of day that I'd found Caddy's body in the water.

I smiled to myself at the thought of all that tripwire outside on the pontoon and hoped to God I would remember it was there when I went back to the *Revenge of the Tide*, otherwise I was likely to take a dip in the mud myself, head first, duvet and all.

I listened to the noise of the birds and the gulls and the distant roar of the traffic heading up the M2 towards London and I was just drifting off to sleep when a sudden thought struck me. Malcolm had been fully dressed.

# Twenty-five

When I headed back towards the lounge, I became aware that something wasn't right. The door was open and through it I could see Arnold sprawled on the sofa with two of his men; there was no sign of Fitz, or Dylan, or any of the girls.

From somewhere upstairs I could hear raised voices, the sound of something heavy falling.

I put on my best Viva smile and entered the room, closing the door discreetly behind me. 'Gentlemen,' I said, 'can I get anyone a drink?'

Waitressing wasn't strictly speaking part of my duties, but they didn't seem at all perturbed by this, and one by one I served them various spirits, mostly neat.

I sat on the arm of Arnold's chair. He put his hand on my backside and gave it a friendly pat.

'While we're waiting,' I said, 'would you like me to dance, or would you prefer it if I left you to carry on your conversation?'

'A dance would be good,' Arnold said. 'Especially since I missed the last one. I've heard some very good things about you, Viva.'

'In that case,' I said, working my way through the list of music on the laptop, 'I'll have to make sure you get something very special indeed.'

I didn't know if they were expecting me to be naked, or to strip, but if they were disappointed that I kept my skimpy black dress on they didn't show it. Especially given that they could have trotted off upstairs and sampled something far more tactile if they'd chosen to do so. Instead they sat and watched, and I held their absolute and total attention until, four tracks and twenty-two minutes later, the door opened and Fitz came in.

He was surprised to see me and for a moment he stood there in the doorway, hands in his pockets, as though he'd forgotten what he came in for. He looked lost, his shoulders slumped. My heart sank for him. He looked so defeated. Much as I didn't want to know what this deal was all about, I wanted it to work out for him.

*There must be something I can do to help*, I thought. *Something to give his confidence a boost...*

Arnold and the others didn't even stir. I had their undivided attention and now I had an extra audience member I upped the game a little bit more, until the track finished.

Dylan got to the laptop and paused the player before it moved on again, and I took Fitz by the hand and said, 'Can I have a word?' while Dylan turned to the assembled men and asked them if they wanted another drink.

I steered Fitz out of the door into the hallway and, casting a quick glance to make sure we were alone, I pushed him firmly back against the wall and kissed him.

Whatever he was expecting, it wasn't that.

Just at the moment where he finally cottoned on to what I was doing and started to respond, I backed away.

He was staring at me, his breathing fast, the beginnings of a smile.

'You can do this,' I whispered.

'What?' he asked.

'Whatever you want to. With Arnold. You can get the deal. Just go and do it.'

He stroked my cheek gently. 'Do you have any idea...?'

'What?'

He just shook his head.

'Fitz,' I said, 'go and sort it out. This is exactly what you're good at, you know it is. Go on.'

He went back into the lounge and I closed the door behind him. Dylan was in the act of topping up Arnold's glass with whisky.

He looked up at me, and for a moment I thought I saw something in that look, unguarded. And then the shutters went up again, and it was gone.

They did their deal. I didn't know what it was exactly, had no wish to, but the likelihood was some importation, or a big supply. Nothing I wanted any involvement in.

After the discussions had finished, Arnold and his associates left in several cars at about half-past four. Gray called taxis for the girls – three cabs turned up round the back of the house at five and they all went. All except Caddy. She was sitting in the kitchen.

'Caddy,' I said, touching her arm.

'What do you want?' she asked, in the tone of voice that suggested she wasn't interested in my response.

'You know there's nothing going on between me and Fitz, don't you?'

She looked up at me then, looked at me properly for the first time since we'd been having drinks before dinner and Fitz had kissed me on the cheek. Looked at me as though she couldn't trust me, didn't believe me, and would be happy if I'd just fuck off and leave her the hell alone.

'Don't give a stuff what you do with Fitz, personally,' she said with emphasis.

'Why are you pissed off with me, then?'

An exaggerated, drunken shrug.

'I thought you were my mate, Caddy?'

Dylan was watching all this with the merest flicker of amusement behind his implacable blue eyes.

'I know what he's like,' she said miserably. 'You don't realise it 'cos you're new. I know the signs.'

'What signs? What are you talking about?'

'He wants you. Since you arrived, he's not looked at me twice. Know how much that hurts? Any idea?'

'Caddy, this is ridiculous. I don't have any intention of doing anything with him.'

I saw her eyes narrow and felt the venom when she next spoke.

'You would do if he paid you enough.'

It hurt more because she was right. I knew it and so did she. And then, in Fitz's multi-million-pound house, in his marble kitchen, I felt cheap and ashamed of myself for the first time since I'd started down this road. What was I doing? It was a boat, it was just a boat. I was in a hurry to get the money together because I'd become greedy and mean and single-minded. I'd slipped into a dangerous spiral of consequences, wanting to buy the boat to escape from all this, and getting into it deeper still so I could earn the money in the first place.

Gray came into the kitchen then, started banging about making coffee, and Dylan went to join Nicks in the lounge drinking and discussing the finer points of the deal.

I went back to the bathroom to get my stuff together, leaving Caddy in the kitchen. Fitz was in the hallway at a big glass table, counting money and stuffing it into envelopes. We exchanged looks. Then he followed me, bringing one of the envelopes with him. My pay for the evening. He put it on the top of my bag. It looked fatter than last time. I felt sick at the sight of it, and at the same time felt a sparkle of excitement in my belly. I could hardly wait to get home so I could count it all.

'You were great tonight,' he said. He shut the door behind him and sat down on the chair, watching me while I packed away make-up, towels, dresses and shoes.

'I enjoyed it,' I said. 'I'm glad it turned out okay.'

'You're not worried?' he said.

'About what?'

'The deal,' he said. 'You know that's just between us, don't you?'

'Of course.'

'I trust you,' he said, nodding.

I was nearly done, zipping up the case and standing it up on its wheels. I was looking forward to going home and sleeping for the rest of the day.

He stood up, between me and the door. I waited. He was buzzing; he could hardly keep still. I wondered what he'd taken.

'I was thinking,' he said, taking a step towards me and running a finger quickly up my arm, 'about our discussion the other day.'

'Yes?'

'You want to hang around for a while?'

'Now?'

'The guys will be going soon. You could stay. We could – er – have some fun. What do you think?'

If it hadn't been for Caddy, I just might have said yes. Despite the tiredness, despite the physical exhaustion, if I'd just taken a moment to consider, staying here with Fitz – he wasn't bad-looking after all – I would have done it and I would have enjoyed it, and maybe everything that happened after that would have been different.

But my head was heavy with the night and the need to lie down alone, undisturbed.

'I'd like to,' I said, 'but honestly, I'm so tired. I just need to go home and sleep. Another time, maybe?'

'I've got some good stuff here, you know – something to wake you up a bit?'

'No, thank you. I just want to go home.'

He looked at the floor, a muscle moving in his cheek. 'Yeah.' He stepped back and opened the door for me. 'I'll get Nicks to drive you.'

When I finally left Fitz's house, it was broad daylight. Thank God it was a Sunday and there wasn't much traffic. I would be home within about an hour.

# Twenty-six

Josie and I were sitting on our old bench in the shelter of the wheelhouse, listening to the sounds of Malcolm tinkering with the engine of the boat. Other than his unexpected appearance in the early hours, the night had passed without incident. The tripwire had not been needed.

'Did I ever tell you,' she said, 'about the time he set fire to the boat?'

'No,' I said, sipping my coffee.

She chuckled at the thought of it.

'He was welding a porthole shut. Only he'd decided to weld it shut just after he'd finished all the cladding inside. He had the full face mask on, you know, and he was sitting on the pontoon welding away quite happily, oblivious to the clouds of smoke billowing off the boat. Liam had to pat him on the back and tell him the boat was on fire. Liam told him to go and look for something to put water in to douse it and he was in such a panic he came out with the lid from his shaving foam. He said he hadn't wanted to use any of my china cups.'

I laughed. 'Presumably you've got a fire extinguisher in there now.'

'Too bloody right,' she said. 'No idea where it is, though.'

Malcolm had undone his elaborate system of trip wires before Josie woke up, winding the wire back into neat coils. He'd offered to re-do this every night before bed, but I'd declined – sod's law was that some innocent person would fall over it and claim massive amounts of compensation.

'He's a flaming liability,' she added, although this almost went without saying.

A shout came up from the hatch under the wheelhouse. 'Right, try starting it!'

I went over and peered down at Malcolm's grubby grey T-shirt hunched over the engine, then turned the key.

A rumble from the engine, a shudder, a series of congested coughs, and the whole boat shook itself alive. From the stern came the sound of splashing and churning water.

'Right, that's enough, turn it off!'

I turned the key again. 'What do you think? Is it okay?' I called down.

'Oh, yeah,' he said brightly. 'Needs an oil change, filters, basic service. There's no leaks or anything. In fact, she's in bloody good nick considering.'

I left him to it and went back to sit with Josie.

'He seems happy,' I said.

'Yes,' Josie said, 'he loves all this. You just need to check him for stupid mistakes – like for instance it's just pure luck that he got you to start the engine with the tide in. Can you imagine if the prop had started spinning at low tide? Mud everywhere. Not pretty.'

'I didn't realise he was quite so accident-prone,' I said.

'It's not that he's accident-prone, just that he doesn't think. When we first moved on to the boat, he dropped his keys down the side into the water. Did he tell you about that?'

'He told me to always make sure my stuff had a float on it.'

'Ha!'

'So what happened? Did he get the keys back?'

'The tide was coming in and it was just over waist-height. So he went down in the water and stood with his ankles in the mud and of course he couldn't quite reach the bottom, even with his arm in up to the shoulder. So he had to get a broom

219

and force himself down the handle head-first until he found the keys.'

'Lord. Was he alright?'

'He smelt foul. And he was puking in the night. Doesn't do you any good to put your face in this river, truth be told.'

'I can hear you!' came a shout from inside the wheelhouse.

We laughed at this. I felt more relaxed than I had for ages.

'Why are you wanting to get the boat started, then?' Josie asked, giving me a gentle dig in the ribs. 'You moving on?'

I blushed. 'No, nothing like that. Well, not yet, anyway. It just seemed like the next step in the process.'

'I thought the bathroom was the next step in the process.'

'Yeah, that. Or the conservatory. I keep changing my mind.'

I slept in the back of the car, jolting awake every time it turned, braked or accelerated. I couldn't bring myself to make small talk and I was so shattered I found it hard to think straight about all the things that had gone on.

The main thing was that it had ended well. The deal had been done, and when Arnold left, kissing me delicately on the inside of my wrist, he had given me a smile and shaken Fitz's hand warmly. And, of course, I was financially one step closer to the boat. Maybe I could have another talk with Caddy when she was sober, try and get our friendship back on track.

I was planning to take Thursday and Friday off to visit boatyards in Kent, on the river Medway. There were a couple of boats for sale at one residential marina, then a much larger yard further up the river had several more. The Medway seemed as good a place as any. Near enough to London to be able to come back if I wanted a night out, and yet far enough away that I could escape from the city and from all the shit that came with the job. I also had it in the back of my mind that, if I wanted to find another job at the end of the year, being a short train ride away from London would be a bonus. I might not have to sell the boat after the year was up. I might even be able to carry on living on my boat and work in the city again if the money ran out.

I had enough money to buy a boat, preferably one that was at least partly fitted out, so that I could live on it while I was finishing it off. I probably had enough cash to at least start the renovation, as well. As things stood at the moment, I would have to carry on working, or at least find a part-time job, to be able to keep myself going while I worked on the boat.

I wished I could fast-forward, speed through the last few months of earning, saving, dancing, struggling for bonuses at work.

I was ready for this all to come to an end.

I opened my eyes and glanced out of the window to see a familiar row of shops. Nearly home, at last.

'Cheers for the lift, Nicksy,' I said, as I got out of the car and took my wheelie case from the boot.

As soon as I slammed the boot lid shut he sped off towards the main road.

An hour later, and Malcolm declared the *Revenge of the Tide* fit to travel. Of course, by that time the tide had gone out and there was no hope of trying it out today.

'You can't do it tomorrow either,' said Josie.

'Why not?' asked Malcolm, looking disappointed.

'Because we've got things to do!' said Josie, smacking him around the shoulder. 'Anyway, what's the great rush all of a sudden?'

'Well, the boat's fixed,' I said. 'I'd love to just go for a little motor upriver, just to see what's there.'

'Well, you can wait until after the weekend,' said Josie firmly, and that appeared to be that.

She went up to the laundry to unload the machine, leaving Malcolm packing up his various tools into a filthy canvas bag. When he was done, he sat back on the bench with me. The smell of him reminded me a bit of my dad – engine oil, sweat, effort.

'Thank you,' I said.

'What for?'

'Fixing the boat, of course. You've been great.'

'Ah, it's nothing,' he said. 'Be good to get her out for a motor, anyway.'

As though the *Revenge* were a little pleasure boat and not a hulking great seventy-five-foot-long barge with all my worldly possessions on it. But it was what I needed to do, after all. I just wished he weren't quite so casual about it all.

Josie was heading back down the slope to the pontoon, a plastic laundry bag weighing her down. When she'd nearly reached the *Scarisbrick Jean*, Malcolm eased himself up and went down the gangplank to help her. When they'd gone into the cabin I went inside, washing up the mugs and the plates from the sandwiches we'd had at lunchtime.

On the table, the two mobile phones were lying side by side. I hadn't remembered them being there, like that. They were in the bag I'd taken to the *Aunty Jean* the night before. Had I taken them out of my bag? I couldn't remember.

I checked the phones and saw two missed calls.

On one phone, a missed call from Carling's number – an hour ago.

On the other, a missed call from GARLAND. I hit redial.

*The number you have dialled is currently unavailable. Please try later.*

I shouted at it in frustration, threw it on to the sofa. Why the fuck couldn't he leave his phone switched on? Was I ever going to speak to him again? At least it meant he was still alive, still out there somewhere. And he hadn't entirely forgotten about me.

# Twenty-seven

The following Saturday night, the Barclay was busy, busier than I'd ever seen it. Norland and Helena were both in, but there was no sign of Fitz when I arrived. Caddy was there too, already out in the club with some of her regulars as I went into the dressing room to get ready.

The club was packed with people: stag nights, groups of men crowded at the bar and the stage. I had private dances in the Blue Room booked, and even the VIP area was full. Dylan, Nicks and Gray were there too, but they were busy – the crowd was rowdy and they ended up helping out the door staff with removing those who had drunk too much.

The atmosphere in the club felt very different. Maybe I should have seen it as a warning; maybe I should have felt it. It reminded me of one of the first weekends I'd danced in the club, when Caddy had steered me away from a group of men in suits who were already tanked up on champagne and vodka.

'Not them, love. They're no good.'

'Why not?'

'They're discussing business.'

'How do you know?'

'You get to know these things. They'll call us over when they're ready. And when they do, be careful with them, alright? Just in case I'm otherwise engaged.'

'Be careful how?'

Caddy had taken a deep breath in and spouted one of her classics. 'This club is full of men who think of themselves as dangerous. In reality, very few of them are. But it really helps if you can spot them.'

I'd steered well clear, left the group to the other girls who were watching them from a distance and waiting for them to finish their business deals. Besides, I had plenty of other guys to entertain.

The club smelled of danger tonight.

By half-past two it was beginning to quieten down; the rowdy ones had all been ejected or had run out of money and gone home. Those that were left were a mixture of regulars and tired-looking businessmen. I wound down with some slower moves. I was tired tonight; I had hardly had time to drink water between dances and I was starting to get a headache.

During my last dance I noticed two of the men who had been with Arnold at Fitz's house last weekend. They were in one of the booths. I made eye contact with one of them and gave him a smile and a wink while I gyrated and swung around the pole.

At the end of the routine, when the last bars of Portishead's 'Glory Box' were fading, I saw Leon Arnold. He was talking to Caddy and Norland at the bar and he was watching me over Norland's shoulder. I considered going over to join them, thought about whether I could get Caddy on her own to try and sort things out.

I had a ripple of applause from the remaining audience as I handed over control of the stage to Chanelle, who was coming on for her last dance.

The dressing room was almost empty; many of the girls had already finished and left. I started to pull off my shoes, looking forward to putting my jeans on and going home, when the door opened.

It was Norland. 'You've got another private dance,' he said.

'What? You're joking,' I groaned. 'I'm worn out.'

'I'm not fucking joking. Get on with it.'

I was half-inclined to leave it, to slip away and pretend that Norland hadn't told me. But I put some lip-gloss on and made my way down the corridor to the Blue Room, thinking about the money, always the money – it was the only thing that made all this worthwhile.

I didn't know who I'd been expecting – one of my regulars perhaps – but in the room were Leon Arnold and the two men I'd seen in the VIP booth earlier on. One of them closed the door behind me.

I felt uncomfortable for a moment but he gave me a warm smile and they didn't seem to be drunk. I cast a quick glance up, to the corner of the room, the CCTV camera, hoping that someone was in the office upstairs keeping an eye on me.

'Hi, guys,' I said, trying to look and sound as if I'd just started work and was ready to give them their money's worth and more besides, 'take a seat.'

I'd said this to the guy who was still standing by the door, but he ignored me.

I was too tired to mess around so I left the music selection screen and went over to the doorway. 'What's your name?' I asked him. He was standing the way Dylan did, still and impassive, as though he were there for my protection. I didn't feel protected.

'His name's Markus,' said Arnold, amused.

'Come and sit down, Markus. You won't get much of a view from there.'

He looked at Arnold, who was sitting on the sofa with his feet up. I raised a questioning eyebrow at him, and there was a nod in response – either to me, or to Markus.

Whatever. Markus left his post on the door and went to sit the other side of Arnold.

I went back to staring at the screen, wondering what I'd already danced to this evening... then I had it. Madonna – I definitely hadn't done any Madonna for a long time.

I started my routine by getting as high up the pole as I could, then spinning slowly back down to the floor.

Arnold was paying attention, thankfully. The other two were talking amongst themselves – nothing they hadn't seen before. I was going to have to do something really spectacular to get them going. Question was whether I had enough energy left, and whether I could be bothered. It wasn't them I was interested in, and it certainly wasn't their money paying for my time – so I turned my full focus on Arnold. I wondered why he wanted them there. He would have had to pay for them, too.

Before the song finished, some signal must have been given that I wasn't aware of, or didn't notice, but Markus and the other guy got up and left the room.

I got to my feet for my final twirl and felt a grip of alarm. Arnold wanted me on his own.

I held out my hand to him and he kissed it, but he didn't let go. 'Come and sit with me for a minute,' he said.

The music automatically switched over to the lower volume, slow-time background noise that they left running in here when there weren't any dances. I picked up my clothes from the floor and slipped back into them as quickly as I could. 'I need to go and get changed,' I said in a voice that I hoped left no room for discussion, 'but thank you. It's been lovely to see you again.'

'Sit down,' he said again.

I sat, at the other end of the sofa. Without a word he moved closer to me, his thigh touching mine. I wriggled out and tried to stand but suddenly, before I really realised what was going on, he was on top of me, his hand up my dress, pulling at my underwear, his mouth on mine.

I pushed him off with a shove and screamed as hard as I could, kicking out with my heels and making contact with something, a shin maybe.

'Get off me!'

'Ow, you fuckin' bitch!' One hand on my shoulder, his knee in my groin pinned me to the sofa by my own stupid dress. 'No need to be so unfriendly,' he said.

'There's CCTV,' I said. 'They'll be in here in a minute…'

'No, they won't,' he said, breathless.

His hands were all over me and I couldn't think what to do. I'd been groped before, I'd had men shouting disgusting suggestions to me while I'd been on the stage and all I'd ever had to do was say something like, 'Please don't speak to me like that,' or look over to one of the guys, and before you knew it they would be being carried off towards the exit.

Now I was on my own.

At the back of my head I was replaying the previous weekend, wondering if I'd said or done anything that might have given Leon Arnold the idea that I wanted this, that I wanted to be on my own with him. Or maybe that this was some kind of set-up, that Fitz had told him I'd be okay with it, having neglected to mention it to me before or since...

'Leon,' I said in a voice that I hoped was both calm and firm, 'please – this isn't right.'

'Shut up,' he said mildly, trying to kiss me while I turned my head left and right and crossed my arms over my chest to try to stop him getting so close, so horribly close.

I looked up again at the CCTV, praying for someone to come and help me. That was my only hope. Even if I screamed or shouted, nobody would hear me. The noise from the club; the dressing rooms were empty; there was nobody in the offices upstairs.

'Please,' I said, 'you really need to stop this. If you want to talk to me this isn't the right thing to do.'

He was hurting me now, his hand gripped around the fabric of my dress, pulling it tighter and tighter against my skin. In a moment it would tear away. Where were they? Surely there was someone watching the CCTV? Surely someone would come? I started to panic, writhing and trying to bring my knees up to throw him off. He covered my mouth with his free hand, pressing me down, pushing my head into the sofa cushions so I was fighting for breath while I clawed at him, trying to find skin that I could scratch. The panic was rising inside me, making me shake, weakening my efforts to get free of him.

I heard a muffled sound, like a bang, and seconds later felt clean air above me as Arnold was pulled away. There was shouting, but I couldn't make out words… I found myself taking long gasps of air as though I'd been drowning. My chest hurt.

I managed to sit up and the room was empty. I was shaking, my hands tingling, my knees knocking together. I tried to push myself up but my legs wouldn't support my weight.

The audio system was still playing at low volume and in front of me the pole rose from the laminate floor, shiny in the lights, gleaming and innocent, oblivious to what had just happened.

I sobbed then, trembling on the sofa, thinking about how they'd made such a big thing about the girls being safe here and how, actually, we weren't safe at all.

And then Dylan was there, hands twitching into fists by his sides, breathing hard as though he'd been running.

He held out a hand and pulled me to my feet, then he put his huge arms around me and held me. Inside the circle of his arms I was sobbing and shaking. He patted me reassuringly on the back. 'Come on,' he said, 'you're alright now. Let's get you to the dressing room.'

There was nobody in there, nobody in the corridor on the way to the dressing room either.

'Where is he?' I asked, when I could speak.

Dylan was sitting on the stool next to me, waiting patiently for me to stop crying. 'He's gone.'

'And the others?'

'They've gone too.'

'What happened, Dylan?'

He shrugged. 'He thought he could get away with it, I guess.'

'What about the CCTV? Isn't someone supposed to be watching it all the time?'

He grimaced. 'Supposed to be.'

'It's not fucking good enough.'

'No.'

The door opened and Norland came in.

'Don't you ever fucking knock?' I demanded, finding myself angry, furious, where seconds ago I'd been falling apart.

'What's up with you?' Norland asked with a sneer.

'She just got roughed up,' Dylan said.

'By Leon Arnold? You're joking.'

'Do I look like I'm laughing? Norland, you shit, why wasn't someone on the CCTV?'

Norland didn't look remotely concerned. It crossed my mind then that Arnold might have paid him something to look the other way.

'Where's Fitz?' I said. 'I want to talk to Fitz!'

'Fuck off,' Norland said, 'he's not here. And in any case, do you think he's gonna listen to you whining? Who do you think you are?'

Dylan stood up and filled the space between Norland and my seat. 'You're not helping,' he said quietly. 'Go back to the office.'

Norland gave me one last filthy look and left, leaving the door to the corridor open behind him.

'Come on,' Dylan said. 'I'll call you a cab.'

He left me to get changed into my jeans and jumper and when I went downstairs he was there, sitting at one of the empty tables in the bar with a glass on the table in front of him.

'Dylan,' I said.

He looked up.

'Thank you.'

'No problem,' he said. 'Cab'll be here in a minute. You want a drink?'

'Vodka,' I said.

He helped himself behind the bar and poured me a glass. In deference to my femininity he shoved a handful of ice and a slice of lemon in there too.

I drank two big gulps, intending to finish it off in one go but not quite managing it before it started to burn my throat.

'I don't know if I can do this any more,' I said.

'It's a rough business sometimes. You know that.'

'It's not like he was just a regular customer, Dylan. It's Leon Arnold. What the fuck's Fitz going to say?'

'That's not your problem,' he said. 'Let them fight it out amongst themselves.'

On the road outside a black cab pulled up to the kerb and I got to my feet. 'Thanks again,' I said.

By the time I got home I was too exhausted to think but I felt grubby, so I ran a bath while I sat at my dining table drinking cold water. I was aching all over, head to foot, as though I'd been beaten up rather than simply held down, and my head was pounding.

I opened my bag to look for some painkillers, and as I did so I felt my phone vibrate, an incoming text. Not a number I recognised.

*Meet me 6pm Monday upstairs food area Victoria Station*

I felt a momentary panic. Who the hell had sent that text? My first thought that it was Arnold, wanting to get me on my own somehow… but then why would he want to meet me in such a public place?

I sent a text back:

*Who is this?*

But there was no reply.

# Twenty-eight

I slept badly, worrying about Arnold and wondering what I was going to say to Fitz the next time I saw him. I had dreams about Victoria Station, about meeting some faceless person who meant to do me harm. I got to work even more exhausted than I usually was on a Monday morning, not looking forward to working my way through the day. To my surprise, Gavin was in the main office, sitting at his old desk, with Lucy next to him.

'What's going on?' I asked.

'He's back,' Lucy said.

'Who's back?'

The door to the manager's office opened then and to my horror Ian Dunkerley came out. He'd lost weight, but his smug expression hadn't changed. He fixed me with a defiant stare that looked as though it had required some effort to produce.

'Genevieve,' he said. 'When you have a moment…?'

I stared at him, mouth open, while he collected papers from the printer and went back into his office, leaving the door ajar.

Oh, God. Not him, not him again.

'Don't keep him waiting, whatever you do,' Gavin said helpfully. 'He's not in the best of moods.'

I didn't even put down my bag, or take off my coat. I went into Dunkerley's office and stood in the doorway.

He was behind the desk, tapping away at his keyboard as if he'd never been away. 'Shut the door,' he said.

'I'd rather leave it open, if it's all the same to you.'

'You're half an hour late,' he said. 'Why's that?'

I didn't reply. It felt as though the world was caving in around me.

He stood up, straightened his trousers, and came around the desk towards me. I took a step back, away from him, at the same moment wondering why I was afraid of him. If anything, he should be afraid of me.

'You thought I was gone for good, huh?' he said, so quietly I could barely hear. He was close enough for me to feel the warmth from him, smell his powerful aftershave.

'I hoped you were,' I said.

'Well, unlike you, I am a professional. I take my career very seriously. And I should point out that I have been working with the police to prosecute your – *friends* – for their assault on me. And the police have been very interested in you, too.'

I bit my lip. He had to be lying. Whatever else he was, Dunkerley wasn't stupid – there was no way he'd report the incident to the police, not after the warning he'd had.

'Now, I'm prepared to put all this behind me. I suggest you do the same.' He turned and went back to his desk.

I felt sick to my stomach as I left the room, closing the door behind me. Gavin and Lucy had gone out somewhere, and the main office was empty. I sat down at my desk and logged on to the network, my head in my hands as I waited for the emails to load. I looked at the list of unread emails in the inbox: four or five from customers, relating to contracts I was working on. And then twelve emails from Ian Dunkerley, one after the other, starting at 07:24 this morning. The subjects of the emails included 'New working practice'; three called, simply, 'Meeting'; one at 09:01 entitled 'Timekeeping'; and finally, as I watched, a thirteenth: 'Office dress code'.

I closed the email window without reading any of them and opened a new Word document.

Ten minutes later Gavin and Lucy returned with their cardboard lattes from the coffee shop on the ground floor, laughing about something and chatting without a care in the world.

'Everything okay?' Lucy asked, seeing my face.

'Not really,' I said, retrieving the single sheet from the printer.

'What's up?'

I couldn't even bring myself to answer her. I folded the letter, not bothering to put it in an envelope, and took it with me along with my bag and my coat to the CEO's office on the next floor. There was a meeting going on.

'Will it take long?' I asked.

Linda, the PA, looked at me blankly. 'Could be ages,' she said. 'Anything I can do?'

'I'll wait, if that's okay,' I said. I couldn't face going back downstairs; the thought of having to see Dunkerley again, or even explaining any of this to Lucy and Gavin, was almost too much.

I watched the clock above Linda's head creep slowly round. Was I really going to do this? Surely this wasn't me – I'd never given up on anything in my whole life. Was I going to let that horrible man get the better of me? I should be fighting this. And yet, the thought of having to carry on...

Ten minutes.

The lift doors opened and Lucy emerged. I thought to myself, *You took the lift?* She looked at me and handed over some reports to Linda.

I don't know if it was Lucy's presence that made me move, or simply that I couldn't stand being here for a minute longer. I got up and went to the office door, opened it wide. Simon Lewis, the CEO, was sitting at his conference table with three other people, one of whom was a client I'd worked with on a major project last year. The conversation stopped abruptly and they all turned to look at me. I strode over to them and put the folded letter on the table in front of Simon.

'Genevieve? What's going on?' he said, and despite my dramatic and unannounced visit his voice was so kind I almost

233

regretted it, almost took the letter back and apologised for the intrusion.

'I'm sorry,' I said. 'I've got to go.'

I shut the door behind me and walked straight past Lucy, who was standing by Linda's desk with her mouth open. I took the stairs – not the lift – and by the time I got to the ground floor I was almost running. I went out of the building through Reception and, despite my heart thudding with the enormity of it all, the relief that I was never going to go back there was sudden, and immense.

The cab took me straight home. I had a hot bath and, after lying awake for a while thinking about everything that had happened in the last two days, I finally managed to sleep. When I woke up in the afternoon, I put on a skirt and sandals with a denim jacket and headed out with my sunglasses to catch the bus to Victoria Station.

It was busy, packed with commuters making their way home. I took the escalators to Victoria Place, and then up again to the part of the mall where various food and drink outlets circled a central, open-plan eating area.

I looked around but there was no sign of Arnold, or anyone else I recognised. Not sitting anywhere obvious, anyway. I bought a coffee from the burger place and sat down on a hard plastic seat bolted on to the table, where I could see the escalators and anyone coming up them. I was still early.

A few seconds later, someone tapped me on the shoulder and I looked around, startled.

To my surprise and relief, it was Dylan. I barely recognised him; he was wearing jeans and boots, a shirt unbuttoned with a dark grey T-shirt underneath. I'd never seen him in anything other than a suit.

'Come with me,' he said.

I took my coffee and my bag and followed him around the other side of the complex to a few tables and chairs that were tucked away behind a coffee kiosk.

'This is a nice surprise,' I said, sliding down into a seat opposite him.

He nodded. 'Yeah. Never seen you in daylight before.'

'And?'

'You could do with getting out in the sun.'

'Cheers. And you look like you could do with laying off the vodka for a while.'

It was true, he looked rough, his skin lined and his eyes red and tired. He hadn't shaved and there was a rasp of stubble over his face as well as over his head, showing the shape of where his hairline would have been, if he'd ever let it grow.

'What can I say? It was a late night.'

I couldn't get over how different he looked, how – normal. He was like any other bloke out having a coffee on a Monday afternoon.

'How do you feel?' he asked.

'I've felt better,' I answered. 'I've had such a crappy few days.' There were no bruises visible from where Arnold had grabbed me, even though the skin around my mouth felt tender. My arms were sore too, where he'd held me down, but nothing you could see.

'How's the boat-buying going?'

'I went to look at some last week,' I said, 'thank you for asking.'

'So you've got enough money, then?'

'No. I've got just about enough to buy the boat, but not enough to renovate it properly and take time off, which is all part of it. I can't do one without the other. So I need to do a bit more saving. I'll have to ask Norland if he'll increase my hours. Or maybe Fitz will ask me to do another one of his parties.'

He was watching me steadily, evaluating.

'What?' I said at last, feeling worried about the intense expression on his face.

'I could help you,' he said, his voice low.

'Help me with what?'

'Help you with the money side of it.'

I ran through the possibilities. Whatever we were doing here, it wasn't something he wanted to discuss in front of Fitz. Which meant he was taking a huge risk.

'What do you mean?'

'How much would you need to be able to leave London by, say, the end of this month?'

Two weeks away. In other words, how much money did I need now?

'At least fifty grand,' I said, after a moment, feeling my cheeks flush.

'I can do that,' he said, without hesitation.

I wondered what I'd got myself into. If it hadn't been for Dunkerley, I would have probably said no. 'So…?'

'I need you to look after something for me.'

'What?'

'It's a parcel. Not very big. I need someone to hide it for a couple of months. Maybe not even that long. You're the best person I know.'

'That's it?'

'Just hide it and don't let anyone get it. That's it.'

'And for that I get fifty grand? Like, to keep?'

'Yours to keep.'

'What's the catch?'

'The catch is, it's not something you want to be caught in possession of. And after you leave, you won't be able to come back. You'll have to walk away from the club for good. You get me?'

I paused, drank the last of my coffee while I considered his offer. He watched me without blinking. He wasn't nervous at all, which made me wonder what was at stake here.

'Where are you going to keep your boat, anyway?'

I shrugged. 'Depends where it is when I buy it, I guess. The boats I saw on Thursday were in Kent. There was one I liked.'

He nodded, 'Kent. That'd be alright.'

'Does that make a difference?'

'Far enough away for it to be safe, near enough for me to come and collect it from you.'

'When will you collect it?'

'I don't know. I'll give you a phone. When I'm ready to come and get it, I'll ring you to arrange a meeting. Is it a yes, then?'

It had been a yes from the moment he'd agreed to fifty grand.

'I guess it is, Dylan.'

He smiled his best Dylan smile and offered me his huge meaty hand to shake. 'Deal.'

I felt a curious sense of release, as though I'd been holding on to a thread somewhere that had finally snapped. I could go. I could afford to buy a boat, and I had enough money to take a year off, maybe even more than a year.

# Twenty-nine

I was back to planning my fantasy bathroom on the table in the dinette when I heard steps on the pontoon followed by steps on the deck and a woman's voice that called out, 'Genevieve Shipley? Hello? Can you come up, please?'

I went up to the wheelhouse.

On my deck were two people, a man and a woman, both of them wearing suits. The woman showed me her card. 'I am DS Beverley Davies; this is my colleague DC Jamie Newman. I wonder if you have a few moments to talk to us.' She spoke fast, as if she was in a tearing hurry and had no time for dissent or explanation.

I felt afraid, as though I had been caught in the act of doing something I shouldn't.

'What's it about?'

'It would be good if you could come with us, Genevieve. We need to have a talk.'

'What – now?'

'Yes, right now.'

'Where did you say you were from?'

'We're from the Metropolitan Police Serious Crime Directorate.'

'But – Jim Carling – '

'DC Carling knows we are here. He told us where to find you. He did say you wouldn't mind helping us out with a few questions, Genevieve. It won't take long.'

238

I guessed she was trying her hardest to be encouraging, but all I could think of was how I could persuade her to fuck off and leave me alone.

It wouldn't work, though. Maybe if I went along with her and answered her stupid questions they would go away and not come back.

'I'll just get my shoes,' I said.

'Mind if I come with you?' Jamie Newman asked me. 'I'd like to see your boat.'

'Sure,' I said, and went down the steps into the cabin, leaving the door open for him to follow me.

He stood there watching me while I pulled on my boots and did up the laces. He wasn't interested in the boat at all, for other than a cursory glance around the cabin he hadn't taken his eyes off me.

They knew about the package, I thought. Or at least, they knew I had something on here to hide. Carling had told them. Newman was here to make sure I didn't move or destroy whatever it was.

I gave him a tight smile, grabbed my keys and the two mobile phones from the dinette table and went back up to the wheelhouse.

'Two phones?' he asked, while I locked the door.

'One of them's got a crap signal on the boat; the other one's got a crap signal everywhere else,' I said, as if that explained everything.

'Where are we going?' I asked from the back seat of their Volvo. I'd never been inside a police car before, marked or unmarked.

'Medway police station,' Newman said. 'They've kindly offered to let us use one of their interview rooms. Saves us a trip back to town with you.'

'Oh,' I said. 'Couldn't we just have had a chat on the boat?'

They didn't answer. I wondered if they'd got other people on there now, searching it.

I watched the streets of Rochester as they passed, thinking of the boat and the package and what it could possibly be. Something I didn't want to be caught in possession of, he'd said. Which meant drugs, several kilos of them, hidden on my boat and waiting to be found.

The following weekend at the Barclay was my last.

It wasn't even a proper weekend, just the Saturday night, and even that was cut dramatically short.

All week I'd been working up to going back there, telling myself that Arnold wouldn't be there, that I'd be careful about private dances from now on, I'd check that someone was in the CCTV room when I was dancing, I'd ask who it was who had booked me – all of that crap. In reality I was going to hand in my notice. I was working up to that, too.

The club was quieter, as it often was towards the middle of the month. Some of my regulars were in, men for whom payday was a bit irrelevant, and I knew I'd be getting some private bookings later on. Would I be able to dance for them without freaking out? Dylan had said he would keep an eye on me, but I hadn't seen him. What if he wasn't even here? Who would watch out for me then?

When I had a spare moment between my dances I went to the bar to find Helena. They were short-staffed and Helena was doing a bit of waitressing. If that was what you called it – there was an awful lot of socialising and chatting up going on at the same time.

'Is Fitz in tonight?' I asked.

She shrugged. 'Not seen him. Go upstairs and ask Nicksy; he's in the office, I think.'

I was halfway up the stairs when Nicks appeared at the top. Someone was watching that CCTV camera, at least, I thought with irony, looking at the camera that covered the staircase.

'What's up?' he asked, folding his arms across his chest.

'I'd like to see Fitz,' I said.

'He doesn't want to see you.'

The answer came back so quickly, I was shocked. He didn't want to see me? Why the hell not? Had Arnold said something to him? Had someone seen me meeting Dylan at Victoria Station?

My heart started thumping with alarm. 'Why doesn't he want to see me?'

Nicks shrugged and didn't answer.

'Could you go and ask him? I only want a minute.'

The wall of muscle didn't move. I looked behind him, down the corridor. All the office doors were shut. If I tried to get past him, he would stop me. There was no way I'd be able to get down there, not now.

Nicks gave me a look that invited me to try. I wondered if I would end up being thrown back down the stairs if I did.

I turned around, but instead of heading for the dressing rooms I went into the main part of the club, scanning the VIP booths for Fitz, in case he was down here after all. No sign of him. Then to my relief Dylan came upstairs from the public bar. He was dressed smartly again, freshly shaved, immaculate.

He saw me and hesitated, as though he was unsure whether he should talk to me or not. I gave him a smile I hoped was encouraging. He smiled back and his eyes travelled upwards very briefly to the CCTV camera above our heads.

The meaning was clear. We were being watched.

I walked over to him and said sweetly, 'I'd like to see Fitz, but Nicks won't let me in. Would you ask him for me, when you get a minute?'

'Sure,' he said in reply, and then he was gone, into the crowds of suits, heading for the bar. If they'd watched that little exchange they wouldn't have found anything unusual in it. I hoped not, anyway.

After that I felt odd, panicky. I sat by myself at the end of the bar, ostensibly scanning for customers but at the same time trying to avoid them all. Across the club in one of the booths, I could see Stephen Penrose. He was a company director, the owner of a chain of estate agents: I only knew this because I recognised him from an interview he'd done with the *Financial Times* a few months ago. Here I knew him as Steve, and I would never have let on that I knew exactly who he was. He was staring at me, smiling.

I was on the list for the pole but for some reason I wasn't called, or, if I was, I didn't hear it. It wasn't the thought of Dylan's money, that sudden pile of cash that made everything here seem so much harder; since Arnold's assault, being here wasn't fun any more. The few people here I recognised, even the ones I liked, the ones I had a laugh with week after week – they all looked different tonight, sinister, strong, threatening. *I can't do this any more*, I thought. *I don't want to be here*.

Stephen Penrose, a man who wouldn't hurt a fly, who paid me double for our private dances in the Blue Room and always sat there rigid, his hand over his crotch like a small boy who needed a wee, was staring at me, his smile of encouragement fading each time I cast a glance in his direction. In normal circumstances he would not have had to wait; I would have been by his side the moment I'd seen he was here. He probably thought I was waiting for someone, waiting for a better prospect than him.

He was safe, surely? Why wasn't I over there, talking to him, easing him out of his working-week shell, making him feel wanted and happy and attractive?

When he stood up and crossed the club towards me, weaving his way through groups of people, I got up off my bar stool and made for the door, walking with purpose and almost breaking into a run. If he called my name, I didn't hear it. I went straight to the stairs, and this time there was no Nicks standing guard at the top. Maybe I'd taken them by surprise; maybe they hadn't considered I would have the audacity to do this; or perhaps they'd all gone out somewhere and I'd find the doors locked.

I was almost expecting this to be the case, so when I reached Fitz's office door I didn't even knock, just tried the door and to my surprise it opened easily, propelling me into the room.

They were all in there. Fitz, Dylan, Nicks, Gray, even Norland, who looked skinny and pathetic next to this group of tough men. I had a second to take this in – Norland, Nicks and Gray sitting on the sofas, cash on the desk in bundles, a holdall on the floor, Fitz perched on the edge of the desk, Dylan standing as though he was about to leave.

Nicks stood up abruptly and took a step towards me.

'Oh,' I said.

'Viva,' Fitz said, holding up a hand which stopped Nicks in his tracks. 'Might be nice if you could think about knocking next time?'

'I'm sorry,' I said, not looking at the others, deliberately not making eye contact with Dylan. 'I just need to have a word with you. It's important.'

Fitz was watching me steadily. I stared him out, feigning a confidence I did not feel. My heart was thumping with panic, the need to get this over and done with so I could get out of here.

'Alright,' he said. 'What is it?'

'In private,' I said.

He laughed, a single laugh of disbelief at my cheek, but even so he looked at the others and said 'Gentlemen, would you give us a minute?'

They all left. Dylan was the last to go. He hesitated in the doorway, and for a moment I had the terrible thought that he was going to say something, do something. Fitz gave him a nod, and then he went.

I took a deep breath. 'Did you know Leon Arnold was here last weekend?'

He shrugged. 'No. And?'

'He attacked me. He booked a private dance and then got his two heavies – Markus and the other one – to wait outside while he jumped me.'

At last Fitz looked up and met my eyes. And he laughed. 'Did he really? Sly old git.'

So it was true, then. I'd seriously pissed him off somehow.

Surely my disagreement with Caddy wouldn't have done it? I racked my brains to think what it could be. Maybe Dylan had been followed at Victoria Station? He was too careful for that.

'There was nobody watching the CCTV, Fitz. He could have killed me.'

'He didn't, though, did he? You're still here, aren't you? Toughen up, princess.'

I waited for more. His eye contact was steady and for a moment I saw only defiance, coldness, until he looked away and a fraction before that I saw something I hadn't expected to see, not in a million years: hurt.

And then I knew what it was, what had happened to turn him against me.

I'd turned him down.

'Fitz...'

'You should go downstairs,' he said. The shutters were back up.

How could someone so tough be so vulnerable at the same time?

'One more thing,' I said, chancing my luck. 'I'm sorry. I need to give you my notice.'

He didn't even look up from the paperwork this time. 'Talk to Dave or Helena about that.'

He didn't seem remotely surprised by it. I got to my feet, left the office and shut the door quietly behind it.

I went to see Helena in the bar. She didn't seem surprised either. I'd been there longer than a lot of the girls – some of them only stayed a couple of weeks, especially if they hadn't managed to get themselves any regulars in that time – but even so, I was expendable. I hadn't even made the house fee tonight so I had to get some notes out of my bag in the dressing room before I went. And then I was free to go.

I walked away from the Barclay feeling unexpectedly relieved. I hadn't realised quite how afraid I'd been, how tense, since Arnold had attacked me. I'd thought Fitz was someone who cared about what happened to his employees, maybe even cared for me, but I'd been wrong.

It was definitely time to go. I had something to look forward to now: Kent, the River Medway and the *Revenge of the Tide*.

# Thirty

The police station in Gillingham was new, a big modern building that could have been an office block, a school, or a college.

I was shown into an interview room that contained a table and four padded reception chairs, a wall-mounted recorder, and a window that was just about too high to see out of. It was bright, though. And very small.

I sat there on my own for half an hour before Beverley Davies and Jamie Newman came in and sat down in front of me. All the interview rooms I'd ever seen on TV had been cavernous by comparison, shadowy, with light from above illuminating the interviewers' faces in a suitably dramatic fashion. This felt more like a job interview. I straightened in my seat. *Concentrate. Think about everything.*

'Sorry about the wait,' DS Davies said. 'Do you want a drink or anything? Coffee?'

'No, thank you.'

'Am I under arrest for something?'

Jamie Newman stepped in. 'No, you're not under arrest. We just need to ask you some questions and it's easier if we do it officially. That's all.'

Beverley Davies continued. 'We want to talk to you about Candace Smith, the woman who was found dead in the river next to your boat.'

'Yes.'

'You told my colleagues that you didn't recognise her, is that correct?'

'It was dark and I had just woken up. I didn't really see much other than a body, a face. It was afterwards that I thought it looked like Caddy.'

'But you didn't share this information with DC Carling or any of the officers from Kent Police?'

'No. It was just a thought. I didn't want to mislead them. When DC Carling told me it was Caddy, it gave me a bit of a shock to think it was someone I knew after all.'

'Can you tell us how you knew Candace?'

'I met her through work.'

'What work is that?'

I looked from one of them to the other, at their calm, impassive, expressionless faces gazing back at me. Waiting for me to slip up, to tell them something they didn't already know. This was nerve-racking, trying to second-guess them.

'I used to do some dancing – in my spare time. She was one of the other dancers in the club I worked in.'

'The name of this club?'

'It was the Barclay.'

'How long did you work there?'

'About seven months.'

Jamie Newman was writing, the notepad on his lap so I couldn't see it. He held the biro with his fist scrunched around it. 'Were you friends with Candace?'

I hesitated, just for a moment. 'I guess so. Not really the sort of place you make friends, though. People come and go all the time.'

'Some men attacked you on your boat,' Davies said, after a few moments.

'Yes.' I wondered if Carling had told her everything, whether he'd relayed our conversation word for word, if he'd even been making notes or recording it. Did she know about him staying the night? Would he have managed to keep that bit to himself, at least?

'What do you think they wanted from you?'

'I don't know.'

'You must have some idea.'

'I thought they were looking for something, maybe. But I don't know what.'

'Why did you think that?'

I took a deep breath in, trying to stay calm, trying to feel as though I was still in control.

'Because they turned the boat upside down, that's why. They came on board and chucked everything around. So either they were looking for something and they didn't find it, or they just felt like making a mess.'

'Why didn't you report it?' Davies asked.

I had no answer. I knew now why the window was so high up. If it had been any lower, I would have been able to see out, to see trees and fresh air and people going about their normal business; but all I could see was a small patch of darkening sky. I wanted to be out there. If the window had been at normal height I might have considered throwing myself out of it. I guessed I wasn't the first person to sit in here and contemplate something like that.

'Why didn't you report it, Genevieve? Could you answer the question?'

'I don't know. There didn't seem to be any point. They were long gone, whoever they were.'

'After you left London, did you keep in touch with Candace Smith?'

'I spoke to her a couple of times. I asked her if she wanted to come to a party I was having. She said she'd think about it, but then she didn't turn up.'

'When was this party?'

'It was – the night I found the body next to the boat.'

They looked at each other then, Newman and Davies. I wondered what they were thinking. My heart was beating fast. I wiped my palms down my jeans and then clasped my hands together to keep them still.

'Right. Let's just go back a bit. You invited Candace to your boat? When did you ask her?'

'I don't know. A few weeks ago, I think.'

'And how did she seem, when you talked to her?'

'Alright. Normal, really.'

'So she was planning to come?'

'I told her when and where. She said she'd think about it. I don't think I really expected her to turn up.'

'Why not?'

'Like I said, we weren't really friends. She was just someone I knew from the club.'

'Did you invite anyone else from the club?'

'No.'

'So what made you invite Candace?'

'It was a spur-of-the-moment thing. I was talking to her, and thinking about the party, and I asked if she wanted to come along.'

'Did you phone her, or did she phone you?'

'I can't remember.'

I must have answered her too quickly.

'You said you weren't in contact with her very often, so speaking to her would have been unusual, wouldn't it? So think again. Did you phone her, or did she phone you?'

'I guess I phoned her.'

'What did you call her for?'

'Just to see how she was.'

There was another pause. Newman was still taking notes on his pad, to my right. I could hear the scratching of his pen on the notepad. He might have been doodling for all I knew.

'You said that Candace didn't turn up.'

'That's right.'

'Are you sure? I mean, if you were busy with the party – talking to your guests, drinking, that sort of thing – maybe she turned up and you didn't realise?'

I considered this for a moment.

'It's not a very big boat. Lots of people were up on the deck.

Someone would have seen if she'd been there. Someone would have told me.'

'We'll need you to give us a list of everyone who was there that night, with their contact details.'

'I already gave it to that bloke – the one who interviewed me – I can't remember his name.'

'Even so, I'd like you to write another list.'

She tore a sheet of A4 paper off the top of a lined pad which was on the table behind her and pushed it and a ballpoint pen over the desk towards me. I stared at it for a few moments and made two headings: 'Marina' and 'Other'. As I wrote each name I thought about how they'd all react to being questioned by the police. Lucy, Gavin, Ben. What would they think?

When I'd finished, she gave me a smile, the first time she'd softened. 'What was Candace like?'

'She was nice. She helped me out a bit when I first started working there.'

'She looked after you?'

'Yes, you could say that.'

'Took you under her wing?'

'I guess so.'

'Did you see much of her outside work?'

'Not really.'

'Did she have any other close friends?'

'I don't know. Nobody I knew.'

'Boyfriends?'

'I don't know.'

'You never talked about it? About guys you liked?'

I shook my head. 'No.'

I hadn't lied to them, not directly. Not yet.

'What about Fitz?'

'What about him?' My heart was thudding at the sound of his name, my cheeks colouring.

'You knew him?'

'Of course. He was the owner of the club.'

'Did you get on with him?'

'I didn't see him very often. He was usually at his other clubs when I was there.'

'What did Candace think of him?'

'She told me that he was alright unless you pissed him off.'

'What do you think she meant by that?'

'Just that I shouldn't piss him off. I don't know. As I said, I didn't see him very often.'

'Did she ever say what happened if anyone did "piss him off"?'

'No.'

'Did you ever see anyone else cross him?'

'No.'

'Were you afraid of him?'

'No. I didn't know him. I just got on with the job and went home.'

'Were the other dancers afraid of him?'

'Not that I saw. If they were, they would have left, wouldn't they?'

'Why did you leave, Genevieve?'

'I was only working there to save up enough money to buy a boat. I'd saved up enough, so I handed in my notice and left.'

'When was this?'

'It was the middle of April.'

'And you never went back for a visit?'

'No.' I still wasn't lying. Not directly. I tried to keep my breathing steady, even though my cheeks were burning, my hands icy cold, as if I had a fever.

'How long had you worked there?'

'You already asked me that question.'

'Even so, I'd like you to answer it.'

'About seven months.'

There was silence apart from Newman writing his notes. Davies was staring at me curiously, as though I were some kind of unusual animal in a zoo and she was expecting more from me, something more interesting, more entertaining.

'These men who attacked you on your boat – did you recognise them?'

'No.' The first real lie. It felt as if I was shouting. Had I answered too quickly? Surely they must realise? I swallowed the lump in my throat, took a deep, steadying breath in.

'Aren't you afraid they'll come back?'

'Of course I am. Look,' I said, 'Malcolm – my neighbour – he's been helping me service the engine. I was planning to take the boat upstream a bit. Just somewhere out of the way. I haven't told anyone.'

'I see.'

'I was going to call DC Carling and let him know. In fact, it was his idea.'

'It was his idea?'

'He asked me if I'd ever taken the boat on a trip anywhere. I said I hadn't. But it gave me the idea. I mean, it's not like living in a house, is it? Why live on a boat and never move it?'

After that they ended the interview and left the room. I didn't ask how long it was going to be before I could go home, but I wasn't under arrest. I could have walked out if I'd wanted to, but there was no point. I could stay and answer their questions until they were as bored as I was of it.

But they came back after ten minutes and said I could go. The Metropolitan Police Serious Crime Directorate had asked me all they needed to, for now, anyway.

I started walking back home. I could have found a bus, or called a taxi, but for the moment I wanted to walk. I was desperate to talk to Dylan, to find out what the hell was going on. In all the confusion, there were two indisputable facts: Caddy was dead. And Dylan wasn't answering his phone. Dylan was the only person connected to the club, other than Caddy, whom I'd told where the boat was moored. Had he killed her?

I was packing boxes in the flat I was renting and drinking a cup of cold coffee when there was a knock at the door.

I'd been expecting Dylan for so many days that I'd almost given up. I was afraid he'd changed his mind about the package, about the fifty grand. I didn't know what I was going to do if he didn't come through with the money, but there was no going back: I'd left work, given notice on the flat, handed over a substantial deposit and marina fees to Cameron. I had to go, whatever happened.

'Can I come in?' he said.

About bloody time, I wanted to say. I wanted to smack him and ask where the fuck he'd been, why he'd left me waiting without so much as a phone call. He was wearing his non-work disguise, jeans and a shirt, navy blue this time, with a tatty-looking jacket over the top of it. He wasn't carrying a bag, which made my heart sink. He didn't have the money with him. He must have changed his mind.

He followed me into my kitchen and I moved a box off the chair to let him sit. 'You're moving out already, huh?' he said.

'I'm putting most of it into storage,' I said.

'I came to see how you were.'

'Oh. I'm alright, thanks. How's Caddy?'

He smiled at me. 'Same as usual. Sometimes happy as Charlie, sometimes a grumpy little fucker.'

I wondered if I should offer him a drink. Did he ever have anything other than vodka? I had no idea where the kettle was, in any case.

'So – you found yourself a boat, then?'

I smiled happily. 'Yes, I have. It's called the *Revenge of the Tide*.'

'No kidding? Weird name.'

'It suits it. You should come and have a look.'

'Is it one of the ones you were looking at? In Kent?'

'Yes. In Rochester.'

He nodded approvingly. Then, 'I thought Fitz might have given you a hard time.'

'Not really,' I said. 'I think I overestimated my own importance.'

'He never said you'd left. He never mentioned you after you burst into the office that night.'

'I think he was pissed off because I complained to him about Arnold jumping me.'

'Ah. That would do it, yeah. And probably coming in to the office without an invite didn't help.'

There was a strange silence for a moment. He filled the room with his bulk, even sitting down.

'So – you still want to do it?'

'Yes.' There was no question over what it was I was still willing to do. Mentioning the package would have been a waste of breath.

'Right,' he said. 'You got a car?'

'No. I'm hiring a van tomorrow, though. To take all the stuff down to the boat.'

'Alright, then,' he said, 'You know Brands Hatch, the motor racing circuit? There's a hotel there, the Thistle. On the A20. Think you can find it?'

'Sure.'

'I'll meet you in the bar of the hotel. Nine o'clock tomorrow night.'

'Alright. What if something happens? I mean, what if I get held up?'

'I'll wait till you get there.'

He stood up to go and I had a sudden urge to ask him to stay for a while. But he didn't hesitate or give me time to ask. He didn't even look back.

# Thirty-one

I was ten minutes late getting to Brands Hatch, mainly because I approached it from the wrong carriageway and had to go down a junction to turn the van around.

It had been a hectic day, and I was tired out with moving more stuff into storage, supervising some removal men who had taken a load down to the boat – mainly furniture. Now it was just me and a Transit van packed to the roof with boxes.

Dylan was in the bar, strategically positioned to the side where he could watch the entrance without making it obvious that he was waiting for someone. I bought a bottle of beer and slid into the armchair opposite his seat.

He gave me of his best Dylan smiles. He looked so different, beautiful almost, when he smiled. 'Thought you weren't coming,' he said.

'Sorry,' I said, 'I took a slight detour on the motorway.'

He nodded slowly. On the sofa next to him was a big plastic carrier bag. He placed a hand on it. I wondered what it was. Cocaine? Heroin? It was best not to think about it too hard, so I thought about the money instead.

'It's all in there,' he said. 'With a mobile phone.'

'Okay,' I said.

'The phone has one number saved in it, under the name Garland. When I'm going to come and collect the parcel, I'll ring you on that number. Only answer the phone if you see that the caller ID says Garland.'

'Why Garland?'

'It's just a word.'

'Is it your name?' He'd never told me. I only ever knew him as Dylan.

'No.'

'Can I use the phone to ring you?'

'No.'

'What if there's an emergency?'

'There won't be an emergency. Nothing is going to happen. You just need to put the parcel somewhere safe, keep the phone charged up, and then in a couple of months I'll call you on that number and arrange to come and collect it. Yeah?'

'Alright.'

The feeling crept up on me before I realised what it was. I wasn't going to see him any more. It was going to be that one call, that one meeting to hand over the parcel, and that would be it. Somehow I'd just assumed that we would always be friends. The thought of not seeing him was making me feel uncomfortable – no, more than that. Desolate.

'What's the matter?' he asked.

I had no reason not to tell him the truth. 'I'm going to miss you,' I said.

Dylan laughed at that and it hurt me. Maybe I was just tired, maybe it had just been a traumatic couple of weeks, but the tears were falling down my cheeks before I realised, and I rubbed them away crossly with my sleeve.

'It's not funny,' I said quietly.

'You won't miss me, Genevieve. I'll be lucky if you remember where you've left the phone after a couple of hours.'

'That's not fair. You're always taking the piss, Dylan.'

He sighed as though I was just some troublesome female he was going to have to deal with, picked up the carrier bag and put it on the floor by his feet, making space on the sofa next to him. 'Come and sit here,' he said, and his voice was softer, almost gentle.

When I got to my feet and sank on to the cushions next to him he put his arm around my back, awkwardly patting my shoulder. I moved closer to him, against him, feeling his bulk, instantly comforted by him. It reminded me of the moment he'd held me after he'd got rid of Leon Arnold. Whatever had been wrong had disappeared and everything was alright again.

We stayed like that for a long time and I relaxed into him. His hand, his huge hand which had been patting me on the shoulder like an inexperienced father trying to wind a new baby, had changed pace and was stroking my upper arm, slowly. And then it was just the tips of his fingers, running from my shoulder to my elbow, and back again.

At last he said, 'We should go.'

I pushed myself up off the sofa and away from him and he brought the bag and walked with me out of the main entrance and across the car park to my van. I unlocked it and opened the door for him to put the bag inside, on the passenger seat, but he didn't move. I turned to face him, about to say, *What are you waiting for?* but the words died in my throat because of the way he was looking at me. He placed the carrier bag carefully at his feet, and without taking his eyes off me pushed the door of the van shut, not with force but with a kind of purpose. He moved forward and with no other warning kissed me, one hand around my back, pulling me against him, the other cradling my neck, his thumb on my jawline.

It was as though I'd been waiting for it, waiting for the longest time without realising, and now it was finally happening my legs were giving way under me and he pushed me gently back against the side of the van to prop me up.

When he finally moved away I couldn't see his face in the darkness but I heard his voice, the emotion in it. He said, 'You want to stay?'

I nodded. I wasn't even sure what he meant, then, but I did want to stay if the alternative was going to the boat on my own, or going anywhere that wasn't with him.

We walked back to the hotel and I waited by the lifts while Dylan went to the reception to see if he could get a room for us. All I could think was that I needed a shower: I'd been lugging boxes and furniture around all day and I felt filthy. But not tired any more – I was energised by that kiss, breathing from the very top of my lungs, fizzing with anticipation.

We went upstairs and along a corridor that went on and on, me following Dylan who was carrying that stupid bag which looked heavier by the minute and was probably full of cocaine.

He was walking fast and I struggled to keep up with him, until he stopped abruptly and I almost ran into the back of him. He opened the door to a room and we went inside; he dropped the bag on the floor, pushed it with the toe of his boot into the bottom of the open wardrobe, and closed the door with the other hand, putting on the security chain.

I was already taking my clothes off, my top tangled around my arms, trying to kick my boots off without undoing the laces, jeans around my knees; anyone would think I had no idea how to take my kit off in an erotic and beguiling fashion.

'I need a shower, I'm sorry,' I said, my voice muffled by fabric as I felt his mouth on my skin, his tongue on my naked stomach.

'Like I care,' he said.

That was all he said.

I was made breathless by how much I wanted him. His physique was powerful, the tailored suits he wore hiding the tattoos that covered his left arm and both shoulders: a black dragon snaking around and across the back of his neck; a tribal pattern, a sun, all black ink, intricate and lovely on his nocturnal skin. And how pale my fingers looked, gripping the inked skin of his shoulder.

It was the way he looked at me, so differently from the way he'd looked at me before, in the Barclay. It was as though he'd opened his eyes and was seeing me for the first time. And I'd been waiting, waiting unknowing for him to look at me in exactly that way. Why hadn't I realised it before? Why hadn't I seen him as he really was, this beautiful quiet man who looked out for me? His body fitted against mine seamlessly; everything he did was at the right moment, just the right pace, just the right pressure. I loved how he tried so hard to make everything perfect and slow and sensual, and then, the way he lost control.

And hours, hours later… we'd fucked and showered and had a drink from the minibar and fucked all over again; I was so tired my body felt as though it was separate from me… it was starting to get light and I was lying stretched against him, fingers threaded through his. He was so quiet and still, I thought he was asleep.

I couldn't stop smiling. It felt as though my life had lurched back on to the right track; as if everything that had been wrong was suddenly, magically right. I would live on the boat, and during the week, when the club was quiet, Dylan could come and visit me. He could help me with the renovations, and if he didn't want to do that we would get quietly drunk together sitting on the deck of my boat, watching the sun go down, and then go down into my cabin and make love for hours and hours. Maybe in a few months' time he would give up working in London and move down to be with me on the boat…

'This was a bad idea,' he said.

The sound of his voice after hours without speaking almost made me jump. 'Don't say that,' I whispered.

He kissed the back of my neck slowly and ran his hand from my thigh over my hip to my waist to my back and my shoulder and my face and I turned my head to look at him again, and he kissed me.

'You could come and visit me,' I said, hopefully, but even before I'd finished the sentence he was shaking his head.

'That's exactly what I meant when I said it was a bad idea,' he said.

'But why, Dylan?' I said, my voice hoarse.

'Because of the package,' he said.

'So give it to someone else!'

He pushed me away and sat on the edge of the bed. 'I'm just trying to keep you safe,' he said.

'Safe from what?' I asked.

He didn't answer.

'You're getting me involved in your dodgy deal, whatever it is, asking me to hide stuff for you. How's that going to keep me safe?'

'It's not what you think,' he said.

'You're ripping off Fitz? Is that what this is about?'

He stood up and started to find his clothes where they were scattered and I wished I'd kept my big mouth shut so I could hold on to him for a few moments longer. The pain I'd felt last night at the thought of leaving him was back, but it was worse now, much worse, because of what we'd done. He was probably right. It had been a bad idea. I could feel the anger coming off him like a scent, fizzing like an electric charge.

I tried again. 'I'll be safe wherever you are,' I said.

'No, you won't.'

'I don't understand,' I said miserably, sitting up in bed.

He already had his trousers on. 'Exactly,' he said. 'You don't understand. You don't understand any of it. Remember when you let that bloke touch you while you were dancing, at Fitz's house, and I was pissed off with you afterwards? You didn't understand about that, either, did you?'

He was looking at me with so much hurt in his eyes, as though I was wounding him still, just by sitting there, just by existing.

'You made me watch,' he said. 'You said you'd do it on condition that I was there. You made me stand there and watch you.'

I think my mouth dropped open with surprise. 'I did that because I thought you were my friend,' I said. 'I thought you'd look out for me.'

'I had to stand there and watch him with his fingers inside you,' he said.

'You were looking at me as if I was a piece of furniture.'

'I had no choice. If Fitz had had any idea how I felt about you he would have had my bollocks for it.'

'He said you liked me, so it seems he knew anyway.'

'Yes,' he said. 'And now look at us. Fitz doesn't trust me any more, Genevieve, because he knows how I feel about you. It makes me a liability as far as he's concerned, especially now you've left. He's going to be watching me like a hawk. And I need him to trust me.'

'You never told me how you felt. How was I supposed to know?'

'I need to work at sorting things out with Fitz,' he said, 'and you need to forget this happened, right?'

'Dylan!'

He was tying his shoelaces, his boots resting on the edge of the bed. Ten minutes ago we had been lying here naked, locked together as if we would never be able to be apart. How could we go from such bliss to conflict in such a short space of time?

When he was dressed I thought he was just going to go, to walk out without so much as casting a glance back at me, but he came back to the bed and took me in his arms and held me against him fiercely. I was crying by then. I tried to touch him, to kiss him, but he was holding me too tightly to move.

'Keep yourself safe,' he said. 'Be careful who you trust. Right?'

I nodded, sniffing, my face buried in his shirt.

'It might be okay. In a few months, if it works out. If you can wait that long. Alright?'

'I can wait,' I said.

He pulled back and wiped my tears away with his thumb. 'Just keep safe,' he said. 'Hide that package somewhere. Be safe. And I'll come and find you.'

Then he left me. He grabbed his jacket and he was gone.

Later, when I had showered again and dressed, I looked in the bag and saw what it contained. A rectangular parcel, wrapped in a heavy-duty grey plastic bag and bound tightly and neatly with black gaffer tape. A small black mobile phone, new, and a charger. And two thick bundles of fifty pound notes. I'd never seen so much cash in my life, but even so I stared at it with no emotion.

In the space of a few hours he'd gone from being a mate, a friend, someone I was doing a favour for, to breaking my heart by leaving me behind.

# Thirty-two

I had almost got as far as the town centre when the rain started – big, heavy drops that threatened to soak me. I made a dash across the pedestrian crossing near the bus station and nearly ran into the back of a silver car that had stopped right in front of me. I went to pass it and the driver's window slid down.

'Genevieve!'

It was Jim. He looked as though he'd had a busy day already: tired eyes, sleeves folded back to his forearms, tie loosened.

'What are you doing here?'

'Thought you might need a lift.'

'No, thanks.'

I stood in the rain, staring at him. A car behind him tooted, making me jump.

I got in the car. It was warm, and almost as soon as I was inside the car started to mist up. He switched on the fan heater. I was already starting to shiver, my hair dripping. I wasn't angry at him, not really. He had a job to do the same as everyone else. I'd forgotten that police were never off duty and so nothing you told them that was of any interest or relevance would ever be classed as private.

We sat in the car staring at the stationary traffic waiting to go through the one-way system, the windscreen wipers scraping noisily back and forth across the rain-spattered screen. The multi-storey car park looked as if it was sagging under the weight of its own ugliness. I bit my lip, my shoulders rigid, resolutely looking out of the window at the rain.

'Everything alright?'

I didn't answer. What possible answer was there?

'Genevieve,' he said, 'I had to tell them. You know that.'

'Did you tell them you slept with me?' I said with venom. 'No, I didn't think so. Funny the bit you left out.'

I glanced across at him. His cheeks were pink. 'There are good reasons why I can't tell them that. Reasons that have nothing to do with you.'

'What the fuck's that supposed to mean?'

There was an awkward silence, broken only by the noise of the rain, the wipers squealing across the windscreen.

'Did they tell you what I said to them?' I asked, at last.

Carling shook his head. 'It's their investigation now. Nothing to do with me.'

'Why?'

'Caddy Smith was from London, so she's their victim. It's complicated. You're the only thing linking her to Kent, so they've come down here to tick you off their list.'

'Oh. You know, I thought they were going to arrest me.'

'They probably would have done, a couple of days ago. But they've got two people in custody, and they've just charged them, which makes things a bit different. It's about evidence-gathering now.'

'They've got people in custody?' I asked. 'Who?'

He shrugged, as if to say he didn't know, but what he meant was, he couldn't tell me. For a horrible moment I wondered if they'd arrested Dylan. Maybe that was why he wasn't answering his phone – maybe he was in some grotty London police station, locked in a cell.

'So what did you say to them?' he asked.

'They wanted to know how I knew her. I told them I met her when I was living in London. I worked at weekends at a club – the Barclay. Caddy worked there too. That's about it.'

'I know the Barclay.'

'Do you?'

'Were you a dancer?'

I looked at him sharply but his eyes were on the road. 'Have you ever been there?' I asked. 'To the Barclay, I mean.'

He shook his head. 'No, some of my mates went for a stag do and I heard all about it. I couldn't afford it, at the time. Bastards went without me.'

I hesitated and then said, 'Yes, I was a dancer. That's how I managed to buy the boat.'

'You have a dancer's body,' he said.

'I haven't done it for a long time,' I said.

The line of traffic was creeping forward, metre by metre.

'Look, I can walk if it's easier,' I said. 'We might be stuck here for ages.'

'Chatham town centre,' he said. 'It's pretty much guaranteed we'll be stuck here for ages. It's not even as if there's any real traffic, it's just the bloody lights slowing us down. There must be ten sets of lights along this one stupid stretch of road, all timed wrong so it just brings everything to a standstill. I mean, what sort of arses think that changing a town designed entirely around a one-way traffic system into a two-way system is a good idea?'

I thought for a moment that he'd finished and I nodded in agreement, but he was only pausing to get his breath.

'You hope that when the government starts cutting costs the people making these sorts of stupid decisions will be the ones to go, but no, there's always enough money to keep a bunch of retarded planners employed so that they can deploy their million traffic cones for a short stretch of roadworks... And even if they do ever finish it, it's still Chatham so no bugger is going to want to come here anyway, not unless they live somewhere with a severe shortage of pound shops.'

'Finished?'

'Sorry,' he said. 'I was coming this way anyway, to be honest, despite the bloody roadworks. And besides, I wanted to see you again.'

I took a deep breath. 'I do like you, Jim. But it's no good us pretending that this is going to work.'

'Whoa,' he said, at the sudden change of tone.

'You can't get involved with me when they still aren't sure if I'm a suspect or not.'

'I'm aware of that.'

'And afterwards, well…'

'Well?'

'By then you might have met a nice girl, or changed your mind about me, or… well, anything could happen. I'm just saying.'

'You've got someone else,' he said. As though there could be no other possible explanation for my rejection of him.

'No. I just – there was someone, but I haven't seen him for months, since I moved here. I don't even know if he still thinks about me.'

'What's his name?'

I pretended I hadn't heard his question, looking out of the window at the dirty, rainy streets. I couldn't believe it was so dark in the middle of the afternoon. The pavements were full of Saturday shoppers, umbrellas, grey coats and soaking trackie bottoms clinging to wet legs.

'What was she like?' Carling asked.

'Who?'

'Caddy.'

I didn't answer at first, wondering how I could do her justice in just a few words. I thought back to some of the good nights we'd had, dancing and working, yes, but having as much fun as if we were on a girls' night out at the same time. I pictured her laughing, doubled over, because one of the Russian girls was trying to chat up some lad from Streatham who thought she was from Scotland. Patting tears out of the corners of her eyes and flapping her hand in front of her face to give herself some air.

'She was beautiful, clever, funny… And she was kind to me. Despite everything. She was kind.'

'Despite everything?'

'She thought…' I said, and stopped short.

'She thought what?'

He was sitting there looking casual, looking as though he didn't care very much what I was about to say, but I could tell he was paying attention to every single word.

'Is this an interview?' I asked.

'No, of course not.' His response was quick. 'You don't have to answer. I was just interested in her.'

'She thought I was trying to steal her boyfriend,' I said at last, watching Carling's face for his reaction.

He looked back at me, his expression hard to read.

'And were you?'

Two weeks after I'd moved on to the *Revenge*, I went back to London.

Caddy lived in a flat in Walworth, not all that far from my old place in Clapham. I found it easily enough, taking my time about it, not even sure if being here was the right thing to do. It was Sunday afternoon. There was no telling if she'd be awake, but it was a reasonably civilised hour to call, even for a nocturnal person like Caddy.

To my surprise she answered the door quickly. She was dressed in jeans and a grey fitted T-shirt that showed off her chest and narrow waist.

'Oh,' she said.

She looked completely different with her hair loose, wavy down her back, no make-up. She looked young. I realised I'd never actually asked her how old she was, just assumed she was about my age, but, looking at her in the bright light of an April Sunday, she looked almost like a teenager.

I thought for a moment she was going to shut the door in my face, but curiosity seemed to get the better of her and she stood aside to let me in.

Her flat was spotlessly clean and I must have interrupted the process of making it cleaner: a mop and bucket were in the kitchenette and the tiled floor was wet. The wide, bright main room smelled faintly of bleach. Patio doors were open on to a small balcony. From below, faint noise of traffic from the South Circular.

'You want a drink or something?'

'That would be nice, thanks. Water'll do.'

I perched on the edge of a white corner sofa looking at the feature wallpaper, a dramatic black and white design. It was starting to make me feel dizzy.

'Fitz was mad that you left,' she said, handing me a glass of water with two chunks of ice clinking in it.

'He didn't seem that bothered when I told him.'

She sat opposite me, her legs crossed, her bare brown foot flexing and circling. 'So what happened? Why did you just take off like that?'

'I'd just – had enough, I guess. I bought a boat.'

She laughed. 'What – like a yacht?'

'No. It's a barge. I'm going to live on it.'

She was looking at me, mystified, shaking her head slowly. 'You always were a bunch of surprises.'

'So were you. I just wanted to come and say sorry if things were bad between us. You were my best buddy. I don't want to lose touch with you.' There. I'd said it. I'd apologised for whatever it was she thought I'd done.

She pulled her feet up on to the chair so that she was cross-legged, biting at her lower lip. 'I don't know,' she said. 'This is all weird.'

'Weird how?'

'You leaving. Did you hear about the raid?'

'The what?'

'Last Friday. The club got raided, loads of police all over the place. Fucking nightmare, it was. We didn't get to leave until gone ten in the morning. I was knackered.'

'Shit! Did they find anything? What happened?'

'I don't know. Nobody tells me shit any more. The club was closed Saturday night – we all got the night off and a pathetic handout from Norland to compensate us. Then business as usual on Sunday.'

All I could think about was Dylan. He hadn't called me, even though I'd almost expected him to. I'd kept his phone with me all the time, kept it charged up, waiting for it to ring. No wonder he hadn't called. If there had been a raid at the club, he would have been preoccupied to say the least.

'You know Fitz was having a joke about it: how you left and the next minute the club got raided. He thought it was you.'

She laughed as she said it, but even so my whole body felt suddenly cold. 'He's always suspicious about something,' I said.

'Yeah.'

'You love him,' I said, trying for a subtle change of subject.

'Yeah, well, I do make that a bit obvious sometimes. Stupid.'

'He doesn't know what he's doing,' I said. 'You deserve so much better than that.'

'Unrequited love,' she said. 'It sucks.'

I drank the last of my water and thought about leaving. I'd come here to sort things out with her, to make sure she was alright, and I'd achieved that. It would be good to keep in touch with her.

'Bit like poor Dylan,' she said.

'What?'

'Well. Me and Fitz, you and Dylan. Don't tell me you didn't know he likes you.'

I couldn't answer that one.

'He's very careful, Dylan is, about not giving anything away. But you could tell by the way he looked out for you. And by the way he watched you when you weren't looking.'

'Really?'

'Absolutely. And he's been fucking miserable since you left.'

'Poor Dylan,' I said. 'He needs someone to look after him.'

We both laughed – the thought of Dylan needing to be taken care of was ludicrous.

Then she said, 'I think about leaving sometimes. I thought about it when I heard you'd gone, in fact. Trouble is, girls leave but they always end up coming back. You get used to the money, you know?'

'I've been saving up,' I said.

'Yeah. That's why you were always borrowing my stuff, huh?'

I got up, taking my glass through to her kitchenette.

'You can come and visit me,' I said. 'When I've got the boat straightened out. Come and stay.'

'Sure,' she said. 'I'd like to.'

'I'll have a boatwarming party,' I said. 'I'll give you a ring.'

She took me to the door of the flat and gave me a hug. Without her heels on she was tiny. For a moment I wanted to ask her how old she was, but it felt rude.

'I'm glad you came round,' she said.

'I want to tell you to keep yourself safe,' I said. For some reason I felt tears start.

'I can look after myself,' she said.

'I know. But they're – you know. They're doing all sorts on the side. The place got raided, Caddy. The police must realise what's going on. It's only a matter of time before Fitz gets caught doing some deal or other.'

'You think I don't know that? I just do what you did – keep my nose out of it. It's the only way.'

Once we'd got on to New Road, the traffic started to ease off. It slowed again for all the traffic lights in Corporation Street, at the back of Rochester High Street, and finally we turned left on to the Esplanade before the bridge. Jim had gone very quiet. Eventually, he pulled in to the car park and sat waiting for me to get out.

I was staring at the wipers, wondering what to say.

'Thanks for the lift, it was very kind of you.'

'No problem.'

'You want to come in for a coffee or something?'

He hesitated, clearly debating with himself, and then, 'I don't think it would be a good idea.'

I gave him a half-smile, but he wasn't looking at me. I got out of the car and shut the door, ran down towards the pontoon, splashing through the puddles, expecting the car to roar off up the hill to the main road, but it didn't. When I got to the boat and looked back, he'd parked the car properly and was following me, hands shoved in the pockets of his trousers, head down.

'Changed my mind,' he said gruffly, when he'd caught up.

The boat was freezing cold. I busied myself with the woodburner while he brewed coffee. I glanced around the cabin when I thought he wasn't watching. The boat looked the same as it always had – untidy, cobwebby in places, but not as though it had been searched.

The fire crackled and spat, the flames brightening the room. I shut the glass door and watched the fire for a moment.

'You should think about putting central heating in,' said Carling.

'I know,' I said. 'It didn't seem that important in the summer. It's daft really: the weather's turning, I should be sorting out the bathroom but the next thing that's going to get done is the conservatory.'

'I'll help you with the bathroom, if you like.'

I smiled. 'Thanks. That's a kind offer.'

He put two mugs of coffee on the table and sat down with a sigh.

'I'm just going to get changed,' I said. My jeans were soaked.

I left him in the saloon and padded down to the bedroom. Waited for a second, then carried on to the hatch – just to see the box, if nothing else... I just needed to look. I could check properly later.

The space was cavernous and dark. I opened the door enough and stood away a little to let the light shine in. I could see the shape of the box at the end. Had it moved? Was it more visible than it had been? I'd thought the other boxes had been grouped around it, hiding it, but from here I could just about make out the words written on the side…

'Everything okay?'

'Yes, yes, fine,' I said quickly, shutting the hatch door with a bang. 'I was just – um – looking for something.'

My cheeks flushed. I must have looked about as guilty as it was possible to be.

He gazed at me steadily, then a quick but deliberate up and down my body, taking in my wet socks and my wet jeans and my wet top, then he said, 'Your coffee's getting cold,' and turned to go back to the saloon.

I went into the bedroom with my heart thumping in my chest. I would have to be careful. I'd almost given it away just then – so stupid. He wasn't daft, he must know there was so much I hadn't told him. And Dylan, too – I'd almost told him about Dylan…

I wrestled my sodden jeans down my legs, then got my socked foot caught on the hem of the other leg of the jeans and before I knew what had happened I'd slipped and landed with a crash and a yelp against the chest of drawers.

Jim was in the doorway within a second; he stood there looking at me for a moment, in a heap with my jeans bunched up around my knees, and then he laughed.

'It's not funny, you piece of shit!'

He crouched down next to me. 'Yes, it is,' he said, still laughing.

I couldn't help laughing too, even though my back hurt from landing against the drawers. He offered me his hand and hauled me to my feet. 'Come and sit down, I'll give you a hand.'

He helped me shuffle over to the bed and while I sat on the edge he pulled my jeans down. They were so wet, the denim was heavy and glued to my skin. He tugged and heaved and I held on to the edge of the bed, but not tightly enough because the next thing I knew he'd pulled me right off the bed and I landed with a thump with my backside on the floor.

I was laughing and crying at the same time, and he could hardly move, his shoulders shaking. 'Oh, God… I'm sorry… are you alright?'

I nodded and shook my head, and then before I could say anything he was kissing me, hard, catching his breath, pulling me against him.

'You are so sexy,' he said quickly, 'so sexy. You don't even know what you do to me…'

I was lying on my back, looking at the dark night sky through the skylight over my head, and feeling the *Revenge of the Tide* moving gently as the water rose up the estuary from the sea and lifted the boat from its muddy cradle.

Jim had woken me, climbing out of bed. I watched him turn left out of the door, heading for the bathroom, and turned over in bed, pulling the covers up.

I dozed for a while, and when I opened my eyes again he had not come back. I wondered if he'd gone home, then I caught the sound of his voice – where? On deck?

The skylight was grey now, light enough in the room to see Jim's T-shirt and sweater on the chair, his jeans missing. I sat up in bed and strained to hear. Silence. And then – a few words. A laugh?

Just as I was considering getting up and going to see if I could hear any better from the doorway, I heard his footsteps in the cabin and I lay back down again quickly, covers up. I listened to the sounds of him taking off his jeans, the chink of the belt buckle as he folded them and put them back on the chair. Then the creak of the bed as he lifted the covers and got back in beside me. His cold hand slid over my stomach. 'I know you're not asleep,' he said softly. 'I can tell.'

'How can you tell?' I murmured, still half pretending.

'From how you breathe.' He was kissing my neck, my throat, my shoulder, pulling me round towards him.

'Who were you talking to?' I asked, my voice muffled against his skin.

'Work.'

'Mm. What do they want at this time of the morning? Your hands are cold.'

He didn't answer my question. I sat astride him, reached up to the wood cladding over my head, put both my hands flat against the ceiling to give me balance, and he cupped my breasts with his hands and watched me move, and let out a sound that might have been a word, or might just have been a groan.

# *Thirty-three*

The sunlight streaming through the skylight on to my face woke me up. The bed was empty. I squinted across to the chair. Jim's clothes had gone.

I lay still for a few moments, enjoying the warmth of the sun, remembering what we'd done the night before. He was good at it. He was getting better and better, in fact.

I heard noises coming from the galley – washing-up noises. Then the radio went on, the sound down low. Just enough for me to hear the music.

I got up and found some clothes, ran a hand through my hair to flatten the bits that were sticking up.

When he saw me he put the kettle back on the stove. 'Morning,' he said.

'Good morning to you too.' I leaned over him and kissed his jawline. He smelled of warmth and yesterday's aftershave.

I took a tea towel from the railing on the door of the stove and dried the cups he'd washed up, putting them away in the cupboard. I felt all domesticated and homely, the sunshine streaming in through the skylights, creating shafts of light and warmth. I loved my boat. Even the wooden boards under my bare feet were warm.

He poured me out a coffee and put the mug on the table.

'I could do with a shower,' he said.

'You could go and have one over by the office.'

'By the office?'

'There's a shower room. It's quite nice, and clean. Better than my hose, anyway.'

'I should really go home. I need clean clothes, and I'm back at work this afternoon.'

'Oh. Alright.'

He was staring at me, his dark eyes unfathomable.

'What?' I said, thinking I might have said or done something wrong.

'I don't want to go.'

I smiled, kissed him again. He had two days' worth of beard, his chin scratchy. 'I don't want you to go, either.'

'How about,' he said into my throat, his hands up under my top, 'I go and have a quick shower now, and later I can just dash home and get changed on the way to work?'

I made a noise that might have been assent; it was enough to satisfy him. When he let me go I went to find him a clean towel, some shower gel. He took it and climbed the steps to the wheelhouse.

'Want me to come with you?' I asked.

'Not unless you're going to shower with me,' he said.

I let him go.

I went back to the bedroom and made the bed, shaking the tangled duvet over the creased bottom sheet. I opened the skylight to let in some fresh air. I was cleaning my teeth a few moments later when I heard it – a buzzing noise. Toothbrush sticking out of the corner of my mouth, I went into the main cabin. It was louder in here.

On the seat of the dinette, a mobile phone on vibrate was buzzing and flashing. I picked it up and my first instinct was to answer it, but it wasn't my phone. It was Jim's.

I stared at the phone in my hand, at the number that was illuminated on the display. Caller ID was listed simply as 'd'. On the table was a pile of papers, envelopes, receipts. I grabbed a pen from a broken-handled mug on the shelf in the galley and wrote down the number on the back of my credit card bill just as the phone stopped vibrating.

*One missed call.*

I put the phone on the seat, chewing my toothbrush thoughtfully. I went back to my poor excuse for a bathroom and rinsed my mouth. In the mirror above the sink I caught the look in my eyes. My heart was pounding.

I found yesterday's jeans in the bedroom and, in the back pocket, Dylan's phone. I scrolled through to the address book. Looked at the number for GARLAND. And then at the number written on the back of the credit card envelope.

I jumped up the steps to the wheelhouse and peered across the boats towards the office. No sign of anyone. The marina was deserted, the boats bathed in bright sunshine. I couldn't see the door to the shower room from here, but there was no sign of Jim.

Back in the cabin, I picked up Jim's phone, activated the screen. He didn't have a password.

*One missed call.*

I worked my way through unfamiliar menus – call history? That was it – and there it was... missed calls. And the last number, the one I recognised.

I selected the icon that looked like a handset and within a few moments I heard a ringing tone as the call connected.

And then –

'Yeah?'

I stood there immobile, the phone pressed to my ear. Just that one word – could I be certain?

'Dylan?'

'Who is this?'

It was him; all my doubts vanished with those three words. 'It's me.'

There was silence on the other end. I half-expected him to ask, *Who?* but he didn't. He knew my voice as well as I knew his.

'Where's Jim?' he asked.

'Hang on – how the hell do you know Jim? And why is your phone switched off all the time? And where the hell are you? And what am I supposed to do with this… this parcel you left here?'

I heard him sigh, above the noise of the wind blowing across the phone.

'You're supposed to trust me,' he said.

'How can I trust you when you never answer your bloody phone? Some men came on to the boat. They tied me up.'

There was a pause before he answered. He probably already knew, after all. He spent enough time with Nicks and the others; he knew everything that was going on in Fitz's world. Still, he played dumb.

'What do you mean, they tied you up? Are you alright?'

'I am now. But I'm afraid, Dylan! What am I supposed to do? What do you want me to do?'

'Is Jim there?' he asked then.

'No, he isn't!'

'Get him to ring me when he gets back,' he said.

'Dylan! What's going on?'

But he had disconnected the call.

There was something – a noise – some small sound behind me. Jim was standing at the foot of the steps, hair damp, towel in one hand and his shoes in the other. He was looking at me with an expression that might have been reproach.

'What the fuck's going on?' I demanded.

'Is that my phone?'

He took a step forward, took it from my hand, fiddled with the buttons. I thought he was going to say something, shout back at me, but instead he held the phone up to his ear.

'Yeah, it's me,' he said, as the call connected. 'I know. Where are you? … Yes, you know you can…'

He looked up at me then. I could hear Dylan's voice through the phone, but couldn't make out the words.

'She's alright. No, of course not. It's what we said, yeah? When? … Alright. I'll sort something out. Okay, mate. Bye for now.' All through this he didn't take his eyes off me. All my righteous anger at having been somehow set up, made a fool of, was dissolving into feelings of unqualified guilt at picking up his phone in the first place. And what made it all worse was that he was standing in my cabin, his jeans unbuttoned, his hair wet.

'Genevieve – ' he said.

'No,' I said. 'This is all wrong. Why…?'

He shook his head.

'You're using me,' I said.

'No.'

'You're using me to get to Dylan.'

'How? Don't be ridiculous. Who did he phone just now, you or me?'

That hurt, more than if he'd slapped me across the face. 'You shit. You complete bastard.' Tears stung my eyes, my hands balling into fists.

'Genevieve. I didn't mean it like that…'

'Why does nobody ever tell me the truth about what's going on?'

I couldn't stand to look at him any more. I went back to the bedroom, pushed the door shut behind me. But he caught it, caught me by one arm, pulled me round to him.

'Don't walk away,' he said.

His face was close to mine. I could feel his breath on my cheek.

I struggled against him, but he held me tighter, bruising my arm. 'Let me go!'

He released his grip. And I stood there like an idiot, looking up at his impassive face, tears of fury and misery pouring down my hot cheeks. 'You didn't tell me you knew Dylan,' I said, sobs catching every other word.

'Neither did you.' He was so calm, so infuriating, I wanted to smack him.

'You knew about me and Dylan. You knew all along…'

'I didn't know how you felt about him.'

'Did he tell you about me?'

He nodded.

'What did he say?'

'He asked me to look after you.'

'What?' I said. I was so angry I could barely get the words out. 'When?'

'He rang me when he heard about Caddy's body being found here. He asked me to keep an eye out for you, because he knew – I mean, he thought that things might get difficult for you. After that he turned his phone off and went out of contact.'

'Why?'

He looked at me for a moment, as if debating how much of this he was prepared to share with me. 'He's done this before. When things get a bit tricky, he switches his phone off. He's a pain in the backside sometimes, you know that, don't you?'

'So you came here and thought it would be a good idea to fuck me, yeah? Is that what you thought he meant by looking after me? Give me something to take my mind off him?'

'It wasn't like that.'

'Why are you here? What do you want from me?'

He looked at me and didn't reply at first, then he ran a hand through his hair and turned away from me, took a few paces. Then he seemed to find the most appropriate answer.

'I was looking for Dylan. When he turned his phone off after he told me about Caddy, I thought he might have still been in touch with you.'

'I don't understand. He just rang your phone, didn't he?'

'He's only rung me twice since that day. Both times, he was in a public place, somewhere busy, impossible to get a trace on him. The rest of the time his phone's off.'

'Well, I think that means he doesn't want to talk to you, doesn't it?'

'Or you, it seems,' he said.

I bit my lip and glared at him.

'Genevieve…' He touched my bare arm, running his hand up under the sleeve of my T-shirt to my shoulder.

'Don't touch me,' I said, pulling away.

'Look,' he said, 'he always thinks he knows what he's doing, right? He does things his way. Much as I try to help him out, try to get him to play by the rules, he's always done it like this. Despite that, I trust him, and you should too.'

He took a step towards me again. I wanted to move away but I couldn't. There was something different in his eyes now. I wanted to believe every word, but it was so hard.

'You should have told me all this before,' I said, trying not to sound imploring. I wanted to sound cold, pissed off, mad at him. But instead, through sniffs and tears, it sounded weak.

'I didn't think this was going to happen.'

'What?'

'You know what I'm talking about; don't play games.'

I raised an eyebrow at him. 'You still should have told me that you knew Dylan.'

'I don't have to tell you about anything, much less something related to an investigation.'

'Oh, fuck off! You're investigating Dylan? Think it's a good idea to be fucking me, then, do you?'

'Of course it's not a good idea!'

'So – what? You were just going to wait for Dylan to show up, and then piss off and leave me behind?'

'I hadn't thought that far ahead.'

I grabbed my jeans from the chair and pulled them on roughly. They were still damp but I didn't care.

'Where are you going?' he asked.

'Just – just leave me alone.'

He caught up with me just as I was about to go up the steps to the wheelhouse. Both arms around my waist. He pulled me back, pulled me tight against him, and as I struggled he held me tighter.

'Genevieve,' he said, his voice just a whisper against the back of my neck. 'Don't.'

I felt myself melting, softening against him. He held me. And I turned in the circle of his arms and put my arms around his neck and rested my face into his chest, breathing him in.

He pulled my T-shirt out where it had been tucked into my jeans and pressed his hands into the small of my back. Without thinking about what I was doing, I slid my hands under the waistband of his jeans, pulling him closer. His mouth was an inch away from mine, his warm breath on me. I could have moved a fraction towards him and our mouths would have met. But I wasn't about to give in. He leaned towards me. I moved back – just slightly. He hesitated, his breath quickening. I could feel him, hard against my body. Inside his jeans, my hand squeezed his backside, my nails digging in. Then he moved one of his hands from my back to my neck, holding my head so I couldn't pull away.

He pushed me back, stumbling, against the steps. My hand felt for a step I could perch on as he pulled my jeans down, then his. When he pushed inside me I gasped, my head back against the top step. For a second the thrill of it held me steady, but there was something wrong with this position, frustrating – I kept slipping down. I pushed him, and when he didn't respond immediately I pushed him harder, pushed him away so I could turn around, kick my jeans off and kneel on the third step, presenting him with my rear view at exactly the right height. He didn't pause but slid inside me, gentler this time, but for just a second. And then it was hard and fast and powerful, pushing me against the steps with his whole body. It didn't take very long. When he came inside me he let out a sound against the back of my neck, through gritted teeth.

For a moment neither of us moved. Nothing but the sound of his breathing against my hair, the pounding of my blood through my ears.

He slid away from me. I turned awkwardly on the stairs, my knee aching from where it had been scraped against the cladding by the force of him driving into me. He pulled his jeans back up.

He held out his hand to me. 'Come with me.'

I took his hand and he led me back to bed, took his clothes off again and climbed in beside me, pulling me close. For a long time we kissed and didn't speak. Eventually his hand between my thighs made me forget everything: the anger, the million questions buzzing around my head, the sound of Dylan's voice on the other end of Jim's phone.

Over our heads the skylight showed clouds across the deep blue of the sky; white clouds, then grey... darkening to an ominous black, threatening rain.

Jim was holding my hand against his chest. I thought he might be falling asleep. I thought about getting up, getting dressed.

'You're still angry,' he said. He was stroking his thumb against the back of my hand. 'I can tell. You're so tense.'

'I feel like everyone's been using me,' I said.

'I prefer to think that we're just helping each other out.'

I moved, sat up in bed, hugged my knees. I wanted to be able to see his face. 'Why did Dylan ring you to tell you about Caddy? I don't understand. Didn't you know already?'

He took a deep breath, ran his hand over his forehead. 'I'm not – well – I'm not part of the investigation team.'

'So who are you, then? You mean you're not police?'

'I am a police officer. I just work on different things, and I'm Met Police, not Kent.'

This didn't make sense. 'How come you're allowed to turn up and interfere with an investigation you're not a part of? Don't you have to do what you're told?'

He smiled. 'I'm not, strictly speaking, interfering. And if you're going to get pedantic, I'm not actually on duty at the moment.'

'Does Dylan have something to do with Caddy's death? Is that why he's not answering his phone?'

He didn't answer.

'He wouldn't do that,' I said. 'He wouldn't have hurt Caddy.'

There was something in his expression, something that he tried to hide.

'You think he killed her?' I said.

'I don't think he killed her,' he replied. 'But I don't know why he's been out of contact for so long. Do you know?'

I shrank back a little, unprepared for the focus to be turned in my direction. 'I have no idea.'

'You knew Dylan from the Barclay,' he said. 'You must have some feeling about what he was like.'

'Dylan was different: he wasn't like the others. He was kind. Well, he was kind to me, anyway.'

Jim grinned. 'I've never heard him described quite like that.'

'Well, maybe you don't know him as well as you think you do.'

He must have noticed the edge in my voice because he sat up, then. He didn't pull the duvet up around himself and he was sitting there, on my bed, arrogant in his nakedness, totally at ease with his body.

'I don't want to fight with you any more,' he said.

'We shouldn't talk about it, then.'

'I'm just trying to keep you safe, Genevieve.'

'Bollocks you are. You're trying to find Dylan. And I don't need anyone to keep me safe, thank you very much.'

He laughed at that, and it stung.

'Another thing that's been bothering me. How do you know Dylan? I mean – he doesn't exactly move in police circles, does he?'

He got out of bed, abruptly, and pulled his clothes on. I watched him, wondering if I'd managed to hit a nerve. He didn't answer straight away, which made me think he'd lied to me and he wasn't friends with Dylan after all. What if he was trying to find him because he was going to arrest him? What if that was why Dylan was keeping away from me? Was Jim using me as bait?

'We were at school together,' he said. 'We've gone our separate ways over the years, but we're still mates.'

'Where?' I said, trying to catch him out. Not that I knew the answer. 'Where were you at school?'

'Don't, Genevieve,' he answered. 'You're just going to have to trust me.'

'Why should I trust you, when you kept something that important from me?'

He looked me straight in the eye. 'You're still keeping important things from me,' he said, 'and I trust you.'

I stared at him, furious.

'I'd better go,' he said, pulling his socks on.

I didn't answer.

'You know what your trouble is?' he said, looking back over his shoulder at me briefly and then turning back to pull on his other sock.

He was clearly going to tell me anyway, so I didn't see the need to respond to this question either.

'You don't have a clue what you're mixed up in. You're flitting around the edge of this – mess – not knowing just how fucking dangerous it is. You think you can take care of yourself, but actually, you have no idea. No fucking idea.'

I glared at him. He was right: I had no fucking idea – but that was because nobody ever fucking told me anything. A few moments later he was putting his shoes on in the galley, and after that there was a bang as he pulled the door of the wheelhouse shut behind him.

# Thirty-four

It would have been easy just to go to bed, to hide under the covers and cry, for what was left of the day if I needed to. But instead I went and had a shower, got dressed, went to the woodburner and tried to get a fire going. It gave me something to concentrate on, with my shaking hands, trying to get the fire started and then sitting in front of the open door, watching it in case it died down again, feeding it until it grew strong enough for me to build the wood around it. And then I shut the door to the stove and sat looking at the flames and the logs starting to glow.

I was still sitting there an hour later when I heard a noise outside, and a few moments later a knock at the door of the wheelhouse.

It was Malcolm, complete with an ancient box of tools. I looked at it doubtfully.

'I thought I'd take a look at your generator,' he said.

'I've got tools,' I said indignantly.

'Yeah. So – er – what happened to your new fella? Saw him earlier, didn't look too happy.'

'Oh, he's fine. He had to go to work.'

Malcolm gave me a look that said he didn't believe me. He lifted the hatch in the wheelhouse that gave access to the engine and peered down into the engine space.

'The batteries should be all charged up,' he said. 'Then once I reconnect them you can transfer over – here – like this…'

I looked and tried to pay attention while he showed me a series of buttons and switches.

'The generator will run off your fuel supply so that'll go down quicker than normal. But you won't need to use it all the time, like, during the day and stuff. You've still got gas bottles for the stove, haven't you?'

I nodded. 'And I've got the woodburner.'

'Exactly. Electricity is overrated,' he said with a smile.

He went back to tinkering with the generator, connecting wires and tubes and bashing things. I clambered over him and went down into the cabin.

'I need to turn the power off,' Malcolm shouted down the steps.

'Alright,' I called back.

The saloon was nice and warm now from the woodburner. I sat in front of it, hugging my knees, trying not to think about Dylan and Jim and thinking about nothing else. I'd thought about Dylan every day since that last time, but not like this. I wanted him to come back for me. I wanted him to be here, with me. I wanted it so badly it was like an ache, like a void inside me.

And Jim – what was I supposed to do about Jim? The thought of him made me shiver. There was something irresistible about him, some force that made me lose my senses and want him, no matter what he said or did. And he was maddening at the same time.

I would ring him tomorrow, once I'd had a chance to catch up on some sleep and get my head straightened out.

'Genevieve!' Malcolm shouted from the deck.

'What?'

'It's all connected.' He came down into the cabin.

I didn't turn around. It must have looked a bit odd, me sitting there on the floor facing the stove.

'You alright?' he said.

I didn't answer and he came to sit on the sofa. 'Gen? What's the matter?'

'It's been a tough day,' I said.

'What happened? Is it that policeman? He been bothering you?'

'No. He's been fine, Malcolm, honest.'

'Maybe you should go and stay with him for a bit, then, till it all quietens down again.'

'I'm not leaving the boat.'

'No one else been around – you know, like before?'

'No.'

'I've not seen anybody,' he said, quickly.

I looked at him then, turned my head slowly. He was sitting on the edge of my sofa, hands hanging between his knees. He looked wired. His left knee was jiggling up and down.

'Malcolm?'

'What?'

'What's happened?'

'Nothing, nothing.' He looked almost afraid, just for a moment.

'Hey,' I said.

He looked back at me. There was something in his expression; I should have been able to tell what it was. But I was too tired and too numb to think hard enough about it.

'I just wanted to say thanks, for helping with everything.'

'Okay,' he said.

We stood awkwardly in the cabin, Malcolm shifting his weight from one leg to the other. 'You know I used to live in London,' he said at last.

'I didn't know that,' I said.

'Before I met Josie. I lived all over, but for a while I lived in Leytonstone. In a squat. Well, digs. I guess it was a kind of a squat, anyway, since we didn't pay anyone any rent. But still.'

'What were you doing in London?' I asked, wondering where this was going.

'Oh, this and that, you know – a bit of construction work, a bit of plastering sometimes when someone would take me on. Just earning enough for beer really. It was alright.'

He looked at me sideways.

'What is it, Malcolm? What are you getting at?'

'Well, I knew of this Fitz. The one who was your boss at that club.'

'You knew Fitz?'

'I never said that. I said I knew *of* him. Some blokes I knew from the pub, they was talking about stuff one night, where to score drugs mostly, and they was complaining about the quality of the gear on the streets at the moment, and they said it was because Fitz had moved on to something else.'

'Something else?'

'Like he wasn't supplying any more. Or he'd moved on to supplying different gear.'

'Oh,' I said, sitting back. 'Doesn't mean it was the same Fitz, though.'

'He used to hang around with this guy, Ian Gray. He was a hard bloke, like his protection, you know, his muscle.'

'Gray?'

'Big bloke, tattoo on his neck. He was missing half his earlobe.'

That was Gray, alright. No wonder Malcolm had been so interested in hearing about life at the Barclay.

'I should have said something earlier,' he said.

'Yes, you should,' I said.

'I was thinking – you know – I might be able to call a few people, find out who it is who's putting the pressure on you. Tell them to lay off.'

'Are you fucking kidding? If you know of Fitz then you know these people aren't going to lay off just because some nice bloke rings them up and asks them not to.'

'Yeah, all right!' he said, affronted. 'I'm not a complete fuckwit. I just meant – you know – I could do some digging for you.'

'I somehow doubt that's going to help,' I said. 'But thanks anyway. They might just get bored.'

'Or they might come along tonight and kill you.'

'If they were going to do that, they would've done it by now,' I said.

'Yeah, you say that. But they never got their hands on that parcel of yours, did they?'

'No,' I said.

'I'd better go,' he said, heading for the steps. 'You just shout me if you need anything.'

'Are we still going to move the boat?' I said. 'How about tomorrow?'

'Sure, yeah,' he said. He was already at the door, and moments later he'd waved goodbye and disappeared.

I looked at my phone and thought about ringing Jim. I sat in front of the stove for a while, allowing the warmth from it to take the chill out of my bones. I couldn't stop thinking about Caddy. I kept coming back to Caddy's last moments, how she must have felt. Had it hurt? Had she had time to feel pain, fear? Had she known she was about to die? And all the time I was so close by – and I'd had no idea she was even there.

I got to my feet and stretched. Everything felt achy, my neck so stiff I could hardly turn my head. I turned off the lights and locked the wheelhouse door, and went to bed.

# Thirty-five

I woke up early and lay still in the greying light from the skylight, wondering what had woken me. And then the scrabble on the deck above, and the cry of a gull, fading as it took off. I tried to go back to sleep but couldn't, and the boat felt too quiet to be lying still waiting for morning.

I got up, dressed and lit the woodburner while I was waiting for the kettle to boil, the crackling of the logs keeping me company while I made coffee. I looked doubtfully for something to eat for breakfast, and made a piece of toast with the last of the bread that was on the verge of being stale. I definitely needed to do some shopping later.

I wondered if there was anything I could do to the boat that didn't involve power tools this early in the morning, and I thought about the black plastic bag full of fabrics I'd thrown into the storage compartment when I was tidying up for the party. Maybe I could make some curtains for the portholes, something to cover over those black circles which had never bothered me much before.

When I finished my coffee I put the mug in the sink and went to retrieve the bag of fabric. I opened the hatch and in the darkness crawled down the three steps, along the pallets to the bow, until I was sitting next to the box. KITCHEN STUFF.

I pushed the box with my finger. It moved. I pushed it again, and it tilted.

No, no! That wasn't right at all.

Without a second's thought I grabbed hold of the box and tipped it upside down, the contents spilling all over my lap, over the pallet, some bits falling through the gap into the smooth curved space of the hull.

The false bottom of the box came away, and with it – nothing.

It was gone. The parcel was gone.

I pushed the empty box to one side and sat there in the semi-darkness, trying to think. My brain felt fried by all this, exhaustion, fear making me irrational. Who had been in here? I tried to think when I'd last checked the hatch before Saturday night – whether I'd actually felt the box or just seen it, like last time when Jim was here, and thought it was fine. It was Thursday, I was pretty sure, and today was Monday, so it might have been empty for several days. Could it have been the police? If they'd found it, why the hell hadn't they arrested me?

I crawled out of the bow again and shut the door firmly behind me. I went back to the saloon, found Dylan's phone and dialled the number. I didn't expect it to ring, and I got the same voice telling me that the phone was switched off. Damn him!

I paced up and down in the cabin, waiting for dawn, wondering what to do next. Dylan had given me the parcel to look after, and it was gone. Someone had taken it. Someone had come on to the boat, maybe when I'd been at the police station, or maybe last night when I'd been hiding, and taken it. I'd let Dylan down. It was all a mess, a complete hideous mess.

I thought again about phoning Jim, but what would that achieve? I couldn't tell him the parcel was missing, because to do so would be to admit to its existence, to implicate myself in whatever it contained.

I wanted to get off the boat, then. It was daylight now. I needed fresh air, to be outside in the real world where shitty things like missing parcels full of cocaine did not exist. It would be a good idea to go shopping and get some food. I couldn't live off stale bread forever. And there was nothing left on the boat that needed my protection.

I took my jacket and hat and locked up the boat behind me. When I got to the car park Cameron came out of the office. I didn't want to talk to him but he waved at me and shouted hello. 'How's it going?' I asked.

'Not bad,' he said. 'What's this Malc was telling me about you going for a trip?'

'Yeah. I just thought I'd try taking the boat out for a bit.'

He stood there a full head taller than me, kicking at a tuft of grass that was growing up through the tarmac. 'Just be careful out there, won't you?'

'Oh, don't worry. Malcolm's going to help me. I wouldn't go out on my own.'

'Technically you can't take the boat out without a licence. It's really easy to run aground,' he said, 'especially if the tide's on the way out. And it's not easy steering a boat the size of yours. I know Malcolm thinks he knows what he's doing, but your boat's fifteen feet longer than his.'

'Malcolm's licensed, isn't he? And he's taken the *Scarisbrick Jean* out for trips?'

'Not for a while.'

'Is there something you're not telling me?' I said with a smile.

'No, no,' he said. He looked shifty. 'I just – I think you need to be careful, that's all.'

'Of Malcolm?'

Cameron's cheeks were colouring. 'No, Malc's alright, you know that. He just... sometimes he does things without thinking through the consequences. You get my drift?'

'Would you help me move the boat, then?'

'If you really wanted to, sure. But I don't see why you need to go anywhere.'

'It's a long story,' I said. 'Really, it's just because – I don't know – it seems a bit silly having a boat and never going out on the river. And I want to have a look upstream before the winter comes. That's why.'

'Have the police been hassling you?'

The dramatic change of topic bothered me. He was standing there with his back to the office door, arms folded across his chest. I wondered what this was leading to.

'No, not really. Why?'

'I saw them come to see you, day before yesterday. Those two from London.'

'Do you know them, then?'

'No, they called at the office. They were asking after you.'

I looked at my feet. 'They were okay. That body I found – turns out she was from London. They're doing the investigation.'

'Right.'

'Look,' I said, 'I'm going to get some shopping in. Want me to get anything for you?'

'Just that there's been a lot of strange things happening since then, haven't there?'

'What do you mean?'

'Like the cable to the light being cut.'

I stared at him for a moment. I couldn't think what to say, and the conversation was taking an awkward turn.

'Just saying,' he said. 'Thanks. Don't need anything.' He turned and went back into the office.

I got my bike out of the storage room and pedalled forcefully out of the gate and up the hill.

The supermarket was just opening, a small crowd of early birds gathered around the entrance waiting for the shutters to rise. I wandered up and down the aisles distractedly, bought the bare minimum of provisions and stuffed the shopping into my rucksack.

When I got back to the marina it was deserted. The office was closed; even the door to the laundry, usually hanging ajar, was firmly shut.

I stepped aboard the *Aunty Jean* to see if Malcolm and Josie were home, but their hatch was locked. The tide was going out, the brown, silty water caressing the hulls of our boats.

Nothing for it, then, I was all on my own. I went back to the *Revenge of the Tide* and stoked the remains of the fire that was smouldering in the woodburner. While I waited for it to warm up I looked for the parcel. I started in the storage space, with my torch this time, opening boxes and moving them methodically from one side to the other, lifting things out of the way, taking it slowly to make sure – what? That I'd not accidentally misplaced it, that I'd not absent-mindedly moved it myself?

It was pointless. The parcel was gone.

Nevertheless I carried on, checking everything and sorting things out as I did so, putting things into some kind of order so that when I next came in here I could find what I was looking for. The bag of fabric and the tins of paint near the door mocked me and I decided that it would be better if I just got on with things, kept busy. My hands were trembling slightly. Not good for sewing: painting was a much better option.

By the time I'd emerged again, the boat was sitting on the mud. I went to look at the spare room. It was just as I'd left it: two coats of paint. The walls looked pale and almost transparent in the grey afternoon light.

I got the paint and brushes out of the hatch and levered the lid off the tin of paint with my gooey screwdriver. There wasn't a lot of paint left. Even if the tins claimed to be the same colour, on wooden cladding like this the slightest variation in shade would show up. I would start with the berth; that way if I ran out of paint I could always do the final coat of the walls with a different tin and it wouldn't look as odd as if one wall were a slightly different shade.

The rest of the tin just about lasted for the berth. By the time I'd finished I was wiping the inside of the tin with my brush, dragging every last drip of paint from the sides.

When I was washing the brushes in the galley sink I heard noises outside. I went up the steps and opened the wheelhouse door. Malcolm was on the deck of the *Scarisbrick Jean*. He saw me and ducked out of sight. I didn't have to ask where he'd been. He looked as though he'd had an argument with a strimmer, his scalp showing pink through the short grey spikes.

'Malcolm!' I shouted. 'I like your hair.'

His face popped up again and looked so depressed I thought he might actually cry. 'Never again,' he said.

I went down the gangplank and over to the *Scarisbrick Jean* so I didn't need to shout. He stayed where he was, one foot on the step down into the cabin, right hand on the roof.

'Is this Josie's revenge for the fact that you didn't notice her hair the other day?'

'Let's not mention that,' he said. He was gripping the roof of the cabin so hard that his knuckles were white.

'How is Josie?' I asked. 'Has she got a hangover?'

'Yeah. She's having a kip.'

'Oh,' I said. Then I added, 'Is everything alright, Malcolm?'

'Yeah,' he said.

I didn't believe him.

'Sounds like you're a bit busy today, then…'

'I am a bit, yeah.'

'Maybe we could move the boat tomorrow?'

'Maybe, yeah.'

I tried not to look disappointed, but lack of sleep and general misery at the situation was starting to get to me. Malcolm was watching me intently, his body blocking the doorway, his whole bony posture rigid.

'Alright, then,' I said. 'Tell Josie I said hi.'

I left him and went back up the gangplank to the *Revenge*. When I turned to shut the wheelhouse door, he was still standing exactly as I'd left him, fixed and motionless, staring straight ahead.

The boat was quiet, and still.

I went back to washing the brushes, and when they were clean I stood them on their ends in an empty jam jar to dry. I should really go back to bed, I thought, try to sleep for a little while. I felt numb and empty. I felt as if I was waiting.

The sound of the mobile phone ringing, loud and discordant, made me jump. The phone was on the shelf behind the dinette, under some papers. It took me two rings to find it.

GARLAND.

'Hello?'

'Genevieve?'

The relief, at hearing his voice. 'Yes! Dylan?'

'Yeah. You need to get out, now. Right now.'

'What?'

'Get off the boat. Take your phone. Ring Jim – understand?'

'What's going on?'

'They've been watching you. But they've gone, I don't know how long for. Fitz is on his way to meet them. Get off the boat. *NOW*!'

# Thirty-six

I grabbed my fleece, the keys, and my two phones. Jumped up the steps to the wheelhouse, locked the door behind me, as if that was going to stop anyone who wanted to get in. I ran across the pontoon to the storage room and unlocked my bike.

Pulling it from the rack, I heard sounds from outside. I stopped what I was doing. I hid behind the door of the storage room in case someone was coming inside. Snatches of conversation. Through the crack in the hinge I could see two men standing at the closed door of the office. One of them had a mobile phone in his hand.

I didn't recognise either of them. They were both wearing jeans, one with a grey fleece, the other with a black leather jacket. Both of them were over six foot, and almost as wide; standard 'enforcer' haircuts. They were engaged in some fervent conversation that I couldn't make out. The bigger one, with the leather jacket, seemed to be giving the one in the grey fleece a telling off. In between the verbal assaults and finger-pointing, he would rock back on his heels slightly so he could see around the corner of the office – down towards the water. Towards the *Revenge*.

I didn't hear the phone ring but just then the bigger man held the phone to his ear, ordering the other into silence with a raised finger.

I held my breath. I still couldn't hear what he was saying, just the tone of it. Urgent. Angry.

He ended the call, shaking his head with frustration. The grey fleece was asking him something. More head-shaking.

Without any further discussion they turned and started to walk away from the office. I shrank back against the wall of the storage room, into the shadows, hoping that they would not hear my breathing, my heart thumping.

As they passed, I heard one of them say, 'He needs to fucking decide, that's all. I've fucking had it with being pissed about…'

And, getting softer as they walked around the side of the building, the other: '…been here for days already…'

I stood there for a moment. My legs were shaking, and my hands. I looked around the storage room, which was just as it always was – boxes that belonged to Roger and Sally, a chest freezer, an old tent packed into canvas bags that had been here so long nobody really knew who owned it; and, in the corner, Cameron's ancient Triumph motorbike – he was supposed to be renovating it, but none of us had ever seen him go near it.

The familiarity of it all brought reassurance and my legs were starting to feel steadier. I peered through the gap in the hinge of the door – nobody in sight. I couldn't hear anything other than the distant traffic. I moved to the doorway, then out on to the unmade path outside. No one there. The door at the bottom was shut, the office in darkness. Beyond, the boats lay silent, sleeping on their muddy beds.

The men had gone to the left. I followed them, crept around the corner of the building in case they were just the other side. Nothing. I went to the corner. The car park was empty.

They had gone.

I went back to the storage room and got my bike. For a moment it crossed my mind that I could go back to the boat, collect some clothes and a few other things that I might need. *Get off the boat*, he'd said. *NOW*.

I cycled up the hill towards the main road, looking all the while for the men, for parked cars. But until I got to the road there was nothing, no one.

I got as far as the castle, the outer wall clad in fiery Virginia creeper like lava pouring from the battlements. I carried my bike up the steps and into the castle grounds, and found a bench. Took both phones out of my pocket. I wanted to call Dylan again, but something told me that his phone would be switched off. Instead, on my phone, I called Jim.

It took him a while to answer.

'Hello, Genevieve.'

'Hi.' He sounded as if he was still angry with me.

'Dylan called me.'

'What did he say?'

'He told me to get off the boat. He said they were watching me, and that I should get off the boat and ring you. So, I'm ringing you.'

'Where are you?'

'Rochester Castle. I've got my bike. Can I... can I meet you somewhere?'

There was a pause, a muffled noise as though he was holding the phone against his shoulder.

'Gen, I'm working; it's going to be difficult to get away. Are you safe right now? Are you sure you weren't followed?'

'I didn't see anyone. There's nobody here. Nobody suspicious, anyway,' I said, looking across at the couple walking across the green, pushing a buggy. By the steps to the castle, an elderly couple sitting on a bench. The woman was laughing, clutching her chest. A few students with matching backpacks were sprawled on the grass. I could hear faintly the tinny noise of music, played through a mobile phone.

'I'm going to send someone to get you, alright?'

'You don't need to do that. I'm alright here, there's loads of people,' I said. 'Jim, what the fuck's going on?'

'I don't know for sure. Just keep your head down, I'll get to you as soon as I can. Keep your phone with you. Stay where you can see other people, and, if you need to, ring 999. Alright?'

'Sure,' I said.

He rang off.

I sat on the bench, feeling the beginnings of righteous anger bubbling up inside me. Fury at being told what to do, where to go.

Well, safe or not, I wasn't going to stay here waiting for my hero to come and rescue me. I got back on the bike and pedalled down the hill, into the flow of traffic.

# *Thirty-seven*

Rochester High Street was deserted, bunting fluttering in the narrow space between the historic buildings the way it always was, heralding the next festival or mourning the end of the last. My bike tyres bumped over the brick paving.

I propped the bike up against the side of the Dot café, ordered a latte and a bacon sandwich and sat at one of the metal tables outside, tucking the bike behind my seat. It was breezy and I was the only one sitting out here, but it gave me some fresh air and time to think.

I hadn't told Dylan that his parcel had gone. I wondered why he hadn't asked me to bring it with me. Maybe he already knew. I couldn't shake the feeling that he might have been on the boat and taken it back.

The waitress brought my bacon sandwich outside to me and I ate it, big mouthfuls that filled my cheeks. I hadn't realised how hungry I was until my stomach growled and churned at the prospect of hot food. It was delicious, and hardly touched the sides, as my dad used to say. I washed it down with the coffee. I kept looking up and down the High Street, half-expecting to see the two blokes who'd been at the marina.

I realised my phone was ringing. I pulled it out of my pocket, the display told me it was Jim Carling.

'Hello?'

'Gen, it's me. Where are you?'

'Rochester High Street. Where are you?'

'I'm still in London. I'm coming to get you now, but it will take me a while to get there. Are you okay?'

'I'm fine.'

'You could wait for me at the police station.'

'No, thanks,' I said. I could think of better places to hang around.

He sighed as though I was being difficult.

'Is my boat in danger?'

'What?'

'Dylan told me to get off the boat. Are they going to torch it, or something?'

'No, of course not,' he said, far too quickly.

'You mean you don't know.'

He didn't answer right away. Then, 'I've got to go. Don't go back to the boat, alright? Promise me?'

'Would you please tell me what the fuck is going on?'

'I don't know, alright? If I knew, I would tell you.'

'Right.'

'I'll see you in a bit, okay? I'll get there as soon as I can.'

I walked up the High Street towards the cathedral, pushing my bike beside me, wondering how I was going to fill the next few hours. I was at the end of the High Street. The bridge stretched out in front of me, traffic flowing across it towards Strood, a train rattling on its way to London. I was finding it hard to think straight. Everything in me wanted to go back to the boat. I had a longing for it now, a need to go back there, as though I'd been away for months instead of half an hour. A need to go home. I could jump on my bike and be there in ten minutes, maybe less.

The doors to the Crown were open, inviting me in. I thought about going inside and getting wrecked; that was another option. Or I could cycle a little further down the Esplanade, to the playground and the gardens, sit on a bench or something and watch the river. I wouldn't be able to see the marina from there, but at least I would be close to it.

I got on my bike and was just turning into the gap in the low wall to the gardens in the shadow of the castle when Dylan's phone buzzed in my pocket. I freewheeled over to an empty bench, leaned my bike against it and answered.

'Hello?'

'What the fuck do you think you're doing?'

It was Dylan.

'You told me to get off the boat!'

'I didn't tell you to fart around in the city centre where anyone can see you. Have you completely lost it?'

He was watching me. I looked around me, as though he would be standing right there. There was no sign of him. 'Where are you?'

'Never mind. Where the fuck's Jim?'

'He said he's working. In London. He's going to come and pick me up.'

I heard him sigh heavily. There was a pause.

'Dylan! I really need to talk to you.'

'Go back to the road. There's a white van. See it?'

I looked back to the Esplanade. There was a huge oak tree between me and the road, and behind it I could see the rear end of a white van. 'Yes.'

'Fucking hurry up, then!' he said, and disconnected the call.

I jumped on to the bike and cycled back to the road. By the time I got there, the van's side door had opened. Dylan was in the driver's seat. He didn't smile, or look at me. His eyes were watching the road, looking across to the mirror to see what was coming up behind us. Through the half-open window, he said, 'Put the bike in the back. Get in, shut the door, hold on to something.'

I did as I was told, lifting the bike awkwardly over the step and pushing it into the dark space. There was nothing to secure it to, so I laid it down on its side. Shut the door with a slam. Before I could even sit down on the bare wooden floor, the van was moving.

I sat down quickly and held on to the bike by the saddle as it slid towards the van's rear doors. It was dark in here, a chink of light showing around the door hinges. The van turned sharply to the left and then to the right. I tried to think, my heart thumping. It must be the little roundabout. We were heading towards the marina. On the straight road I shuffled back against the rear of the cab, found a wooden rail to hold on to. One hand on the bike, the other on the rail, I braced myself for the sharp turn at the end of the road, the steep hill up towards Borstal village, the bike heavy and desperate to throw itself at the back doors.

I'd only caught a glimpse of him. He looked rough, rougher than he used to after several nights of too much vodka and no sleep. I was surprised by the force of excitement I felt at seeing him again.

I heard his voice, raised above the rattle of the engine, through the wooden partition separating the back of the van from the cab. 'You alright back there?'

'Yes. Where are we going?'

'Not far. I'll stop in a minute.'

At the top of the hill the van stopped. I could hear the click-click of the indicator. As I'd thought, the van swung to the right. Still heading towards the marina. Slight downhill and then up again. In the darkness I pictured the same route I'd cycled this morning, past the church, past the shop. Any minute now he'd slow down and turn right.

But the van didn't slow. In fact it accelerated slightly, with a crunch as he changed up a gear. Where were we going? I tried to think about what was beyond the turning for the marina but I never went this way – there was a road which led to Wouldham village, a winding road through the fields that snaked under the Medway bridge and followed the curve of the river for miles, heading towards Maidstone.

Then, abruptly, a turn to the right.

It caught me out. I'd relaxed my grip on the wooden rail and I gasped as the bike and I swung round, the tyre banging off the side of the van, my foot out to brace against it as I slid across the splintery wooden floor. The van was driving slowly now, bumping over pot holes and then over some sort of bump that felt like a mountain and crunched against something metallic at the back as we crawled over it.

The van stopped. The engine shuddered and cut out. I heard the driver's door open, and slam shut with a hollow clang. Then the side door of the van opened, and I blinked in the sudden light. He filled the doorway, brightness behind him. I let go of the bike and shuffled to the open door, intending to put my arms around him, but by the time I got there he'd turned and sat on the edge, his back to me.

I sat next to him. My legs dangled over the side; his reached the rocky rubble on which we were parked.

'Where are we?'

All around us were bushes, trees; through a gap in them I could see the river. I could hear the traffic on the motorway bridge just as I could from the deck of the *Revenge*, but I couldn't see it until I jumped down from the van and picked my way through the uneven ground to the gap in the bushes.

The bridge rose up, mountainous, to my right, one of the pillars just a few metres away. The traffic roared overhead.

'Stay out of sight,' Dylan said.

Tearing my eyes away from the soaring height of the bridge, I realised where we were – on the bend in the river past the marina. I could see the back of the *Revenge of the Tide*, the edge of the *Scarisbrick Jean*. If I went a little further, I would be able to see the whole boat, and most of the marina. A few steps out on to the muddy shore, and I might be able to see right up to the car park and the office. A thin pontoon made out of pallets held together with bits of rope stretched out across the mud. I remembered the tracks I'd seen in the mud leading to the porthole. This was where whoever it was had started their walk to my boat. It must have been Dylan, then.

I saw movement out of the corner of my eye. On the deck of the *Scarisbrick Jean*, Malcolm's shorn grey head popped up and then went below again. I moved quickly back into the shelter of the bushes and turned towards the van. He'd driven it through a gap and parked it in a space tucked away in between two trees. From the rocky, unmade road the van would have been invisible; from the northern bank of the river, it would have been possible to see the back of it sticking out, but little more than that.

'Is this where you've been all this time?' I asked.

He shook his head. 'On and off. I've been here solidly for the last couple of nights. But I had to go back to London, too, last week. And I was over there for a bit,' he said, pointing directly across the river to Cuxton. The public waste site was on the opposite bank and I could just about make out the queue of cars waiting to dump broken furniture, hedge clippings and whatever else into the skips.

I sat next to him again. His shoulders were bowed, and when I looked at his hands, gripping his knees, I realised they were shaking. I put my hand over his, squeezed it. His skin was cold, rough to the touch, the knuckles scarred and dirty. I looked at his face, but he was staring resolutely out across the bit of river we could see in the space between the greenery.

'What's going on, Dylan?' I asked quietly.

He made a noise, like a grunt of sheer hopelessness. A *Where do you want me to start?* kind of noise.

'What happened to Caddy?'

'Wrong place. Wrong time.'

'What do you mean?'

'Fitz thought he had a leak. He thought Caddy was it – he was having her followed. They followed her all the way to your boat. Apparently they lost her at the marina, then she suddenly popped up in front of them – don't ask me how or why, I don't know. She started yelling. One of the fuckwits punched her and she went down. That's what they said to Fitz when they got back to the club, anyway.'

I stared at him, the thoughts spinning and whirling around my head. 'You mean it was an accident?'

'No, it was them being complete fucking idiots. It was an accident that it happened near your boat. A coincidence, I guess. Apart from the fact that you invited her to your party.'

It was all my fault, was what he meant. I was still processing this when I realised he was saying something else.

'...thing is, Fitz didn't know where you were. In fact, he'd almost forgotten all about you. And then when the fuckwits went back to the club and told him what had happened – when he'd come down from the ceiling – he started wondering what she was doing in a boatyard. And he found out you were here.'

'So what?'

'So, now he thinks you and Caddy were in on some scheme together. He doesn't know what. But sooner or later his paranoia will bring him to bloody invent something. Which is why you're in big trouble.'

'I thought it was the parcel,' I said, vaguely.

He gave a short laugh. 'The parcel? You mean the one I gave you? I don't think so. Not unless you've been waving it about.'

'Dylan. Someone took it. I don't know when. I'm sure it was there on Thursday, then this morning when I looked it was gone.'

He was staring at me with an amused smile on his face. Whatever I'd expected in reaction to the news that his precious parcel was missing, it certainly wasn't this.

'You never looked in it?' he said.

'No. Of course not. I just hid it, like you told me to.'

He rubbed a hand over his scalp and sighed. 'Put it this way. Whichever idiot has got it will get a big shock when they finally open it up.'

The clouds were thickening over the bridge, moving so fast it looked as though the bridge was swaying and might fall at any minute. It was dizzying. It was starting to get dark.

'Why are you here, Dylan? If you're not here to pick up the parcel, what are you doing here?'

He didn't answer at first, looking out across the grey-brown river to the opposite bank, to the trees and the grass and, in the distance, the cars queuing to get round to deposit their rubbish in the public waste facility.

'I'm here because of you, of course,' he said, so softly that I wasn't even sure I'd heard him.

'Me?'

'I was watching out for you.'

My first reaction was to blurt out that he hadn't been doing a very good job, considering the number of times I'd felt threatened and afraid in the last few days, but I bit my cheek instead. 'Does Fitz know you're here?' I asked at last.

'Of course not.'

'Where does he think you are, then?' I asked, remembering how Dylan was like Fitz's shadow, the one out of all of them who seemed to be completely trusted, always there.

He shrugged miserably. 'Told him I was going to Spain to see Lauren.'

'You won't have much of a tan when you go back.'

He laughed then, a throaty laugh that ended in a cough. 'Not much of a one for sunbathing, me,' he said.

'No, I guess you're not. Jim said you'd done a runner.'

'Did he now?' he said. 'That's interesting.'

'You weren't answering when he called you, same as you weren't answering me. Why did you do that?'

'I rang him when I needed to.'

'And why did you ring me the night after Caddy died? I answered the phone and you didn't say anything.'

'I wanted to check you were okay. Then Fitz turned up and I had to pretend I was listening to voicemail. It's not that easy to make private phone calls in that place, you know that. Always someone watching. Anyway,' he said with finality, 'I'm not going back.'

'What?'

'It's a long story. But I'm not doing it any more. I've had enough. Like you.'

'What are you going to do?'

'I'm going to go to Spain,' he said. 'Set up my own club, a bar, something like that.'

'Sounds like a really good plan,' I said. 'I almost wish I could come with you.'

He looked at me properly for the first time. His eyes were dark, and the twinkle behind them I'd always thought made him look cheeky, not dangerous like the others, wasn't there any more.

'That wouldn't be a good idea,' he said.

'Why not?'

'Fitz will come looking for me,' he said. 'He doesn't take kindly to people who let him down.'

'Like Caddy?'

'Yeah, if you like. You need to stay where you're safe.'

'I'm not exactly safe here, am I?' I said. 'Why should I stay?'

I felt him tense up next to me and for a moment I wondered if I'd said completely the wrong thing. I was almost expecting him to lose his temper, shout at me.

But when he spoke again, his voice was even quieter. A calm, measured response.

'It won't be forever.'

'What won't?'

'You're only in danger because of Fitz. Once he's sorted out, you'll be fine.'

'Sorted out?' I echoed. 'What do you mean? Who's going to sort him out?'

'Christ!' he said, raising his voice for the first time. 'You and your fucking questions! And to think the reason I liked you so much is that you knew when to keep quiet about shit like this!'

'I'm sick of being the only one who doesn't know what's going on! Why don't you trust me?'

'I do trust you. There's just a lot of stuff you're better off not knowing.'

'What's in the parcel, Dylan?'

When he answered, his reply was so unexpected I thought I'd misheard him and I had to ask him to repeat it. 'What?'

'Flour. It's just bags of flour. Self-raising.'

# Thirty-eight

It was starting to get dark already, the grey clouds moving overhead getting greyer and darker, until the streetlights on the opposite bank of the river came on. I was standing at the edge of the bushes, looking through the giant concrete bridge supports to the marina, to my beautiful *Revenge of the Tide*, and the smaller shape of the *Scarisbrick Jean* next to it.

'Why the hell would you give me bags of flour to look after?' I asked, and when he didn't answer straight away I stood up and walked away, trying to work it out for myself. None of it made sense. Fifty thousand pounds, to look after a parcel full of flour?

'I needed you to get out of London,' he said.

I looked back at him, still sitting in the open side of the van.

'You wouldn't have gone,' he said. 'I couldn't trust Fitz to keep Arnold out of your way. You'd gone and got yourself implicated in Fitz's deal because you were at his house that night. And as if that wasn't bad enough, they were going to raid the club and I didn't want you to get caught up in all that shit. Without the money you wouldn't have gone. And you wouldn't have just taken the money if I'd offered it to you, would you?'

'Wait. You knew about the raid before it happened?'

He stared at me, not answering. Somewhere, the light was dawning. 'You're working for the police,' I said.

I remembered what Jim had said. He'd told me he'd known Dylan for years. He was a friend. And as I started to process it, I realised something else. 'You're the leak. You're betraying Fitz.'

'Yeah,' he said.

'My God. He'll kill you.'

'Yes, he will. If he finds me.'

'He doesn't know yet?'

Dylan shrugged. 'Maybe he does, maybe he doesn't. It was easier when he suspected Caddy, to be honest – he wasn't even thinking about me. Then, when those idiots killed her, he started looking at you.'

'If you'd stayed in London, he wouldn't have had any reason to suspect you. If he finds out you're not in Spain after all…'

'Yeah, well, that's why I've been sleeping in a fucking van for the past few nights.'

'Jim told me you'd been friends for years. He said you were at school together.'

'Yeah, well, what was he supposed to tell you? It's not something you can just slip into conversation.'

I turned my back on him and looked over the rocky ground and the expanse of mud and water to the boats. Everything was so quiet over there, as though nothing could possibly disturb the peace. I went back to the van, and sat in the doorway next to him, out of the wind.

'Why did Fitz's men want to search my boat? And why did they kill Oswald?'

'Who the fuck's Oswald?'

'Malcolm and Josie's cat. They killed him and left him on the pontoon next to my boat.'

'No idea,' he said. 'Maybe one of them was allergic. When did they search your boat?'

'Nearly a week ago. Remember, I told you yesterday when you rang Jim's phone? They tied me up and knocked me out. When I came round the boat had been turned over.'

'Hold on,' he said. 'They knocked you out?'

'Yes.'

'They were only on there for a few minutes. That fuckwit next door scared them off.'

'What?'

'You mean Nicks and Tony? Wednesday night? They were supposed to ask you what you'd been talking to Caddy about, give you a gentle warning. That was all. I watched them go on board your boat and three minutes later that guy with the frizzy hair had seen them off.'

'I was out cold. Nicks hit me on the side of the head.'

'Fuck's sake. No wonder they keep killing everyone and everything, it's ridiculous. Why can't they just talk to people?' He lifted his hand to my head, stroked my hair. It was the first time he'd touched me.

*Three minutes later that guy with the frizzy hair had seen them off...*

'I've got to get back to the boat,' I said.

'What, now?'

'Yes, now. And you're coming with me.'

'Don't think so.'

'Yes, you are. I've just worked out which idiot took the parcel. And if we don't hurry up, they'll kill him.'

# *Thirty-nine*

We were standing by the office, looking down towards the boats. There was no sign of life at all – nobody skulking in the shadows, watching; no one in the office, or the showers, or the laundry. Nobody around the boats. All was quiet and silent.

I rang Jim again, and this time his phone was switched off.

'What shall I do?' I asked Dylan. 'Shall I leave a message?'

He shrugged, all his attention focused on the boats. He started walking towards the pontoon.

'Jim, it's me. Just to tell you I'm with Dylan. We're going back to the boat. Come and meet us there, okay?'

There was blood on the deck of the *Scarisbrick Jean*. I saw it as Dylan and I made our way down the pontoon towards the *Revenge of the Tide*.

It was a smear, a long streak of brown and red, along Josie's proudly scrubbed wooden deck, as though something large or heavy had been dragged through it. It went into the cabin through the doorway that was now tightly closed and locked. And a smear, maybe a handprint, on the gunwale as if someone with bloody hands had steadied themselves while leaving the boat.

'Oh, God,' I said. 'Look – there's more...'

There was another handprint on the gunwale of the *Revenge of the Tide* as well, a smear. Spots of blood on the deck.

Dylan went first. He was different now, tense, his body solid and even bigger than it had been just a few minutes before. He was readying himself.

The lock on the door was broken off. I followed him down the steps into the cabin and they were there. The saloon was crowded with people. It was like some kind of fucked-up Barclay reunion. Fitz, very different in a pair of jeans and designer trainers, and Nicks, lounging on the sofa, making themselves at home. In the galley, to my horror, Leon Arnold, leaning against the cooker, and the one who'd watched the door for him that night he'd attacked me – Markus? Sitting on the table at the dinette, swinging his feet and looking cheerful.

I looked away from them.

And on the floor, his wrists tied behind his back and not moving, was Malcolm. His short grey hair was stained red. His eyes were closed.

'What have you done?' I said to Nicks, breathless with rage. 'What did Malcolm ever do to you, you bastard?'

Fitz smiled at me. 'He thought he had a brain. Didn't you, you little piece of shit?'

He aimed a kick at Malcolm's back and Malcolm arched away from him, groaning, an animal sound.

'Don't do that!' I said. I crouched down, touching his head, trying to see where the blood was coming from.

His eyes opened, panic in them. He whispered, 'Sorry…'

'It's okay,' I said. And added, pointlessly, 'Don't worry.'

'And Dylan,' Fitz said. 'Nice to see you, mate. Spain not quite to your liking, was it?'

Dylan didn't answer immediately, just kept his bulk between Nicks and me, his back to the door. 'You shouldn't be here, Fitz. Wherever you think your leak is, it's not here.'

Fitz laughed then and Nicks did too, both of them, like a couple of school bullies. 'I know exactly where my leak is, Dylan, old boy. You think I'm here for her? You seem to think I'm thick or something. Do you?'

He got to his feet, then and came towards Dylan, who stood his ground. He wouldn't try anything, surely? Dylan was at least a foot taller, and twice as wide.

'I'm here for *you*,' Fitz said. His voice was almost gentle, but as he said it he dug his index finger into Dylan's ribs.

'What's he doing here?' Dylan asked, his voice still casual, casting a single glance over to the galley.

'I'm looking after my interests, mate, same as you are,' said Leon.

Dylan snorted. 'What interests?'

'We had a deal going,' Fitz said, 'before you went and fucked it all up for us.'

Where was Josie? Maybe they didn't know about her. Maybe she was safe, shopping somewhere. On the floor, Malcolm let out another groan, longer this time, louder.

'I *said*, shut the fuck up!' Fitz said, kicking Malcolm in the shoulder.

'Dylan's just here to see me, no other reason,' I said.

'I know that, love,' Fitz said, looking at me properly for the first time. 'He's been a bit distracted lately, haven't you, mate? Can't keep your mind on the job? Funny, that. And you disappear off to the wilds of – where are we? – Kent, and, what a surprise, there's Dylan all ready to keep an eye on you. Touching, I call it.'

'Must be love,' Nicks said. And they laughed.

'Look,' I said, my patience wearing thin, 'I'm getting sick of all this. Whatever it is you want, just take it and get off my boat. Leave us alone. Leave us all alone.'

'We've got things to sort out first. Right, Dylan?'

Dylan turned to look at me then and for a second I saw the old Dylan, the guy who used to watch me dance with a face like a rock, not giving anything away with his expression but somehow saying a lot more with his eyes.

'You need to go,' he said to me quietly. 'Take Malcolm with you, and go.'

'I don't think so, sunshine,' Fitz said.

317

'Let her go,' Dylan said. 'You don't need her here. You've got what you came for.'

'Not yet.'

Like a petulant child demanding attention, Malcolm let out another cry, a sob, moving his legs.

I didn't know what I had been expecting. I was alert, aware that this confrontation was not going to be easy or straightforward, but I wasn't at all ready for what came next.

'Will you fucking shut up, you annoying little shit?'

Fitz pulled a gun out of the waistband of his jeans and aimed it at Malcolm. I saw the gun a second before he fired it. The noise of it was deafening in the small space and I jumped back without even realising it, just as Malcolm's body jerked on the floor. Blood started seeping from a wound in his shoulder. He cried out, just once, and then he was silent and still.

Both my hands clasped over my mouth with the shock of it. Struggling to breathe. And then it all got much, much worse. Fitz was pointing the gun directly at Dylan's head. I screamed, started shouting, 'No! No, no!' and Markus took me by the arm and pulled me towards the bedroom.

Dylan took a step towards me and for the first time I saw real fear in his eyes. 'No!' he said.

And then Leon Arnold stood and blocked my line of vision as both of them took me into my bedroom and shut the door. Markus turned on the light and I wriggled free of his grip and lunged for the door.

'Now, now,' Arnold said, putting himself in my way. 'You don't want to watch him do it, do you, Viva?'

I tried to push past him to get to the door. And then he hit me, casually, across the face. It hadn't looked as though he'd put much force behind it but even so my feet left the floor and I ended up in a heap against the berth. I pulled myself up into a sitting position, my head spinning. From the saloon I heard a yell – Dylan's voice or Malcolm's? A noise of such pain and accompanied by a crash, as though something heavy had fallen –

'Dylan!' I shouted, as loud and hard as I could, sobbing at the end of the word as Markus came for me and dragged me to my feet before smashing his fist into the side of my head.

I heard Leon Arnold laugh as I fell to the floor, and then ringing in my ears, and blood in my mouth, and for a moment I passed out.


I was being dragged up, off the floor. I gasped and coughed, pulling with weak fingers at the hands that gripped under my arms. Then I was thrown back on to something soft – my bed? I opened my eyes. Everything was a confusing whirl and the emotions behind it all were alien – and then, my pounding heart, and the realisation that I was in my bedroom with these two men, and the door was shut. And out there, in the saloon, noises – shouting…

'Dylan,' I said.

'Never mind him,' said Markus. 'He is a dead man.'

I think it was the first time I'd heard him say anything. He had an accent, from somewhere in Eastern Europe. The words and the way he said them chilled me to the core.

'Let me go,' I said, 'please let me go.' My own voice sounded odd, dulled above the ringing and surging in my ears. I touched a hand to my jaw; the side of my face was throbbing.

Leon Arnold was looking through my clothes. He had opened the drawers and was pulling out bits of underwear. I tried to get up off the bed but Markus pushed me back with a single hand.

'What are you doing?' I said, my voice high and panicky. 'Leave that alone, it's mine.'

At the back of my drawers, he had found something that stopped him. 'What about this, Markus? What do you reckon?'

From the tip of his finger, a sequinned thong dangled. I'd even forgotten it was there – the last few bits of skimpy underwear from my dancing days.

I felt sick at the sight of it.

'Put that back,' I said, trying to make my voice stronger, more in control.

He seemed to notice me then, and came over to the bed. 'Are you going to be difficult, Viva?'

'Get the fuck off my boat, you disgusting little man,' I said.

He laughed. 'That's a yes, then.'

He pushed me back and before I could move or struggle he'd put one forearm across my throat, leaning over so close to my face that I could feel his breath on me. I clawed at his arm, scratching him with my pathetically short nails, kicking with my legs. And then, someone holding my legs. While I fought and bucked, I felt someone – it must have been Markus, although all I could see was Arnold – undoing my jeans.

I thought about Jim. I wanted him to come and save us, so badly. I wanted him to be here and take these horrible men away. I thought about him until I could almost hear sirens, too far away, fading and getting closer and fading away.

I tried to speak, tried to say no. But I couldn't breathe, or speak. When he relieved the pressure on my throat I heaved in air, coughed, gasped.

Arnold sat companionably next to me on the bed while Markus pulled my jeans down. I kicked him as hard as I could, aiming for where I thought his face would be.

That was a mistake. Arnold pushed me back again, this time spreading his hand across my throat, squeezing with his fingers.

'Viva,' he said, 'if you carry on fighting, you're going to get hurt. Do you understand?'

Panic was rising inside me. I nodded, my eyes wide. He let go of my throat and as I gasped and sucked air in, I heard the unmistakable sound of the engine starting. Abruptly Arnold got up off the bed and left the room.

It gave me such a shock that I half-sat up. The whole boat rattled and shook. I could hear the water churning at the stern, and the splashing of the water against the hull. The keys were still in the pocket of my jeans. They must have bypassed the ignition somehow. What were they doing?

Markus was sitting on the edge of the bed, looking towards the door.

In that moment I could have tried to fight back – choked him, maybe, hit him with something – but there was nothing within reach. My hands were shaking and there was no fight left in me. No fight. Only fear.

I shrank away from him to the corner of the bed, hugging my knees. Trying to disappear.

There was a shout from the saloon, something I didn't quite catch. Markus went to the door and looked out down the corridor – was he talking to somebody? Then he shut the door behind him and stood facing me with his back to the door. Guarding it.

I moved slowly to the edge of the bed. My jeans were on the floor. I reached down for them, expecting at any minute he would stop me, shout at me, hit me even. I stretched out my arm for them and pulled my jeans towards me slowly, as though he would only notice quick movements, as though he was some kind of wild animal I was trying not to disturb.

But he still wasn't looking at me. It was as though I had ceased to exist for him, as though he was there to guard the room and anything in it.

The sobbing started again when I was dressed. I curled into a ball in the corner, my back to the door, my body shaking with it.

I was still curled up like this when Arnold came back. 'Get up,' he said.

I didn't move and he grabbed my arm, digging his fingers in and dragging me backwards over the bed. I yelped in pain and fear, gripping the waistband of my jeans, horrified at the thought of being undressed again. But he needed me for something else now.

'Get up on deck. Fitz wants you to drive the boat.'

*Drive the boat?*

I stumbled through to the saloon. The boat was swaying and rocking in a way I'd never felt before. The tide was rising, but not quickly enough – every few moments I felt a jolt and a scrape when the hull brushed against the riverbed.

There were two bodies on the floor. Malcolm's and Dylan's. Standing over them, Fitz: the gun he was holding aimed at Dylan's head.

My hand covered my mouth in horror. Holding back a scream. I had no words left for him.

The whole scene was alien to me. My boat, my beautiful boat, was a strange place now with these people here, with these events taking place inside it.

Then I realised something. If Fitz was still pointing the gun at Dylan, that meant he was alive. And in that moment I heard him make a noise. His head was covered in blood, as though they'd kicked him over and over. He was lying awkwardly, half on his back, his legs sprawled wide. And his foot moved. Very well, then. He was alive. And then I saw Malcolm's hand, lifted and moving in a vague, graceful wave before falling on to his chest.

'Get up there,' Fitz said, jerking his head up to the wheelhouse. 'Get up there and I might not kill your fucking shit of a boyfriend. Yet.'

As I hauled myself up the steps, I could hear the sirens. Nicks was waiting for me at the top of the steps. He had his hands on the wheel but it was jerking out of his grip, as first the tide took it and then the silt, the rudder catching against the bottom. The engine roared and rumbled and I could hardly hear myself think.

'You,' he yelled, 'steer this thing. Get us to deeper water. Right?'

'You need Malcolm,' I shouted back. 'I've never done it before.'

'Who?'

'Malcolm. The guy he shot. Down there. He knows the river.'

The *Revenge* was adrift, maybe fifteen metres from the pontoon. I could see blue flashing lights, coming towards us down the hill. The marina was in darkness.

The boat jolted again, harder this time, enough to make Nicks lose his footing.

'I said you need Malcolm!' I yelled at him.

He stuck his head through the door to the cabin and shouted something at Fitz. And then, a few moments later, Malcolm was being shoved up through the doorway. Conscious, bloody, but still it was Malcolm. He looked at me, squinting and frowning as though he had no idea what was going on.

'Are you okay?' I said, trying to get him to focus on me.

'Yeah, yeah...' he said.

'You need to steer,' I said, putting his hand on the wheel.

He looked blank. Nicks was in the doorway to the cabin, talking to Fitz. I got close to Malcolm, close enough to smell the sweat and the blood and the fear.

'You need to steer. Right?'

Finally he got it. He gripped the wheel and turned it gently, and the *Revenge* started to move away from the pontoon again. Blue lights now, flashing outside the gate to the marina. One car pulled into the car park, then a second.

The *Revenge of the Tide* eased off the mud and rocked into the flow of the river. Malcolm steered the boat round, back towards the Strood bank. Nicks stepped back as Fitz came up the steps and into the wheelhouse. I moved out of the way. He had blood on his hands, blood down the front of his jeans. The gun was still in his hand. The boat was roaring out into the midstream now, away from the bank and the police officers who were gathering on the pontoon, torches shining over us, flashing into the wheelhouse.

'Where do you want to go?' Malcolm shouted at them.

Fitz was slapping Nicks on the shoulder as though they'd done something smart, outwitted the gavvers, escaping from under their very noses. 'I dunno, mate. Just keep driving for now, right?'

Malcolm was turning the wheel slowly, bringing his hands back to the two o'clock position each time. And Fitz and Nicks had to move to the stern to keep watching the pontoon. I wondered what Malcolm was playing at. The *Revenge* was heading straight for the other bank now.

Fitz was laughing, cupping his hand to his ear as the officers on the pontoon shouted things that none of us could hear. Nicks was next to him, almost leaning over the edge.

'What did you think you were doing, Malcolm?' I asked him, trying to get him to look me in the eye.

He shook his head.

'Malc! Did you ring him?'

'I was trying to help, okay? I was trying to get rid of it for you.'

'By *selling it to Fitz*?'

'I know, I know,' he said. 'It wasn't my finest moment, alright?'

I looked over his shoulder at Fitz, who seemed to have given up on taunting the police. He looked joyous, as though he'd just done the best deal of his life. 'What are you two gossiping about?' he shouted. 'Get on with it, you fuck!'

I turned back to Malcolm and he looked determined, focused, a gleam in his eye that I hadn't seen before. 'Get ready,' he said, and I didn't understand what he meant until there was a great bang, like an explosion. The boat stopped dead and I was catapulted sideways, down the steps and into the cabin, landing on my back with a crash. I skidded backwards along the floorboards and hit my head on something, one of the cupboards in the galley.

My ears were full of the grinding of the engine, louder than ever, vibrations coming through the floor and rattling the cups and plates. A book, papers, a bowl fell off the top of the galley worktop and landed on my head. Above it all, shouting, yelling, noises from the deck.

I struggled to my feet and hauled myself upright. The boat was listing to port and the saloon was at a crazy angle. Dylan had rolled over and was lying in a jumble of limbs and broken bits of furniture, cushions from the dinette, against the bottom of the sofa. I crawled over to him.

'Dylan? Can you hear me?'

His face, his poor face. Even in the darkness I could see so much blood on him. I touched his cheek, crying.

'I'm so sorry,' I sobbed. 'I should have listened to you, I should have listened.'

He made a noise then, not quite a groan. A cough, above the noise of the engine churning. And he said something – I couldn't hear him.

'What?' I put my ear next to his mouth. 'What did you say? Say it again.'

'I said alright.'

I kissed his cheek and tasted blood. He coughed again, raised an arm and pushed me away. I was going to have to leave him here.

A weapon – I needed a weapon. I scrambled back to the galley. All the knives had fallen out of the knife block except for one: a small vegetable knife. It wasn't going to be much good against Fitz's gun, but it was the best I could do.

I pulled myself back up the steps. Malcolm was there, leaning back against the wooden wall of the wheelhouse, holding his head. Blood was pouring from a cut above his eye. Fitz was lying in on the ground in a heap, not moving.

'What happened?' I yelled. 'Where's Nicks?'

He waved a hand to the deck and I went to look.

Nicks had fallen from the deck into the water below. But we had run aground. In the dim light I could see him, half-swimming, half-wading towards the boat. The water was coming in almost visibly, the tide tugging at his legs and pulling him backwards. The more he struggled in the mud, the more it pulled him back. And then he fell forward into the water. Pushing himself upwards with his hands in the mud now, his legs stuck up to his knees, he was never going to make it.

I shoved the knife into my pocket and went to the storage locker on the deck, found a lifejacket, pulling it clear. They'd come with the boat. I had no idea if they'd ever been used, or worn.

'Hey!' I shouted.

Nicks was flailing in the water, struggling to remain upright. He tried to turn but that made him lose balance and he fell again.

I threw the lifejacket at him. It flew through the air and landed in the water a few metres away from him, but it might as well have been a mile. He stretched and tried to reach it, and one of his legs, miraculously, came free of the mud and he fell backwards into the water. At that moment the stern of the boat caught against a surge of tide and, with nobody at the wheel to guide it, turned in a slow, graceful arc. The momentum of it was powerful and fast, and before I realised what was happening I saw Nicks's face illuminated in torchlight from the pontoon, saw the fear in his eyes as the hull came towards him.

There was a thud, a bang, and the boat passed over him. I raced to the port side, hoping to see him come up, but there was nothing. Nothing.

And then there was another sound, a shout from behind me, a crash. Fitz was wrestling with Malcolm on the deck, the two of them rolling over and over on the slope until they ended up in a heap against the port gunwale. Fitz was punching at Malcolm's face, over and over again, his fist coming away bloody, blood spraying in droplets.

'Stop it, stop it!' I yelled, my voice drowned by the churning engine and carried away by the wind.

I pulled at Fitz's back but he was slippery with mud, and cold. I felt for the knife. It was small, just a little kitchen knife, but before I could think about it too hard I jabbed it into his upper shoulder. Not hard, or deep, just enough to make him stop.

Blood started seeping from the wound into the fabric, blooming into a wide crimson flower, and he turned, struggling to his feet. Malcolm lay still, his face away from me against the storage locker on the port side.

'What the fuck did you do that for?' Fitz yelled at me, trying to reach behind his shoulder to feel the wound. 'Are you fucking mad?'

I still had the knife in my hand but he swiped at it, grabbed for it. I kept hold of it and as Fitz turned his body towards me there was a bang, a shot, loud above the noise of the engine, echoing across the empty space. I didn't feel any pain. I looked down at my body in shock, expecting to see blood, expecting to see a hole somewhere. Then Fitz let out a scream and crumpled into a ball.

Malcolm was still. Fitz was on his side in a foetal crouch, making high wailing noises.

Above that, and above the painful grinding noise of the engine, I could hear more sirens. They seemed louder, the vibrations passing through my feet and into my chest with a discordant rhythm. And another sound, distant, a helicopter... but too far away?

Dylan. I wanted Dylan.

I ran down the steps. It was dark, the cabin was a mess and the floor was wet, slippery with blood. I looked across to the bottom of the sofa. He wasn't there.

The engine finally spluttered and cut out. Then I could hear it, the definite thud-thud of a helicopter, and a spotlight shone down on to the deck of the boat and in through the open wheelhouse door. I could see blood on the walls, on the floor. A bloody handprint on the wooden cladding near the door to my bedroom. And noise – I could hear movement. And a sudden bang, the noise of wood cracking and splintering.

The door was open. The bedroom was a mess, a tangled angled mess with bedding and dark blood on the walls. On the floor, against the bed Leon Arnold lay still, his leg twisted beneath him. He wasn't moving.

The noise, again. I looked to my left, to the open doorway of the second bedroom. The two figures inside it fighting, a tangle of bodies, fists, and it took me a moment to realise that it must be Dylan, must be Markus – but which one – and what could I do?

In the corner of the room, tipped on its side, was my crate of tools. I lifted the nearest – a plane, heavy and solid. And at that moment the light shone through the porthole and Dylan was on the floor, and Markus with his knee on Dylan's chest, a piece of wood he'd broken away from the edge of the berth, a big lump of two-by-four raised back at shoulder height ready to swing it into Dylan's skull.

I must have hit him with the plane. I had it in my hand and then he was lying on the floor, slipping a little on the smooth floor and sliding to a stop against what was left of the berth.

I dropped the plane. I was on my knees next to Dylan, not knowing where to touch, not knowing how to help him.

Noises from the cabin, shouts and steps, lights shining down the corridor. I thought it was Fitz. I put my body across Dylan's and held him, protecting him.

# Forty

The hospital in the middle of the night: a soul-destroying place to be.

Josie and I had been sitting in the same hard plastic chairs bolted to the floor, for the past two hours. Before that, we'd been allowed in to see Malcolm, or at least Josie had. I'd watched through the doorway, a police officer standing next to me in case I did something, or said something, or tried to run – I didn't even know. But they were here in any case. I stopped paying attention after a while and the next time I looked the male officer had gone and a female officer was there in his place. She spoke to me, random words that made sense at the time, and I nodded to her and said, 'Yes, okay,' and that seemed to satisfy her because she was quiet after that.

The police officer had brought me a cup of brown liquid that might have been coffee. It burned my throat but I scarcely noticed. My head was trying to sort through what had happened, but none of it made sense. It churned in my brain and every version that came out was somehow wrong, faulty, failed.

Josie had given up asking me questions. Every time she mentioned Malcolm's name, I cried. She told me that she'd gone into the *Scarisbrick Jean* and found flour, several bags of it, piles of it tipped up on the floor. Flour everywhere. She had no idea what that was all about.

That was the one bit that made sense to me. Malcolm had taken the package out of the hatch, expecting it to contain drugs. Then he'd phoned them, had made contact with Fitz, believing the parcel to be a shipment of drugs belonging to the criminal gang. And Fitz had come down himself to sort the mess out, thinking maybe that he'd finally discovered that someone was skanking him, taking a cut of the drugs he was importing, and that the stash was in Malcolm and Josie's boat. And of course when they opened the package in front of Malcolm, poor Malcolm who was as crap at being a criminal as he was at everything else and hadn't thought to look inside the parcel himself first, the kilos of cocaine they'd all been expecting turned out to be six bags of self-raising flour.

'It's that one from before,' Josie said, and I looked up.

Jim Carling was striding up the corridor towards us.

He was dressed in jeans and a brown jacket, frowning and looking left to right as though he was lost somehow and cross with himself for not knowing what was going on.

I rose to my feet, wanting to call to him or wave, but not sure what he would say, how he would react. But when he saw me he smiled. He touched my arm gently, as though he wanted to hold me, but I moved away. We stood awkwardly a few feet apart. This was, after all, a professional meeting rather than a social one. 'Where were you?' was the first thing I said.

'I tried to get there. As soon as I got your message I got patrols to go out to the marina…'

'They nearly killed him, Jim. They nearly killed Dylan. And Fitz shot Malcolm. It was so awful, it was…' I was crying again, the tears that didn't seem to stop for more than a few moments at a time.

He took me in his arms and this time I didn't pull back. I sobbed loudly, out of control, and he held me tighter, and stroked my hair, and made soothing noises that somehow made it all worse, not better.

In the end he said to me, 'Come for a walk.'

The sobs had subsided to jerky breaths, my hands shaking. He put his arm around my shoulders and steered me down the corridor, past the reception desk to the entrance.

Outside it was chilly, the air crisp. I breathed it in deeply. I thought that I would never take breathing fresh air for granted again. We found a wooden bench and sat there for a few moments in the darkness. I wondered if he'd come to tell me Dylan was dead. They'd taken him away in an ambulance. Every time I asked, nobody seemed to have any idea what had happened to him.

'You know they're going to arrest you,' he said.

'I think I hit him with a plane.'

'Yeah, don't tell me anything, I don't want to know about that. I'm just letting you know.'

'How's Dylan?' I asked. 'Have you heard anything? They won't tell me.'

Jim's face was grave. 'He's going to be fine,' he said.

'Have you seen him? Is he really okay? I thought they'd killed him. I thought Fitz had killed him.'

'No, he's alright. Fitz is in a room somewhere upstairs. You know he shot his own bollock off?'

'What?'

'Accidentally, of course. Occupational hazard, keeping your firearm tucked into your waistband. He's been arrested. They've got a guard on him.'

'And the others?'

'Leon Arnold's just got concussion, would you believe? The other one is upstairs with head injuries. Not as bad as it looks.'

I waited for him to say something about Nicks, but that was all he said.

'What about my boat?'

'The marine unit's getting a tug and they're going to bring it back to the boatyard at high tide. I think it's alright.'

'You know they were after Dylan,' I said.

'Yes.'

'You need to keep him away from them, Jim.'

'Yeah, that's kind of what I spend my whole working life doing, keeping Dylan out of trouble.'

'You told me you'd been at school with him. I knew you were lying; I just didn't know why.'

He looked at me steadily, his cheeks flushed. 'I wouldn't have lied to you without good reason.'

The sky was turning grey at the edges, the shapes of the trees standing out now against the clouds and the sky. I was tired, numb, cold. I wanted to go home and sleep forever.

'What's going to happen now?' I asked.

'Fitz will be charged. You'll be interviewed and, with a bit of luck, bailed. And then you and Dylan can do whatever it is you want to do, and I'll quietly disappear and think about what might have been.'

I felt my cheeks flush. I'd behaved very badly, towards both of them. 'I'm sorry,' I said.

He was quiet for a moment, then he gave a short laugh. 'Yeah, well, I should have known I'd never be that lucky. Besides, you're one of the most infuriating women I've ever met.'

I looked up at him then and saw the hurt there, despite the smile. 'Me, infuriating? Bloody cheek! You were the one who wasn't around when I really needed you.'

That was the wrong thing to say. I saw him almost flinch.

'Look, I didn't mean that. You did your best, didn't you? It wasn't your fault I decided to go back to the boat, when you'd told me not to. I was an idiot.'

'No, you're right. I let you down. Both of you.'

An ambulance pulled up outside the entrance around the corner, sirens screaming and then abruptly silent. We got up off the bench and walked back towards the doorway.

'Can I see Dylan?' I asked.

That look, again. The hurt behind his eyes. 'I'll see what I can sort out,' he said.

# *Forty-one*

The morning of Caddy's funeral brought bright blue skies across London. I caught the train from Maidstone East and now I was waiting outside Bromley station, wondering if I should have worn lower heels, tugging my skirt down a little. Opaque tights made the outfit more sober.

The black BMW pulled up next to me without a sound and, while Dylan got out of the driver's seat and went round to open the door at the back for me, I opened the passenger door and jumped in. Despite the occasion I smiled to myself as I watched him through the wing mirror. He stopped, rolled his eyes, shook his head slightly and came back to the driver's side. He got in and shut the door.

'Alright?' I asked.

'Yeah.'

That was it. The engine started up and we moved off into the traffic.

At first I stole sneaky glances at him out of the corner of my eye, and then I gave up and twisted in my seat so I could look at him properly. His gaze remained resolutely ahead, and, while he seemed perfectly relaxed and calm, both hands were gripping the steering wheel. Dark glasses, partly hiding the mess they'd made of his face. He was wearing a suit the way he always did, even though he wasn't supposed to be going to the funeral. He'd offered to drive me there and wait for me, and, because it was the only time he'd agreed to see me since the night I'd nearly managed to get him killed by taking him back to the *Revenge*, I'd readily accepted.

'You should come in with me,' I said at last. 'They probably won't even notice.'

'They'd notice,' he said. 'I don't exactly blend in.'

I wasn't even sure why Caddy's family had extended an invitation to me, since I was possibly the only one who could have saved her, could have got to her in time. But it seemed that Caddy had talked about me, and, since I wasn't a dancer any more, that was it: I got an invitation.

'You, on the other hand,' he said, nodding towards my black skirt, 'will fit in just fine. You look like a solicitor.'

'Do I?'

'Maybe a solicitor who pole dances in her spare time.'

'Why won't you see me?' I asked, out of the blue, since he seemed to be relaxing at last. 'Why are you being so distant?'

'I'm here now, aren't I?' he said with a deep breath in, as though I were some tiresome child asking the same question for the hundredth time. The car had stopped at traffic lights, the sound of the indicator's subtle click on-off-on hypnotic and soothing.

'You heard from Jim?' he asked.

'Not since the hospital,' I said. 'You know he's been suspended.'

'Yeah, I heard. He told me they arrested you.'

'Yes. Not going to help me get another job, is it?'

'They charge you?'

'They charged me with assault and then they gave me a police caution. Could have been much worse, I guess, but it's still given me a criminal record.'

'You should talk to your boyfriend Jim,' he said. 'Might be able to take it off for you, if you ask him nicely.'

'He's not my boyfriend. And in any case, he's not supposed to talk to me.'

'Well, I guess it will give his eardrums a chance to recover.'

'Why did you offer to give me a lift, Dylan, if you're going to be a rude, grumpy bastard?'

He laughed then, and I thought he might be softening again. 'Why d'you think? Wanted to see you in a skirt. Been a long time since I saw you in a skirt.'

'You're such a tease.'

'Yeah, you love it. Anyway, we're here.'

We drove slowly up a long, curved driveway between manicured lawns, trees, wooden benches and flower beds and over speed bumps. There was a car park discreetly tucked behind a large yew hedge, and as we pulled in other cars were disgorging their occupants. Everyone was looking around the same as I was, wondering if they should recognise each other and offering hesitant smiles.

'I'll wait for you here,' he said.

'Please come with me,' I asked. For some crazy reason I wanted an excuse to hold his hand.

'I'll wait here,' he said again.

So fucking stubborn, the man. I slammed the door as hard as I could, but it still only made a reassuring clunk.

The funeral was very quick. While I waited outside the chapel at the crematorium with all the people I didn't recognise, the mourners from the previous service were filing out of a different door on the other side of the building. There were about forty people, maybe a few more. A woman of about fifty could only have been Caddy's mum – she was exactly like her: petite, curvy, beautiful, with dark hair scraped into a neat bun. She was crying a lot, silently, dabbing her tears away while a girl who might have been Caddy's younger sister stood by with no expression on her pale face to give anything away. Trying to establish the family relationships passed the time.

I stood awkwardly on my own, wishing I'd worn flatter shoes, wishing I'd not worn quite so much black.

The car arrived with the coffin, and as the funeral directors positioned it on their shoulders I recognised Beverley Davies,

335

the officer who'd interviewed me, standing at the back. She looked different today, smartly dressed in a grey trouser suit and a grey, grim smile.

The service was over in half an hour. I sat at the back and listened while they talked about Caddy, and for a while I wondered if I was in the wrong chapel after all because everything they said related to a different woman, a woman I'd never met; she was a loving sister, a talented pianist and singer; she'd got a good degree in English and had completed a PGCE. She'd done a year of teaching and had loved it, and then had taken time off to work in London. They didn't mention that she was also an accomplished dancer. They didn't mention the Barclay.

I stopped listening. When the curtains started to close around the coffin, I shut my eyes.

We all filed out of the back of the chapel while they played Adele, which made me want to cry. And then I found myself stifling a hysterical giggle when I had the thought that they should have actually played the Pussycat Dolls' 'Buttons' – which had been Caddy's favourite dancing track.

I joined the line of people waiting to speak to Caddy's mum and sister. I tried to run through what I was going to say. What possible things were there, in those circumstances? *I'm sorry I didn't save her? I'm sorry I invited her to the party? I wish things had been different?*

'I'm so sorry,' was what I actually said. 'Your daughter was a beautiful person.'

'Thank you for coming,' Caddy's mum said. She was already looking past me to the next person in the line.

Caddy's sister was crying now, a boyfriend, with earrings and a straggly growth of beard, providing a comforting shoulder.

People had started to head back to the car park and I followed them.

'Genevieve?'

It was Beverley Davies. She tried for a smile and then gave up, walking alongside me.

'How are you?' she asked.

'I'm alright, thank you. Do you know how Jim is?'

'I can't – sorry.'

'He didn't do anything wrong,' I said.

'They'll take your statement into account. I just wanted to say thank you for coming. I know the family – they've had a very difficult time of it.'

'Yes.'

'Are you coming to the pub?' she asked.

'I don't know – I don't think…'

'Well – if I don't see you… Take care.' She went off towards a dark grey Vauxhall that was parked at an angle half on the grass verge and got into the driver's seat. I watched her drive away.

The BMW's windows were open and I could see Dylan watching me through the gap in the hedge as I walked back towards him.

'They're having drinks in a pub,' I said through the open window, 'do you want to go?'

'Nah.'

'Suit yourself,' I said, climbing into the passenger seat. 'In that case, you can drive me there and wait for three hours or so while I get pleasantly hammered.'

The Bull's Head in Chislehurst High Street was crowded with people and, although most of the people dressed in black seemed to be outside in the garden, in the end, I managed to persuade Dylan to come in and mingle. I'd already spent twenty minutes standing on my own, like a lost soul, necking vodka. I wanted some company.

'You don't need to talk to anyone,' I said. I was dragging him in.

'Too right I don't.'

He waited at the bar to get me another drink and I spotted Beverley Davies again. I turned away. Dylan had talked to Jim, I knew he had. Jim had worked with Dylan for years, but their alliance went deeper than that. I'd almost expected there to have been some sort of argument between them, some sort of dispute over me; but it seemed I'd overrated my own importance in that respect. Dylan seemed to be utterly convinced that I should be with Jim now. Despite risking his life to keep me safe, since they'd let him out of the hospital he'd avoided me, ignored my calls, refused to talk to me, and above all given me no indication about how he felt, whether he still liked me, or even if he ever had. And the cooler he was, the more he pushed me away, the more I wanted him. It was a big, horrible mess that seemed to have no solution.

We stood awkwardly in the beer garden, my heels sinking into the grass so that I was constantly perching on my tiptoes.

'So,' I said, 'when are you going to Spain?'

'Soon.'

'What if I need to get hold of you?'

'You won't.'

'But what if something happens? What if I need to talk to you?'

He sighed heavily.

'Fuck's sake, woman. Jim knows where I'm going. He's the only one who knows. So if there's any sort of emergency – not that I can imagine there will be – but if there *is* – Jim knows. Alright?'

'Can I see you again, before you go?'

'You don't give up, do you?'

'No,' I said. 'I don't. Unlike you.'

He swallowed three big, slow gulps from his pint. 'What's that supposed to mean?'

'You've given up on me.'

'I never had you in the first place,' he said.

'I'm not going to stay here without you, Dylan.'

He waited for a few seconds before answering, scanning the faces in the beer garden as though he was expecting to see someone he knew.

'You've got Jim,' he said.

'Jim's being investigated for some sort of misconduct because of me,' I said.

'That'll all be over with soon enough.'

'He doesn't want me anyway, Dylan.'

He raised his eyebrows. 'That's what he wants you to think. Poor bastard's fallen in love with you, and to make it worse he blames himself for what happened.'

'Well, it wasn't his fault. It was mine. The whole thing.'

'Would have probably been a lot less drama if you hadn't slept with him.'

That hurt. My cheeks flushed and I gritted my teeth to stop myself answering him back. I took it in and felt tears stinging my eyes, looking away from him, across the crowded beer garden at the blurred faces.

'Well,' I said at last, 'since you don't care about me, it doesn't really matter any more.'

'Who said I don't care?'

'Why are you such hard work? What is wrong with you?' I demanded, trying to angle my face into his line of sight. 'Dylan?'

He finished his pint, put it down on the top of a plastic bin and headed through the gate and out into the car park. I ran behind him, trying to keep up, but he was already in the car with the engine on, the tyres sending an arc of gravel flying as he accelerated towards me.

I stood firmly in the middle of the car park as the car headed straight for me at a heart-stopping speed. Then the brakes slammed on and the car stopped, the bumper about a foot from my knees.

I got in the passenger seat and pulled the door shut with force.

Neither of us spoke.

He was heading for Bromley, back to the station. It felt as if I was running out of time. 'Look,' I said at last, 'can you give me a lift back home? I don't want to go on the train.'

'Public transport beneath you now, is it?'

'No. I've had too much to drink. I don't want to be on a train drunk like this.'

He let out a short laugh. 'You want me to drive you all the way to Kent?'

'It's not that far. Please?'

He let out a heavy sigh that implied I'd just ruined his day, but at the next junction he turned back towards the A2. The fact that he'd agreed to drive me home gave me a fraction of hope, despite his hostility. I leaned my head back against the headrest and closed my eyes, trying to think. The alcohol had filled my brain with a cloud. Everything I thought of saying sounded stupid, or desperate, or selfish. How could I begin to deal with someone so stubborn? What could I possibly say that would make him change his mind?

I had to fight the urge to reach out and put my hand on his knee. I wanted to touch him so badly, thinking that if words weren't going to work, then maybe some kind of physical contact would do the trick. But he would have just removed my hand, deliberately placed it back on my side of the handbrake.

I opened my eyes and looked at him.

We were on the dual carriageway now, speeding past the Black Prince. Another forty minutes or so, and I'd be home and my chance would have gone. I'd never see him again, after this.

'I was worried about you,' I murmured.

I thought he wasn't listening because he didn't react; staring straight ahead at the traffic, he might as well have been alone in the car.

'I thought you were dead. I thought Fitz had killed you.'

He took a deep breath in through his nose. If all this was such an ordeal for him, why had he agreed to give me a lift home?

'Well, he didn't. I'm still here.'

'Do you miss the club?' Oh, so many stupid questions. I couldn't think of the right one.

'No.'

'What are you doing?'

'What?'

'I mean, are you working?'

'No.'

Silence again. I closed my eyes, half-wishing I'd not asked him for the lift after all. If he'd dropped me at the station, this torture would have been over with by now.

I must have dozed, because the gentle click of the indicator woke me. I sat up straight and looked out of the window.

'Oh, don't turn off here.'

'What?'

'I've moved the boat.'

The BMW moved swiftly out of the exit lane for Rochester and Strood, and back on to the main carriageway. A car behind us beeped. Dylan looked in his rear view mirror at the driver.

'Right,' he said. 'So where the fuck is your boat?'

'Allington. Near Maidstone. It's the next exit. Sorry, I should have said.'

We were on the Medway bridge by this time. Beneath us, the marina where I'd lived for six months in total, where I'd made some good friends, and where it had all fallen apart. I couldn't see it from up here. Just the straight lines of the motorway and, in the distance to the left, Rochester Castle, a flag flying from the battlements.

'When did you move the boat?'

'A few weeks ago. Bloody ordeal that was, I can tell you. I had to go through a lock. I had to pay Cameron to help me move it.'

He didn't say anything. At the next exit he turned off towards Maidstone, down a long, steep hill with a view over the Medway valley. 'It was difficult,' I said, even though he'd not asked. 'You know, with the people in the marina. They're lovely, all of them, but they've chosen this quiet life, you know? Or at least, that's what they were hoping for, until I turned up and ruined it for them. And Malcolm and Josie... We

341

did try. We were talking about it all. But Josie blames me for everything that happened. And I blame myself.'

'It wasn't your fault,' he said at last. 'He was the fucking idiot that brought Fitz to your door.'

'No,' I said. 'I did that. Malcolm just hurried him along a bit.'

He fell silent again, concentrating on the short stretch of the M20 that would take us back towards Maidstone. I couldn't bear the quiet. The minutes were flying past, the precious time I had with him was slipping away like sand through my fingers.

'It's a nice place, anyway,' I said. 'Not a marina. Just a few moorings, and there's a nice pub too, with a restaurant. There's even a shower block; it's supposed to be for kayakers I think, but I used it anyway until I finished the bathroom last weekend. And the river isn't tidal because I'm above the lock. I get ducks and swans now, instead of bloody seagulls. It's a nice place. You'll like it.'

'I'll like it?'

I smiled at him, hopeful. 'I think you will.'

'I like the sound of the pub.'

'You have to walk across the lock to get to it. I'm on the wrong bank.'

'And it's alright there? Safe?'

'Yes. I feel safe.'

'Good.'

Maybe it was the fact that we were a long way outside London now, but I could feel him thawing. His shoulders were not as rigid, his grip on the steering wheel more relaxed.

'Your boat's alright?'

'Yes, I think so. I'm still repairing things. But now I'm just getting it straightened out so I can sell it.'

'Why?'

He looked at me properly for the first time since we'd left Chislehurst.

'I can't live there any more. I moved the boat because I thought it would help, but it hasn't. So much happened on that boat, Dylan. Everything I look at reminds me of that night. Of Malcolm getting shot, of what Arnold was going to do. Of you nearly getting beaten to death.'

'You can't just give up on your dream. You need to give it time.'

I shook my head. 'It won't change how I feel. I can't stay there. You need to take the next turning on the left. That one, there, look.'

The car turned into Castle Road and slowed as the road narrowed, towards the end. Minutes, that was all I had left. Just a few minutes with him.

'What will you do?' he asked.

I couldn't cry, not now. I forced the tears back. 'I don't know what I'll do.' I wanted so desperately to hear him say the words *Come to Spain. Come with me.* But he didn't.

At the end of the road was a turning circle, with the entrance to the lock-keeper's cottage and, beyond it, the car park which served the slipway into the river. And we were there. The car's tyres crunched on the gravel and we pulled to a stop. The *Revenge of the Tide* was moored against the concrete bank, a few feet from where we were parked. It was sandwiched between two narrowboats and it looked huge and out of place, crouching like a grown-up between two kids, dominating the bank.

I took a deep breath. 'Will you come inside?'

He shook his head.

'I can't,' he said. He was actually gritting his teeth.

'Can't what?'

He paused, ran a hand over his forehead. 'Can't – do this any more. Why won't you just leave me alone?' And he finally turned to look at me, properly, for what felt like the first time.

I reached across to him, put my hand up to stroke his cheek. 'Because I love you,' I said. 'And I know you love me, even though you won't say it. I know you do.'

He stared at me for a long moment and I stared right back at him, challenging him to refuse, or make a joke about it, or laugh. When he did none of those things I put my hand up to his cheek, stroked it gently, and then clambered over the central console of the BMW and kissed him, ignoring the wince as my weight fell against his bruised chest, pushing him back against the door so that I could pretty much climb on to his lap, and put my arms around his neck so he couldn't get away, couldn't move until I'd finished, until I'd made him change his mind.

## Author's Note

Readers who are familiar with the Medway may well recognise some of the locations mentioned in this book. However, the marina where the *Revenge of the Tide* is moored is an imaginative blend of several of the boatyards along the river and therefore does not exist as it is described in the story. The Barclay is also entirely fictional.

## Acknowledgements

The first draft of *Revenge of the Tide* was written in November 2010 for National Novel Writing Month (NaNoWriMo) and was excitedly presented to my editor, Vicky Blunden, as a 90,000-word draft. The transformation of that tangled mess of ideas, characters and plot into the final book is thanks to her, and to the brilliant team at Myriad, including Candida Lacey, Corinne Pearlman, Linda McQueen, Anthony Grech-Cumbo, Adrian Weston, Dawn Sackett and Emma Dowson. Thank you all.

I would also like to thank Vanessa Very and Linda Weeks for reading early drafts and making invaluable suggestions which changed the course of the story completely. Vanessa, who seems to be making a habit of resurrecting characters I try to kill off, saved Dylan from just such a fate.

Whilst I was conducting research for the book, Jill Vago very kindly let me spend some time on her boat, *Tobias*, and helped me with all my questions about living aboard. Thank you very much, Jill!

Two reference books in particular were also invaluable, and I can highly recommend them to any reader: *A Home Afloat* by Paul Cookson, with wonderful photographs of boats which provided inspiration for the interiors of the *Revenge of the Tide*, and *Living Aboard* by Nick Corble and Allan Ford, which helped me with the practical aspects of converting a barge to living accommodation.

I would also like to thank Jane Salida, Louise Payne and Keli Stephenson of the fabulous Pole Saints, who introduced me to pole fitness, and to the other class members who let me draw stick figures while they did all the hard work. Thank you, too, to Nikki W, who kindly answered my questions about working in London clubs. For a detailed account of a dancer's life, I can highly recommend the excellent book *Girl in High Heels* by Ellouise Moore.

So many people provided support and encouragement while I was writing this book that it would take several pages to list them all. So thank you to all my wonderful friends and colleagues at Kent Police, especially to Lisa James and Mitch Humphrys who kindly checked my manuscript for procedural accuracy. To the talented Medway Mermaids, and to the inspirational Rochester and Chatham book club – thank you, ladies. And for all my online friends, especially the Kent NaNoWriMo participants who went through the madness of November with me – thank you.

The last and best thanks of all to my boys, David and Alex, I love you.

If you liked *Revenge of the Tide*, you might
like Elizabeth Haynes' bestselling
debut novel *Into the Darkest Corner*.

**AMAZON BEST BOOK OF THE YEAR 2011**

**WINNER OF AMAZON RISING STARS 2011**

**LONGLISTED FOR THE
CWA JOHN CREASEY DAGGER 2011**

**FEATURED ON THE SPECSAVERS
TV BOOK CLUB 2012**

Friday night, Hallowe'en, and the bars in town were all full to the cauldron's brim.

In the Cheshire Arms I'd drunk cider and vodka and somehow lost Claire and Louise and Sylvia, and gained a new friend called Kelly. Kelly had been to the same school as me, although I didn't remember her. That was no matter to either of us; Kelly was dressed as a witch without a broomstick, all stripy orange tights and black nylon wig, me like the bride of Satan, a fitted red satin dress and cherry-red silk shoes that had cost more than the dress. I'd already been groped a few times.

By one, most people were heading for the night bus, or the taxi rank, or staggering away from the town centre into the freezing night. Kelly and I headed for the River bar, since it was the only place likely still to let us in.

'You are *so* going to pull wearing that dress, Catherine,' Kelly said, her teeth chattering.

'I fucking hope so, it cost me enough.'

'Do you think there will be anything decent in there?' she said, peering hopefully at the bedraggled queue.

'I doubt it. Anyway, I thought you said that you were off men?'

'I said I've given up on relationships. Doesn't mean I'm off sex.'

It was bitterly cold and starting to drizzle, the wind whipping the smells of a Friday night around me, blowing up my skirt. I pulled my jacket tighter around me and crossed my arms over it.

We headed for the VIP entrance. I remember wondering if this was a good idea, whether it might not be better to call it a night, when I realised Kelly had been let in already and I went to follow her. I was blocked by a wall of charcoal-grey suit.

I looked up to see a pair of incredible blue eyes, short blond hair. Not someone you'd want to have an argument with.

'Hold up,' said the voice, and I looked up at the doorman. He wasn't massive like the other two, but still taller than me. He had a very appealing smile.

'Hello,' I said. 'Am I allowed to go in with my friend?'

He paused for a moment and looked at me just a fraction longer than was seemly. 'Yes,' he said at last. 'Of course. Just…'

I waited for him to continue. 'Just what?'

He glanced across to where the other door staff were chatting up some teenagers busy trying their hardest to get in.

'Just couldn't believe my luck for a moment, that's all.'

I laughed at his cheek. 'Not been a good night, then?'

'I have a thing for red dresses,' he said.

'I don't think this one would fit you.'

He laughed and held the velvet rope to one side to let me in. I felt him watching me as I handed my jacket in to the cloakroom; chanced a glance back to the door and saw him again, just watching me. I gave him a smile and went up the steps to the bar.

All I could think of that night was dancing until I was numb, smiling and laughing at people with my new best friend, dancing in that red dress until I caught the eye of someone, anyone, and best of all finding some dark corner of the club and being fucked against a wall.


### Thursday 1 November 2007

It took me a long, long time to get out of the flat this morning. It wasn't the cold, although the heating in the flat seems to take an age to have any effect. Nor was it the dark. I'm up every day before five; it's been dark at that time since September.

Getting up isn't my problem; getting out of the house is. Once I'm showered and dressed, have had something to eat, I start the process of checking that the flat is secure before I go to work. It's like a reverse of the process I go through in the evening, but worse somehow, because I know that time is against me. I can spend all night checking if I want to, but I know I have to get to work, so in the mornings I can only do it so many times. I have to leave the curtains in the lounge and in the dining room, by the balcony, open to exactly the right width every day or I can't come back in the flat again. There are sixteen panes in each of the patio doors; the curtains have to be open so that I can see just eight panes of each door if I look up to the flat from the path at the back of the house. If I can see a sliver of the dining room through the other panes, or if the curtains aren't hanging straight, then I'll have to go back up to the flat and start again.

I've got quite good at getting this right, but it still takes a long time. The more thorough I am, the less likely I'll find myself on the path behind the house cursing my carelessness and checking my watch.

The door is particularly bad. At least in the last place, that poky basement in Kilburn, I had my own front door. Here I have to check and re-check the flat door properly six or twelve times, and then the communal front door as well.

The flat in Kilburn did have a front door but nothing at all at the back, no back door, no windows. It was like living in a cave. I didn't have an escape route, which meant that I never felt really safe in there. Here, things are much better: I have French doors which lead onto a small balcony. Just below that is the roof of the shed which is shared with the other flats, although I don't know if anyone else uses it. I can get out of the French doors, jump down to the shed roof, and from there down onto the grass. Through the garden and out the gate into the alleyway at the back. I can do it in less than half a minute.

Sometimes I have to go back and check the flat door again. If one of the other tenants has left the front door on the latch again I definitely have to check the flat door. Anyone could have been in.

This morning, for example, was one of the worst.

Not only was the front door on the latch, it was actually slightly ajar. As I reached for it, a man in a suit pushed it open towards me which made me jump. Behind him, another man, younger, tall, wearing jeans and a hooded top. Dark hair cropped close to his head, unshaven, tired green eyes. He gave me a smile, and mouthed 'sorry', which helped.

Suits still freak me out. I tried not to look at the suit at all, but I heard it say as it went up the stairs, '…this one's only just become available, you'll have to move fast if you want it.'

A lettings agent, then.

The Chinese students who'd been on the top floor must have finally decided to move on. They weren't students any more, they graduated in the summer – the party they'd had had gone on all night, while I lay in my bed underneath listening to the sound of feet marching up and down the stairs. The front door had been on the latch all night. I'd barricaded myself in by pushing the dining table against the flat door, but the noise had kept me awake and anxious.

I watched the second man following the suit up the stairs.

To my horror the man in jeans turned halfway up the first flight and gave me another smile, a rueful one this time, raising his eyes as if he was already sick of the letting agent's voice. I felt myself blushing furiously. It's been a long time since I made eye contact with a stranger.

I listened to the footsteps heading up to the top floor, meaning they'd gone past my front door. I checked my watch – a quarter past eight already! I couldn't just go and leave them inside the house.

I shut the front door firmly and unclipped the latch, checking that it had shot home by rattling the door a few times. With my fingertips I traced around the edge of the doorframe, feeling that the door was flush with the frame. I turned the doorknob six times, to make sure it was properly closed. One, two, three, four, five, six. Then the doorframe again. Then the doorknob, six times. One, two, three, four, five, six. Then the latch. Once, and again. Then the doorframe. Lastly the knob, six times.

I felt the relief that comes when I manage to do this properly.

Then I marched back up to the flat, fuming that these two idiots were going to make me late.

I sat on the edge of my bed for a while with my eyes lifted to the ceiling, as if I could see them through the plaster and the rafters. All the time I was fighting the urge to start checking the window locks again.

I concentrated on my breathing, my eyes closed, trying to calm my racing heart. They won't be long, I told myself. He's only looking. They won't be long. Everything is fine. The flat is safe. I'm safe. I did it properly before. The front door is shut. Everything is fine.

Every so often a small sound made me jump, even though it seemed to come from a long way away. A cupboard door banging? Maybe. What if they'd opened a window up there? I could hear a vague murmur, far too far away to make out words. I wondered what price they were asking for it – it might be nicer to be higher up. But then I wouldn't have the balcony. As much as I love being out of reach, having an escape route is just as important.

I checked my watch – nearly a quarter to nine. What the fuck were they doing up there? I made the mistake of glancing at the bedroom window, and then of course I had to check it. And that started me off, so I had to start again at the door, and I was on my second round, standing on the lid of the toilet, feeling my way with my fingertips around the edge of the frosted window which doesn't even open, when I heard the door shutting upstairs and the sound of footsteps on the stairs outside.

'…nice safe area, at least. Never need to worry about leaving your car outside.'

'Yeah, well, I'd probably get the bus. Or I might use my bike.'

'I think there's a communal shed in the garden; I'll check when we get back to the office.'

'Cheers. I'd probably leave it in the hallway.'

Leave it in the hallway? Bloody cheek. It was untidy enough as it was. But then, maybe someone other than me would make a point of locking the front door.

I finished off the check, and then did the flat door. Not too bad. I waited for it, the anxiety, the need to go round and start again, but it was okay. I'd done it right, and only two times. The house was silent, which made things easier. Best of all, this time the front door was firmly fastened, indicating that the man in jeans had shut it properly behind him. Maybe he wouldn't be a bad tenant after all.

It was nearly nine-thirty by the time I finally got to the Tube.

# MORE FROM MYRIAD EDITIONS

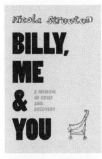

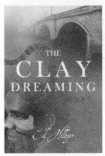

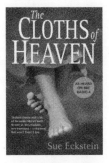

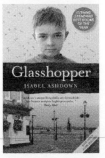

# MORE FROM MYRIAD EDITIONS